J0604174

Also By Ward Howarth

River City Blues

SHINE *A* LIGHT

by Ward Howarth

A Frontside Press Book

Copyright © 2024 by Ward Howarth

www.wardhowarth.com

Frontside Press Logo designed by Vaughn Howarth

Cover photo by Patrick Tomasso on Unsplash

This book is a work of fiction. Names, characters, places, and incidents either are the products of the author's imagination or are used fictitiously, and any resemblance to actual events or persons, living or dead, is entirely coincidental.

Print edition ISBN 978-0-9976098-4-4

E-book ISBN 978-0-9976098-5-1

for Frank Howarth, my father,
for always believing in me

PART ONE

VICTORY IN EUROPE DAY

TUESDAY, MAY 8, 1945
RICHMOND, VIRGINIA

1

A distress call hit the Annex just after midnight. The panicked owner of a five-and-dime on Boulevard reported a burglary in progress and said to come quick. The switchboard op rang Bennie's office, jolting him from his catnap.

"Sorry to disturb you, sir, but no one's picking up at Second Station and the trouble's in their jurisdiction. Shall I keep trying?"

Bennie stifled a yawn and cracked his back. Memo to self: stop sleeping in the office chair. He had fallen out waiting for official word from the War Department. A full German surrender was imminent and he was intent on keeping the peace once the public heard the news.

"No, I'll take it from here, Annie, but radio for available units to head to the scene, stat."

Bennie hung up, stood up, and stretched. The thought of leaving the office jazzed him, but he was nap sluggish and in need of a lift. He unlocked his top desk drawer, bagged his pep pills. Two months back, Bennie nailed a medical doctor for pushing narcotics. When Bennie threatened to suspend his license, the doc traded *up* — a simple slap on the wrist in exchange for Bennie's round-the-clock supply of oomph. Bennie popped two and chased them with stale coffee. With crime stats on the fritz and City Hall breathing down his neck, he kept a steady stream pumping through his veins. "Even I need juice to stay in the pocket," Bennie told Imogene once, but she chided him for using, said they were ruinous to his already fragile mental state.

As usual, she wasn't wrong.

Bennie hit the washroom next. Water on his face, mouthwash, tie pulled taut. Gotta look sharp, set an example. A check on his reflection — a little rundown, maybe, but still the same old

Bennie. He had short black hair that was loosely trimmed, just a bit longer than his old military cut. His nose and chin were unpronounced — regular features on an even face. His dark brown eyes, though, were the prodding kind. Perfect for a cop, his dad always said. They asked questions just by looking your way.

No time to lose — Bennie double-timed it to the main foyer and made a quick stop by the firearms locker. He grabbed a single-barrel shotgun, a Winchester 37, and pocketed shells. Too much firepower, maybe, but it never hurt to make a show of force. Down the hall then, a peek into the detectives' lair. He found two Victory Squad bulls kicking papers around their desks. Eddie Haden out of vice, Shane MacDonald from robbery.

"You two, with me, now."

Both men came to their feet and followed Bennie out of the room. Pulling on their jackets, glad to be off late-night busy work. Eddie had fifteen years under his belt, working himself up the ladder from flatfoot to top cop. Young gun Shane was just home from the war, having retaken his old job after a stint with the Navy.

"Where to, boss?" Shane asked.

Bennie cut through the squad room and led the three of them down the staircase. "A smash-and-grab out west, near Broad and Boulevard. If we get there soon enough, we might catch 'em in the act."

Eddie popped bullets into the cylinder of his revolver. "That's Second territory. What are we doing on it?"

"No one's picking up there. The switchboard rang me."

Eddie and Shane shared a knowing look. Second Station let too many calls slide by. Shane said, "You're here awfully late, boss. You should powder, we can take it."

"Relax, MacDonald, no need to shoo me off. I just want to get out of the office, stretch my legs. Plus, waiting on war news is putting me to sleep."

They exited the Annex and spilled onto the sidewalk. Bennie watched a taxi drive by and wondered if Imogene had grabbed a shift for the night. He turned to Eddie and tossed him a set of car keys.

"Be a doll, would you, Haden, and grab us a set of wheels?"

Eddie flipped him the bird and hustled for a black-and-white.

Bennie rolled his neck and shook out his legs — a buzz had set in already. He suddenly felt as if he could run to the scene faster than they could drive there. He looked over at Shane and found him smiling big. Wanting to say something but holding back. Bennie just shook his head, he knew what was coming. "Come on, out with it."

"She kicked you out again, didn't she?"

"In a manner of speaking."

"But it's your house What'd you do this time?"

Bennie sat on it for a beat, loading shells into the Winchester. "Asked her to marry me."

Shane howled. "So I guess that's a no?"

"She didn't say, one way or another. Just told me to leave."

"I'd say that's a no, boss."

"Really? I'd say that's progress."

Shane fought off laughter. "How? How is that progress?"

"Well, like I said, she didn't say *no* exactly, just… to leave."

Shane let it sit for a moment. "And you don't think that's a no?"

"No, I don't. Look, I know her. If she'd wanted to say no, she would have said it."

"But she didn't say yes."

"No, she didn't. She just told —"

"Yeah, yeah, she just told you to leave. When was this?"

"Last night."

"Have you talked to her since?"

Bennie shook his head and looked away, hiding his embarrassment. He had no idea what he'd say to her next. They had a date set for later tonight, for the Wells' big party, and he was terrified to see her. Haden pulled up then, almost racing to a stop. The tires screeched on the street.

"Let's go, ladies!"

Bennie grabbed the front seat and fired up the siren. Shane slid in back, ecstatic. "You owe me a dinner, Eddie!"

Eddie shot Bennie a disapproving look. "Really, boss? Again?"

Bennie couldn't help but smile.

"Just drive."

Eddie put the car in gear and sped off, taking Broad Street west at breakneck speed. The siren at full blast, everything a blur. Cool night air hit Bennie's face and suddenly he was back on Guadalcanal, hunting Japs in the jungle from the shadows of overgrown brush. Call it growth: moments like these used to send his nerves into overdrive, but now they just sparked his inner soldier back to life.

Horn blares — *LOUD*.

Eddie dodged late-night drivers while Shane bellowed war cries out the window. Traffic was light and they made good time, reaching the five-and-dime in six minutes flat. Bennie was glad: there was a black-and-white already there and a patrolman out front. Eddie braked curbside, the car tires squealing as headlights cast wide light on store windows. All three men spilled from the car and zoomed for the patrolman, Jimmy Knight, a new Annex recruit with only six months in. Check his face — a worried look, sad going on angry.

"What happened?" Bennie asked.

Jimmy steadied himself against a front window, shadowed war bond posters and weekly specials his backdrop. "It's a woman, sir. A gunshot to the chest. I'm on my way now to call the morgue."

"Anyone else inside?"

"Just my partner, sir. Henderson."

"Use our car and radio the Annex direct. Have the switchboard call it out and tell them to send a wagon and lab men, stat. Eddie, stay with Jimmy and get what he knows after the call. Shane, with me."

Broken glass and busted lock fragments were scattered about the outer entryway of the store. Bennie and Shane sidestepped the mess and threw open the two front doors in tandem. Eerie vibes inside — the headlights spread harsh light on picked-through food-aisles while music played from an overhead radio. Woody Herman was on now, belting his way through 'Caldonia.' Foodstuffs littered the ground — boxes of cereal, canned vegetables — what was left of them knocked from ransacked shelves. Shane fumbled his way to a wall switch and flooded the room with overhead light. Scanning the room now, they both caught the gist. Call the robbery a regular rush job gone bad, the perp/perps in a hurry to get what they could and scram.

A shaken voice called to them from the other side of the store. Make it Jimmy Knight's partner, Henderson.

"She's over here."

The woman was spread out on her back behind a side counter, her vacant eyes staring off to the side. Her head rested against the wall and tilted up some, just enough for them all to see the crude swastika someone had fingered in blood on her right cheek. Perhaps it was her own blood, having spread from the gunshot wound in her chest throughout the shin-length smock she wore. She looked to be about sixty and Bennie's gut sank at the thought. Someone's mother, probably, maybe even someone's grandmother. She looked formidable, this woman with a bandana pulled across her forehead, with her pale skin and curly black hair. Bennie guessed 5'6", 110 pounds. A little scrawny, maybe, but Bennie saw a strong build inside that dress. It wasn't hard for him to imagine her as someone who had held her own in life, who had etched out a place for herself and worked hard to excel there. Her smock sleeves had been pulled back to her elbows — check those forearm muscles. She had been a strong woman, indeed, and in the last hours of her life, she looked to have been working hard. Cleaning perhaps, or preparing the store for tomorrow. The smell of bleach was not far off and there was a broom nearby.

Shane knelt down near the counter. "Two .22 shell casings, right here."

Bennie stepped back and scanned the ground, glad for at least one clue. Something odd caught his eye. "Is that… *hay*?"

Shane leaned over for a closer look and flashed his penlight. Sure enough, there was a straw of hay, right there on the ground. "Damn, boss, good catch."

"Sh… She looks like my mother," Henderson said.

Bennie and Shane looked at the stunned young cop. Early twenties, easy. A putrid shade was spreading across his face. *Give him something to do*, Bennie thought, and quick.

"Henderson, have you and your partner ID'd the woman yet?"

"Uh, no, sir. We only arrived a few minutes before you did."

"There must be an office here somewhere. Chances are there's a purse or a handbag, something with her identification in it. Find it. And while you're at it, look for anything business related. A checkbook, a bill. Something that could help us identify her."

"Yes, sir." Henderson perked up some, glad to be given a useful task, and started off.

Shane cracked his knuckles, antsy. "I know we're waiting on the photo men, boss, but I hate to leave her like this. Permission to close her eyes?"

Bennie nodded. Shane knelt down and gently eased the woman's eyes shut with his thumbs before closing his own eyes, crossing himself, and whispering a Hail Mary. Bennie said a silent prayer for the woman as music from the radio turned melancholy. Jo Stafford on now with 'It Could Happen to You.' *Imogene's favorite singer*, Bennie thought, as memories and emotions hit him from all sides. He thought of Skipper Holly, his old friend, dying in his very arms some fourteen months back. And not on the battlefront, but right here at home. He thought of the troubles that led to Skipper's death and the trail of bodies that followed it. He thought of men in the jungles of a Pacific island he hoped never to return to. He thought of their bodies laid to rest there and their souls concurrent.

Shane pointed at the woman's neck. "Hey, boss, look."

Bennie tracked Shane's line of sight and watched as he slipped his penknife just inside the woman's smock. Watched as he lifted up the ball chain of a necklace with a sterling Star of David pendant dangling from its center. "Shit," Bennie whispered to himself, the circumstances of this crime taking shape in his mind.

Noise swarmed the room as Eddie led a throng of men toward the body — two men with a gurney and Rooney from the lab. Print gear in his hand, a camera hanging around his neck. He stopped next to Bennie and did a double take.

"Christ, she looks like my aunt. Is that really a swastika on her face?"

Bennie loosened his tie. Crime scene heat gave him the sweats.

"Yes, and it's crucial you not disturb it as you print her. When you're done with the room, I believe there's a straw of hay near the counter, along with two .22 shell casings. Bag it all."

"Yessir."

Rooney set his print gear on the floor and started snapping photos. Brilliant pops of white light followed in rapid succession, each one fading into the next. It was as if they were suddenly ringside at a prize fight. Bennie squinted and rubbed his eyes. He was both tired and wide awake at the same time. He heard Imogene's lovely, raspy voice say, "Those pills won't save you."

Eddie sidled up to him, crossing himself at the sight of her. "Patrolman out front, Knight? He's a little too shaken up to give me anything solid. Says he and his partner here didn't see shit."

Bennie sighed. "Figures."

Almost on cue, Henderson appeared before them both, clutching a handbag. Excited, proud. "I found it, sir."

Bennie took the purse. "An ID inside?"

"Of sorts, sir. There's a letter."

Bennie shuffled through its contents. Nestled in with the loose dough, make-up products, and keys, Bennie found a V-Mail letter addressed to Mr. and Mrs. Harold Kleinfeld.

"Good work, Henderson. Find anything else?"

Henderson handed him a business license. "Found this tucked inside the register. Which has been cleaned out, by the way."

"No surprise there," Eddie said as Bennie skimmed the license top to bottom. Sure enough, Harold and Ruth Kleinfeld had owned 'The Sunshine Five-and-Dime' since 1938. Bennie gestured to Rooney and handed the license to Henderson.

"Have him photo both this and the handbag, then check it all in as evidence."

"Yes, sir!"

Henderson took the purse and fell in with Rooney, leaving Bennie, Shane, and Eddie to stew on the scene.

"What's your take, boss?" Shane asked.

Bennie looked around the store, his eyes tracking an imagined path for the robbers as he spoke. "For argument's sake, let's say there were two of them. It's not hard to imagine them entering the store unaware of her presence. They start in on the aisles, they grab cans, boxes of food. They hit the register, empty it. Maybe they're ready to leave when — "

Shane made like a ghost. "Boo! Boss Lady over there surprises them."

Eddie fought with it. "But the swastika? When'd they know she was Jewish?"

Bennie shook his head. "Maybe they questioned her, taunted her."

Eddie scoffed. "That's thin. They're in a rush, going for everything they can, they're not the thinking type."

"Then maybe they knew already," Shane said.

Eddie was skeptical. "How would they know?"

Shane fought for it. "They could have found out beforehand, targeted the store."

Bennie nodded, reluctantly. "They were making a statement."

Eddie sighed. "If that's the case, there'll be more just like this."

Rooney signaled to Bennie with a thumbs up — all set. Bennie gave the gurney men the go-ahead and found himself face-to-face again with Jimmy Knight.

"There's a call for you outside, sir. From your car radio, I mean."

Bennie thanked him and moved off, wiping sweat from his brow. He steadied his stride and left the five-and-dime in a rush.

Dig that cool night air, washing over him.

Dig that dead man juju, creeping up his spine.

Jap ghosts, nipping at his heels.

And now, Ms. Kleinfeld's soul, clawing at his back.

A sales ad inside a front store window caught Bennie's eye — a quart of milk delivered was a steal at 13 cents — and he wondered: just how many golden teeth *had* he pulled from the severed heads of dead Jap soldiers?

Was it twelve or thirteen?

Bennie slid into the front seat of the patrol car and grabbed the receiver.

"This is Sherwood."

Static on the line. Then, Annie's voice. "I hope I'm not

disturbing you, sir, but I have… good news and bad news."

"It's hard to think of anything worse than what we've just seen, Annie. Let's have the bad news first."

Annie cleared her throat. "Ms. McKenna has just called, sir. She says for you not to pick her up for the Wells' party tonight, that she will just meet you there."

Bennie almost laughed. *And just like that, we're on the outs again.* "And the good news?"

Annie choked up. "A… a teletype has just come through, sir. From the mayor's office, it's direct from the War Department. The Germans accepted terms. The war in Europe is over."

Bennie hung his head and fought the urge to smile.

"That's wonderful, Annie, thank you. I will share the news with the men here immediately and please, no matter what you're doing, who you're with, find a way to celebrate."

Annie eked out a joyous "Yes, sir" before Bennie dropped the receiver and brought himself to stand just outside the black-and-white, his arms resting against the driver's side door for support. A weightless feeling had come over him suddenly and he thought he might fall over. He watched as the men cleared the five-and-dime and collected on the sidewalk, their faces grim and solemn. He called up an authoritative voice, like his father used to do on the baseball field, and formed his words.

"Listen up, everyone, I have news to share."

The group quieted down and turned Bennie's way.

"We've all been expecting it, but it's official now. The Nazis took a knee."

One by one, the men registered the news. They laughed and whooped and hollered and made joyous sounds Bennie had never heard them make before. Shane howled at the moon like a prairie dog while the two gurney men danced arm-in-arm, moving in a circle like two prospectors who'd just struck gold. All Bennie could do was sink into the driver's seat, too stunned to fully embrace his own joy.

Shane rushed over, his rakish grin in full swing.

"What do you say, boss? Can Eddie and I fire off a few victory shots?"

Bennie nodded as Shane hustled back to the crowd. He and Eddie fired off an entire cylinder a piece into the sky. Six shots each, the rest of the men just eating it up.

Bennie smiled, the noise complaints be damned.

It was twelve, he remembered.

Twelve golden teeth.

2

Knox sat on the edge of his cot and waited for them to let him out of his cell. His back upright, his feet planted firmly on the floor, his hands folded in his lap like some schoolboy awaiting dismissal. Surprisingly, Superintendent Visel had allowed him a shave and returned his clothes, not that they fit anymore. Everything was loose and airy on account of the ten pounds he'd lost since going inside. *Fear burned off those pounds*, he thought. Fear of the guards, fear of solitary, fear of the kitchen slop they served up three times a day. He was almost sick just thinking about it, but he held it in, steeling himself. *It will all be over soon, one way or another*, he thought, fingering the makeshift blade that rested against his right leg. He'd fashioned it out of a thin, angular piece of slate stone he found in the yard. It was sharp now, sharp enough to pierce flesh, and if they tried to keep him here, tried to work him over and say he provoked *them*, he would stab the two guards, Ghostman and Scangili, and then he would never get out. He'd have to force his own hand then, stab himself maybe, or cut his very own throat, because today was his getaway day. He was done, time served — four years, three months, and seventeen days for armed robbery and assaulting a police officer — and he would not be kept here any longer.

The waiting made Knox jumpy, so he pulled Sadie's picture from his pocket once more for comfort. It was a black-and-white snapshot, sent to him by Constance some years back in her last letter to him. Knox guessed it had been taken in the apartment they once shared, after he'd been sent up, and he was careful not to tear the frayed edges any further. Sadie was a mutt, some mix of hound and terrier, her dark fur mixed with uneven patches of grey. The blend gave her an exotic, almost feral look, as if she were a beast of the wild. Sadie would be about nine years old now, maybe ten. A good life for a dog. Knox wondered if she'd remember him after all this time.

CLANG, CLANG, CLANG.

Knox shook at the all too familiar sounds and shot to his feet. There they were, right outside the cell, Ghostman and Scangili, rapping their batons across the bars. Knox stuffed Sadie's picture back into his pocket quick — they'd confiscate it if they saw it, call it contraband. A chorus of aggressive shouts echoed throughout the corridor — the guards' presence riled up the other inmates something good. Ghostman spoke above the noise.

"You are one lucky jailbird, you know that?"

Ghostman reeked of rotgut liquor. Heavyset but quick with his hands, he got a kick out of working over the inmates. He held his baton up now, tapping it against the cell like a drumstick.

Tap, tap, tap.

Scangili just laughed, his icy cackles like metal scrapes across hard ground. He was the smaller of the two, more bones than skin, his grin too wide for his face. He looked at Knox and said, "But what if he puts up a fight, eh? What then, Ghostman?"

Ghostman peered through the bars now, moving the baton in a suggestive manor.

"Then he'll get *this* in a place it don't belong."

Scangili whooped and hollered, disturbingly elated by the idea, but still Knox held the blade to his side, keeping it just out of sight. Both his voice and body quaked as he spoke. "Gonna put it to me one last time, are you? Yeah, well, come right on in here, boys, I got somethin' for ya!"

And now they're in the cell, on him, just like that, a two-man attack. Knox dodged the first blows, but the ones that followed caught his ribcage and knocked him against the wall. He righted himself and choked out a breath.

Shouts echoed throughout the corridor, egging Knox on.

"Get 'em, Knox, put it to 'em!"

"Don't let 'em snuff you!"

Ghostman threatened with more. "You talk pretty big, jailbird, but you ain't much, are you?" Scangili just howled, bowling over with glee. Knox shielded his right side, holding the blade tight. They still hadn't seen it. He shot Ghostman a defeated look, stroking his ego. *Come on, big man, take the bait.*

But Ghostman just pointed his baton at Knox and snarled. "You know what, jailbird? I think it's time to put you with the rest of 'em, because you're just a whiny shit, like they are, and we're gonna pound you into a good little *schütze!*"

Knox made a face. Was that… *German?*

Suddenly, footsteps and movement rushed the cell. Someone tore the baton from Ghostman and threw him against the bars.

An angry voice rang out. "I said hands off, you heel! Hands off!"

A stunned Knox stood back from the fray and watched as Superintendent Visel loomed over Ghostman, walloping him with the baton. Visel stood at six feet even, muscular and lean. They say he'd been a railroad man.

Ghostman cowered, shielding himself from the blows. "Alright, alright!"

Visel turned to Scangili. "And you! Haven't you done enough, you mangy wop?"

A disappointed scowl took over Scangili's face, his hands balling into fists. "I didn't mean for it to happen that way, I swear! I know I can do it, please, just give me another chance!"

Visel wasn't having it. "Enough. Kitchen and laundry, now!"

Scangili threw a helpless look at Ghostman, his protector, before throwing the cell keys at Visel, spitting at him and storming off.

Visel let it go and threw the baton at Ghostman. "I'll deal with you later," he said, turning his attention to Knox. "And *you*. It's true what they say. You are one lucky jailbird."

Knox flashed his stone blade. "The hell I am. *This* is my day. I did my time. I see the outside of the gate, or it's you and me."

Visel just laughed. "Got a weapon, have you? Yeah, well, keep it, Sutton, because where you're going, you might need it." He motioned toward the corridor and said, "This way, please. To the right." Like it was all so natural, a pleasant walk in a pleasant place.

Knox pocketed his blade and stepped over a moaning

Ghostman as he left the cell. *Quick now, before they force you back in, tell you it was all a joke.* He looked to the right and said, "That's not the way to the release desk."

Visel followed him out. "No, Sutton, it's not, and you're not going to the release desk. But don't worry, you're getting out, alright." He gave Knox a rough shove from behind and said, "Now come on and move. We're late."

They snaked through the rear of the cell block, Visel overtaking him. The man in a hurry, checking his watch. They moved past the boiler room and the solitary lock-ups and came to a door in the rear of the penitentiary. Visel unlocked it and suddenly there was piercing sunlight, so bright Knox had to shield his eyes. Visel calmly slipped on a pair of sunglasses and stepped outside.

"Harsh, isn't it, Sutton? Yeah, well, just you wait. Come on."

Knox followed Visel along a narrow dirt path and let his eyes adjust, looking around. They were outside the prison confines now, no gate in sight, the ground littered with cigarette butts and candy wrappers. They dodged a scrap heap of metal and a pile of discarded tires, both overgrown with weeds. Collected for the war effort, no doubt, but never passed on to the rationing board. They skirted an open end metal drum with a crude red swastika painted on its side. A burn barrel, it looked like, and Knox peeked inside. It reeked of gasoline and was lined with the ashes of charred prison garb. *Christ*, he thought, *here's my getaway day and I'm walking through a goddamn trash yard.*

"*Where* are you taking me?" Knox asked.

Visel outstretched a hand and pointed. "To them."

Knox followed his aim and saw three men leaning against a prewar Ford just up ahead. The ride looked old and rusted and sported an uneven Mercury Blue paint job. Two of the men wore dark suits and hats and came off tough. Icy stares, greaseball mugs. The other man Knox easily recognized as Walter MacKeye, his old cohort in all things illicit. Bootleg liquor, numbers, breaking and entering. Knox took up with Walter's crew before the war and together, they pulled some real doozies. Big hauls, good memories. *Not that they mean a damn thing now,* Knox thought, looking at Walter across the way, the man showing his age after all these years. Weathered lines on his face, not as much of that short, white hair on his head. He still had a firm build, though, like Tarzan in the movies. Probably still had trim lined up all over town. He always did well with the ladies.

Walter stood and clapped as Knox and Visel came to a stop. "You came through, Visel, but you're late. We've got to cut and run if we want to get a jump on this spook's outfit."

Knox almost laughed, the gist of it coming to him. "Good to see you, too, Walter. Funny, but I don't remember asking you for a getaway day ride."

Walter grinned like a snake oil salesman. "What are friends for, eh, Knoxy?"

"Knoxy, that's cute. Haven't heard so much as a lick from you since I been inside and here you are with the nicknames. Guess you're still too busy ratting off your numbers' competition to the cops."

Walter snarled as his greaseball pals shared a concerned look. "I don't do that no more."

Knox rolled his neck, feeling looser now. Fresh air all around, freedom within reach. "Oh, that's right. You and the Sherwood kid had a dust-up and now the heat's on. Heard all about it inside, that's too bad."

Walter took a step forward, smirking. "If I remember right, his old man was the one that sent you up."

Knox felt himself go tight again. "Yeah, and I wish I could say I shed a few tears when I heard someone eighty-sixed him, but then I'd be lying."

Visel stepped between them. "Enough! You two can jaw like old ladies at a tea some other time. Pay up, MacKeye, and let's get a move on."

Knox gave Visel a hard look. "What is this? Why aren't I going out the front, like everybody else?"

Walter eased up. "Think about it, Knoxy, what do you get when you leave out front? You get a few bucks from the prison board, something to make a start with, not a whole heckuva lot. You get a scratch of paper scribbled with the address of some halfway house you wouldn't want to be caught dead in, and what do you get there? You get a hot and a cot and a roof over your head for a few nights and then you're out on the streets, all alone. It's nothing a decent man would stand for, that's the truth. It's the gutter. You know it and I know it. But what am I offering you? A hundred bones, straight up, for nothing but an hour of your time. You were a great wheelman, back in the day, I know you remember. I need you, right now, and I'll pay you, don't worry. Just keep her running, and we'll all come out ahead. What do you say?"

Knox looked from Walter to Visel to the two toughs leaning against the car, weighing his options. Could you pull your blade, shut 'em all down, grab the wheels and go? Not a chance. You're slow, frail, and outnumbered four to one. "And if I say no?"

Walter cracked his knuckles. "You could go out the front, sure, but then, who knows? Maybe you're seen doing the wrong things with the wrong people."

Visel nodded. "Happens all the time. Guys get out, they cross paths with an old friend, and boom — parole is shot and they're right back inside."

Knox let out a nervous laugh. "That's some racket, but you just try and put me back inside and we might all kick off."

Visel flexed fists. "You really want to take that chance?"

Walter shook his head and started for the car. "I had you figured wrong, Sutton. Thought maybe these years inside had given you some sense. It's too bad, really. I hear the guards are even worse on repeat offenders."

Knox looked at Visel — the big man, calm and menacing.

Knox looked at the car — his one chance at freedom.

The choice is clear, he thought, stepping past Visel and walking carefully toward the driver's side of the Ford. His pulse up, his hands clammy. *Christ, do I even remember how to drive?*

Walter smiled. "Glad you came to your senses, Knoxy. Now, if you'd be so kind as to get into the fucking car, we need to leave."

Knox slid inside the Ford and took the wheel. It surprised him, how it felt just like coming home. The familiar washed over him, guiding him. He ran his hands along the steering wheel, the dash, the seat — he'd never felt more at home.

Time was ticking. Walter slid into the car, smug, and smacked the passenger door a few times. "Now let's go already!"

Knox fired up the car, the engine coming to life on the spot, and started to pull away. He turned and gave the prison one last look as they drove off. *Goodbye, darkness. I'll die before I ever see your shadows again.*

Walter leaned his head out the window and looked back at Visel. He raised his left hand toward the sky, holding it up straight like the Nazis do when they salute.

"Hey, Visel!" he called out. "Heil Hitler!"

Walter roared and the two in the back started to laugh, too, the three of them getting a real kick out of it. Knox felt like a heel, not being in on the joke. He came to an intersection and started to brake.

"Where to?"

"Second and Leigh," Walter said.

Knox thought it over. "Jackson Ward?"

"Very good, Sutton. Four years in the clink and you still know your way around."

Knox heard familiar sounds coming from the back seat and turned to look. Sure enough, Walter's pals were loading bullets into their guns. He shot Walter a knowing look.

"This ought to be fun. Good for you and bad for someone else, if I remember the way of it."

Walter pointed his own gun at Knox.

"Just quit your yammerin' and *drive*."

Knox coasted to a stop off Leigh on the south side of the street, just east of Second, and let the Ford's engine purr.

Look, dead ahead: an easy exit route down a one-way street.

Look, to the right: a dirt-and-gravel alleyway, a surefire dead end.

Look, one street up: an alternate route if the cops show.

Angles, exits, getaway paths. *Wheelman shit*, Knox thought. In his blood, in his bones. He learned it firsthand from the old man, the best there ever was, running moonshine through the backwoods of southwest Virginia. Real father-and-son bonding: out the window shootouts at 90 miles an hour, hiding out in tin roof shacks for days at a time, living the good life once the coast cleared. Knox had never been happier.

Walter spoiled the memory, reaching over and grabbing him by the shirtsleeve like he did, pulling him in close.

"Remember what I said, Sutton. Keep it running and stay put, or we'll put you back inside." Knox flinched as Walter tapped his left cheek, like an uncle might do, before he and one of the toughs darted from the car, taking the sidewalk at a full clip and making a beeline up Second Street.

Knox brought his window down and took in the fresh morning air, a few deep breaths to calm his nerves. Behind him, the other tough oozed tension. Tapping his fingers against his leg, fidgeting with his gun. Knox wondered: can I get my blade out, lunge for the back, and stab him before he gets a shot off?

Suddenly, joyous cheers filled the air.

Knox gripped the steering wheel, ready to jet. All around the car, it seemed, the world was coming alive. Negro men, women, and children hugged one another and ran across the streets to embrace their family and friends. It couldn't be more than ten o'clock in the morning and here was a party starting like it was a Saturday night.

"It's over!" they screamed. "It's over in Europe!"

And then, from somewhere, a man's deep voice rang out. "Excuse me!"

Knox looked to his left. Coming toward him now was a tall, imposing black man with a patch over his left eye and a clerical collar around his neck. A one-eyed preacher man that leaned over some, crouching down to get a better look at the two in the car.

Knox turned his head and whispered into the back seat. "What are we gonna do?"

The tough in the back cocked his gun. "Just keep her running, jailbird, I'll deal with the preacher."

Yeah, and I bet it'll be as raw a deal as there is, Knox thought as the preacher stormed his way toward them, saying to Knox, "Yeah, that's right, I'm talking to you, son. Whatcha' come 'round here for?"

Knox felt his nerves rattle. From behind him, he heard,

"Goddamn spooks." Then, shouts came from up Second Street. *BAM, BAM, BAM* — gunshots, too.

Suddenly, Walter and his pal came around the corner in a hurry, the two of them racing toward the Ford. They both hobbled some, holding one another up as people in the street began to scurry in a panic. Their joyous cheers turned to cries of horror as both men waved their guns and threw themselves into the car, leaving a trail of blood behind them.

Walter screamed, the man clearly in pain. "Go, go, go!"

Knox turned to his left again and locked eyes with the preacher man, both men getting a good look at the other. *Damn it*, Knox thought, it's too late to hide my face. And now, *what the --*

Knox was stunned as the preacher stopped in the middle of the street and pulled a gun. Knox laid into the gas and tore away, almost taking out a family of four. Parents and kids dove every which way as bullets rattled off the rear end of the sled.

Knox put Constance and Sadie first in his mind and blocked the rest of the world away.

You goddamn fool, he thought.

You goddamn fool.

3

Timony raced her Packard One-Twenty down Grove Avenue in a frenzied bid to meet the caterer at her home and threw a quick look back at the open boxes of champagne and liquor crammed along the back seat. The bottles clinked against one another as she threaded her way through the neighborhood and turned into their private cul-de-sac. Five boxes, eight bottles a piece. A mix of brandy, rum, gin, and bubbly, the liquor now on the ABC ration-free list, thank the heavens. *But my goodness*, she wondered, with everyone coming, would it really be enough? Approaching the house now, she slowed and steered her car into their cobblestone driveway, breathing a sigh of relief. No caterer yet, but there's a truck and some men unloading musical instruments onto the back patio. *That* would be Johnny Pepper and his band, The Salt Shakers, the hottest ticket in town. A giddy feeling rushed through Timony as she pulled her car to a stop. Oh, what a party this will be! She gave herself a quick look in the rearview, checking her hair and makeup and adjusting her black short-brimmed chiffon hat just so. Pleased with herself, confident. *Yes, they love to talk about your weekly bridge parties, Timony Wells, but this is a party they will talk about for years to come!*

She grabbed her purse and the Thalhimer's bag with her new cocktail dress from the front seat, snagged a bottle of bubbly from the back, and moved with excitement from the car to the house. She exchanged waves and hellos with Johnny and his band as she scooted along the patio, twirling and dancing with herself in celebration of today's wonderful, wonderful news. She sprinted through the sunroom and the living room in a flutter and came into the kitchen where two of her servants were gathered, her arms open wide, ready to hug the entire world.

"Oh my dears, my darlings, it's all happening! Tonight, we're going to throw this town's largest, wildest party and cheer this glorious day until our lungs burst! Can you believe it?"

Macy, her maid and friend and secret confidant in life, looked up from the dishes she was washing and shook her head. "We're excited just like you are, Miss T, but I don't know how we're gonna fit all these people in this house!"

Timony dropped her purse and bag to the floor and handed the bottle of champagne to Christian, Macy's young, handsome brother and their man-of-all-trades. "Christian, be a darling, please, open this immediately and pour us each a glass!"

Christian made a face, because after all, it was only 11 o'clock in the morning. "Are you sure, Miss T?"

Timony laid her hat gently on the counter. "Yes, yes, open it, please!"

Christian smiled and went about opening the bottle as Timony freed Macy from the sink and moved her about the kitchen in a two-step.

"Now, my dear Macy, you know as well as I do that we have all the room in the world here! We have the patio and the driveway and the drawing room, even Harrison's study if we need it!"

"Oh, you know he won't like that, Miss T! And people in the driveway? At this house? The friends you keep won't ever let you forget it! Can you imagine, the mayor, enjoying himself from out there? My lord!"

POP! went the champagne bottle and the cork sailed through the air, ricocheting off the ceiling as Timony gave Macy a spin. "Oh, nonsense, they'll love it! And I'm going to be sure all three of you get to enjoy the party, too! This news is for all of us, *everyone* must celebrate! Now, where are our drinks?"

Christian set three tall champagne flutes along the middle counter and began pouring from the bottle. The ladies broke from their dance and made for either side of Christian. He finished pouring his own and they each took their glasses in hand, Macy and Christian raising theirs to meet Timony's as she made a toast. "To all the soldiers and the generals and the nurses and the wives, to all of them and all of us, that's one front down and one to go!

Hear, hear!"

Macy and Christian repeated the expression in unison and took slight sips of their drinks while Timony downed hers with a single tip of the glass.

"Now *that* is how you celebrate!" Timony exclaimed.

Macy wasn't so sure, the rush of the moment catching up to both her and her brother as they giggled, still in awe of being offered a glass of champagne this early in the day. Macy set her flute down on the counter and gave Timony a strong look. "Maybe that's how *you* celebrate, but I'm not having anymore of that, not this early, not with all we have to do." Macy was a middle-aged, full-bodied Negro woman who had learned to stand her ground with anyone, anywhere. She might be Timony's maid, but she was no pushover.

Timony went about pouring another glass of champagne for herself. "Oh, fiddlesticks, both of you. You've earned it! Hell, we all have. Now, where is your cousin? He deserves a drink, too."

Almost at once, the joy drained from both Macy and Christian, their faces suddenly as gray as a stormy day.

Christian fought with the words. "Miss T, Robinson is upstairs with Mr. Wells, they're — "

"Say no more, you two, not a word!" Timony downed her second helping of champagne in a flash, handed the empty glass off to Christian, and started from the kitchen without missing a beat. "Both of you, enjoy those drinks and then get to it! The caterer will be here any minute!"

Macy called after her. "Timony, wait."

But Timony was in the hall now, rushing off. "Oh, don't try and stop me, Macy, you buzzkill! Your cousin deserves to celebrate, too! Hell, I might even offer Harrison a glass!"

Timony raced up the stairs and started down the causeway that led to the bedrooms, calling out for the two of them.

"Robinson! Harrison! Where are you two?"

No answer. She called out again and got the same, so she moved further down the hall and began to peek into the rooms as she passed each one. First into the guest bedroom and then into Harrison's. No one in either. She checked her own bedroom next and smiled, finding it cleaned, her bed made, her dressers straightened, but no, they were not there either. Puzzled, she stood for a moment and felt herself grow tight and hesitant.

He wouldn't dare, she thought.

But a noise from around the corner gave her pause and she stepped back into the hallway and looked south, to the rear of the house, toward Nolan's bedroom. Sure enough, there was a light on and something happening inside his room.

Timony started that way, moving slowly, careful not to run in heels, especially on the carpet. *That's just what you need*, she thought, to slip and fall and embarrass yourself in front of him. To feel slighted. No, she said to herself, I won't let that happen, I won't let him get the better of me, not today. She continued down the hallway and held herself in check as the anger within her began to blossom, the joy and delight she had known all morning slipping away. She brought herself to a stop just outside the doorway to Nolan's room and watched as her husband and Robinson moved their son'sf furniture about his room. Pushing his bed against the wall and stacking chairs from the living room on top of it. The pillows crumpled, the covers all a mess, as if their son were finally home and had slept in his own bed. Neither Robinson nor her husband noticed her standing in the doorway. Harrison was too busy barking orders, speaking to Robinson the way he did.

"No, not like that! Turn the chairs *this* way, toward the wall. Christ!"

A dejected Robinson did as he was told, the young man clearly at odds with the task he was being commanded to carry out. Timony calmed the rage inside her and took a deep breath before she spoke.

"Robinson."

Both men froze, the look on their faces like that of cat burglars caught in the act. Timony cleared her throat and continued.

"Please take the chairs off Nolan's bed and take them to the guest house nearest the driveway, along with whatever else Harrison has instructed you to put into this room. Christian is in the kitchen, tell him I said for the two of you to do this together.

And see Macy before you work too hard, she has something for you."

Robinson came to life, eager to right the wrong. "Yes, Miss T."

Timony gave her husband a sharp glare before she turned and retreated to her bedroom, forcing calm into her legs as she made her way down the hall. She felt herself grow flush, the champagne catching up with her. Tears welled in her eyes, her entire body was on the fringe of a dizzy spell. *Finally*, she thought, stepping into her room, steadying herself against the wall. She quickly threw a light on and went straight for the phone on her bedside table. Sitting on the edge of the bed now and peeling off her heels as she dialed the kitchen, speaking in a hurry.

"Macy, it's me Please bring up a pitcher of ice water and the Thalhimer's bag with my new dress. Thank you."

She hung up before Macy could respond. She was too embarrassed to address the episode or admit her foolishness. She closed her eyes and massaged her temples, whispering to herself. "Harrison, you jackass."

Had Macy and Christian tried to warn her? Yes, that's right, a call from the kitchen had followed Timony to the main foyer of the house, but by then, she was so caught up within herself that she didn't think to heed that little voice in her head that said, *wait, something might be wrong*. She was rushed and impulsive, her instincts compromised by the champagne.

Timony heard the carpet shuffle outside her bedroom door. That would be Harrison, right on time. Ready to tell her like it really is and how it should be. So cocksure and justified all the time.

"It was just for one night, Timony."

Timony let out a sigh and moved from her bed to her dresser, keeping her eyes to the floor. Unable to look at him straight on.

"I won't have it for one night, Harrison, I won't have it for a hundred. I have told you again and again that we will not use our son's room like some common storage closet!"

"It's been eight months, Timony, we have to face the facts."

She looked up then and addressed his reflection in the mirror. Sure enough, he was standing tall, as if he'd done nothing wrong.

"Eight months, two days, and something close to twelve hours, to be exact. Or did you think I'd forgotten?"

"Oh, for God's sake, Timony. He's my son, too."

Timony took to removing her jewelry. "Really? Well, pardon me if I needed that affirmation, but I wouldn't call cramming our son's bedroom with the living room furniture to be the most fatherly of gestures."

Harrison took a cautious step into her bedroom. "You think you're the only one who wonders if he'll ever come home? You, who parades around the city in tomorrow's fashions and hosts weekly parties that cost more than our servants' wages for the entire month!"

"That's certainly one way to change the subject. To be honest, it's nice to hear you consider my social calendar at all. Funny thing, being as you hardly ever notice me or my comings and goings, at least not until they interfere with your business meetings and evenings at the club."

Harrison spoke with a forced conviction. "Oh, come now. You know as well as I do that you're welcome with me anytime. At the Commonwealth, at the Westwood. But the meetings, they just wouldn't interest you. It's all figures and the war and what's to come next."

"How would you know what interests me?"

"What?"

Timony watched her husband in the mirror. Saw his eyes dance and his confidence flutter. *Let's test him*, she thought, feeling impulsive again. That champagne rush, still with her. She turned to face him and went about taking off her day dress. Undoing her collar and then the three front buttons one by one before unfastening her belt. Pulling the dress open across her chest and watching his eyes find her breasts. Slipping one arm out and then the next before edging her hips out of it completely. Putting on a real show, like a seductress, just like she imagined Rita Hayworth might do. She let the dress fall past her legs and rest on the floor, standing before him now in nothing but her slip.

"You were saying… something about what interests you?"

Timony wanted to believe her husband liked what he saw, but

the smirk on his face told her otherwise.

"Nice try, Timony. Who's changing the subject now?"

The squeal of metal wheels stole their attention and they turned to find Macy suddenly there in the hallway, rolling a serving tray to a stop just outside the doorway and resting a pitcher of ice water atop it, saying "Here you go, Miss Timony," as if the act itself were reason enough to be glad. But Timony was anything but, embarrassed and angry now at having been rejected by her husband once again. She grabbed her wrap-around robe from the dresser and rushed to cover herself. She spoke curtly. "Thank you, Macy. Please let me know when the caterer has arrived."

Macy set the Thalhimer's bag just inside the room and shared a knowing look with Timony. The two women had known each other for over fifteen years and it was almost second nature, the way Macy could read Timony's mood by the tone in her voice. She could sense trouble brewing, sure enough, she was no stranger to their challenges as husband and wife. "I'll call you just as soon he arrives, Miss T." Macy eased the door shut and excused herself. Timony waited until she'd gone and then sank into her vanity chair, suddenly exhausted.

"It's hardly midday, Timony, and here you are, nearly spent," Harrison said, pouring himself a glass of ice water. "I can smell the champagne. You're drinking already, this early in the day?"

A parched Timony watched him drink. "I was celebrating."

"There'll be plenty of time for that later, don't you think?" He downed the rest of his water and set the empty glass back on the tray. Looking altogether refreshed now, with not a care in the world. He didn't even offer her a glass.

"Speak for yourself. It's been almost three and half years since this mess began, I'm more than ready to enjoy myself."

"Tell that to the Japs."

Timony scoffed. "My god, Harrison, must you be such a bore about it all?"

"It's my job, in case you've forgotten. Hell, I've been fielding calls from defense plants all morning, trying to negotiate this and resell that. I wouldn't say surplus is a bad thing, but everybody wants a piece. And they're all coming after me to get it."

"You were at the office this morning?"

"Yes, bright and early."

"I wondered where you were. I missed you at breakfast."

"I am sorry about that, but I knew with the party tonight, I wouldn't be much help for the next few days. Offices all over town are closed tomorrow and Thursday."

The phone by the bedside rang then, startling them both. Harrison made his way around the other side of the bed, being careful to avoid even so much as brushing against his wife, and picked up the phone. "Yes?"

Timony went for the serving tray and poured herself a glass of water, downing it slowly and letting the cooling rush soothe her nerves.

"I'll tell her," Harrison said before he hung up the phone. "The caterer's here."

Timony couldn't be more appreciative, glad that something new had arisen and would take her mind from all this and put it back on the real business at hand, tonight's party. She perked herself up and strolled into her spacious walk-in closet, pulling on the light and marveling at her many outfits. A few hundred, easy, certainly enough to rival the likes of Joan Crawford, she hoped, maybe even Betty Grable. She called out to Harrison as shoe pairings with her new cocktail dress ran through her mind.

"Tell me who you've invited to the party, Harrison, so I can make sure the caterer has enough."

Harrison leaned against the closet doorway. "Everyone from the office, plus spouses and dates, so that's about two dozen."

"And your mother?"

"She was planning to come, but turns out she's busy attending to some friends at our old synagogue. Rotten business, really. A woman we knew has been killed."

"My God, who?"

"Ruth Kleinfeld. She and her husband owned a store in town. Gosh, I've known her since I was ten, maybe eleven. She taught us all Hebrew and made jewelry for almost everyone."

"That's awful. Did I ever meet her?"

"If you had, it would have been some time ago. I can't even

remember the last time I saw her, but while we're on the subject of awful, I should tell you, I've invited Stolmy."

"Reed? My goodness. You know Imogene is coming, so of course I extended an invitation to Bennie."

"They're still getting on?"

"I never know with those two. They're on, they're off, they're on again. And now, apparently, he's asked her to marry him."

"What'd she say?"

"She says he has to quit his job first, stop running around and playing cops and robbers."

"Well, I say there's fat chance of that. In any case, I'll keep Stolmy with me, you keep the two of them with you."

Timony grabbed her favorite pair of black Mary Jane pumps from the shoe rack and scooted from the closet, slinking past Harrison like a ghost. *You had your chance,* she thought. "Jedidiah's always been good about keeping the peace and he knows them both very well. I'll let him intercede if need be."

"I should have known he'd be coming."

"And why wouldn't he? He's one of my closest friends, so of course I want him here with us tonight. And he's bringing a date."

"What's his name?"

"Oh, stop. He says she's an old friend who's in need of a new scene. I'm looking forward to meeting her."

"You'll certainly have plenty of people to entertain."

"As if I'd have it any other way," Timony said, smiling as she took a seat at her dresser and started to freshen up for the caterer. She watched then through the mirror as her husband milled about the center of her bedroom, unsure of what to do next or what to say. *Clearly too chickenshit to make a move now,* she thought, before he finally piped up.

"I guess, then, that you've, uh, got it from here. The party, I mean."

Timony forced a smile. "Don't you worry, dear. It'll be a party like we've never had before."

Harrison almost laughed. "That's what I'm afraid of."

"Just shut the door on your way out, would you?"

Harrison let the abruptness of her words sink in before he

turned to leave the room.

"And Harrison?"

"Yes?"

"Don't ever put furniture from our home or anything else for that matter into our son's room, ever again."

And then he was gone, just like that.

MIA, they called it.

Missing In Action.

First her son, now her husband.

How I wish it were but an affliction or a curable disease, Timony thought, something to be diagnosed and treated with medication. But no, this was something far worse. A void that had taken root within both her home and herself and continued to grow since her son's disappearance.

Eager to fill that void, Timony laid her makeup brush on the dresser and looked at herself in the mirror, her hair falling over half her face like Veronica Lake's peek-a-boo cut and suddenly she was some kind of mystery woman. A woman to be desired, perhaps, maybe even written about. Slowly, she slid her right hand down underneath her stocking to the folds between her legs and massaged her spot in a circle, gently at first and then a bit harder, desperate for a release. She watched herself as she kept at it and gripped the surface of the dresser with her other hand, squeezing it so hard it might crack.

4

Marlon squeezed his tattered bible with both hands and tilted his head back to better see the heavens. All he could truly see with his one good eye was another St. Philip Hospital ceiling in dire need of repair. The paint cracking, the plaster flaking over his assembled flock like that desert dust back at Fort Huachuca. *It's tempting*, he thought, to let it get the better of you, to let the anger boil your blood until you run over. But he'd been at this game his whole life and he knew when to look beyond the devil's work and see the truth. He closed his eye and called up his sermon voice.

"Come 'round, Lord, come 'round, because we're down here so very low today, so very low indeed. A vicious hand has struck down our friend and brother Cornell and he bleeds, Lord, oh how he bleeds! And it's today, of all days, this day of joyous news that we gather here in support, gather together to heal one another and pray. Oh Lord, how we pray!"

A round of "Amen!" circled the hallway.

"So come 'round with your strength, Lord, and build our brother *up*, but do not pity us Lord, do not pity us this day, for as we come together in prayer, know this, Lord, we will not be quieted down."

"Oh, no!"

"No, we will not be silenced in our suffering, and for that, we ask your forgiveness, Lord."

"Oh, Lord!"

"With your blessing, we will rise."

"Praise Jesus!"

"Please, Lord, grant our brother the strength to heal and forgive us our transgressions, for we are ever in your service. Ah-men."

"Amen!"

Marlon opened his right eye and adjusted the eye patch over his left. Beads of sweat and phantom pains needled the knotted crater of skin where his left eye used to reside something fierce. Marlon was young for his twenty-nine years and looked it, and yet, he often felt as if he aged several years in a day, the way trouble compounded for his kind. He loosened his clerical collar, wiped the sweat from his brow, and thought back through the day. The morning had started with prayer, celebrating the news from Europe. V-E Day, here and now, Praise Jesus! The celebrations started in the church gathering hall, hugs and cheers and even some libations, too. Oh yes, a few bottles of ol' Garrison's firewater had been passed 'round, yes indeed. Just a few pops, though, nothing over the line. Soon, though, the congregation's joy was too much for the church alone and they spilled onto Two Street, the sight of them like a New Orleans parade, the lot of them dancing and singing at the top of their lungs. All the typical hootin' and hollerin' you'll find north of Broad and west of Fifth on any given Saturday night, only this time its ten something in the am on a Tuesday. And then all that joy, all that love, was spoiled in an instant by an evil hand come 'round. Can't let Negro folk have too much fun, now, no sir. Show us a world where they give out peace, love, and happiness to all and we'll show you a sign that says 'blackie no can have.'

Cornell's sister Mary came over to Marlon, on the verge of tears. He brought his arms down around her, held her tight. Marlon caressed her hair and spoke to her gently. "Now, now, what do the nurses say?"

"They just don't know. They say he's lost a lot of blood." She cried like a baby and buried her face into his chest.

"That he has," Marlon said, "that he has." As a matter of fact, much of Cornell's blood was caked to Marlon's own shirtsleeves, having dried there in the hours since he carried Cornell from his poolroom to Garrison's pickup and then to the hospital lobby.

Marlon's cousin Charles came over to them now, wiping tears from his deep-set eyes. Charles was not an imposing man but he was a *fierce* soul, the look on his face now like that of a wildcat out for blood.

"Come on, now, what's the plan? Let's get after 'em!"

Marlon's look told Charles *to keep your voice down*. He gave Mary a squeeze and whispered a comfort into her ear before pulling Charles to the side and speaking in a low voice.

"You best be careful what you say and when, you hear me?"

"Oh I hear you just fine, brother Marlon, but that don't change a thing. What're we standing 'round here for? We needs to be on the move, now."

"Not yet. Right now, we wait."

"For what? For 'em to come at us again? Mr. King didn't say nothing about all this."

"He didn't have to. We take on a situation like this, we assume these kinds of risks."

"Then who was it? You said you got a good look at the driver."

Marlon called up his memory and saw the eyes of that wheelman again, saw him pick up those two that robbed Cornell and speed off.

"That I did, that I did. He was a hard boy, of sorts. Rough on the outside, but a little soft in the eyes. Like he'd been around some but maybe not too sure of himself."

"Maybe he was a soldier, come home already, like you."

"Nah. Any soldier seen any action worth a damn gonna have it right there in their eyes, whether they've come home in one piece or not. This one, he's like somethin' left out in the sun too long. All burnt up on the outside, inside nothin' but mush."

"Make way, make way!"

Threatening voices from near the lobby doors put Marlon and Charles on edge, and with good reason. Two city cops had entered the hospital and were headed right for them, carrying their air of menace like a stinkbug holds a stench. Both in uniform, packing heat. One a little taller than the other, both of them sporting that holier-than-thou look the police take on when they roll up on black folk. Marlon could see they meant to make a scene so he jumped out in front and cut them off before they made the crowd.

"Officers, officers, pray tell, we're into a grave situation here with family and friends, so if I may, allow me to intercede on behalf of my constituents. What brings you 'round this glorious day?"

The cops came to a halt and shared a look. The shorter one looked Marlon over, sizing him up. The taller one said, "I'm Officer Strickland, this is Halifax. And you are?"

"Jefferson, Marlon Jefferson. Although some folk just call me Preacher."

Strickland got right to it. "Did you fire a gun this morning, around 10 o'clock, in the vicinity of Second and Marshall?"

Marlon was stunned — no one in *his* camp would have called the cops, how could they know? He knew he shouldn't, the devil be damned, but he lied. "Why, no, officers. What on earth would give you such an idea?"

Halifax, the shorter of the two, rested a hand on his holstered gun and got tough. "Don't play dumb with us. Do you have a gun on you now?"

The crowd behind Marlon went hush. He could hear nothing but hospital sounds now. Babies crying, patients moaning, nurses hustling.

"Officers, officers, please, what's this all about?"

Strickland sighed, a smile taking shape on his face. "If that's the way you want it, then, preacher, face the wall."

"I really don't see as that's necessary. Please, we're in the middle of — "

Halifax moved quick, turned Marlon around and threw him against the wall. "Enough talk, n____! Now put your hands on the wall, spread your legs."

Gasps rounded the hallway. Charles was having none of it, charging the cops with balled fists. "You bring that rough stuff to us, you gonna get it right back!"

"The hell we are," Strickland said, decking Charles with a haymaker. Charles hit the floor, choking for breath. Strickland stepped toward the crowd and brought up his gun. "Nobody say a word or you'll get the same!"

The crowd whimpered and shuddered. Marlon hung his head in embarrassment, the shame washing over him like a tidal wave. There he was, on display, for everyone to see. Marlon forced himself to stay quiet as Halifax took to patting him down, talking to him all the while with liquor on his breath.

"I don't know who it was, preacher man, but somebody sold you out. Made an anonymous call and said a one-eyed man of God was so excited this morning he took to firing a gun at strangers. Now, now, who could have made that call? Any ideas?"

Marlon had an idea, alright, but that could wait. What most worried him now was that Halifax was about to find the pistol he had tucked into the back of his waistband and that would most definitely mean a trip downtown and some more roughhousing care of these two fist-happy cops here.

And just like that, Halifax shook his head, saying "Boy, you're in for it now" as he pulled the pistol out from under Marlon's shirt and showed it to Strickland, the two of them happy as could be at the sight of it. The crowd gasped some more as the cops brought Marlon's arms back and cuffed him tight, so it hurt right good when they grabbed him by the shoulder and forced him to move. Marlon kept his head up like the strong preacher he was as the cops marched him toward the lobby, the assembled crowd parting for him like he was Moses at the Red Sea. He told everyone as he passed, "Gonna be alright, gonna be ok. I got that Holy Ghost by my side, don't you worry." Kept saying it even as Halifax ribbed him with a blackjack and told him to shut his mouth.

The cops took Marlon to a basement, somewhere dark and remote. Didn't run him through Central Booking like they should, no sir. He'd done all that before and knew the fun that came with being held for hours on end with no food or water until the judge finally got 'round to seeing you. And only then it was to tell you what you already knew, that you were guilty and sentenced for such and such a time and oh, there's a fine, too, so don't forget to pay that before they haul you off to the city jail.

No, this time they went straight to bruising and bloodying Marlon with a rubber hose before dropping him into a hardback chair. Something with no give at all. Tough as bricks on his back, as uncomfortable as they come.

Strickland took up at a desk across from him. "Makes no difference you're some preacher man. You fired a gun, in broad daylight, so now you just sit there and think about what it is you need to be telling us. There's some good news out there today and we aim to be a part of it, so that means we ain't gonna let no pistol firing ne-gro take that away from us, you hear me?"

Marlon could hear him just fine, the words of this Southern white boy coming through clear and righteous, but he himself could hardly speak, what with the blood running down from his nose and into his mouth, clogging up his airwaves. He spit onto the floor so he could breathe.

Halifax circled him with the hose. "Oh, that's good, preacher. Dirty up our floor. We'll make you clean it up, just you wait."

Strickland leaned across the table. "So whatcha' got to be firing a gun about, preacher?"

Marlon coughed out a few breaths and called upon the Lord to help him find the words. The spirit within him told him to give them *some* of it, but not all, so that's what he did.

"Couple of hard boys came through the neighborhood. Tore up my friend's poolroom and shot him in the gut. We get that from time to time and don't like to stand for it, so I carry something with me."

"And just what exactly did you fire the gun *at*?"

"Getaway car."

"Is that right. Make?"

"Ford, prewar. Mercury Blue."

"Get a look at the driver?"

For the second time that day, Marlon lied and said, "No."

Strickland glanced at his notepad. "We understand there's a numbers operation going on in your buddy's poolroom. Maybe a few slot machines, too. Maybe this mess you talk about has something to do with all that."

Marlon didn't say anything.

Strickland smiled. "That's interesting. Suddenly, you've got nothing to say."

Halifax came 'round to face Marlon, taunting him with the hose. "We go 'round a few more times with this, I bet you'll have plenty to say."

Marlon rolled his neck, let his muscles relax. That's one good thing the Army taught him: don't stiffen up when you engage the enemy, it makes you more vulnerable to defeat. "Well, if we're gonna get into it, Mr. Policeman, let's get on with it, then."

Halifax came right up to Marlon's face then, fuming. Swinging the hose around, making him flinch. The short man probably more pissed about his meager size than anything else. "Oh, you want to test me, is that it? Didn't get enough of this the first time?"

Strickland stood up and walked around the desk. "Look, Mr. Jefferson, you're going to jail, one way or the other. If you help us out here, give us some good info for our report, we can see that you get into a good cell, maybe get before a judge sooner than some."

Marlon felt his back stiffen again. *You test me, Lord, how you test me.*

Strickland leaned back and took a seat on the desk. All relaxed, like he was a teacher. "Mr. Jefferson, does the name Walter MacKeye mean anything to you?"

Marlon felt pain in his chest and wondered if there was blood in his lungs. "I've heard of him."

"And what have you heard?"

"He a thug, making trouble for your kind."

"My kind?"

"Po-lice."

Strickland smiled. "What about Jedidiah King?"

"He I know."

"Is that so?"

Marlon coughed and grabbed his ribs. The pain was sharp. "Mr. King's a regular on our side of town. Comes 'round often, even owns a stake in one of our hotels. He's good to our community, too. Donates to my church, helps out. He's a good man, Mr. King. Was there for me when I come home."

"Come home from where?"

"The war."

Strickland was surprised. "Really, you were a soldier?"

"So what if I was?"

Halifax got up close. "Talk back to us and you'll lose that other eye, right quick."

Marlon almost jumped up and took Halifax down to the floor with him, but if he wasn't in bad enough already, he knew it would be worse if he did.

"Yes, I was a soldier."

Strickland wanted more. "Doing what?"

"I made bombs."

Strickland and Halifax howled. Strickland couldn't wait to say it. "Well, what do you know, a bomb-making n____. Doesn't look like you were too good at it now, does it? Whatcha' do, set one off right in front of you?" The two howled some more.

Marlon took a deep breath and fed them another lie, his third of the day. "No, this was a Jap bomb, come onto our ship."

Strickland was impressed. "Is that so? Well, is that what you do now, make bombs?"

Marlon took a deep breath and looked at the ceiling. He knew what was coming.

Strickland looked at Halifax. "Cause that sure would explain some things, don't you think, partner? Preacher man here making bombs, running numbers, getting into it with the big boys."

Halifax grinned, spinning the hose around. "I don't like his attitude. I say we get more out of him."

Strickland came to his feet. "I'll hold him down."

Marlon felt the spirit guide his fury and was about to spring himself from the chair when a white woman dressed to the nines tore into the room and said, "You will do no such thing!" Two beat cops were at her heels, stumbling over themselves. Marlon guessed they had been unable to stop her, the way she carried herself. Head up high, walking fast in shiny two-inch heels.

Strickland was stunned. "Who the hell are you?"

Marlon, too, was stunned as this woman came straight for him and began to help him to his feet, this woman in her long black gloves and form-fitting evening dress. He couldn't help but admire her sleek, thick brown hair, styled like a fashion model. She wore bright red lipstick and smelled like a bouquet of spring flowers. Marlon winced as he stood, impressed with this woman's fortitude, and guessed that because of it, her cheeks had known the back of a man's hand a time or two.

Halifax scowled. "Hey, we're talking to you, bitch! Who are you?"

The woman pulled an official-looking letter from the pocket of her handbag and handed it to Halifax. "Who I am is not important, but I *am* here today on behalf of one Jedidiah King, who, by special arrangement with Acting Lieutenant Sherwood, has authorized *me* to procure this improperly detained and horribly mistreated man. In that letter, you'll find a directive authorizing me in this capacity *and* the signatures of both misters, King *and* Sherwood."

Strickland almost laughed. "That's a bunch-a shit. Only person we take orders from is *us*. Not you, and certainly not King. Why, he ain't even police!"

The woman began to lead Marlon from the room, speaking to the cops over her shoulder. "Yes, well, in this very moment, that's just not a point we're going to contest. Now, if you please."

All Strickland could do was watch as this mystery woman and the preacher hurried off. Halifax looked plain dumbstruck, trying to make sense of the words on the page. He looked up from the letter. "Hey, now, this ain't shit!"

One of the beat cops made a move for the preacher, but the woman turned on the quick and kicked him in the balls. He fell to the floor, turning blue. And then the woman and Marlon were gone.

Strickland grabbed the letter from Halifax. "The hell is this?"

Halifax threw the rubber hose to the ground. "It ain't no official nothing, just some kind of paper trail bullshit!"

Sure enough, all Strickland held in his hands was a delivery notice from King Tobacco Company. Nothing on it but an address and some instructions. No signatures, not a one.

Strickland balled it up and threw it across the room.

"Goddam!"

The woman hustled Marlon into the passenger seat of a Buick Century, ritzy wheels. He winced, grabbing his ribs, and fell into the seat, watching as she ran 'round the front end, this slender but capable woman making haste. Throwing herself into the car and firing it up. As they sped away, she pulled a short dog of Old Crow whiskey from under the front seat and handed it to Marlon.

"Now, I don't know if this offends you, Mr. Jefferson, but it might help numb the pain some."

Marlon took a few sips, grateful for both the gesture and the whiskey.

"Don't offend me none, m'am. Obliged."

Sirens rang out behind them — Strickland and Halifax were giving chase. The woman winked at Marlon and smiled as she laid into the gas. One look at her and Marlon had no doubt that she would lose the cops. Marlon couldn't help but admire the ease she had about her. All nice like, driving a beaten black man from his near incarceration to, well, somewhere.

Marlon cleared his throat. "If you don't mind me asking, m'am, where we headed?"

The woman took a hard corner at top speed, the tires righting from the skid. The woman sure of herself behind the wheel. Probably sure of herself in other ways, too. "Why you poor thing, you must wonder who I am. Well, I am Miss Constance Lee, a friend to you and a good friend to Mr. Jedidiah King, yes sir. He wants me to take you to the hospital your friend is at, what's it called again?"

"St. Philip."

She grinned and winked at him like it was a come on. "Yes, St Philip Hospital, have no fear. We'll be there in a jiffy."

She really leadfooted it then and Marlon leaned back into his seat, grateful for the comfort it gave him, but overtaken by fear, praying to the Lord all the while.

Please, God, don't take Cornell from us just yet.

5

Bennie surveyed the goings-on at police headquarters and rubbed sleep from his eyes. He'd grabbed a quick snooze on a basement cot until a call from City Hall woke him. Stolmy on the horn with a pep talk. "Continue to keep it quiet, Sherwood. No parades, no Victory dance hubbub, we've still got Japs to kill. And this business with the Jewish woman? Wrap it up, fast."

So much for sentiment, Bennie thought, watching as his people worked hard, their emotions split down the middle. Joy for V-E Day, anguish for Mrs. Kleinfeld. Bennie shook his head at the thought of her lifeless body and made a beeline for the new and improved detective's lair, now in a more spacious setting with newer desks and even a few windows. Stolmy insisted they move from the old, cramped office to roomier digs down the hall. "There's a shitload more crime going on, and we can't have the men working on top of one another, now can we?" One holdover remained, without protest: wall-to-wall pinups, carefully transferred to the new den by horny cops. Unsurprisingly, approval of the decorations was met with universal acclaim, since nothing could lighten the mood of a city detective quite like the inviting look of a half-dressed Hollywood starlet. Bennie scanned the wall — fresh cheesecake caught his eye: Linda Darnell and Yvonne De Carlo, both looking flush and delicious in next-to-nothing. Bennie felt himself stir — make up with Imogene quick and see what's playing at the Byrd, go for a night on the town.

Excited talk in the lair stole Bennie's attention. He rounded a corner and found Shane holding court at the blackboard, chalking up crude dot lines and stick figures for the benefit of the other case men assigned to The Victory Squad. Eddie Haden sat atop a desk and gnashed peanuts, studying the markup with his seen-it-all eyes. Bennie had made Shane lead on the investigation and Eddie his backup, much to Eddie's chagrin. Haden had fifteen years on the force to Shane's two, he thought he should be in charge.

Shane mocked up a bullet's trajectory on the board. "And then they surprised Mrs. Kleinfeld and ended her life."

"Why 'they'?" a vice bull asked.

Shane leaned against a desk. "It's a pattern we're noticing and we think it fits. Breaking and entering perps working in teams of two."

Bennie spoke up, made his presence known. "Does Mrs. Kleinfeld's husband have an alibi?"

Shane nodded. "Home asleep. The Kleinfeld's maid confirmed it, but both she and the husband were too devastated to give us much else."

Eddie went cross. "She's working late while he's catching zzz's? What a bum."

Bennie didn't like it either. "Still, let's give him a few days to mourn and make arrangements before we follow up. In the meantime, just to be safe, let's run his name by gun dealers around town and hope he doesn't own a 22."

Shane wrote in his notebook. "Check."

A homicide detective cracked his knuckles. "Nine times out of ten, it's the boyfriend or the husband."

Bennie held his hands up, as if to stop traffic. "That's true, but the swastika, the B and E pattern, Jewish business owners — let's not make any assumptions here."

Shane agreed as Eddie brushed peanut crumbs from his hands and popped off the desk, ready to get to it. "I say we play off our informants while we're waiting on the lab, see what shakes out."

Bennie liked the idea. "Yes, run with that, but be discreet and don't get sloppy. We need movement on this and fast. Where are we with evidence?"

Shane read from his notepad. "Rooney pulled several print sets from the five-and-dime and scoped the file index. No matches yet."

Bennie sighed, not entirely displeased. "Every second counts, gentlemen. You know what to do."

Shane rolled his neck. "You can count on us, boss. When we know, you will, too."

Bennie turned to leave, his knees quaking at the thought of seeing Imogene at the Wells' party. Hell, tonight, he'd choose hand-to-hand combat over a face-to-face with her.

Eddie called after him. "You gotta be kidding me, Sherwood. A big case like this, where're you off to?"

Bennie tried to think of a wisecrack, something to amuse the men and soften his edge, but he never had been much good with humor. And he was too spent from the day to conjure any wit.

"It's a party, The Wells are hosting. I need to make an appearance."

The men just nodded, no big deal.

Shane asked, "You taking Imogene?"

"Meeting her there." It just raced out of him and he didn't hear it until after he'd said it, but by then, it was too late. The men started to laugh and whistle, as if they'd just watched a .400 hitter whiff an easy pitch. Well, now. Shane and Eddie must have shared his tale of romantic woe with everyone on the squad. He shot them both a playful glare. "Gentlemen, you didn't."

Eddie roared while Shane played coy. "Oh, come on, boss, we're all rooting for you!"

"I'll bet you are. I'll remember this come assignment time, the both of you."

Bennie grinned and shot them all the bird as he turned to leave. The lot of them returned the gesture in kind. Eddie bowled over. Shane pleaded for him to take his word for it, he meant no harm.

Bennie's grin faded fast, to hell with them all. Seventeen hours into this day and he still wasn't through. He still had to conjure up the *cajones* to face Imogene, a swell gal that knew firsthand how he tossed and turned in bed and cried out in his sleep. What woman in her right mind would say yes to that.

Timony held her martini high above the crowd as she threaded her way through the throng of people crowded into her living room, brushing up against the bridge club ladies and their husbands as she inched her way from one side of the room to the other.

"Hello, hello," she said, risking a sip of her drink before raising it up again, careful not to let it splash. "There's food and drink, please make yourself at home!"

My God, she thought, *my home*. I'll have to hire more help just to have it *clean* —

Timony threw a sudden look behind her, both shocked and a little delighted. Did someone just pinch *my ass?* She locked eyes with one of the bridge club ladies' husbands. He shot her a suggestive wink before the crowd swallowed him up. Well, well — at least *someone* is interested.

Waves of excitement filled the room as Johnny Pepper and The Salt Shakers broke into radio hit *Ac-Cent-Tchu-Ate The Positive*, the music spilling into the house from the patio, everyone joining in for a sing-a-long. Timony squeezed her way out of the crowd and leaned against her living room wall, exhausted. Her legs spent, her feet aching. *Enjoy this moment of respite while you can*, she thought, but you best keep your face up, her mother always said, don't let your troubles show. Timony forced a grin and watched as her friends and neighbors danced and kissed and stumbled about her home in drunken revelry, the floor quaking with movement. The walls shook from everyone singing. She closed her eyes and joined in, belting at the top her lungs: *"You've got to spread joy up to the maximum, bring gloom down to the minimum, have faith or pandemonium, liable to walk upon the scene!"*

Pandemonium, indeed — this party rivaled *any* night of the week at Tantilla Garden, Richmond's most favorite place to dance the night away. Timony wiped away the beads of sweat that had pooled along the back of her neck. "Why, there must be enough heat in this room to warm all of Europe!" she announced to no one in particular. Strangers necked all around her now, no one she knew. Where Harrison was, she had no idea. And Jedidiah, her dear friend, had canceled on her, something had come up. She downed the rest of her martini in a single gulp and let it race down her throat, savoring the rush. She could have another, but it won't be enough. Ten more won't be enough. Why, there wasn't enough party in this whole world to fill the emptiness inside her.

How can I be whole, she wondered, *while my husband ignores me and my son is lost?*

A hand touched Timony's shoulder and gave her a start. She looked up to find Imogene McKenna, right there, with a glass of champagne in her hand and a smile on her beautiful face. Timony threw her arms around her dear friend, ecstatic. "Oh, you're here, you're here! Finally!" Imogene hugged her right back as Timony marveled at Imogene's luscious mane of auburn hair and drank in the comfort of another human body so close to her own. She watched as Imogene downed her first drink on the quick. "That's my girl, more on the way!" Timony motioned for one of the servers to bring them another round.

"Good, because after the day I've had, I'll likely have several more."

"Oh no, more trouble with Bennie?"

"If only. For starters, one of my fares stiffed me. And then, when I tried to chase him down, I get pawed in the street by a sailor."

"No."

"Oh yes. And then he has the nerve to ask me, would I like a 'Victory boink' in honor of us knocking off the krauts."

"My God!"

"It's true."

"What did you do?"

"Kneed him where it counts and told him I was saving myself for a Marine."

"You did not!"

Imogene winked. "I did so."

Timony laughed so loudly that others in the room turned to look their way. A waiter brought their drinks and they drank heartily, reveling in the day, the party, the moment.

"So, *are* you?" Timony asked.

"Am I what?"

"Saving yourself for a Marine."

Imogene laughed. "Hell, it's illegal just to *think* about some of the things Bennie and I do in bed. But that's my biggest problem, you know? I see him and go all squirrelly inside, just wishing he'd put his hands on me right then and there."

Timony sipped her champagne and blushed, wishing she had stories of her own love life to share. "Do I hear wedding bells?"

Imogene scoffed. "He'll have to get a divorce first."

Timony almost spit up. "What? From who?"

"His job! Hell, he's either playing war in his mind or cops-and-robbers in real life. Either way, he's only half with me when we're together. Unless we're, you know."

Timony thought she heard the phone ring when Imogene caught her deflated mood and wrapped her arms around her shoulders.

"Oh, come now, Harrison loves you, you know he does. You and I, we've just picked two men who need work as much as they need us, if not a little bit more, you know?"

In my case, perhaps a lot more, Timony thought.

Imogene finished her drink and took another from a waiter's tray as he passed by. "Enough about me. How was *your* day?"

Timony tried to forget her morning and put on a smile as something caught her eye from across the room. More like some*one*. She touched Imogene's arm. "He's here."

Imogene followed her gaze and found Bennie on the other side of the crowd, looking quite sharp in a crisp button-up and that navy suit jacket she'd bought him. She felt her knees go just a little weak at the sight of him — his face freshly shaven, his hair slicked back, Bennie looking less like a cop now and more like a prom king, waving across the room to her with an apologetic grin.

Timony even felt herself stir. "Goodness me. I get it, sister, I get it."

Imogene freed herself from the wall and started his way, in a hurry to embrace him, but Timony held her back.

"Oh, no no no you don't. Make him come to *you*."

Imogene leaned back against the wall and laughed, happy beyond words to have such a friend, when sounds of chaos from the kitchen made their way through the room — dishes falling to the floor, a scream, a woman crying.

Oh, dear, Timony thought — Macy.

She excused herself from Imogene and pushed herself through the crowd, keeping her face on as she said "Pardon me!" and

"Excuse me!" to everyone she passed, hugging one person and kissing the cheeks of another until finally she came into the kitchen. There she found Christian and Robinson consoling a most distraught Macy, her face strewn with tears. Timony rushed over to them.

"My God, what's happened? What is it?"

Macy buried her face into Timony's chest and sobbed, unable to speak.

Christian looked up at Timony, his face pale and sullen.

"It's our uncle Cornell. He's… he's dead."

Marlon gripped the sides of the pulpit and looked out at those who had assembled in the wake of tragedy, the sanctuary pews so full that churchgoers spilled into the aisles. The lot of them swayed and cried and held one another up, so much sadness in the room that smiles seemed a factual impossibility.

Go on, then, someone call the water board, we got your reserves right here. Why there's enough tears in this here church to flood the James River, and none more so than his own. But tears alone aren't enough to make things right, now are they? Marlon dried his right eye with a handkerchief, stalling as he tried to find the words and his sermon voice, both lost to him now in the face of such unspeakableness. But find them he did, speaking now as a lion roars, the spirit come through him.

"Oh, Lord!"

Marlon's words rang out through the sanctuary like a shot from a rifle, the entire room holding its breath until he took up again.

"How you have saddened us today, taken a precious soul from our lives and brought him into your kingdom. Where he most certainly belongs, oh yes."

"*Lord, have mercy!*"

"*Have mercy, please!*"

Marlon spoke through his tears as best he could. "And we are grateful, Lord, *GRATEFUL* that he is with you today, but his absence from our lives cuts like a knife to the very bone!"

Cornell's sister Mary fainted. Women screamed and swarmed her body. They fanned her with their hat brims.

Marlon closed his right eye and raised his head up high.

"So send your angels down, Lord!"

"Send 'em down, oh yes!"

"Because we're in need of healing, Lord, like we have never needed before!"

The congregation sobbed and weaved, the emotions running through the room like a great storm, pushing those assembled past the brink of anger and pulling them back again into the open arms of the spirit. Marlon felt himself go limp, the weight of the day too much for him to bear any longer. Bruises had set in on his face and body, the sting of the police beating even sharper now then it was just a few hours ago, and he felt as if he could preach no longer. He motioned for Miss Ruby to start up on the piano as he stepped down from the stage and disappeared into the rear of the church, padding along the sanctuary's dim and cavernous back hallway, his hands on the walls for guidance and support. He could still hear the voices from above, crying their way through a spiritual in unison. *It's a me, O Lord, standing in the need of prayer. It's a me, O Lord, standing in the need of prayer.*

Finally, Marlon came to the very private room he kept, shouldering the door open like a man in a mood and finding the three gathered there — his cousin Charles, lookin' madder than a landlord when you're three weeks late with the rent; Miss Constance Lee, leaning against the far wall with her arms wrapped around herself, her cheeks damp from crying; and the one and only Jedidiah King, as dapper as can be in a tux with his hair done just so, smoking one of his famous cigarettes and looking none too pleased. Marlon ignored them all and went straight for his drink cabinet. The Devil in him now, the world be damned as he grabbed his precious corn whiskey and drank straight from the bottle, walking about the room in a stir.

"I'm truly sorry for your loss, Marlon," Jedidiah said.

Marlon took another drink. "Are you, now?"

"I'll cover funeral expenses, hospital bills, whatever you need."

"Whatever I need, huh? What I need... what *we* need is some goddamn protection from your kind on this here business arrangement!"

"I never said it would be easy."

"No, you did not. You did not say that, you're goddamn right. But you failed to mention just how *determined* your competition is!"

Jedidiah stubbed out his cigarette. "I'm at a loss, Marlon, really. I wanted out of all this and saw a money-making opportunity for you. I had no idea it would come to this."

Charles looked ready to blow. "An opportunity? An *OPPORTUNITY?* This was a member of *OUR CHURCH!*"

Constance stepped into the center of the room, her arms out like she was trying to stop traffic. "I think what Mr. King is trying to say is that he had hoped this arrangement would offer you a means of growth. Numbers thrive in this city, good as anywhere, but there was no way to know it would come to this."

Marlon felt the whiskey mix with his bloodstream and shoved a chair out of his way. "Who was it, then, done us like this?"

Jedidiah and Constance shared a knowing look.

Charles kicked the chair over. "Come on, now, *out with it!*"

Jedidiah let it out slow. "If I tell you…"

Marlon took a step toward Jedidiah, his stolid 6′ frame enough to put the fear in any man. He looked like a football player to Jedidiah's slim businessman. "*If* you tell us? There is no 'if,' friend, not now, not ever. Give it up, *now.*"

Jedidiah wiped sweat from his brow, a rare occurrence. The man hardly ever lost his cool. "I believe the man you want is Walter MacKeye."

Marlon was stunned. "Is it, now? Might surprise you, but I done already heard that name once today. Those policemen, roughed me up? They ask'd me 'bout him, too. You think it was him?"

Constance looked right sour at mention of this man's name. "I knew it J, he's coming after us, the heel. All because of me."

Marlon fumed. "Sounds serious."

Jedidiah hung his head. "He's a major player in everything from B and E to illegal gambling to ripping off your grandmother, and I'm sorry you had to find out about him this way."

Marlon took another drink. "Don't mind about that now. Just

tell me where I can find him."

"Marlon…"

"Don't you Marlon me, *friend*. We go back aways, oh yes, but there is gonna be some re-tri-bution tonight, oh yes indeed."

Charles made like a choir singer and raised his hands up. "Praise Jesus!"

Marlon got right into Jedidiah's face. "Now, where… can… I… *find* this Walter MacKeye?"

Jedidiah thought it over for a moment before gesturing at Constance.

"I think it's best I let her tell you."

Marlon looked over at the woman and found all the signs of revenge on her lovely, delicate face.

"Where he is right now, I'm not entirely sure," she said, "but I can think of one way to get his attention."

It was the smell that woke Knox.

Something putrid and rotting he hadn't noticed before.

He covered his nose with his shirt and came up off the mattress, wondering how long he'd been asleep. Six, maybe seven hours, he guessed, looking around the bedroom. What he could see of it, anyway. It was dark outside and there were no lights on in the house. Walter had said to keep them off so as not to attract attention. And it was definitely late, Knox figured, peering out a front window into a pitch black night.

Knox yawned and tried to remember where he was. Somewhere in Church Hill, he recalled, in a house at the end of a street. Walter had left him here after the mess they'd made in Jackson Ward. Said it was one of his many hideouts around town and that Knox should just lay low, get some rest, he'd be back soon.

Goddamn, that smell!

A dead rat, maybe, Christ.

Knox left the room and felt his way along a hallway and down some stairs. His stomach growled something fierce, a real hunger setting in since he'd not eaten all day. Way to go, champ. Your first day out of the pen and you didn't even go for a real meal. *Maybe there's an icebox here with some food*, he thought. With any luck, something to drink, too. He seemed to escape the smell some and breathed a little easier as he left the stairs and wandered through a few rooms. His shoes were still upstairs, he'd have to go back for them when Walter showed, whenever that was. Said he'd be back after awhile, after he'd called the cops on that preacher man and tried to get him rung up for firing at their wheels.

Knox found what passed for a kitchen and was disappointed to find that the icebox wasn't even hooked up to an electrical circuit. Nothing in the cupboards, either. *This really was a hideout*, Knox thought. Keep costs down, use only when needed. Pretty smart, really. If Knox played his cards right, maybe he could own his own house someday. Get back with Constance and finally go legit. Get out of the life for good and into the real estate game. Probably it's own kind of racket, really. Rent the pads out, get working stiffs to pay *you*.

Just listen to yourself, Knox thought, dreaming big. Not a full day out of prison and you're stuck inside a vacant house that smells like the sewer. So what do you do, get your shoes and go it alone? Walter hasn't paid you. That one-eyed preacher could make you, *easy*. And Walter's pals would surely put the word out if you ran. Knox would have a price on his head, the entire city would know. He almost laughed — he was more free inside than out.

Somewhere in the neighborhood, a dog howled.

Knox thought of Sadie and almost cried when he heard the sound of a car approaching. Walter, probably, come back for him at last, but just to be sure, Knox crept to the side of a front room window and peeked outside. He watched as the sled cut its headlights and slowed to a stop near the edge of the front yard. The engine kept running as someone got out of the car. Knox peered as best he could, his eyes adjusting to the darkness outside.

It's… not Walter.

It's a man, yes, but taller, a little more to him, creeping toward the house as if he doesn't want to be seen.

Getting closer now, the man's features framed by the moonlight…

The fuck?

Knox felt his heart and lungs give out. *It can't be.* He blinked to be sure, but there was no mistaking it. None other than that one-eyed preacher man was standing just a few yards from the front of Walter's hideout, holding what looked like a glass bottle of some sort. Liquid inside it, a rag hanging out its end.

No...

Preacher man lit a match and set the rag on fire.

Oh, God, no...

Knox forced life into his legs and darted up the stairs for his shoes just as the bottle came crashing through a window into the front room. He heard the fire spread behind him and the crackle of flames as true panic set in, his motor functions jagged now as he tried desperately to find his shoes and then struggle to put them on, stumbling and tripping over himself.

Christ, that smell!

Come on, *think*.

Even if you could get downstairs, you sure as hell can't go out the front now. You gotta go out the back, *somehow* — Knox hit the upstairs hallway, searching, his shirt over his face to breathe. He felt the heat rising now and swatted at wafts of smoke. Look there, *a door*. A back room, maybe. Knox flung it open and caught that smell full on.

Holy fuck, what is that —

That's a body on the floor, is what it is. With a shot to the gut, it smelled like. Nothing else could smell like that. Goddamn it, Walter, you put me in here with a dead body? *Don't look at it*, Knox thought, *just get to that window*. Knox rushed over and looked out —

That's a second floor fall, all right.

And there's more smoke now, coming up behind him like a fog. He could hear the flames close behind. This old house, going up quick like dried pine. Knox felt his eyes burn as he yanked up the sash and straddled the sill. Don't look down, don't think, just go — he couldn't help but turn back as he brought both legs out, his eyes meeting the dead body's lifeless gaze.

Holy what the —

That's Scangili!

Knox almost fell to the ground, processing it — not fifteen hours ago, they'd been brawling in his cell, and now here was the guard Scangili, his hollow soul finally laid to rest. *Yeah, well, good fucking riddance,* Knox thought, pushing off the house and dropping to the ground like an anvil, his instincts screaming *bend your knees* as he hit the ground and fell backward, his body contorting into a ball and somersaulting to a stop.

Pains up his legs. Pains up his back. Quick, run a body check — nothing broken. Knox stumbled to his feet and backed away from the house, watching as more and more of it burned, confused and half-broken and altogether enraptured by the all-consuming beauty of fire.

So uncontrollable, so free.

Sirens in the distance — fire, maybe police.

Run, you fool.

Run.

HOME FRONT HORRORS CONFOUND
RIVER CITY HERALD / MAY 10, 1945
BY ARCHIE SMITH

She was strong of soul and a revered member of her community.

He was withdrawn and cruel, feared by almost everyone he knew.

Tethered by tragedy, the two make an unlikely pair, but the recent murder of a Jewish five-and-dime store owner and the discovery just one day later of the charred remains of a state penitentiary employee in a fire-ravaged East End home has many of our city's residents wondering: have the horrors of war finally come home to roost?

Speaking at yesterday's press conference, however, Acting Lieutenant Bennie Sherwood sounded optimistic as he spelled out the department's progress. "While I can't go into specifics, I *can* tell you the Victory Squad is making rapid progress daily. Answers are coming, and soon."

Ruth Evans Kleinfeld was murdered during a robbery just hours before the official announcement of Victory in Europe. A proud wife and mother, Ruth was also a business owner, managing The Sunshine Five-and-Dime on Boulevard alongside her husband, Harold. And to no one's surprise, she was a cherished member of their synagogue, known for her keen wit and her peerless recipe for matzoh ball soup. "She was the light of everyone's day," a near inconsolable Harold remarked as he made plans to honor her life.

Councilman Harrison Wells wiped tears from his eyes as he remembered his former Hebrew teacher. "I just can't believe she's gone," he said, adding that he and his wife, the socialite and society columnist of this very newspaper, Timony 'Thursday' Wells, were donating a significant sum to Mrs. Kleinfeld's synagogue and establishing a study program there in her name.

No such arrangements are in place for Carmine Scangili, the ex-prison employee found amongst the remains of a house fire that continues to stump police. While Sherwood was mum on details surrounding the surprise discovery of Scangili's body, state penitentiary superintendent James Visel, Scangili's former boss, had plenty to say. "Carmine was a good egg and deserved a better end. Sure, he had his ways with the inmates, but it gets rowdy in here and Carmine was always up to the task of maintaining order." Visel ignored this reporter's follow-up questions about rumors of inmate brutality at the penitentiary, pausing only to crack his knuckles and add, "I'm a betting man and I'd say it was an ex-inmate that did ol' Carmine wrong, may he rest in peace. Tell the police to ring out their dragnet because whoever did it can't be far."

Speculative words, perhaps, but Director of Public Safety Stolmy Reed appeared to agree. "Given the state of the city these days, we'll take any lead we can get. I don't want our fighting brave to come home to a city where anything goes, because, let's face it, we're practically breeding criminal activity in Richmond these days, not containing it." Pressed, then, to comment on the performance of Acting Lieutenant Sherwood, Reed was dismissive, at best. "It's not pretty, is it? But it is a temporary posting, as he well knows. I've known Bennie Sherwood his entire life. He's got the pedigree of a policeman and the instincts of a soldier and he's doing just fine. But let's be fair, eh? Once we knock the Japs off, we'll find a new Chief and right the ship for good."

As many will recall, Acting Lieutenant Sherwood took over light command duties of the police department last April in the wake of an investigation into the devastating Jefferson Hotel fire of last March that left seven dead, among them Reed's only son Jack, himself the former chief of detectives. While the elder Reed has moved easily into his new role as Director of Public Safety, Sherwood's transition has been anything but smooth. Since the start of this year, robbery, domestic assault, and petty crime have been rising steadily. Sherwood attributes the uptick to wartime fatigue and says things may get even worse before they get better. "Look, we're all breathing a little easier now that the European front has died down, but let's face it, Richmond gets hot in the summer, so I expect tensions — and crime — to rise with the mercury." When asked to speculate on whether City Hall might offer him a more permanent post, Sherwood simply shrugged. "If City Hall decides I'm no longer fit for this job, so be it, but until they promote me or can me, I'll be out in the streets with badge and gun."

PART TWO

FALLOUT

6

Horror stories from inside the state penitentiary made Bennie's skin crawl. Beatings, whippings, involuntary sterilizations. Sunlight-deprived inmates gone asylum-crazy from it all.

Bennie thought of more stories the old man used to tell about the state cooler and got chills. A frigid wind blew up Spring Street and made it even worse for he, Shane, and Eddie, the three of them moving with trepidation under the mid-morning shadows of the prison's four-story concrete facade, a temple of doom and death.

Shane burrowed into his jacket. "We know anything about this guy, the super?"

Bennie pulled his steno and read off his notes from Visel's City Hall employment file. "James Monroe Visel, 43. Born in Indiana, February '02. He worked the Ohio railroad as a teen, graduated to supervisor at 21. Drifted west during the Depression and did time for bank fraud in California before turning his life around. Came back east in '38 as a foreman on a convict train, started here at the prison in '40."

Eddie whistled. "That's some pedigree. I'm surprised his con man beef didn't disqualify him from this line of work."

Bennie steered them through the front doors and into the lobby. "I agree. Either way, he's our best chance at info on Scangili, so let's play nice."

Eddie nodded, ready to go along, even as Bennie clocked him scowling at the idea. Seen-It-All Eddie didn't trust anyone and Bennie wasn't entirely sure he trusted *him*. Eddie's rise to king of the vice desk had been anything but by-the-book and there were rumors he was still just a little too friendly with some of his informants. Still, the department was stronger for his experience *and* his familiarity with Richmond's cadre of riff-raff, so Bennie looked past his misgivings — for now — and assigned him to The Victory Squad. The department's wartime unit was a mix of detectives from every desk formed to meet the needs of Richmond's troubles during wartime. And what better way to balance the old than with the young. Bennie glanced at Shane, just twenty-five years old and fresh from the Navy. His young-gun, do-anything, go-anywhere attitude was *also* just what the department needed. There would be more men just like him coming home in the next few months. Men looking to displace auxiliary cops and take back their old jobs, as well as misguided men looking to fuel their newfound fighting spirit within the guise of a police uniform. Bennie hoped he could tell the difference and looked forward to the challenge of working with them, learning from them, perhaps even leading them.

A gruff, familiar voice called out to them from up ahead.

"Ladies, so glad you could join us."

Bennie winced at the sound of Stolmy Reed's voice and what the department did *not* need — The Cane watching over their chit chat with Jimmy Visel. Bennie's nerves pulsed as The Cane tapped his walking stick in tandem with their approach, as if to suggest they should hurry and avoid being late, which they were not. Standing next to Stolmy were two men. One was tall and imposing — make him Superintendent Visel — while the other was shorter and thicker and, by the looks of him, bred to scare off laughter for miles. A real goon-type, the kind of man children run from and women avoid. Bennie came to a stop and shook off his nerves, trying to remember the last time he was here. Eddie and Shane came to just behind him.

Bennie stood tall. "Stolmy. Clearly, you felt your presence was needed here. Lest I assure you, it is not."

Stolmy balanced on his cane with both hands. "Oh, come now, Bennie. I'm merely a spectator to these proceedings, called upon by our city's tax payers to see that protocol is followed and justice is swift. I assure you, my presence here is purely a formality." He twirled his cane like a carnival showman.

"As if there's anything pure about you, my ass," Eddie sneered under his breath.

Stolmy craned his head. "Excuse me? What's that?"

Bennie's memory clicked, *rats* — Eddie and Stolmy harbored a longstanding beef from their time as grunts on the force. Something about a woman.

Noticing Eddie now, Stolmy gloated. "Oh, hello, Haden. Didn't recognize you in a suit and tie. Figured you were still mopping up the drunk tank and cleaning out the cells."

Bennie turned to hold Eddie back, but it was too late.

"You goddamn heel! Martha deserved better than you and you know it. Hell, I bet that walking stick in your hand is the same one you beat her with before she died. Did you beat your son with it, too? Huh, huh now? Did'ya?"

It was like two contenders talking smack before a fight. The Cane fumed and charged Eddie like a bull, his walking stick suddenly in the air. Visel stepped between them, the man used to breaking up fights.

"You all want to want go to the dance together, do it on your own time. But if you want to talk about this business with Carmine, then let's get to it. I got trouble coming and going in this place and no time for this, so, if you please, this way."

Visel gestured for them to follow and led the way to his office. The walk helped to frost tensions. Shane just laughed — at Eddie. "Like kids at the schoolyard, you two. All bark, no bite."

Visel's office was tight, stuffy, too small for six men. Bennie stood against the far wall while Eddie and Shane grabbed seats. Visel took up at his desk while his goon pal loomed behind him, leaving Stolmy to hover in the doorway. A light breeze blew in — the room's one window was cracked open. Bennie peeked out at the prison yard and its makeshift baseball diamond. Chills, a buried memory surfaced — there he was, a teenager out on that very field, playing first base in a pickup game his father had organized. Cops versus inmates.

Visel cleared his throat. "Time's ticking, gentlemen. What do you want to know?"

Bennie addressed Visel. "To start with, Superintendent, please tell us what you know about Carmine Scangili."

Visel rested his elbows on the table, one hand on top of the other. "What can I say? Carmine was easy on life and hard on the job. Just what we need in here. He was always on the straight and narrow, too. Didn't take bribes, didn't bring anything in off the black market. It's a real shame he went out the way he did."

Eddie brought a leg up over one knee and picked lint out of his sock. "Did Carmine ever get rough with the inmates?"

Visel brought both hands behind his head and leaned back with a confident smile — creepy. "We get all kinds in here, so, some days it goes one way, some days it goes the other."

Bennie knew this was not the time to address the depraved elephant-in-the-room that was inmate abuse at the State Penitentiary, a myriad of prisoners' rights violations that stretched back decades and was known throughout the inner circles of city government as a kind of untouchable evil. Still, he pressed, softly. "Sounds plausible, then, that Carmine may have incurred the wrath of some enemies, people that wanted to bring him harm. You know of anyone like that, Superintendent?"

"Of course. It's just like I told the papers. Plenty of recent parolees had a grudge against old Carmine, so I say your best shot is to shake 'em down, 'cause I'm betting it's one of them did him in."

Bennie shot Visel a hard look. "You certainly seem sure of that."

"And why wouldn't I be? Look, I deal with this lot day in and day out, I know 'em better than anybody, and I'm telling you, they never change. In here, out there, they're all the same. Crooked in, crooked out." Visel took a document from his drawer and handed it to Bennie. "I'm sure your office gets one of these from the state parole board, but we've had seven jailbirds released in the last three weeks alone. That's trouble on the street, if you ask me, and it wouldn't surprise me none you find a link from one of them straight to Carmine."

Bennie scanned the ex-con list. Shane breathed on his badge and buffed it with a handkerchief. "Where were you that night?"

Visel looked offended. "Excuse me?"

"Where were you the night of May 8th? The night Carmine got burnt to a crisp?"

Stolmy protested. "Is that really necessary, MacDonald? Sherwood, control your men."

Bennie put his hands up. "Pardon my detective, Superintendent, but please, answer the question. Where *were* you the night of May 8th?"

Visel paused, measuring his words, his face as calm as a still lake. "I was here, where else?"

"Can anyone attest to that?"

Visel motioned over his shoulder. "He can."

Bennie was glad, he'd been waiting for an opportunity. "Is that so? Good, then perhaps an introduction is finally in order. You are?"

Visel's goon surveyed the three cops in the room before answering, his lecherous look full of disgust. "Tommy Müller, head guard."

Eddie perked up. "You a German national, Müller?"

Müller got tense. "So what if I am?"

Stolmy smacked his cane on the ground. "Posturing will get us nowhere, gentlemen."

Bennie glared at Stolmy and turned to Visel. "So you and Müller were here at the prison that night, is that correct?"

Visel nodded. "This is a twenty-four hour operation. Tommy and I are here day and night, working to keep this place running smooth. And anyways, I had no reason to cause old Carmine any harm," he motioned at Müller, "and neither did he."

Eddie cracked his knuckles. "Question. If you're so busy around the joint, how come you let Carmine off for the night? Sounds like you need all the help you can get."

Visel shrugged. "What can I say? It was just his night off."

Bennie folded the parole board sheet and stuck it into his jacket pocket. "We'll need a staff list from you."

Visel looked daggers at Bennie as Shane read from his notepad. "So far, we've been unable to track down next of kin. Carmine have family in town? An ex-wife, maybe, kids?"

Müller just laughed. "Carmine, a wife? There's a better chance you find ice in hell, that's for sure."

Eddie was intrigued. "Why do you say that?"

Müller smirked. "Let's just say Carmine was more… married to the job than anything else."

Shane wrote in his notepad. "What about friends? Guys he palled around with?"

Visel looked surprised. "*We* were his friends."

Bennie, Shane, and Eddie all shared a look: who the fuck would want to be friends with these two?

Eddie saw an opening. "Well, then, being his friends and all, maybe *you* could tell us. Carmine ever come across as an anti-Semite?"

"It could be anything," Bennie added, "an offhand remark, perhaps, or an attitude about the war."

Visel smiled. He clearly didn't mind the question. "Nothing comes to mind."

Bennie pressed. "More specifically, did he ever mention anything about a Ruth Kleinfeld?"

Visel, clearly annoyed now: "And just who might that be?"

Shane spoke with indignation. "She *was* a local business owner, cherished by her community. A Jewish woman."

Visel nodded, dismissive. "Oh, that's right, that woman from the newspaper article, the one that mentioned both her and Carmine? No, he never mentioned her. Why would he?"

Stolmy caught Visel's air and fidgeted with his cane. "I'm sure Bennie and his men are just trying to be thorough, Jimmy. You can't think of anything that would point your former employee towards this Kleinfeld woman? Anything at all?"

Visel, straight: "No, I cannot."

Like a man on trial — Bennie didn't like it. "We'd like to see where Carmine lived. He have a house, an apartment?"

Visel was losing patience. "An apartment."

Bennie opened his steno to a blank page and slid it across the desk. "The address, please."

Visel wrote down the address and handed the steno back to Bennie before he rose from his chair, the man ready to be done with this altogether. "The clerk up front will provide you with an employee roster. If you need anything else, leave a message with him."

And just like that, the meeting was over. Visel and Müller started from the room and the rest followed. Soon they were all out in the hallway, just waiting for someone to speak. Bennie could smell the sting of fear in the air, the prison's essence like bad jungle ju-ju.

"I trust you can find your way out, gentlemen," Visel said, before he and Müller began to walk into the prison. The two men disappeared around a corner and left Bennie to face Stolmy on his own. Eddie and Shane had started off already, the both of them quick to powder. Bennie tried to downplay his irritation — his relationship with Stolmy Reed was difficult and complex.

"Are you gonna babysit us through the whole of this investigation, Stolmy? Because if you are, I'll just turn in my badge now, let you have your old job back. I don't need a chaperone and neither do they."

Stolmy smirked — he was clearly enjoying this. "Careful how you address me, *Lieutenant*. Your performance on this case will play a major role in deciding how we move forward with the police department at war's end."

Bennie wasn't satisfied. "If the papers are to be believed, it sounds like you've already made up your mind on that."

"Oh, that's nothing but a bit of political theater, Bennie. I'm just trying to keep you on your toes, keep your mind on the case."

"It still sounds like you're threatening my job."

Stolmy twirled his cane and tapped it on the ground, like a man on a stroll in the rain. "Bring these cases in and I won't have to."

"You know, I could do my job a lot easier if I didn't have scum like Strickland and Halifax to worry about. They've got to go, Stolmy, it's like the wild west over there at Second Station. It's unforgivable what they're putting folks through. I'm sure you've heard the rumors about that preacher by now."

Stolmy shook his head, disheartened. "If only they were rumors. Look, my hands are tied, Bennie, no major staff changes until the war's up, the mayor's orders. Hell, I'd fire 'em both right now if it was up to me — "

Bennie said, "I want a formal inquiry, I want... "

Stolmy waved it off. "You want world peace in a time of war, son, and you're not even in charge."

"Not yet."

"And you won't get there if you don't close these cases. Never mind this business about the preacher. You just do your job and it'll all fall in line."

Stolmy turned and walked off, another conversation over. Bennie turned and started for the clerk's office, but was startled when, behind him, he heard the faintest of screams, a man calling out.

Perhaps in pain.

Definitely in fear.

Outside, the world had changed. The sun shone bright, morning chill was now early afternoon warmth. Shane and Eddie waited for Bennie as he emerged from the penitentiary and Bennie thought that leaving this place was like narrowly escaping death.

Shane was ready with a quip. "Eddie and I agree, boss. We all need showers to kill the stench we just picked up in there."

Bennie couldn't agree more. "That was the filthiest, most put upon show I've ever seen. I just gave Stolmy an earful about it, too, not that it did a bit of good for us."

Eddie chomped on a toothpick. "What do you want to do now, boss?"

Bennie tore the address of Scangili's apartment from his steno and handed it to Shane. "I want *you* to scout Scangili's pad and see what you can find out. Eddie, I want you to tail Jimmy Visel. I want to know where he goes, who he sees. What he eats and what he doesn't. I want it all."

Eddie nodded, a hint of dread on his face — tail jobs were shit city.

Shane loosened his tie. "What are you gonna do?"

Bennie scanned the parolee list, the staff roster. "Thumb the phone book, see who knows what. If I learn anything useful, I'll put it in a report and leave it on your desks."

Eddie grinned. "Your gal pal give you an answer yet?"

Bennie's look said she hadn't. "You two just aren't gonna quit with this, are you?"

Shane slapped him on the back, playfully. "Not a chance, boss. Not a chance."

7

Carmine Scangili's former apartment was on the third floor of a five story walkup just off an Oregon Hill side street. Shane parked his sled and shot a look around the neighborhood, checking the address in his steno. Oregon Hill was working-class, all the way. Low-rent pads far from downtown but close enough to the pen that Scangili probably walked to work and back. Shane ran through his notes on Carmine, on the hunt for a clearer picture. The coroner's report said he was tall, almost rail thin, and that he had been shot in the stomach and strangled to death prior to perishing in the inferno that charred his body. What a way to go. His employment file listed DOB as 5/20/99. He had one card on file at HQ. It listed a juvie beef from '15, an arrest for robbery hijinks that netted him a year on a rehab farm. No mention of mother or father, but a probation counselor noted that Carmine was 'distraught over brother's death' while serving his time. His juvie charge ended with adulthood, so he was free to sign onto the prison as a guard in '20, the only place he worked until just a few days ago.

Shane tried to piece the man back together. Scangili lived to be forty-five and never married. He had no next of kin, lived alone, and held a job that by most standards was depressing and undesirable. Sad times for a sad sack. Shane hesitated to pursue the matter any further — *maybe we should let old Carmine just be, eh?* Because he certainly wasn't resting in peace, not after being left to rot and burn. But a policeman's burden was to pine for the truth, so Shane tilted his hat up off his face, pulled out his badge, and rapped his knuckles on a first floor door. The sign next to it read 'landlord.' An older man with cautious eyes and wire-rim glasses cracked it open.

"Yes?"

Shane held up his badge. "Mr. Thompson, I'm Shane MacDonald with the police. I called earlier, about Carmine Scangili's apartment?"

"Oh, yes, right." Thompson unlatched the door and proceeded to lead Shane up a flight of stairs. His eyes downward, his attitude dismissive. "It's like I told you over the phone, detective, one minute he was here and the next, he just up and left. And then of course, well, obviously you know what happened or you wouldn't be here."

"On the phone, you said it was Sunday when he cleared out of here. Five days back, is that right?"

Thompson just nodded. "Yes, Sunday when he terminated his lease, that's right. Sunday it was."

Shane smiled to himself, he loved the tells. Repeating yourself was always a dead giveaway that you weren't on the level.

They came to 3C, Scangili's old digs. Thompson unlocked the door and started to back away. "Well, there you go, Detective, like I said, there's really nothing to see in there since it's been cleaned out. Please just shut the door once you're done, I'll be — "

Shane put a forceful hand on Thompson's shoulder. "How about you stay right there while I have a look around."

Thompson wouldn't meet his eyes. "Ok, yes, alright."

Shane left him outside and stepped into the apartment. It was your standard one room flop with a kitchenette in the corner and a bathroom off to the side. A furnished room rental — couch along the wall, coffee table, foldout Murphy bed. Nothing on the walls or shelves. Shane felt an intuitive tug from the kitchenette and checked the cupboard first — nothing but moldy bread crumbs and an old coffee cup. Nothing in the sink, either, nothing in the drawers. Off to the bathroom next — a loose tile on the floor, missing grout in the shower. Note to Mr. Thompson — work on your upkeep, pal, or we'll cite you with a proprietor's violation. Hoping for a bit of luck, Shane checked the medicine cabinet next — empty shelves, again. The spot had truly been cleaned out.

Frustrated, Shane shut the cabinet door and was suddenly staring at himself in the mirror. He was still plenty handsome at twenty-five. Brown hair, brown eyes, his mother's impenetrable smile. He did three years with the Navy down in South America as a radio signal tech and it actually did wonders for his state of mind. All that sunshine, all that beach weather. Hell, he was probably one of the few men who never saw real combat during the war, not that he didn't try. He was denied a posting in the Pacific and was instead assigned to hunt for German subs off the coast of Brazil. When he was brought back to the States this past Spring, the war was as good as won, so he called up his old boss, The Cane, and asked to have his patrolman's job back after his discharge. The Cane did him two better — he helped secure Shane early dismissal from military service *and* netted him a promotion, a spot on the robbery detail of The Victory Squad. The V-Squad was struggling to contain the city's crime wave and The Cane thought a young hotshot from the Navy would help jumpstart the effort. Shane also figured the higher-ups saw him as young and inexperienced, more willing to risk his neck than the older flock, and that was fine by him. Armed robbery was the most dangerous racket going these days and his willingness to go all-in got him status in the squad room and choice looks from the phone-op girls. But that new-job feeling had worn off and he hadn't brought in a real case in weeks. He knew the Lieu was catching flak from both The Cane and the papers over rising stats, so the only thing his handsome mug was good for right now was finding something, anything, that could —

Look there, at the mirror…

At the *bottom right* of the mirror…

Where the ornate painted frame, about a half-inch thick, appeared more *touched*, more worn away from say *skin oil* than anywhere else on the frame. Shane pulled the cabinet open and eyeballed the seam between frame and mirror. *Something* was wedged inside. Shane looked down — a sink, right there. He dug into his jacket pocket for a handkerchief and laid it over the drain in case anything fell out. He pulled his penknife and slipped a blade inside the seam, careful not to pry too hard.

Go easy now, there, that's it…

Bingo — some *things* fell into the sink.

Shane looked down at a photograph and two handwritten notes.

The photo was of a young kid, maybe ten, eleven, and if Shane was honest about it, a halfwit. One eye cocked askew, his mouth half-open. On the back was written 'Giovanni, Sicily, 1912.' Shane shuffled through the handwritten notes. One was a list of German words and phrases and their English translations.

Hallo. Hello.

Auf Wiedersehen. Goodbye.

Ja. Yes.

Jetzt. Now.

Hör auf. Stop it.

Hände hoch. Hands up.

Shane pictured Scangili standing in front of the mirror, reading from the sheet, practicing. But for what?

The other handwritten note was a list of addresses. Local, for sure. Cary Street, Broad Street, Patterson Avenue, wait — Boulevard.

The Sunshine Five & Dime.

A Jewish-owned business, *confirmed*, plus common German phrases…

Goddamnit.

"H… hello?"

Shane had almost forgotten all about Mr. Thompson. He took the photo and the two handwritten notes, slipped them into the folds of his wallet, and met the landlord in the next room.

"Mr. Thompson, when did Scangili clear out of this apartment?"

Thompson put on a blameless face. "It was Sunday, like I said."

Shane loved this part of the job. "Mr. Thompson. I could go about interviewing the other tenants on this floor. And if I did, I bet I'd find out that it wasn't Sunday, after all, now would I? So why don't you do us both a favor and tell me what really happened and when, because if you give me any more runaround, I'll find a way to stick you with an obstruction beef, you hear me? That means court fees, a spot on your record. It could even mean jail time."

Thompson started to quiver. Something had him good and spooked. "Okay, okay, please, I… I don't want any more trouble."

Shane leaned against the wall and pulled out his steno, ready for his tell-all. "Go ahead, Mr. Thompson."

"Two nights ago, I got a call from Mrs. Jenkins in 3B, middle of the night. Maybe two o'clock in the morning. She said she heard noises from here in this apartment. Loud noises, like furniture moving, things you don't expect to hear that time of night. And well, by then, of course we'd heard the news about Carmine and so naturally, I thought it odd that someone would be in here. So I got out of bed, came to see what was going on, and then, well…"

"Yes?"

Thompson took off his glasses, rubbed his eyes. "I found two men rummaging the apartment. When I walked in, the light was off, the men had flashlights. I turned on the light and saw that the room had been ransacked. Things everywhere, the furniture tossed over. I asked them their business and that's when I see they have masks on. Gas masks, like you see in safety films. They pin me against the wall and point a gun in my face. One of them tells me to keep my mouth shut or he'll shoot me, right then and there. So I do as I'm told, I don't want trouble. The one with the gun, he stays with me while the other goes through the room and takes boxes of paper, I think, I can't really see and I'm too scared to look, anyhow. And just like that, they're done, but before they leave, they tell me to clear the room out the next day, make it look like Carmine up and left *before* what happened to him. They tell me to do this right away, that they'd be watching to see that I'd done it, so that's what I did. I had my men clear it out yesterday. And I changed the lock this morning, I was afraid they had kept Carmine's keys."

Shane scribbled notes, writing as fast as he could. "Have you noticed anyone watching your building since then?"

Thompson hugged himself, rubbed his shoulders. He almost had the shakes. "No, but I haven't exactly been looking, either. I really don't want any trouble for my tenants, detective. Or my wife."

"Of course not. You've clearly had a scare here, Mr. Thompson, and I thank you for being candid with me. What can you tell me about your old tenant here, the late Mr. Scangili."

Thompson calmed some, the man having unburdened himself. "Well, he was an odd sort of man, if I do say so. And I certainly don't make a habit of speaking ill of the dead, mind you, but he was often late with the rent and, well, he made the other tenants uncomfortable."

"How so?"

"When he wasn't rude to them, he, uh… he *leered* at them."

"Did he now. What'd he do, put on a stare whenever the ladies walked by?"

Thompson collected himself.

"No. The *men*."

8

Tail-job.

Eddie yawned and stretched his back out best he could, having been sitting in the front seat of his department-issued Ford Roadster for just about three hours now, waiting for Jimmy Visel to make a move. Plenty of time to stew on old grudges and new sorrows. Like Stolmy 'The Cane' Reed, his old partner from days on the beat. Back then, Stolmy buoyed favor with the higher ups and rose like a rocket through the department, leaving Eddie to slum it out on patrol for almost ten years. Stolmy even stole his girl, too, Sweet Martha, may God rest her soul. Martha always wanted to run with the upper crust and since Eddie was more like crumbs on the floor she went big for Stolmy's new clout and fat paydays. She stayed with Stolmy all through the accident that nearly took his leg, too, just like the good wife Eddie always knew she'd be. She even stayed with Stolmy after he began to beat both her and their only son, Jack, the man so angry at his limp he laid his wrath into everyone around him.

I'm sorry the cancer took you, Sweet Martha. You deserved better.

And if Eddie didn't have such a plum spot on the Victory Squad, he'd take Stolmy and throw him back under a Broad Street trolley car, let it take both legs this time. Payback for all the times he struck her.

More yawns, more memory lane.

Eddie remembered how his years on patrol netted him a solid band of informants, men and women well-versed in the give-and-take of Richmond street life. This led to a string of choice undercover assignments and Eddie proved himself worthy every time. Soon he was full time with vice and then he really started to cook. By then, he knew every narco-slinging doc and every whorehouse cooze within twenty miles of the city limits and he closed more cases his first year as a detective than any tec before or since, 29 cases total, still a department record, and all while working for the man who stole his girl. Eddie was a worker, he'd be the first to admit, pride in the job and all that, and boy did he love to put the cuffs on and see the look in perps' faces when he knew he'd gotten 'em dead to rights, when they knew they had no way out. It was probably some entitlement shit he inherited from the old man. Pops worked every day of his life, always on the straight and narrow, even when they struggled to make ends meet. He was a true man of principle, Pops, and he looked down at anyone on the take, at anyone not playing it square.

Well, dad, if I'm really gonna be honest about it…

Shadows flickered in Eddie's purview — there's movement on the penitentiary's front steps. *Well, what do you know* — there's Jimmy Visel, strolling out after a day on the job. Eddie checked his watch, it was just after six o'clock in the evening. So much for that all day, all night routine he fed us in the meeting.

Visel slid into his Lincoln Continental — top-drawer wheels, hard to come by — and zoomed off. Bound for downtown, it looked like. The car would be easy to spot — there weren't many on the roads these days — so Eddie hung back for a few.

His thoughts festered quick.

Memories, regrets.

Say, dad, about those 29 cases…

Eddie tailed Visel to Doris Potter's cathouse on North Adams and watched him disappear inside. He parked a few car lengths away from her front steps, killed the engine, and recalled his own frequent visits to her parlor. He'd been quite the regular those early years on patrol. Trying to forget Martha, trying to fuck away the job. Doris' spot was one of two police-sanctioned brothels allowed to operate within city limits and Eddie had worn so much of his own personal groove into the wood of Doris' front steps she made him repair them himself. And even then he was still delinquent, come to think of it. Too many times with 'please, I'll pay you later' and his credit was shot. Not that it mattered now.

He hadn't been inside her pad in years. Hell, he hadn't talked to an actual woman in months, not since his mother had died from too many cigarettes and the black cloud of loneliness had settled into his heart, his soul. Nothing left to do now but grow old and die alone. Like mother, like son, huh? *Well, here's to you, mom.* Eddie snagged a toothpick from his cigarette holder and hoped it would sate his edge. Smokes were *still* too hard to come by these days, at least on the regular. If nothing else, Eddie wanted the war to end so he could take up his old habit again. Nothing to do but wait now — for Jimmy, for the Japs, for a good smoke. He rolled his car window down, closed his eyes, and tried to push every thought from his mind.

It didn't take. Somewhere on the block, a window was open and radio sounds drifted into the street. News headlines, then music — more of that same old saccharine sound, it all sounded the same to Eddie. He could care less about The Andrews Sisters or Bing Crosby, the lot of them selling the war to everyone a song at a time. All he wanted to listen to was that good ole' honky-tonk. He wanted Bob Wills, he wanted Roy Acuff. Come Saturday night, if Eddie wasn't on duty, he was glued to the radio, listening to the Grand Ole Opry out of Nashville, Tennessee.

Time ticked away — the tail-job blues. Eddie gnashed on another toothpick. More memories came. They haunted him, they stayed too long and turned rotten.

A few minutes later, Jimmy Visel hustled out of Doris' pad and zoomed off again.

Christ, Jimmy, did you even get a look at her face?

Eddie tailed Visel to The Occidental — a downtown grub spot that catered to fat cats — and watched him from a far corner table. The super, fresh off an appetite-inducing tryst, wolfed his dinner. Steak, potatoes, and asparagus, with a martini chaser to boot. *Prison pay must run you to the moon and back,* Eddie thought, comping a scotch and soda off a waiter he busted once for Mary Jane. Watching Visel induced fierce hunger pangs, but Eddie had but pennies in his wallet. A couple at a nearby table got up to leave. Eddie swiped their plates and guzzled their scraps.

A phone rang behind the bar. A waiter brought the phone to Visel, who speared an olive and took the call. Eddie sipped his scotch and watched as Visel listened, nodded, and hung up before ditching his table. Eddie tossed the rest of his drink back and followed suit.

It was an alleyway meet.

East of downtown, just inside Church Hill.

Eddie parked a block away and crept to the scene like he was a window peeper. Just off a front porch now, an angled view all he could get. A car's trunk open — Visel and another man looked inside it. Their voices ricocheted off the alley's brick walls. Eddie caught fragments.

"…more where this came from…"

"…can use it all…"

"…had better come through…"

"…yeah…trainees…"

"…more like slaves…"

A couple of yuks and then both men raised their arms in a Nazi salute.

"Heil Hitler!"

"Heil Hitler!"

Eddie felt his stomach give out and watched as Visel took delivery of whatever was in that trunk, he and the other man moving boxes to Visel's Lincoln. Eddie ducked out of sight after the men moved into view, he could only hear now and what he heard was a 'see you next time' and a car driving off.

Eddie weighed his choices, time running out. He could run to his car, try and spot Visel's sled again, tail him to who knows where. *Or*, peek around the corner, which he did — the other man's ride was some kind of Plymouth it looked like, silver — and tail *that* car, see where the goods are from. Eddie looked around — no call box nearby, no way to clear it with Sherwood.

Think, Eddie.

You can always tail Visel some other time. You know where he works, where he lives, what he does after work. But these two and their salutes to a dead tyrant — whispers of Hitler meant something *big*. Bigger than Richmond, bigger than slugging it out on the same old streets until you die. Eddie smelled a hero's victory — follow the big lead, close the big case. See the future — newspaper articles, a promotion, maybe even Stolmy's job. Send the heel packing.

The choice is clear — *go big or go home.*

The Plymouth drifted east on Route 5 and kept going. Past street lights, past houses on the city's fringe, past Lenny's Lodge. Cutting northeast now, it drifted some more and Eddie panicked — how much gas could this department-issued sled have left in the tank? He caught a sliver of moonlight on the dash and checked the gauge — not much, almost in the red. He looked up at the Plymouth, dead ahead. No way to back out now and look, lights up ahead, *big* lights.

Eddie couldn't believe it.

His department-issued sled puttered out just shy of the entrance to the Army Air Base, a military HQ built around Richmond's Byrd airport for the war. Eddie felt his palms clam up as he watched the Plymouth pull up and stop at an official-looking gate. He killed the headlights and steered the wheels into some brush. He snuck out of the car and stayed low, surprised at the adrenaline fueling his steps, feeling just like Bennie and Shane must feel with their young hearts and young legs. He ducked into a throng of trees and peeked out just in time to see that Plymouth pull past the gate and drive toward the airport. It glided onto the tarmac and disappeared into the night.

My, my, Eddie thought, leaning against a tree to catch his breath. We've got Nazis in town and they're working some angle out of a military installation. *And unless I'm wrong, I'm the only cop that knows.* Screw the headlines, screw the promotion — Eddie saw dollar signs a mile long. Enough to quit the job altogether and buy a big house in the country, just like mother always wanted.

Eddie thought of how many ways he could play this, how he could use it. He walked back to his car, hoping for more luck. Check the hatch, *bingo*. A jerrycan of gasoline, right there. Eddie fueled up, hit the ignition, and turned back to Route 5 with his mind set on another stop downtown. He needed more info and *now*. Time to wrangle one of his informants, see what shakes out.

The Murphy Hotel bar was a local watering hole that catered to a diverse cadre of drinkers, from Richmond's VIPs to those less likely to seek the spotlight. You could find someone you knew there almost any night of the week and after a few drinks, it wasn't hard to come by some useful information you could use or trade up for something more. That's what Eddie was counting on, anyway, as he stepped into the main room and shot a look around. There's Jedidiah King, the tobacco big shot, holding court at a table full of county-club types. Suits, ties, drinks all around, the lot of them just yukking it up. Eddie resisted the urge to pull him aside and bribe him for a carton of smokes. A really sexy woman was sitting to King's right and she was enjoying herself, too. *How could she not*, Eddie wondered. Eddie stirred, just looking at her — she was like a magazine cover model, full of mystery and intrigue. *Way* out of Eddie's league.

Eddie scanned the bar next — *pay dirt*. There's Sykes Caldwell on a corner stool, downing gin like its water. Sykes was the department's go-to informant, easy to pump for page-one skinny. Just feed him more drinks. An empty stool, right there — Eddie sidled up.

"How's it hanging, Sykes?"

Sykes turned his way, friendly. "Well, hello there, Eddie. I'm guessing this isn't a social call."

"You guessed right." Eddied called the bartender over. "A rye for me and whatever my friend's having. On my tab." The bartender balked — Eddie's tab was overdrawn. Eddie shot him a hard look and the bartender put his hands up, he didn't want trouble. He went for their drinks.

"So tell me, Sykes, what do you know?"

"About?"

"About anything. You hear anything new?"

Sykes shook his head, laughing to himself. "You cops are all the same. You think you can just ply me with booze and I'll tell you whatever you want to hear. How 'bout you tell *me* something and

I'll tell *you* if I've heard anything about it?"

Eddie was impressed. "Grown some balls, have you? Well, kudos to you, Sykesy. Try this on — we've got murder on our hands, two of 'em. I'm sure you've read the papers."

Their drinks arrived.

"I have."

Eddie sipped his rye. "So you know we've got a shit show on our hands."

Sykes sipped his gin. "That I do."

"Ruth Kleinfeld. Did you know her?"

"I did not."

"Did you know anything about her?"

"Can't say I did."

"Do you know anyone who *did* know her?"

Sykes shook his head again. "I think you need some better questions, Eddie."

Eddie glared — what a smart ass. "This Scangili fellow. You two ever cross paths?"

"Carmine? A time or two. We weren't exactly friendly, but I'd see him around."

"And?"

"And what?"

"*And* what can you tell me about him? For Chrissakes, why are you making this so difficult?"

Sykes brought his voice down to a low whisper. "Because I want you to work for it, detective. All I know is rumor. Word was, he liked to play for the home team, if you know what I mean."

"He was a homo?"

Sykes put his hands up. "I know not from experience, Eddie. When I say rumor, I mean it. That's just what I heard."

"You think that's why he got snuffed?"

"I don't know. Would it surprise you?"

Eddie's shook his head. "The Kleinfeld woman was Jewish. That mean anything to you?"

Sykes sipped his gin, weighing his response. "The White Shadow."

"The what?"

"The White Shadow. You haven't heard anything yet, I take it."

"I don't have the faintest idea what that is."

"The *Führer* might be dead, but his spirit lives on." Sykes looked over his shoulder, spooked. "The White Shadow, Eddie. It's some kind of local group, looking to cause a ruckus. That's what I've heard, anyway."

Eddie's mind ping-ponged — Visel, Nazis, local thugs, some kind of airfield angle. He got chills — this was *huge*. "You've actually been a big help, Sykes." Eddie downed the rest of his rye in a single gulp.

Sykes raised his gin. "Yeah? Well, maybe one day, you cops will find someone new to bother for this shit."

Eddie grinned and snatched the gin from Sykes' hand. "Not a chance." He downed the gin, tossed the empty glass on the bar, and held his head up high as he walked out the door.

9

Drinks at The Jefferson Hotel bar — Jedidiah's idea. "The only way for us to truly conquer our fears, Bennie, is to confront them head on," he said once. After last year's fire, Bennie wasn't sure he would ever be truly comfortable setting foot in the hotel again, but for the time being, it didn't appear he had a choice. Between police board meetings and afternoon sit-downs with city council members, Bennie was at The Jefferson two, sometimes three times a week, and every visit set him on edge.

The bartender brought Bennie's drink without prompt, an Old Fashioned cocktail with rye. His usual and the old man's favorite, a tradition passed down. He took a hearty sip and thought of his father. An aching melancholy slid down his throat.

Thin crowd at the bar, Bennie was thankful — no reporters hounding him for quotes. He was early, too, and Jedidiah would most certainly be late, the man always coming from somewhere and not long to be someplace else. Jedidiah was part man, part myth, and forever scarred by the events of last March. Bennie replayed the tragic night of the fire and thought of how Jedidiah began that evening as merely an entertainer, playing host to some movers and shakers who were threatening the status quo of Richmond's underworld. He ended it a killer, burying a self-defensive bullet deep into the chest of his ex-lover, Jack Reed. After that, Bennie couldn't understand how Jedidiah managed to spend so much time at the hotel. He was always hosting a party at one spot or another, but he preferred The Jefferson and would often entertain his investors and friends here. And he was instrumental in helping to fund the hotel's repairs, propping himself up as the city's savior while Bennie took the fall for Jack Reed's death. Behind the scenes, however, they grew as friends and became near inseparable as confidants in the shadows. Bennie called it — "We lied to save the world and a brotherhood was born." Jedidiah agreed. They both worked to clean up Jack's loose ends in gangland and watched, sadly, as Stolmy unraveled from both the death of his only son and the loss of his position as Chief of Police, a job he'd held for almost ten years, when Jack's many crimes came to light in the press. It was exhausting, keeping up the front, but it was the right plan, one Bennie and Jedidiah both agreed to, and one they'd rarely spoken of since.

Bennie checked his watch — more time to kill. He pulled Shane's case report from his jacket and took stock of the V-Squad's progress on their investigations. Lots to be proud of. His team worked 'round the clock to produce the following choice bits of information. One, after a thorough questioning of local gun shop owners, it had been determined that Harold Kleinfeld had at no time owned a 22 pistol. And Shane confirmed, for a second time, that Mr. Kleinfeld was home asleep at the time of his wife's murder, so the husband angle was nixed. Two, a partial print pulled from The Sunshine Five-and-Dime notched a police records match, a two-time loser named George Carroll who'd been sent up for attempted rape *and* burning down a church. And three, a *full* print off a car's steering wheel found near where the Scangili body had been found *also* netted a rap sheet match, one Knox Sutton, just out after little more than four years for armed robbery and assaulting a police officer. Of note — Sutton had not, as of yet, checked in with his parole officer. Bennie sipped his rye, impressed, near giddy. With blue-chip scoops like these, they might actually put these cases to bed.

More info on the sheet — a personal note from Shane: 'Interesting tie-ins, boss, thought you'd want to know. One of Sutton's known associates is Walter MacKeye. And the police officer Sutton assaulted? None other than one Samuel Sherwood.' Bennie smiled and sipped his drink. Well, well, dad. Turns out you're on the case, too.

A string of excited hellos and how-are-you's began to make its way toward Bennie and sure enough, there was Jedidiah and his friendly, confident way, charming the shit out of everyone he saw.

He came to the bar, his arms open wide like they were long lost friends, and pulled Bennie into a bear hug.

"Ah, my dear friend, what a lovely sight you are."

Bennie signaled the bartender for a round as Jedidiah took a seat. "It's good to see you, too. And I'm beginning to think there's not a soul in town you don't already know."

Jedidiah grinned. "Oh, I expect there's a few men and women out of my purview, here and there, but it won't be long, Bennie. I'll have them under my fold yet."

"On that, I have no doubt."

The bartender brought their drinks and they cheers'd one another and took their first sips. They sat for a few moments in silence, neither in a rush to speak, to bring up old secrets or new worries. How thankful he was for Jedidiah. Who smiled just then and broke the peace.

"Well, if we are only to speak on the obvious, my friend, you're certainly having a time of it, if the press is to be believed. Any progress to speak of?"

"As a matter of fact, we're learning more and more. Got a couple of wins today, good tips, and I think we're on the right track, finally. Speaking of… " Bennie read from Shane's report. "Do the names George Carroll or Knox Sutton mean anything to you?"

Jedidiah shook his head. "No, but I'll keep my ear to the ground for you, if it'll help. Anything you can tell me?"

"They're both ex-cons and it looks like they're both involved. That's all we know for now."

Jedidiah nodded, weighing a question. "And that business with the body and the fire. Has anything come to light there?"

"So far, just these two names. One day at a time, we'll get there."

Jedidiah leaned into his drink — a gin martini, dirty, with three olives — and if Bennie didn't know better, he swore his friend was holding something back. But after all, the man did have his own life. And his own secrets. Speaking of…

"There's talk going 'round the squad room, J, that you had Constance intercede on that preacher's behalf last week, right in the middle of him getting worked over by two of our worst. He a friend of yours?"

"He is. He'd been at St. Philip Hospital that day, attending to a man that died, when those men arrested him. When I heard what happened, I made some inquiries and felt it was best I send rescue."

"I can't say I'm sorry you did." Bennie scanned Shane's case report again and found the details nestled in with a list of possible connections to Mrs. Kleinfeld and Scangili. There — that poolroom owner's death. That brought the total of local lives lost on V-E Day to three.

"Cornell Johnson?"

Jedidiah grew forlorn. "Yes. Any progress there?"

Bennie sighed. "My gut says it was Walter, but no one on the street that day got a good look at the two men that busted up the poolroom. It was all so much chaos. Same goes for his mugshot, no one we showed it to could fully ID him. So that leaves me with suspicion, which is enough to haul him in for a lineup, only I can't find him. And I'm thin on resources and manpower as it is. Hell, I don't even have the juice to coordinate a manhunt, at that. My only hope is that Walter will slip up and we'll catch him unawares."

Jedidiah nursed his drink. "What about Strickland and Halifax? Can you do anything about them?"

"I pleaded with Stolmy to no avail. My limited scope of power only gives me say-so over 'immediate activity' at the Annex and right now, that means connecting the dots between the murders of a highly respected Jewish woman and some lowlife from the pen. How my father did this job for so many years without losing his mind, I'll never know."

Jedidiah fought the urge to speak. "Bennie, I..."

"Oh, please, J. You don't need to say anything. I just have to get all this out and you're the one friend I can trust. Plus, it saves me from taking it home to Imogene. You know how she feels about it."

Jedidiah appeared relived. "Yes, but I also know how she feels about you."

"She still won't give me an answer."

"Give her time. And if you don't mind me saying so, neither of you need the pressure of marriage right now. McGuire General needs *her*, the city needs *you*, and you both need each other. Let that be enough for now. The right answer will come, for both of you."

Bennie raised his drink, impressed. "You're certainly the sage tonight, J. I think that was just what I needed to hear."

Jedidiah finished his martini. "Yes, well, sadly it's taken me a lifetime of missteps to recognize what really matters in life."

Bennie could just tell, here comes Jedidiah and his confessions. "J…"

Jedidiah lowered his voice. "Oh, my friend, You know, if it weren't for my… indulgences, there would nine more people on this planet, your father among them. Living, loving, and contributing to the world."

"You don't know that." Jedidiah had convinced himself that his rejection of Jack Reed as a romantic partner led Jack down the dark path he followed, a path that included black market profiteering, the Jefferson fire, and the murder of Bennie's father.

"Oh, but I do, sweet Bennie. I do."

Bennie lowered his voice. "Look, my father's death was not your fault. The fire was not your fault. Jack started it, not you — "

"But if I hadn't *spurned* him, he may never have… "

Bennie leaned in close. "Stop. Do you know how many times I think, if I hadn't stepped *this* way in the jungle, if I hadn't taken *that* path, some Jap solider might still be alive today? Or that I might be dead? Look, I don't like to think on it much, but they had families, too, same as us. Maybe it always gets to you, maybe it always will. Maybe it creeps up on you in the worst ways when you're least expecting it. I know it does to me. But you just have to know it, J, that it wasn't your fault. You did what had to be done. Christ, look at me. Everyday I'm this way or that way with some decision or another, and sometimes it's about a life. I can't think too hard on it and neither can you."

"What you did for me." Jedidiah fired the shot that night, but it was Bennie who took responsibility.

"Yes, and I'd do it again. It's like we said, we leave it at that, friend, and *move on*."

Before we're found out, Bennie wanted to say, but he didn't, and instead was glad to welcome the silence that came next and the drinks the bartender brought them even more so. *No more, though, or you'll be in your cups at morning roll call.*

"Let me ask you a question, J."

Jedidiah sat up, ready for a change of subject. "Alright."

"If you were convicted of attempted rape *and* burning down a church, think you'd ever get out of prison?"

"Well, I suppose that depends."

"On?"

"Who I tried to rape. What kind of church I burned down. This is the South, after all."

"I see your point."

"Is this a white man, a black man? Or can you not say?"

"White."

"Well, then I think you have at least some of your answer."

Bennie tried to think of something more to say, but thought better of it. Best to leave it for tomorrow, dig into the case with fresh energy. He looked at his good friend and knew there was nothing more to say, not tonight. They raised their glasses to one another and finished their drinks.

Jedidiah split for a late-night rendezvous. The who/what/where — Bennie knew better than to ask. He'd just get a fib, anyways. But he did have one last order of business on the night, so he asked the bartender for the phone. Bennie dialed out and heard several rings before the voice on the other line picked up, its owner's carefree, devil-may-care attitude a most welcome sound.

"Lenny's Lodge, where the truth is free but the lies'll cost ya. Lenny here."

"It's Bennie."

"Bennie! What's buzzin', cousin?"

Lenny Greenberg — motel owner, tattoo enthusiast, and friend to almost anyone for the right price. Lenny ran a kind of way station for the downtrodden at his lodge, harboring a host of fringe dwellers in exchange for money or trade, sometimes both. Some were on the way up, some were on the way down, but all of them were just happy to be off the grid. From ex-cons to ex-wives, it didn't matter if you were looking to kick a habit or start a new one. At Lenny's, you'd find room, board, and good company, if you wanted it, and you could stay a few days or stay a few years, it was entirely up to you, just so long as you had something to offer. The department even used to keep a few rooms there, for witnesses and CIs, but that all changed when Bennie's former partner was knifed to death by Jack Reed in one of Lenny's unnumbered suites. Bennie cringed, thinking of Niles, and made a mental note to tap the widow's fund and send flowers to Cheryl Lee.

Through the phone, Bennie heard noise in the background at Lenny's, maybe a crowd. He cleared his throat. "Nothing but the same old thing, pal, just trying to keep the streets safe. What've you got cooking?"

"A poker game! You want in?"

"On my salary? Not a chance, but I do have a few names for you."

"You usually do. Shoot."

"Have you run across an ex-con named George Carroll?"

"Can't say I have. What's he to you?"

"Just a person of interest, for now. You catch wind of him, I'd like to know."

"Sure thing."

"The other is Knox Sutton, also an ex-con. Did time for armed robbery."

Pause — it stretched a little too long.

"Lenny?"

"Yeah, yeah, I'm here, just making a mental note of these two names. Look, B, I'll keep my ear to the ground, just like always."

"Thanks."

"And you know, while we're in a doing favors kind of mood, I got a couple of gals out here look like they both wound up on the wrong side of a drunk husband. What would it take to, uh, right those wrongs?"

Bennie thought of someone putting the hurt on Imogene and felt his gut churn. "Just get me names. I'll put someone on it."

"You're a good one, B. Don't ever change."

"Tell that to my gal. She wants me soft and quiet, riding a desk."

"Oh, she'll come around to your charms, eventually. We all do. You make an honest woman of her yet?"

"Working on it."

"Yeah, well, you better gas it and fast, pal, 'cause I've seen your lady and she's the biggest catch there is. I'll get you the husbands' names and let you know if I hear anything on these other two."

"Thanks, friend."

"You got it."

Lenny clicked off and Bennie checked his watch. It was just after one am, Imogene might be home soon, wrapping up a cab shift. He eased off the bar stool and quickened his pace as he stepped out into the night.

10

Knox put his guard up as he sat at the Lodge's roomy and sturdy poker table. *Looks like one of a kind,* he thought, running his fingers along the patches of finish sanded down by so many resting arms over the years. He laid the ten bucks Lenny had staked him over a pair of drink ring stains and caught a whiff of the cheap corn whiskey soaked into the felt. A good egg, Lenny, letting him lay low at the Lodge until he figured out his next move. It had been a week since he escaped the house fire, his body still sore from the fall. He felt aches and pains with every step. With nowhere to go, Knox turned vagrant the first few nights, raiding restaurant garbage bins for food and catching z's in the bushes of a public park. His eyes constantly over his shoulder, fearful that Walter would spot him any minute and blame *him* for destroying his home. Dark thoughts had kept him up nights ever since. Scangili's dead eyes boring through him, that one-eyed preacher man coming after him with a fireball. With no one to call and not the faintest idea on how to reach Constance, Knox considered hopping a train and skipping town for awhile until he remembered Lenny's refuge out Route 5, a kind of hideout for the lost and lonely. Fitting the bill to a T, Knox dug himself into the bed of a produce truck and rode it all the way there, hopping out just in time.

Lenny's Lodge had been like a second home to many over the years, Knox included. He stayed here more than a few times before prison, dodging cops and hiding out after jobs. He even recognized a few of the Lodge's current tenants as they filed in around him for tonight's card game. To his left was Old Butch Donaldson, a B and E man as vile as they come. Knox remembered his crude MO was to woo a woman, knock her out, and steal her jewelry. He acknowledged Knox with a frosty nod and turned to gab with Sykes Caldwell, a man who spent more time on Earth drunk than sober. Sykes kept his ear to the ground, though, and often traded valuable street gossip for booze and places to stay. To Knox's right was a rogue's gallery of the beaten down and dragged out, the usual Lodge clientele. Some ex-cons he recognized, some he didn't. A couple of broads, too, looking worse for wear in over-sized clothing. Call it bruise cover-up. Knox thought of Constance and prayed she was safe.

A short dog of gin made its way around the table, along with a sizable dose of restless energy — everyone anxious to get started and win some money. Knox took the bottle and downed a good sip when he noticed Lenny eyeballing him from over in the corner as he talked on the phone.

Loudmouth Butch, impatient: "Hey Greenberg! Cut the chit-chat, let's get moving over here!"

Lenny shot Butch the bird before hanging up and cruising over to the table, kicking up the volume on the radio as he took up in the dealer's seat. Stan Kenton came on as Lenny called for a fair game — no palming cards, no shorting the pot, no peeking. "Nickel antes, capeesh?" Everyone agreed and the deck was cut, the sound of cards shuffling a real comfort to Knox, something familiar. It reminded him of home, of family, and of how his father used to play cards at the kitchen table with old chums, risking their grocery money for a thrill. Sometimes winning, sometimes not. Over the next hour, the same kind of luck made its uneven way around the table, favoring some more than others. Butch gloated and chomped on a cigar, winning a big pot on just a pair of twos while poor Sykes bottomed out after only three hands. One of the girls, though, Naomi, she won not one but two big spreads and vowed to put the winnings toward divorce lawyers for both her and her friend, Teresa. Knox bet big on a straight that never materialized and then went cold for a few hands before finding a streak and netting a century off four of a kind, more than enough to make a start with. Find an apartment, get back with Constance. Maybe even get some wheels, too. Start up again with a good crew, not that bunch from before that got him all tangled up with Johnny Law.

Chinwag at the table swayed every which way and started with the war. "Roosevelt should just fucking bomb the Japs already," Old Butch barked. Talk soon veered toward back-alley scuttlebutt. Sykes grabbed another beer — his fifth — and leaned back into his chair. "Any of you come across this White Shadow outfit yet? I hear they're out for blood."

Old Butch just laughed. "All's I know is they better steer clear of *me*. I got no time for Nazi rowdies just looking to make noise."

Sykes looked shaken. "I don't know, Butch. I hear they clipped that Jewish woman just for kicks."

Teresa grew hot. "That sweet old lady at the five-and-dime? They did that?"

Sykes nodded.

She threw down her cards. "Goddamnit."

You have no idea, Knox thought. Tingles ran over his skin as he thought of the pictures Ghostman used to pass around the cells — the ones with Klan members draped in rebel flags, murdering and burning in the name of God and Confederate generals. Recruitment for the cause, he called it. The White Shadow. Part Klan, part Nazi. All shitstorm bad.

Lenny caught the boo-hoo buzz circling the table and took a good pull of gin. "Way I hear it, they're a fanatic bunch of Hitler hangers-on, looking to make a stink. Holdouts from the Silver Shirts and German-American Bund. Apparently they didn't get the memo on V-E Day." Chuckles circled the table. *If you knew what I knew*, Knox thought, *you wouldn't be laughing*. Lenny threw a change-up. "Anyone here come across an ex-con named George Carroll? He's newly outta the pen and could be looking to make trouble."

Knox froze at mention of Carroll's name. Inside the pen, George had been in and out of solitary, always on the skids with Visel and the other inmates. Word got around that he spent most of his waking hours memorizing and rewriting Bible verse. Knox knew to steer clear of him, the guy was just *way off*. And he never understood why Carroll and Scangili got so chummy before Carroll just up and vanished, not even finishing his sentence, but now he knew the score. Visel and Walter, running their scam with ex-cons. Well, hide your women and children, people of the world, and fast, because just the thought of George Carroll on the street is enough to make the Devil's skin crawl. And even with all that, even though Knox knew he should just keep his mouth shut, he still said, "I know him."

Lenny wasn't surprised. "I figured you might. You just got out, too, yeah?"

Knox nodded. "We're not pals or nothing, if that's what you're thinking, but yeah, I know him."

"Well, if you or anyone here happens to catch sight of him, let me know, yeah? I got someone who wants to make his acquaintance."

No, they really don't. Knox kept it to himself this time.

Old Butch grinned. "Say, now, that someone wouldn't be your pal Bennie Sherwood, he of the Richmond Po-lice Department, now would it? 'Cause I'd hate to find out you'd gone canary, Len."

Standoff tension came on strong, like a gunslinger standoff in the old West, but Lenny just sat back and chomped his cigar. "Butch, the privileged few I invite to this table know better than to quiz me on anything more than what they can do to earn my trust. So if I were you, if you want to be invited back, I'd put that idea in your pocket and keep it there."

Old Butch sat back and stewed, he knew better than to say anything more, but Sykes, well… Sykes couldn't resist, his eager voice nearly cracking with excitement.

"Is there a-a reward?"

Lenny balked. "For what?"

"Finding this guy Carroll."

Lenny shook his head. "You want to go looking for this joker, that's on you. But, if you happen to put eyes on him before anyone else and let me know, I'll be sure something good comes your way."

Sykes looked ready to jet from the table and get his search on stat when Naomi held up her winnings, leaned into the table, and, to no one in particular, said, "I'll pay someone fifty bucks to beat the shit out of my soon-to-be ex-husband."

It was as if a bomb went off — the room froze and they were all trapped in a museum exhibit, with no agency to say or do anything, before the laughs started to creep in, little by little, circling the table like a cough no one wanted to catch. Save for pipsqueak Sykes, who couldn't help but chime in, again.

"I'll do it!"

The room roared. Sykes, too. Knox thought of how good it felt to laugh, even though he knew Naomi was serious.

Lenny reached out and took her hand. "I got someone working on that as we speak, don't either of you worry. Nobody's gonna hurt you again." And just like that, the ladies' laughter turned to tears. Lenny leaned over to console them with hugs and pats on the back. Smooth, can-do Lenny. Probably gets all the cooze he wants.

Knox thought of his own physical needs as a radio ad for Tantilla Garden came on. His stomach went all wobbly at mention of 'the South's most beautiful ballroom.' He and Constance used to dance the night away there, night after night, under the stars, even, loving it when the Garden pulled back the rollaway ceiling, the drinks and laughter flowing like a river of happiness through the joint whenever they were there, nothing but love and affection between them. Knox counted his winnings again and felt bold. "Say, I've got a name of my own to pass around. A girl I used to go with. Anyone here know Constance Lee?"

Sykes grew excited. "Yeah, I remember seeing you two together! Say, she's moved up in the world. She's doing big things now."

Knox — all nerves. "Doing what?"

Butch collected his winnings. "She works for Jedidiah King now. Handles his affairs, runs the business side of things."

Knox tried to picture Constance schlepping with bigwigs. "The cigarette guy?"

Lenny nodded. "The one and only. You know him?"

Knox shook his head, but he should of known. Naomi gave him a sympathetic look as he thought back two years. Her visits dropped off then. Her letters, too. "All the same, anyone know where I could find her? We had a dog together and anyhow I'd just like to see her again. For old times' sake."

Lenny stood up and stretched. "Anywhere King is, you're likely to find her right there with him. Find him, you'll find her. But I gotta warn you, Sutton, she's moved on from the old life. No more running around with a crew, she's gone legit."

Butch almost laughed. "Yeah, especially after that business with MacKeye, she's done with all that."

A sizable discomfort took up in the room, as most everyone now looked as if too much had been said. Everyone but Knox.

Please, tell me more.

"What business with MacKeye?"

Butch looked around the room and caught himself, 'Oh Shit' all over his face. "Oh, that? That was nothing. It was a while after you got sent up when she took up with him, and then, yeah, when she'd had enough, she got out. That's all it was."

Knox looked hard at Lenny. If anyone in the room would give it to him straight, he would.

"This on the level?"

Lenny didn't look so calm anymore, taking a drag of his cigar and forming his words. "Look, Sutton — she and MacKeye had a thing and it wasn't pretty. A couple of us saw what was happening and we helped her out of it, that's it. But don't worry, King's a good one, he's doing right by her."

It took everything Knox had not to storm the table with a broken beer bottle and force Lenny to tell all. But there were rules here and Knox knew better. So he called up his prison nerves, honed sharp in the darkness night after night, and held his tongue. And then, with all the calm of an approaching storm, Knox collected his winnings and made his way around the table toward the door — handing Lenny back the ten he'd staked him — before strolling out of the room, Knox never more sure of himself than he was right now.

11

Timony held the phone away from her face and laid her Southern charm on thick, kicking her voice up some to drown out the clamor of the newsroom and pretending to be interested, best she could.

"Really? All weekend long? In Charles City County?"

It's just east of town, Mrs. Talmadge told her. Not far.

"At your weekend home? How nice!"

I want to never go there, Timony thought.

"No, Mrs. Talmadge, can't say I have."

What the hell is there to do in Charles City County, anyway?

"And just a spot of rain? Well, now, aren't you lucky."

I'll be lucky when I get off this goddamn phone.

Now, now. Be nice. Timony remembered herself and softened. "Well, all I can say is *that* is just about the loveliest weekend I have heard about all day and I will be *sure* to include it in this week's column, you can be sure of that."

Mrs. Talmadge went on to say that she saw Harrison's picture in the paper this week and read all about his efforts on behalf of the city. How lucky we all are and what a handsome man!

"I'll be sure and tell him you said so. Do call again when you have more to share!"

Timony hung up the phone on the spot, in a way now over mention of her husband's good looks. By a complete stranger, at that! Yes, Harrison is handsome, especially when donning one of his tailored suits and slicking back his hair for publicity photos. Why, just last week, he mugged for the newspapers' cameras after a victorious city council meeting over the whats and wheres of his never-ending war surplus crusade. Timony stirred, thinking of his photo in Sunday's paper and the way he looked so much like

Gary Cooper does in any one of the movie magazines she kept at the house — *Picturegoer, Photoplay, Movie Stars Parade*. And yes, Harrison is athletic, too, keeping fit at the club with their doubles tennis and his swimming. But Harrison is also curt to a fault, speaking his mind when it's most unwelcome. He also chews his food loudly and refuses to do even simple chores at their home, preferring instead to leave his shoes and his clothes and his dishes about for Macy to straighten and clean, even as he complains about her wages and the added stress of even having servants at all. Harrison is also busy and absent from their home of late, which makes him absent from their marriage, as well.

For what reasons, Timony truly did not know. Looking down at her waistline to be sure, she was pleased at how trim she'd kept it these last few years. Why, she had to keep up appearances for society's sake and of course there were her exercise routines and watching what she ate. *And how could I not stay in shape*, she thought, *with all the rationing!* And she was always ready with a smile and a conversation starter when Harrison arrived home after long days at the office, having sparred with the mayor over funding or quarreled with that awful Stolmy Reed over 'new directives in public safety.' What she had begun to suspect, quite depressingly, is that Harrison bore her some ill will over their son's absence from their lives. Perhaps blamed her, even, for Nolan's decision to enlist and serve in the first place. The thought of it now gave her quite a jolt and she reached desperately for the ice water she kept at her desk, downing it quickly, wishing it were vodka or gin — a woman *must* stay hydrated, her mother had always said, for her skin. The rush of the water cooled and calmed her in equal measure as she looked out at the rest of the Herald's newsroom. The symphony of reporters hacking away at their typewriters in a rush to meet the copy editors' deadline was always a welcome sound to her ears.

She'd taken the job of 'society editor' more for amusement than anything else, something to keep her busy between lunches and parties and her never ending social calendar. The thrill of a deadline, however, why it moved her in ways she'd never known it could! Lord knows, she'd didn't need the money, but her inheritance had never been enough to satisfy her mind or her heart. No, Timony 'Thursday' Wells needed to know things and to know people and to know things about those people in just the right ways so that she might be able to connect them to the kinds of enriching activities that would bring them comfort and happiness and joy. From debutante announcements to the Junior League to the Garden Club to the wildly exclusive Women's Club, there was always something for a willing, educated woman of Richmond to do. For if Timony had a true purpose these last several years, these war years, it was to spread joy in places where there was none and to bring happiness to those who didn't have it. And even as she struggled to find balance in her marriage and peace within herself in the shadow of her son's absence, she would continue to bring joy to others — in her society column, in her volunteer work, and at her parties.

The very thought of 'party' gave her a welcome start as she said out loud, to no one at all, "Thank the fucking stars, it's Thursday!" Timony grabbed the phone and dialed the house. Macy picked up on the third ring.

"Wells' residence."

"Macy, sweetheart, it's me."

"Oh, Miss Timony! Why, I wasn't expecting you to call for another hour, at least."

"Yes, well, it's a *slow* day in society news."

Timony was now cross with herself for being so curt with Mrs. Talmadge. The worst of Harrison, rubbing off.

"Listen, do me the grandest of favors, would you? Find the number of a Miss Dorothy Talmadge of Richmond and invite her over tonight, please. I'd be most grateful."

Timony heard Macy scribbling on a notepad before she asked, "Anything in particular I should tell her?"

"Just that it's a bridge party, of course, and that we play as much bridge as you'll find at an all night poker party. And to leave her husband at home, where he belongs."

Macy was aghast. "My Lord, Miss Timony, you really want me to say all that?"

"No, of course not. Just tell her to bring her smile and a good disposition and she'll be sure to enjoy herself. Now, have we got enough to drink?"

Macy giggled. "Like you don't know it's Thursday. Why the liquor man was just here. Six boxes, my Lord. How anyone works on a Friday after one of these parties, I say."

"Did he flirt with you again?"

"Oh, stop now!"

"Well, did he?"

"You know he did."

"And just when are you gonna go out with him? Time is ticking, Macy, don't you let him get away."

"I will be sure and keep that in mind, Miss T, but I'm doing just fine on my own right now, thank you very much."

"Yes, well, you know how I like to bring people together. Now, have there been any messages for me, or any mail to speak of?"

A pause as Macy's tone turned reluctant. "Why, no, Miss Timony, nothing has come today."

The 'nothing,' of course, was in hopes of a very real something — a telegram or a letter or some such notice of her son's whereabouts. MIA for nearly nine months, and no one, not the war offices even, will tell us a goddamn thing. *My God, to think of what he's been through! But this is no time to think of that now, is it?* Come now, she heard her mother say — take a deep breath. Correct yourself and put a face on.

"That's alright, no bother t'all," Timony said as the slightest Southern twang snuck into her voice, the way it always did when she was hiding how she really felt. "Now, have you seen or heard from Harrison, by chance?"

Macy's tone changed again, this time toward the suspicious. "Matter of fact, he just came through here. Rather in a rush of sorts, he was, in an awful hurry to get to his office and then off again he went. It *was* rather curious, I should say."

Timony frowned. Harrison knew to steer clear of her 'bridge' parties, but this sounded odd, even for him.

"Did he say what it was about, this urgency?"

Macy's voice kicked up — she was covering. "Uh, no m'am, he didn't say much at all."

Timony wasn't having it. "Was he rude to you again?"

"Oh, you know how Mr. Harrison is, how he can be. He was just in a way, is all."

"Yes, well, he'll be in such a way he won't know which way is up when I've had a say with him, you can bet your ass."

"Miss Timony!"

Timony glanced at the clock — she had forty-five minutes to wrap up edits for her column and get to the Commonwealth Club for lunch with Jedidiah. She'd deal with Harrison later. "Now, before I go, whatever can we do about this situation with your uncle? I mean, I know he's passed, God rest him, but you've never said, and I've been running ever so quickly to this and that, and what with poor Mrs. Kleinfeld, I'm afraid I've not been as thoughtful with you as I would care to."

Macy took a moment to respond. "It's no bother, Miss Timony, you're so kind to me already. Kind to all of us, really."

"If you think of anything, you'll tell me, yes?"

"I will indeed."

"For the time being, my dear, let's forget our troubles, because it's Thursday, and at my house, you know that means the booze is plenty, the glasses are clean, and there ain't no time for Mr In Between!"

Timony strode into the Commonwealth Club like she owned the place.

Which she did, in a way.

Her father's trust had secured her a five percent stake in the club overall and a seat on the trustees board, two things that mattered to her very little. What did matter to her and *should* matter to everyone there, the room watching her now as she threaded the lunch room in a smart business-like two piece she'd bought only yesterday in a private sale at Thalhimer's, was how much she knew about *them*, and would continue to know about them as long as she was Timony 'Thursday' Wells, purveyor of local gossip and editor of the society column. And that was ownership in a way, was it not?

She sure liked to think so, smiling and waving at everyone as she passed, thinking of what she could print in her column and what she couldn't. Why there's that mayor's aide, the one on the veteran's affairs committee working *so* hard to set up housing for those returning home, the very same one who jets off to Buckroe Beach on the weekends with his mistress. Just look at him, waving back at Timony now with not a care in the world. *And why look, there's even one of my neighbors*, Timony thought, a dear mother of three whose middle child was *most definitely* fathered by a member of Johnny Pepper's band, the Salt Shakers. There she is, raising a glass at Timony as she passed by her table.

"See you tonight!" Timony said to her with a wink as she twirled her way through a pair of waiters, catching whistles as she put on a real show for everyone in the ballroom. And at last, at the table Timony was fast approaching, there was Jedidiah King himself, her dear friend and local tobacco magnate. He rose from his seat with a welcoming smile. He rivaled only Harrison for handsomeness, his weathered face never without a smile and his svelte build rarely inside anything but one of his many custom-fit three piece suits. What a mystery Jedidiah was, a man who never seemed to do without, even in war time. Timony appreciated the way he stood and buttoned his jacket like a gentleman as she made the table, greeting her with a kiss on the cheek and a comforting hug.

"Why you are always a sight for sore eyes, dear Jedidiah, no matter how long it's been since I've seen you!" Timony was flattered at the way he pulled out her chair for her, the attention he paid her.

"And you, my dear, are a bonafide treasure, a welcome sight to all!" Jedidiah motioned for a waiter. Within moments, a tray of martinis appeared.

Three, to be exact.

Only then did Timony notice the other woman at the table and all at once, she found herself thunderstruck, unable to recall any housewives league or social calendar obligations or debutante parties she might have promised to plan or attend. She could hardly remember her own name, trying not to outright stare at this enchanting woman with scarlet lipstick and a seductive smile, a woman who looked so much like a movie star that Timony half-expected Cecil B. DeMille himself to yell "Cut!" and rush to their table for lighting adjustments and line reading corrections.

Jedidiah noticed this, too, of course, and cleared his throat as he took two of the martinis from the tray and handed first one to Timony and then the other to his friend before taking the third for himself. "Timony my dear, allow me to introduce my confidante and business partner, Miss Constance Lee. Constance, this is the estimable and irreplaceable Timony 'Thursday' Wells. who I'm sure you know by reputation and who I so often speak of."

Timony blushed and raised her glass in earnest. "Only good things, I hope!"

Constance just winked. "And a few other things, but don't worry, I won't tell."

Timony was so caught off guard by Constance's wit she nearly spit up her drink and then there was nothing left to do but laugh about it. The three of them giggled and looked from one to another. Timony played along, of course, but she suddenly felt like a silly schoolgirl. Timony Wells, who commands whatever room she's in and steers the conversation whichever way she wants it to go, why she was suddenly so beside herself she started to sweat. And then they really got into the laugh, hell, the moment threatened to become a full on roar as a very overwhelmed Timony had the unmistakeable feeling that after meeting Constance Lee, her life would never be the same again.

12

Marlon grabbed Miss Ruby's hips with both hands and arched his own upwards so that he rose into her even further, the two of them rocking back and forth in the kind of harmonious union that can only come from two bonded souls making love. Within seconds, she made those sweet, sweet sounds he so loved to hear. The both of them cried out and moved the bed as they climaxed together and felt the world fall away for a few brief, precious moments. It was as if the rotation of the Earth paused, as if God himself put a stop to things ever so briefly, just for them. Marlon could still feel the lingering sting of the police beating throughout his ribcage, even though it had been several weeks, and he winced as Miss Ruby came off him and laid down next to him, pulling the covers up over their bodies and running a hand along his chest the way she did. Her soft, adoring touch made him feel confident, gave him comfort. And for a few moments, it was as if there was nothing else in the world, and surely no one but the two of them there, resting and savoring the moment.

But for Marlon, it wasn't long before that dark feeling was back, the one that had been eating away at his soul ever since he lit up that house in flames, the way he so willingly gave in to rage and made a fraud of himself. Now, with every sermon he preached, every heartfelt word he offered to a member of the church, with every hug he gave to a child, he worried they would discover what a phony he was, worried they would discover just how hard he fell the wrong way, and cast him out, banish him like some jackleg preacher and send him away. If they don't call the police first, that is. The guilt of it had been gnawing at him more every day, and if he let it go on any longer, there wouldn't be any more of him left. Certainly nothing to offer this beautiful, angelic woman lying next to him, this woman he hoped to marry and start a family with. So a most fearful Marlon called upon God for courage, took Miss Ruby's hand and held it tight, and forced it out.

"I... I think I may have killed someone."

Miss Ruby let out a sympathetic coo and kissed his shoulder.

"Oh, baby, you poor thing, it's alright. You were in the war, like everybody else."

Marlon felt a sting in his eye and almost laughed. *That's a whole other story, for another day*, he almost said. "No, I mean... a few weeks ago. After Cornell passed, I did something... unforgivable."

Marlon found it was suddenly hard to breathe as Miss Ruby propped herself up on one arm and looked at him with a cockeyed smile, her heavenly, exquisite breasts just there before him.

"You're being silly. What do you mean, you *did* something?"

And then Marlon became a storyteller, the words racing out of him faster than he could speak them, telling Miss Ruby all about how he and Charles had taken over one of Mr. Jedidiah's numbers' operations and set it up in Cornell's poolroom and how that had unknowingly put them in the crosshairs of a man named Walter MacKeye and that it was this man Walter that brought such sadness to their lives and felled Cornell the way he did. And then he went on to remind her that on the same day the war in Europe ended, two white policemen gave him a beating so vicious he could still feel it in his bones, even now, but that it still didn't stop him from guiding the flock that night, the way he found the strength to speak on Cornell's tragedy the way he did. And that it was only later that very same night and only after he'd been weakened by too much of that devil water, that moonshine he loved so, did he go to this man Walter's house, where he'd been told told no one would be, and set it ablaze with a vengeful spirit he never knew he possessed. And with tears in his eyes falling like rain, he went on and told her more.

"And then... then I saw the stories in the paper, about how a man's body had been found, some man that worked at the prison. And my Lord, my God, what have I done? I burned that house, I burned that man, I'm no better than a lynchin' mob!" Marlon crumbled to the floor then, coming to his knees and praying in a fit of desperation. "Oh, Lord! Please come 'round and show yourself to me! Come 'round, Lord, and show me the way!"

And then, ever so slowly, the tears ceased and Marlon's heaving slowed as the frenzy of the moment died away, Marlon feeling quite embarrassed now and even silly at having let himself become so overrun with emotion, of kneeling here naked in his bedroom in the presence of a woman he'd just made love to. He was quite startled, then, when Miss Ruby came 'round the bed and brought herself near, sidling up next to him on the floor and folding him into her embrace, caressing his face and speaking to him softly the way his mother used to do after he'd run afoul of his brothers or, worse, his father.

Ruby closed her eyes. "My Lord, I ask you, how much must we endure? How much must we give of ourselves before we find peace?"

Marlon could hardly believe her sympathy. "You mean, you're not disgusted? With what I've done?"

Miss Ruby took Marlon's head in her hands and looked lovingly into his eyes. "A great man I know once asked of his congregation, who among us has not given in to anger? Who among us has not given in to sin? Now I'm not saying what you did was right, sweet Marlon, but there ain't no crime in being a man."

"But I took a life! How do I live with that?"

Miss Ruby kissed his forehead. "Did you strangle this man?"

Marlon was taken aback. "No, but — "

"Stab him?"

"What? No!"

"Shoot him with a gun?"

"Didn't have to, I — "

"You what?"

"I told you, I lit that house up — "

"That's right, you lit the *house* up, and that's all you did."

CCRRRAAAASSSHHH!

The sound came from just across the street, at the church — something breaking, shattering. Marlon and Ruby came to their feet at once and rushed to his bedroom window just in time to see a throng of young white men and women running through the street and calling for n____s to burn, smashing in apartment windows and slashing car tires. From what Marlon could make out, someone had thrown a rock through one of the sanctuary windows and now, wafting into the outside air, was the sound of a little girl crying.

Miss Ruby shrieked, her face aghast in horror. "My God, *the children's choir practice!*"

Marlon sprinted down Second Street faster than he ever thought possible, his sore ribs like daggers to his core, but still he gave chase, barreling down on these hate-filled teens and wishing he had one of his homemade bombs at the ready to lodge at the jalopy they were all piling into now, the lot of them sneering back at Marlon, calling him jig and darkie and telling him to burn in hell. The teens were about to speed off when one of the boys wanted one last go. He broke from the pack and hurled another rock straight at Marlon, and for a split second, Marlon saw himself back at Fort Huachuca, loading that last explosive onto the truck and wishing he hadn't. And right here and now, Marlon knew he should duck, just hit the ground and hug it, like the Army taught him, but he found the spirit of an outfielder instead and tracked the rock as it sailed through the air, sizing it up with his one good eye and catching it with both hands — never mind the sting and the way it cut into his palm. No, with the fluid motion of a graceful dancer, Marlon became like David to this boy's Goliath, pivoting in that very same moment and throwing the rock right back at him, knowing full well he shouldn't, that he *would* burn in hell, that this again was a vengeful act he would come to regret. But it was so satisfying, this act of release, and it was as if he'd thrown a runner out at home plate, the way the rock hit the boy's leg and leveled him to the ground. Marlon was both ecstatic and horrified with himself as he listened to this boy cry out in pain. His low-rent friends sped off, leaving him behind.

Marlon caught up to where the boy was, on Clay just west of Second, and knelt down, his breath all a flutter. The boy recoiled in true fear, inching himself away from Marlon. He grabbed at his leg and winced in pain. Marlon looked around — onlookers everywhere, *make it quick.* He grabbed this boy by the shoulder and got in close.

"You hear that?"

The boy was true scared, listening and looking around. "Hear what?"

"*Nothing.* No police siren, oh no. They don't come 'round here much anyhow, so there's nobody coming for you or me, understand? At least not soon, so you listen good, son. You're gonna come with me for a time and we're gonna have ourselves a little sit down, you understand? And when I find out what I want to know, then I'll get you to whatever hospital admits white boys like yourself."

The boy spat at Marlon's face. "Fuck you, n____!"

Marlon wiped the spit away and dug his hands into this boy's shoulders real good. "Is that right, now? Do that again and I'll be happy to just up and leave you right here in the street where these good, church-goin' folk will come and descend on you like a pack of wolves. Is that what you want?"

The boy weighed it for a beat before shaking his head like his life depended on it.

"That's what I thought." Marlon lifted the young man from the street just like any good-natured preacher would do, holding him up and hobbling along with him as they made their way back to the church, speaking to onlookers and those affected by the violence as he passed.

"Don't you all mind, now, we're gonna get this misguided young man some help! And then we'll get the police out here to help us, don't you worry, gonna get this all straight!"

Marlon put on a face for everyone. He smiled and waved like he knew he should, knowing full well that when he got this boy away from prying eyes, all bets were off.

Screams.

Tears.

Trauma.

Back inside the church, Miss Ruby gave Marlon the damage report: young India is off to St. Philip Hospital for stitches, but she'll be back at choir practice in no time. The sanctuary window is shattered and there's rain coming, so we need to cover it up stat. And the rocks put some awful splinters into a few pews and the floor, so we need to get that all smoothed over before Sunday.

"Coulda been worse," Marlon said, wiping the tears from her cheeks.

"Yes, it coulda been worse."

AAAHHHHH!

The boy cried out from Marlon's back room. *Best get there before Charles goes too far*, Marlon thought as he turned to go. Miss Ruby called after him.

"Yes, well, just be sure this all don't put a stop to *you*, you hear me? You remember yourself, Marlon!"

They threw the boy against a hardback chair, made him sit. He was Klan-robe white, bone scared. Marlon clocked his eyes as he looked 'round the room, scanning for a way out.

"Where… where am I?"

Marlon had to smile. Come to think of it, his private room *did* have a dungeon-like feel to it. Musty air, old shotguns on the wall, just one bulb giving off light.

"What's your name, son?"

"B-B-B-Billy… Billy Johnson."

"Tell me, Billy. Whatcha come 'round here for, do these things?"

"Well, I… I mean we, it wasn't our idea, I swear."

"Still, sure seem like you enjoyed yourself. Whose idea was it, then?"

Billy grabbed for his leg, wincing. "Please, sir, I'm hurt real bad, I… I need a doctor!"

Charles almost laughed — little miss India was his cousin's daughter. He kicked Billy in the leg where the rock had hit him and they listened to Billy scream like an injured animal. Charles didn't care none at all. "Oh, oh, so… so you need a doctor? My cousin's daughter needs a doctor and she's only *ten years old!*"

Marlon got between them and lied, his first of the day. "Look, son, police gonna be here *any minute*. Now, you can spend that minute in relative peace *or* my cousin and I here can take turns. Now… what's it gonna be?" Billy just looked at Marlon and nodded. Marlon leaned in, got in close. "That's good, Billy. Now, whose idea was all this?"

Billy was parched for thirst, fighting for words. "Some men, there were three of them, I.. I…we didn't get their names. They paid us."

"They paid you? To do what you did?"

Billy nodded.

Charles was livid. "Why?"

"I don't know, I swear. I just… they said go and stir up some trouble. I don't know why, honest."

Marlon tingled. "You get a look at them, yeah? These men?"

Billy fought with it. "Well yes, but I… we, I mean, we didn't get their names, I swear."

Marlon pressed. "What about Walter? You hear that name? One of 'em named Walter?"

"No, no I swear! Please, sir! I'm real sorry 'bout what we done!"

Charles wanted more. "Where? Where can we find these men that paid you?"

Billy swallowed — holding back. "Uh, well, we just… we just run across 'em."

Sounds of commotion came from upstairs in the sanctuary. Police must be here — *dammit*. Marlon got right into Billy's face, devil-spirt angry: "*WHERE?*"

Billy could hardly speak. "It's just a house we go to, in Ch-ch-Church Hill. Please, sir, don't hurt me!"

Footsteps in the hall, knocks on the door, Miss Ruby whispered through it: "Marlon, they're here."

Marlon gave Billy a dagger stare. "You best tell the police the right kinda things, Billy Johnson, or we're gonna come to *your* neighborhood and get biblical, you hear me?"

Billy Johnson just nodded, as if the only thing he knew how to do in this entire world was nod his head.

In the moments that followed, Marlon and Charles helped Billy to his feet and brought him upstairs, telling the police *all* about how they tried to help this young man and repair his leg until the police came, only they didn't have the right kind of doctoring tools like they thought, no sir. Marlon was in such a daze from the events of the last hour, he hardly remembered speaking to the police at all, but he was most grateful that those two policemen who gave him such a beating were nowhere in sight. Only when the important policeman showed, the one he sometimes read about in the paper, did Marlon come to some and perk up, the look on this man's face a look of honest concern, as if he could truly sympathize with those who had endured trouble and tragedy. Marlon adjusted himself as the man approached — righting his eyepatch, standing tall. And then there he was, right in front of him.

"Sir, I'm Acting Lieutenant Bennie Sherwood, with the police. I understand you've had some trouble?"

13

Stakeout — a junkie's hideaway near Chimborazo Park in Church Hill, a little after dusk. Bennie and the men were huddled just off the front porch, waiting to make their move. Bennie wiped sweat from the back of his neck and ran through what they knew once more. Billy Johnson, that scared-as-shit kid they'd cornered at Marlon's church, he gave up this hideout off Twenty-Fourth Street. Somewhere he and his friends got high off uppers and homemade booze. Eddie knew the address already, it was a vice-squad hot spot. A round-the-clock hole-up for drug traffic and illicit hustle-and-bustle. Bennie skimmed an infractions list on their way over, wide-eyed. There had been arrests out the yin-yang — prostitutes, johns, pickpockets. Confiscations through the roof — Maryjane, uppers, downers, dope and dope paraphernalia. Habitués en masse — lowlifes, vagrants, truant teens and bored housewives. *Plus* — ex-convicts violating their parole. Sometimes days from their release, sometimes mere hours.

Call it a win — the ex-con angle ran straight to Scangili, so they moved on it fast and cooked up this bust-in on the quick. Approach the joint under cover of darkness, catch the dopers unaware.

Eddie loosened his collar and kept his voice low. "We gonna do this or what?"

They were all at-the-ready, crouching behind some overgrown brush, the moon's illuminance their only light. Hotshot Shane up front, Bennie and Eddie in the middle, two flatfoots pulling up the rear. Bennie checked the barrel of his gun, wishing for his canteen as a shiver ran up his spine. Jungle vibes, coming in hot. *OORAH*, ride the wave. He nodded at Shane, who smiled and motioned the crew up the steps, guns drawn. They padded onto the porch and flanked the front door — three on one side, two on the other. Sounds inside the house — junkie moans and 'Come to Jesus' cries of ecstasy. Shane gave a flatfoot the go-ahead. The grunt reared back and kicked the door off its hinges.

Shane, loud: "Freeze, Police! Don't anybody move!"

The cops spilled into the living room and caught the scene — seven users getting high. On couches, on the floor. Men, women, black, white. A haze of smoke in the air, thick and drug-laced. Bennie stifled a cough, he could hardly see. Blinks, 20/20, a real jolt — one of the women he knew from a veteran's group he looked in on, a recent widow. She caught Bennie's gaze and looked away. Maybe ashamed, maybe not.

Cue the round-ups, lose the guns. Half-in-the-bag users weren't lucid enough to resist arrest. One of the white men even stuck out his hands, ready for cuffs, and said that Nazis lived in his garage. His girlfriend flirted with Shane and offered herself as trade for a jail skip. Bennie watched as his lead detective considered her offer.

"Shane."

Shane met Bennie's disapproving stare with a devil's smile and a wink. "Only joking, boss. Only joking."

Sirens outside — a wagon pulled up just in time. Bennie told the men to book everyone but the woman he knew, waiting until they were clear outside before he played it easy and knelt down in front of her.

"Christine, isn't it?"

A GI's widow, her husband died in France. Christine let her glassed-over eyes rest on Bennie, her ghostlike face a mix of lax euphoria and sadness.

"You gon' arrest me?"

"No, I'm gonna help you."

"Help me? What 'eye need your help for? Government sen' me ten thousand dollars after Johnny died, you know that?"

Bennie eyed the coffee table — pills, needles, dope dust.

"I wish you wouldn't spend it on this."

Anger crept into her slurred speech. "No? Maybes I should send some of it ta France, then. Army sent me Johnny's *things* 'while back. Nice of them to do that, I thought. B'then I found a picture in his wallet of some French woman and a baby. He was in the service fifteen months. Plennya time to start a new family, innit?"

Bennie could only shake his head and look away — this part of the job, he was no good at. He wished Imogene was here, she always knew what to say. "Listen, whatever that is, whatever it means, it's in the past, but you're here now and we're gonna help you get right."

Christine looked at him with a sunken look. She nodded at the coffee table. "Oh yeah? How's I'm gonna get right, when alls I know is wrong?"

Bennie looked away, ashamed of his own hypocrisy. His treasured pep pills were right there in his jacket pocket. He popped one on the way here. "We'll show you how to keep the wrong at bay, I promise."

Christine offered what passed for a nod and looked away as Bennie called for one of the flatfoots. He came running.

"Sir?"

Bennie gestured at Christine. "Grab one of the black-n-whites and take her straight to MCV. Check her in as 'Daisy Lewis' and have the doc get her cleaned up on my ok."

The grunt paused. "But sir, aren't we supposed to…"

Bennie got up close. "Just do it."

The grunt snapped to and steered Christine out a side door, away from the hubbub out front. Bennie hit the front porch and surveyed the scene. Shane took names and ran interviews. One by one, cuffed junkies stumbled to the wagon on cloud nine.

Eddie mulled about the main room, bored. "It's like I told you, boss. Nothing but junkies and junkie stink, every time we bust this place."

Bennie sighed. Haden's dismissive attitude was yesterday's news. "It's the lead we were given, it's the one we followed. And if you knew so much about this place already, why didn't you suggest we check it out before?"

Eddie shrugged. "Most users don't commit murder. At least not the premeditated kind. Or did you not see the handful of losers limping out of here just now? They pose about as much threat to us as a teddy bear."

Bennie couldn't stand having to spell it out. "Not two hours ago, Billy Johnson ID'd Thomas Müller, the one they call Ghostman, off the photo we showed him. Confirmed that he was one of the men who paid the kids to stir up trouble. And according to the roust sheet, ex-cons run through this place like it's a mandatory stop on their road to freedom. Which means they know where they can go once they're released, which *means* Scangili had to know, too."

"So why don't we just bring Müller in, since the kid ID'd him?"

"Because it'll never stick. A judge catches wind of the kids' drug induced state and he'll toss it. Plus, it doesn't get us to anywhere near arson and murder. Paying kids to stir up trouble amounts to what, disturbing the peace? That's hardly the result we're looking for."

Eddie held his hands up. "I didn't mean to poke the bear."

Bennie nearly slugged him. "You sure about that? Look, I've got The Cane breathing down my neck, Imogene near ready to bolt, and little power over the men in my charge, you included. If I don't narrow our focus, the public will lose all confidence in us, and then we'll both be walking the bread line."

Eddie shoved his hands into his pockets, all laissez-faire. "Suit yourself, boss. I got other plans."

"Do you, now? Perhaps you'll share these plans with me, maybe I can help you with them."

Eddie just smirked. "I work better alone, you know that. And when it's all done, I've got a one way ticket with a single seat. Call it my after life. I'll send you a postcard when I get there."

Shane stood in the doorway and whistled. "I should sell tickets for you two, ringside. You boys need a ref? Look — we've got newshawks outside. A photog, too."

Bennie loosened his tie. "Then we don't have much time. Both of you, help me look through the house before we're descended on by vultures."

Eddie tossed couch cushions. Shane hit the ground, on his hands and knees as he looked under tables and chairs. What a mess — gum wrappers, used napkins, animal hair. Maybe one of the junkies has a dog — poor Fido.

Bennie checked out a side table and found a stack of newspapers, torn up and cut into. *Precise* cuts — meticulous, exact. A few words here, an entire headline there. Straight, clean cuts around bodies of text and articles, getting just what was needed and nothing more. Strange — users were lax, high, floating on air. Who in that mind state has the faculty to cut up newspapers so neat and tidy-like?

Bennie sifted through the stack — war headlines hit him front and center. Dated two days back, the Herald's front page — Jap Kamikaze pilots sank a US ship. Shivers ran up his spine, but he staved off the heebie-jeebies, no time for them now. He palmed the rag and stuffed it into his jacket pocket. Something to read later with a calmer mind.

They hoofed it upstairs next — two bedrooms, three closets, a john. Shane spotted a stack of boxes in one of the bedrooms and rifled through them.

"Bingo."

Hate-tract flyers, newly printed. Klan edicts, Third Reich iconography. Bennie skimmed one and turned to Shane. "Get these out of here quick. I don't want anyone from the paper to catch wind of them."

Shane collected the boxes when Eddie walked in, holding something up in his hand. "More paydirt."

"What is it?" Bennie asked.

Eddie handed him a crumpled piece of paper with both an address and a phone number written on it. "Trash bin findings. That address is right at Allen, not far from the Lee statue." *Finally,* Bennie thought, Eddie was being useful, his years on patrol paying off. "That number, though," Eddie continued, "I don't think I know it."

Bennie started to get a bad feeling, reading it over. "I think I do. You see a phone anywhere?"

Eddie pointed downstairs. "In the front room, by the door."

"I'm gonna run this down. You wait for Rooney, supervise his print of the house." Eddie groaned, but Bennie went on. "Bag anything drug related and have a full report on my desk before noon tomorrow."

"Fuckin' A, Bennie, that'll take hours, I'm — "

"*Your'e* on the V Squad by the skin of your teeth. Miss another briefing and I'll have you back on vice full time."

Eddie held his tongue. The nerve of this kid, ten years his junior.

"Aye, aye, cap."

"Good." Bennie handed Eddie the hate pamphlet he still had in his hand.

"What's this?"

"Some light reading while you wait."

Bennie hustled downstairs and made for the phone. He read the number again and dialed out, dreading what came next. *Please, don't be what I think you are.*

Four rings, a pick up — Holden Taft's eager-to-please voice, on the line. "Confederate Cab, at your service. Where are you and where would you like to go?"

Bennie almost didn't answer. "Holden, it's Bennie Sherwood."

Holden's voice turned hesitant, the same way everyone's did when they heard it was Bennie on the horn. "Oh, hello there, Bennie. If you're looking for Imogene, she's not driving tonight, but she's in for a day shift tomorrow. Want to leave a message?"

Bennie played dumb. "Oh, that's right, she *did* tell me that. I must have forgotten. I'll, uh, try her at home."

"No bother t'all, Bennie. Call anytime!"

Oh, I think I will, Bennie thought, thanking him and hanging up. "Goddamnit," he said, dialing out again, the Annex this time. Crackles through the phone, then Annie's sweet pipes. "Police HQ, this is A — "

"Annie, it's Bennie. I need you to chase down an address for me."

Bennie read it out to her and waited. One minute stretched into three and then she was back on. "That address is The Carter Hotel, Bennie. A halfway house, according to the directory."

Annie gave Bennie the hotel's number. Bennie copied the details into his steno, thanked her and hung up. Shane stepped back inside the house, reading from one of the pamphlets.

"Did you know that Hitler and Jesus are coming back to life to save us, together?"

"It's about time, wouldn't you say?"

Shane laughed. "What'd you find out?"

Bennie told him. "I thought I knew the number and I was right."

"She still drives a cab?"

Bennie nodded. "When she's not at McGuire. She likes to stay busy, that one."

Shane stretched. "And the address?"

"The Carter Hotel. Know it?"

Shane shook his head. "If it hasn't been robbed in the last six months, I'm not familiar."

Bennie yawned. It had been a long fucking day. "Where are you on Scangili?"

"Meant to tell you, I'm meeting a woman tomorrow morning. She saw his mug in the paper and called us. Apparently she knew him when he was kid. With any luck, she'll give us more to go on."

"Get some rest then and call me when you're through. We'll hit the hotel afterwards."

"Roger that."

Shane strode outside and left Bennie alone in the main room. Eddie was right — nothing but junkie stink in the air. Bennie fingered the pep pills he had nestled into his jacket pocket and just *knew* — without Imogene, without the job, he'd end up here, too.

14

Thick, rich sunlight shone through the window of Bennie's second-story bedroom, bathing it in the kind of golden rays he imagined were only bestowed upon on-again lovers and the grand faces of Egyptian pyramids. He rolled to his right, expecting to feel Imogene's warmth, but felt instead the rigid cruelty of his old friend, the floor. Pains all through his back, he felt every one — he must have thrashed in his sleep something fierce. He arched, stretched, rubbed sleep from his eyes. Nothing to do now but shake it off and move on. He reached over to his dresser, snagged a pep pill from his jacket pocket, and downed it straight, no water. Minutes ticked off and zoom, his thoughts were like cars on a racetrack, he'd never catch up.

Shuffles on the bed — Imogene's beautiful faced popped over the edge. "I can hear you thinking, you know? Your brain is like a noisy clock."

"It is in desperate need of repair."

"What are you doing down there?"

"Oh, you know, writing my memoirs, planning the crime of the century, just having a grand old time. Wanna join me?"

Imogene crawled down from the bed and laid next to him. She brought the bedsheet with her and threw it over them. "What happened?"

"We caught a lead and rousted some perps at a house in Church Hill. While we were there, I found this." Bennie pulled his jacket off the dresser and fished out the newspaper he glommed. Imogene saw the headline — JAP PILOTS SINK SHIP OFF OKINAWA.

"You told me you don't read the news anymore. You don't even listen to the radio, so you won't hear about it."

It being the war in the Pacific. "I don't. But I saw this and wanted to know more. I thought I could handle it."

Imogene wrapped an arm around his chest and kissed his cheek. "Then let's not talk about it. Talk to me about something else."

"Well, Shane's following a lead on Scangili this morning, hopefully that gives us something new to go on. The Cane is still breathing down my neck, but that's nothing new. I think Eddie is off on some side case he won't let on about, but I can't afford to fire him and I don't have the manpower to put a tail on him. That's most of it. Your turn."

Imogene pushed her hair from her face and rolled onto her back. "Let's see. My rounds at McGuire are a gas. Some of the men are quite chatty, you know? They'll tell their stories to anyone who'll listen. Some of the others, though, well, they remind me of you." She grabbed one of his hands and squeezed it. "Timony says she and Harrison aren't getting on well at all, that it's really been quite bad between them, but she thinks it'll pass. She says he's just so busy with that city council business he's wrapped up in. And she can't get anyone at the war offices in Washington to tell her anything about her son, which I think is odd, personally. With her money and connections, I'd of thought she could get anyone to talk. And Constance, well, what can I say? She is quite the addition to our group. I mean, she sounds like she's done it all and wants to do it all again, she really is fun. But every so often, I notice her in a private moment, where she looks rather forlorn, like she's thinking about someone else or somewhere she'd rather be."

"Jedidiah hasn't told me much about her."

"Well, she is a bit of a mystery, but she's lovely and I'm glad to know her."

"Speaking of mysteries…"

"Oh, come on now, Bennie. I really don't wanna talk — "

"It's not that, it's something else."

Imogene softened. "Okay."

"It's about Holden."

"Taft? Really?"

"Yes."

"What about him?"

Bennie told her about the note they found. "And it makes me wonder if Holden has maybe a particular kind of clientele that would be good for me to know about."

Imogene propped herself up on one arm.

"So you want me to… spy on him for you?"

Bennie tried to think of something cute to say. "Well, yeah."

Imogene was afraid to say yes right away. "And you really think that would help you?"

"I do. You know, most of the narcotics and drug users we come across, they can't afford cabs, or at least, they wouldn't choose to spend their money that way. It's unusual, and it may be there's more to the story. Or it could be nothing, just a scrap of paper left behind. But I won't know unless I try, and while I could set up something undercover, you already — "

"Sure, I'll do it."

Bennie was ecstatic — he lived for happy moments with this woman. "Thank you."

Imogene kissed him, pretty revved up now by the thought of something so under the table. "I can start right away. I'm on the late shift at McGuire, actually, so I'm stopping in at Confederate to work on a few of the heaps. How will I know what to look for?"

"You won't, really. But I'll give you some names and addresses. We can cross check them against his logs. And who knows, maybe an address or two will stand out, on its own."

Imogene t'sked. "That'll be tricky. Holden is pretty careful. Keeps his office locked up tight. And checks my receipts twice, all the way through, every time I drive."

The phone rang. That'll be Shane, hopefully. Bennie sat up, wincing. The goddamn floor. "Just keep your eyes open. You never know what you might notice." He kissed her forehead and darted for the hallway.

Imogene watched him go. "Yeah, well, I better get paid for this, Bennie Sherwood! I'm no cut-rate Mata Hari, no sir! I'm a bonafide secret agent, the real deal!"

Bennie made it to the phone on the fifth ring. He grabbed the handset. "Shane?"

"Sorry to disappoint, but no."

There was a familiar voice on the line, nonetheless — Archie Smith, Herald reporter on the rise.

"Archie. Must be important if you're calling me at home."

"We're beating up on you pretty bad these days. I thought you could use a friend."

"You thought right. What'd you have in mind?"

"Our usual spot, thirty minutes? Let's find some common ground."

"You're on. See you then."

Bennie hung up. 'Common ground' stirred a fresh memory — Christine, that war widow, drugged up and sad. He rang for the operator.

"MCV, please. The main desk."

Clicks, half a minute later — this no-nonsense voice. "Nurses' station."

"This is Bennie Sherwood with the police. I had a woman sent your way last night, under the name of Daisy Lewis. How's she holding up?"

"One moment, I'll check."

Muffled voices on the line — a nurses' confab. Bennie raced through a set of air squats to pass the time.

The nurse came back on the line. "Sir?"

"Yes?"

The nurse's voice was filled with worry. "I'm so sorry, but she checked herself out this morning, we didn't even see her leave. She broke into the medicine cabinet on her way out, I just can't believe it. Is she a criminal?"

Bennie tensed. This goddamn war. "No. No, she's not."

Bennie hung up and moped back to the bedroom. His spirits rose at the sight of Imogene, already dressed. Runway pretty in cabbie threads. She looked at him, puzzled.

"Why so sad?"

Bennie shook it off. "A favor?"

She puckered her lips — fresh lipstick. "Anything for you."

"If Shane calls, tell him I'm at Third Street? I'm meeting

Archie."

"Oh, good, maybe you can get him to stop dogging you in the papers." She winked. "I'm getting tired of having to defend your good name all the time."

"I always knew you'd save me from ruin."

"You're a star on the rise, Bennie Sherwood." She blew him a kiss. "You just need a little push every once in awhile."

Shane checked the address in his steno — First Avenue and Pollock Street in Highland Park, north of the city proper. An old streetcar suburb that became a hotspot for immigrants from Eastern Europe. He parked and made for a pad just off the intersection. Fancy digs — a big bay window, wraparound front porch, fruit trees in the front yard. Shane even smelled freshly baked bread wafting his way. For an early morning assignment, he could do worse.

The woman he was to meet saw him walking up the entryway and greeted him excitedly, bursting onto the front porch and waving him toward the house. "Ciao, Mr. Policeman! Ciao! Please, this way! Come, come!"

She led Shane into a sitting room and invited him to sit on a firm, cushioned couch embossed with gold trim. He did just that and eyed the room as she poured coffee. It was like a museum. Wide, elaborate paintings adorned the walls. A polished, turn-of-the-century dining table sat off to one side, practically begging for attention. Everything was neat and tidy, nothing out of place.

"You have a lovely home, Miss..." Shane checked his steno. "Domenica?"

She finished pouring their coffee, jerked upright, and struck a pose. Hands on her hips, big smile, raised eyebrows. "Yes, yes, that's me! Francoise Bethanue Domenica, at your service. Some name, yes? My mother was French, my father Italian."

"It's lovely." *What a woman*, Shane thought. She looked to be in her mid-sixties and she'd done up her hair and put on make-up. She wore a rose-colored, shin-length dress and brown buckled heels. She was buoyant and graceful and even did a little twirl before she sat down opposite him on a matching couch.

"Why, thank you." She held up a tray of pastries. "Care for one? They're oven fresh."

Bachelor Shane — stale pickings in the icebox at home, no breakfast. "Don't mind if I do." He took one and wolfed it.

"It's good, yes?"

Shane nodded, his mouth full. Willpower — no seconds. "Now, Mrs. Domenica."

"Yes, yes." She leaned back into the couch and spread her arms along the length of the frame. This grand lady, ready for her big interview.

"You called in a tip. You knew Carmine Scangili?"

She covered her mouth. "Oh my goodness, yes, poor Carmine. What tragedy in his life! I can't bear to think of it, I truly can't, but I see his picture in the paper, yes? Here, let me show you." She jumped up and strode into another room. She was back in a flash, newspaper in hand. "Here, I see this."

Mrs. Domenica held the paper out for Shane to see. A Herald's metro page from several weeks back. Scangili's mug, front and center. She tapped the picture with her index finger several times.

"I see this and say, I knew this face. When he was small, yes?" She extended her hand out into the air, as if measuring the height of someone young. "When he was a boy, I knew him. I knew this face."

Shane got ready to write in his steno. "Tell me about him."

She sat back down. "He was an angel. The sweetest boy."

"Really."

"Yes. Helped his mother, helped his father. Helped his brother, the sweet boy, the poor little child. Carmine was an angel, god rest him." She crossed herself. "Dio lo riposi, yes. God rest him."

"That's surprising, Mrs. Domenica, I have to say. The more we learn about Carmine, well, he doesn't sound like much of an angel to us."

"I can tell you why."

"You can?"

"Yes. His brother." She pointed outside. "Murdered, on these very streets."

Shane sifted through his notes, he was full of questions. "A brother, murdered? When?"

"1922." She said it with authority. "Right out in those very streets. I tell you, Mr. Policeman, the cruelty of young boys is no small thing. The neighborhood boys, they ran wild every day, and I witnessed this, yes, I did. I never want to think of it again, but I see Carmine in the paper and think, I should tell someone. About the real Carmine. And his brother, Giovanni."

Memory click — the name, Giovanni. Shane pulled the photo from the back of his steno, the one he'd found at Scangili's apartment. He handed it to Mrs. Domenica. "Is this who you're talking about?"

Mrs. Domenica took the photo. Seeing it, she nearly bust into tears. "Oh, my, oh my sweet Giovanni, you poor thing. Yes, yes, this is him! Such a sweet boy. See, he was, how do you say," she made a face, as it she were ashamed to say anything about it at all, "a little slow in the mind, ok? Sometimes, it happens. You have a child and it happens, ok?"

Shane nodded in agreement. "Of course."

"But these boys around here, when they got to a certain age? They don't go easy on him, no. They were so mean! They push him, they call him names. And Carmine, well, he fought back. In his brother's honor, yes, he fought back. But then, oh no. It is so terrible to say."

Shane was on the edge of his seat. "Please, Mrs. Domenica. It would really help us to know."

Mrs. Domenica took a deep breath and composed herself. "One day, the other boys? They throw a rock. It hits Giovanni right in the head. He dies in the street that very day. I see it all," she pointed outside again, "I see it happen right out there."

"That's awful, Mrs. Domenica, truly. I'm sorry you had to revisit that."

"I will never speak of it again. But when I see this," she pointed at the picture of Carmine in the newspaper again, "I say to myself, I don't know this Carmine. The things about him, these terrible things? I don't know that Carmine, but I know angel Carmine." She held up her hands. "It's all too much."

Shane made notes and took the photo of Giovanni back from Mrs. Domenica, folded it away. "Mrs. Domenica, I can't thank you enough for sharing this with us. This was clearly a difficult choice."

Mrs. Domenica put on a proud smile. "I'm happy to help. This country has been good to me, I want to help when I can."

"I appreciate that, very much. What can you tell me about the years following Giovanni's death? What happened to Carmine then?"

"He sank into a deep sadness. Like an ocean. He never smiled again."

Shane nodded. "What about his family? Other friends, other kids from the neighborhood? How did they react?"

"They move on. It's too sad for them, so the family, the parents? They move back to Italy. They want to go home, to Sicily. But Carmine, he stayed here. He never wanted to leave his brother, even in memory. It's so very sad." Mrs. Domenica looked away, teary eyed.

Shane's stomach growled — those pastries taunted him. "Did you ever see Carmine act out in revenge, Mrs. Domenica? After what happened to his brother?"

Mrs. Domenica waved the idea away. "After awhile, I don't see Carmine any longer. He moved away, too. Where, I don't know." She gestured towards her front door. "And after Giovanni, well, I shut my door. I don't look out into the street any longer. It's all too much."

"Mrs. Domenica, do the names Müller and Visel mean anything to you?"

She frowned, straight off. "No."

"And did you ever contact or hear from Carmine's family again, after they moved back to Italy?"

She shook her head decisively. There were no more memories of Carmine to share.

Shane rose from the couch. "I can't thank you enough, Mrs. Domenica. I understand how painful this was, truly I do."

She lifted the tray of pastries. "Here, you take."

"No, Mrs. Domenica, I— "

"No, you take." Forceful — near offended if he didn't.

"Yes, of course, thank you."

Shane stuffed a pastry into each of his pockets and balanced three more in his hands, it was all he could manage. She stood and followed him to the front door — a true hostess, courteous to her guests from start to finish.

"Mr. Policeman."

Shane turned to her from the front porch. Awkward, addressing her in the middle of a juggling act. "Yes?"

"You find out why, about Carmine? I want to know. Even if it's ugly."

"Yes, m'am."

Mrs. Domenica stood up straight and proud. She nodded at him with downcast eyes before closing the door on their visit.

Shane left the porch and made his way out into the street. Inside of a minute, he was standing in the very spot where he imagined that Giovanni had been hit by a rock and died. He thought of the joys and cruel ironies of youth. To play without thinking, to act without consequence. He saw an imaginary rock sail toward him and almost ducked. The thought of what happened made him sad, too.

Over to his wheels, fast — a trash bin right there. No more appetite. He dumped the pastries, every one.

Third Street Diner, their usual booth. Last in the row, away from the crowd. Archie was there first, already nursing a cup of coffee. The waitress brought one for Bennie as he slid into his seat. She left them with a flirty wink.

Bennie made himself comfortable. "Nice of you to call."

Archie smiled. "It's the least I could do. How's Imogene?"

"She's wonderful."

"You two still shacking up?"

Bennie nodded. "I'm trying to make it official."

"Oh yeah? You got a date set yet?"

"Working on it."

Archie dialed back the zeal. "I won't hold my breath."

Bennie took a sip — good joe. "I like my chances. Call me an optimist."

Archie raised his cup. "You did make it home from the war."

"As you well know."

Memory lane — last Fall, Archie authored a tell-all about Bennie's time in the Pacific that unfolded over a three-week spread in the Herald. It earned raves for Archie's reporting and sent the paper's subscription rates soaring.

"How's Maryanne?" Bennie asked.

Archie grinned canyon-wide. "She's on the nest."

"Whoa, no kidding? Congratulations, that's great news."

They clanged their mugs in a cheers.

Dead air then — nix the pleasantries.

"Look, Bennie — "

"I'm not asking you to lay off altogether."

"Hey, I'm the one that called you, remember? I want to help. But I don't make the news, Bennie, I just report it."

"Isn't there anything else you can report on?"

"It's the war across the board until we're out, that I can't control. Beyond that, our readers want stories about public safety. They write to us about it regularly."

"Then write about how many cats we pull out of trees."

"We would, if you actually rescued any. Look, as long as there's a killer or killers on the loose, no one in this city cares about anything else. People are afraid, Bennie. And it's been what, three weeks? Did you know the Kleinfeld family is gunning for your dismissal?"

Bennie felt gutted. "No. Wow, is... is that a story you're running?"

Archie put on a friendly look. "It doesn't have to be. I'm here with an offer that comes straight from the top. Feed me something I can use in place of your predicament and we can steer the coverage away from it for awhile, buy you some time. I know you, I know how hard you're pushing for answers. Let me help."

Bennie didn't even have to think it over. He leaned into the table and kept his voice low. "Someone paid bored teens to rough up Negroes in Jackson Ward. And then a lead on those teens steered us to a pad known for rampant drug use on the eastern side of town. I won't tell you where or give you any names, but you can run with those tips and see where they take you, as long as you keep my name out of it."

Archie's eyes doubled in size — what a get. He pulled out his notebook and scribbled fast. "This'll buy you days of coverage, at least. Maybe more."

Bennie sat up and drained his coffee. "I'll take anything I can get. What else are you guys reporting on?"

"Let's see. It's all war, war, war, even if it isn't related to combat in the Pacific. The Seventh Loan Campaign is a hot topic, keep buying more bonds and all that. The Richmond Office of Civilian Defense is closing, not much they can do anymore. And Governor Darden says the state will keep to a 35 mile per hour limit until the Japs cave. Does anyone actually stick to that?"

Bennie shrugged. "Half the time, maybe? Monitoring it means we waste gas, too, so I tell patrol not to bother."

A pause — Bennie caught himself. "That you cannot print."

Archie laughed. "Noted. Let me see, oh — Harrison Wells is in the news. You know, the city councilman?" Bennie nodded as Archie continued. "He's in some kind of kerfuffle about the war surplus out at Camp Lee. Seems he wants to do one thing with it all, the council another. Beyond that, it's all just odds and ends. Nothing too exciting."

The waitress made their table. "Lieutenant Sherwood?"

"Yes?"

"There's a call for you, a Detective MacDonald."

Bennie slid out of the booth, fishing for change. "Thank you, I'll be right there."

Archie waved him off. "Coffee's on me."

"Thanks."

"What is an Administrative Lieutenancy, anyway?"

"It's a short leash, is what it is. Stolmy wants me out when the Japs fall. It's his way of limiting my influence."

"Oh yeah?"

"It's a story for another day. Say, I gotta run. Can't thank you enough."

"It's the least I can do. Stay safe out there." Archie raised his cup once more. "And here's to you and Imogene. Don't let her get away."

Bennie skipped over to the server's counter and grabbed the phone. "Shane?"

"Affirmative. Let me tell you, boss, there's more to Scangili then we thought."

"Yeah? I'll pick you up, you can tell me on the way."

"Where to, that halfway house?"

"The very one. Meet you at the Annex?"

"Ten minutes, see you out front."

The waitress came over to take the phone from Bennie. He handed it back to her. "Thank you," he said.

She handed him a sandwich wrapped in napkins. "Thought you might need some breakfast. It's a fried egg and cheese."

"You're an angel."

"And you can't save anyone on an empty stomach, mister, now get."

15

A sign outside the Carter Hotel advertised clean beds for twenty cents a night. The joint was sleaze city. If rundown was a look you were going for, this spot could win an award. Street grime, chipped paint, the stench of impermanence. A mishmash of ads were tacked up out front — decaying war bond posters and want-ads, crude sendups of Hirohito and Mussolini. Transients and wayward sons mingled on the sidewalk outside. A few of them powdered when they saw Bennie and Shane pull up, their sled clearly a police cruiser. No unmarked today.

They made the entrance and moved through a cramped hallway that led to an unmanned sign-in counter. Just across the way was the flop's modest dining hall. Bennie caught the scent — onions, sweat, and fear in potent wafts. A staircase behind the desk snaked upstairs to the beds. Men made their way up, men made their way down. Bennie caught vacant looks and shifty eyes on them all.

"What can I do for you?"

Bennie and Shane turned to find a thick-set man walking toward them from the dining hall. He wore a stained waiter's smock and sported an uncombed mustache. His hard eyes looked humorless, as if he'd forgotten how to laugh altogether. Life had led him to run this joint and he wasn't happy about it.

Bennie and Shane flashed their badges. Bennie said, "Name's Sherwood, with the police. This is MacDonald with robbery. Are you the proprietor here?"

The man nodded. "Name's Graham."

Shane took notes. "Is that your first name?"

"My given name is Ace, if you must know. What's this all about?"

Bennie put his badge away. "You get many cab drop-offs?"

Graham looked unsure. "Not really. Most of the folks who stay here can't afford cab fare."

Bennie looked around the dining hall and had to agree. More vacant faces, more shifty eyes. Men down on their luck, by choice or by chance.

Shane stood up straight, flexing cop attitude. "Still, it's safe to say you get a few, from time to time, is it not?"

Graham played along, he wanted this over with. "Yes, detective. We get a few cab drop-offs." He shuffled through papers on the counter then, remembering something. He set a ledger in front of them, pointing at a line. "We had one just yesterday, in fact. A man got dropped off here, maybe midday." Graham started from the desk. "If you'll come with me, I think he's in here."

They followed Graham to the dining hall and Bennie felt his pulse notch up — jungle juju, coming in hot. He raised his voice a bit and said, "You ever get anyone here straight from the state pen?"

And just like that, a man near the back of the room jumped up and beelined for the kitchen. Bennie and Shane were after him fast, dodging lodgers and kitchen staff as they followed him, crashing through the kitchen and out into the alley. Outside now, stark sunshine hit them hard.

Bennie shielded his eyes. "You see him?"

Shane yelled, pointing to the sky. "He's on the fire escape!"

And he was already one floor up. Bennie pulled his gun. "Freeze, police!"

The man paused and looked down. His eyes were half-wild, his grin cockeyed. He laughed and raced for the top.

Bennie yelled "Go!" as he and Shane leapt onto the fire escape and started after him.

"It's a four story building, he's not far from the top!" Shane called out.

He and Bennie hoofed it up the escape and spilled onto the roof. There he is, one building over, hauling east, wildcat fast. Bennie and Shane gave chase, the two of them leaping from building to building in a mad dash. Bennie yelled "Stop!" as the man stormed another rooftop, three buildings over now, the last in the row, nowhere left to go. Shane pulled his own gun. Bennie yelled "Just a warning shot!" as Shane fired one off, dinging it off an air vent. The sound of it rang out as the man scrambled for cover with Bennie and Shane closing in.

"There's nowhere left to go, so give yourself up!" Shane called out, following his gun onto the last rooftop. Bennie was right behind him, the two of them suddenly watching in disbelief as the man shot them the wildest of looks, as if he lived for the hunt and the chase, and then disappeared over the edge of the building.

Bennie couldn't believe it. "The fuck?"

They padded to the edge and risked a look down the side of the building. Sure enough, there's their wild man, scaling a drain pipe four stories down.

Sounds of joy came from below — the kind kids give off. Bennie almost didn't see them at first, but there they were, a throng of teenagers playing sandlot baseball in an adjacent lot. All of them truant — school's not out for another few weeks.

"Hey kids, watch out!" Shane yelled.

The kids looked up at Bennie, confused at first, then amused and waving, as if he and Shane were celebrities of some kind, but then a sense of alarm took hold as the wild man dropped from the drain pipe and ran towards them, cackling and waving his arms. The kids scurried and scrambled away from him. Bennie and Shane looked on helplessly as the man knocked a kid to the ground and stole his bat.

"Goddamnit!" Shane said, out of breath and out of time, his entire body in knots. He raised his gun, but Bennie swatted his arm down. "Shane, no, the kids!"

Bennie could only hope and pray their wild man didn't take a swing at one of the kids and when he didn't, when he only locked eyes with Bennie from nearly a hundred yards off, flashing his wild grin and then turning to run, Bennie sank onto the rooftop, so relieved and spent he thought he might pass out.

Shane couldn't believe it either.

"Who the hell was that?"

George Carroll, it turns out.

Bennie, Shane, and Graham stood over George Carroll's bunk in a twelve-bed room on the third floor of the flophouse. The room smelled of bleached blankets and lost time. Midday sun crept through high-walled windows and spoiled the naps of more than a few men. Bennie watched as they tossed and turned, as if caught up in bad dreams. Graham scratched his head and read from the ledger.

"Says it right here, just like I remembered. George Carroll, paid in full for this week and the next. I just can't understand it, he wasn't a bother to anyone yesterday."

Shane paced the room, he was still coming down off the chase-high. "You sure about that?"

Graham shrugged. "Well, I mean, no one complained about him. Then again, we do get all types in here. There's really no telling, I suppose."

Bennie tried to hide it, but he really wanted to punch something, *anything*. "Yeah, well, suppose your crowd ain't the complaining type." Bennie stepped three cots over and looked down on some yokel catching a snooze. He jerked his feet this way and that. The bum snapped awake.

"Hey, what gives?"

Bennie flashed his badge. "What gives is a few questions. Play it smart and I'll let you get back to your nightmare."

The bum groaned, he'd been through this shit before. "So ask, already."

Bennie pulled Carroll's mugshot photo from his pocket and held it up. "Your bunkmate here, you ever chat him up?"

The bum snickered. "Oh, him."

Shane walked over. "What about him?"

"He wouldn't shut up, is what. You ought to hear the way this guy carried on. All about God and this biblical reckoning that's coming. I tell you, the guy is in a *way*. I got so I was playing possum, on account of I couldn't listen to it anymore."

"You remember anything else about him?" Bennie asked.

"When he wasn't spewing crazy talk, he seemed pretty sad.

That news in the paper, about that fire and the body they found? He got pretty worked up over it, kept reading the articles over and over. If I didn't know any better, I'd say he knew something about it, but I'm on parole and I can't be messing with anyone like that, so I didn't ask." The man gestured at Carroll's bed. "He really must have left in some kinda hurry, 'cause he left his duffel behind. He was awful protective of it, I can tell you that."

Bennie pulled the duffel from under Carroll's bunk and set it on top of the mattress, unzipping it slowly, as if it were contaminated. Real-life horror greeted them, right there on top, captured in pristine black and white photographs. A dozen or so, maybe more. Bennie struggled to shuffle through them. The scenes depicted in them were almost too difficult to witness. Klan members celebrating as lynched black men hung from tree limbs. Bare-headed women screaming in horror as they're beaten and branded with electric irons. Stone-faced children watching as animals are mutilated near a fire, the kids most likely drugged. Bennie saw his own hands knife a Jap to death.

Shane crossed himself. "Christ, I might hurl. Who the fuck even develops these?"

Bennie set the photographs to the side and checked out the rest of the duffel's contents. Rummaging though it carefully, he found tattered clothes, a decades-old shaving kit, and a well-read bible that looked more like a scrapbook than a religious text. Thumbing pages, Bennie was shocked. There were crossed-out words every few lines, crude markings in the margins. And look there — those newspaper cutouts, from the junkie hideaway, they've been taped to the pages in very specific ways, the article words and the bible verses merged together now in a kind of mix and match collage. And all around the pages, someone had drawn swastikas and angels and scribbled end-of-the-world proclamations. Bennie was so stunned by one passage that he couldn't help but read it aloud. "The cleansing apocalypse will be orchestrated by God himself and carried out by his loyal blood-fire angels as they reign down upon the Earth, ridding it of Jew vermin and diseased n_____s. Call on me, Lord, for the White Shadow rises, God's will be done."

Poor Graham looked ready to faint. "What in God's name."

Bennie and Shane shared a dark look.

What in God's name, indeed.

16

It was the middle of the morning and Knox could just make out the contours of the State Penitentiary's north wing through the Confederate Cab Company's office window. Soul-crushing darkness was a mere five, six streets over and could be yours for the low, low price of a botched robbery job. Knox shifted in his seat. Uncomfortable, tense. It was his first ever job interview and it was anything but on the level. Lenny had turned him on to the gig as a favor, albeit with caveat. Knox had to kickback ten percent of his fares to Lenny in exchange for securing him a job. Not a bad deal, really. Lenny even secured Knox a chauffeur's license on the quick from someone he knew at City Hall. With a dummy name, no less, to shield him from both the cops and Walter. Lenny sure was some guy. He seemed to have a little bit of everyone in his pocket.

Behind the cluttered desk, Confederate Cab's owner cleared his throat and put on a phony smile. His tabletop nameplate read 'Holden Taft, Proprietor' and he was certainly no stranger to a big lunch. Taft's jet-black hair was slick with too much pomade and his office reeked of cigar smoke and bonded whiskey. *He sure must cook up a lot of deals in this room*, Knox thought, as Taft leaned back into his ragged desk chair. It creaked under his heft.

"So, Mr. Smith. Lenny says you have driving experience?"

"I do."

"In what way?"

Knox flashed on a cherished memory — threading a Franklin County dirt road in the old man's trunkless Chevy hot rod at top speed, the treasury agents' bullets whizzing by.

"Back home, I worked with my father, making deliveries."

"Of what?"

Knox struggled for an answer. "Oh, various necessities. Commodities and the like."

Taft laughed, knowingly, and handed Knox's license back to him. "Is that so. Well, Mr. Smith, you don't appear to be known by the police, Lenny's vouched for you, and your license is in order. Welcome aboard."

And just like that, Knox was gainfully employed for the first time in his life. They left the office and stepped into a three-bay garage that neighbored a modest parking lot. Dig the busy-bee goings-on: a phone op manning calls, cabs coming and going, a mechanic changing engine oil. Knox caught a whiff of gas fumes and got tingles. He learned to change a tire before he ever learned to read.

Taft steered them to a blackboard chalked up with shift times and put Knox on the schedule. Hank Smith — your new 12AM man. "You'll be on overnights for the first few week, Hank, while I get to know you as a driver. Then we can see about a more flexible schedule."

"Works for me." Knox took a good look around, taking stock of his new surrounds. Making note of doors, passageways, exits. Paths to freedom in case he had to make a run for it. And only then did Knox truly notice all the Confederate flags painted along the walls and the cabs themselves. He'd been so nervous about the interview, he hadn't really noticed.

"Say, Taft, why the name? And why all the southern crosses?"

Taft grinned, this was clearly something he enjoyed talking about. "Really, it's just good ol' advertising, but before the war, we catered to the Old Soldier's Home, when it was around. You know, on Boulevard? Where the Civil War vets lived? The last one kicked off in '41, but with all the soldiers from Camp Lee around, I thought it would do to showcase our history to newcomers, so we expanded the business. You know, my grandfather helped install the Robert E. Lee statue. Back when it stood in nothing but a tobacco field."

Knox clocked Taft's proud look. "He did, huh."

Taft beamed. It came off slimy. "Is our heritage something you're passionate about, as well, Mr. Sutton?"

Knox thought of his own recent heritage, traditions to never pass down. Beatings, extended stays in solitary, rat shit in his prison food. Payback from Ghostman and Scangili for his refusal to join their hate gang.

"Sorry, can't say it is."

Taft lowered his voice. "Well, if you ever change your mind, I can certainly point you in the right direction."

Christ, who isn't trying to recruit me? Knox squared up on Taft. He had two inches, plus. "Look, boss, if it's all the same to you, let's keep the heritage out of it. I'm just looking to make some dough, alright?"

Taft's glee deflated. "Noted."

Wham!

Over in the garage bay, the mechanic slammed the hood of a cab shut and kicked one of its tires. Knox did a double take as he realized the op was a *she*, watching her untie the bandana holding up the thick mane of auburn hair that then fell about her shoulders. *The times sure have changed*, Knox thought, watching her wipe sweat and oil grease from her face and neck before she looked their way.

"I tell you what, Holden, I can't wait until they start kicking out new rides with new engines. These old sleds we got? Scrap heap standouts, all the way."

Knox nudged Taft. "She works here?"

Taft laughed. "Does she ever. Imogene's our secret weapon. But a word to the wise, newbie, she's taken. Runs with a copper, even. Here, I'll introduce you."

Taft led Knox over to the garage bay where Imogene was standing. Sure enough, the cab was a prewar Chevy, worse for wear, but she was anything but. Knox wondered what kind of man her cop boyfriend was as she gave them both a hard look and carried on with her rant.

"And I tell ya, Holden, I don't know what's gotten into the men around here since V-E Day, but I've been groped more times than I can count over the last three weeks. So I'm not even gonna ask, I'm just gonna tell you, I'm putting a gun in the glove box and one of Bennie's baseball bats in the trunk. The next gent who paws me is gonna get either a sting in the gut or a lob across the head, maybe both."

Taft put his hands up, it's not like he could stop her. "You shoot someone, Imogene, and your fella'll be none too pleased."

"*He* I can handle, don't you worry. Now, who's this?"

Imogene gestured at Knox as she began to brush back her hair and apply a fresh coat of berry red lipstick. It made both her hair and her fair skin pop. Knox locked eyes with her and stepped forward, offering his hand.

"Hank Smith, a pleasure. I'm on overnights this week."

Imogene smiled and shook his hand. Strong, firm. Knox was impressed. "A word of advice, Hank, have your fares flash their cash *before* you pull off. Drunks, especially."

Knox smiled at the old cabbie adage. "Will do, thanks."

Imogene put her hands on her hips and winked. "What do you say, boys? Does Nurse McKenna pass the test? 'Cause I'm about to do my rounds at McGuire, try and cheer up the down and outs."

Taft blushed. "If that don't put a smile on their face, lock 'em in the booby hatch."

Knox agreed but held his tongue, too impressed to speak. He was just-out-of-prison horny. He needed to find a willing woman and soon.

Imogene put on a flirty look. "Holden, I just remembered, I need to check a few of the addresses I picked up from last week. Mind if I take a look at the log book?"

Pushover Taft — anything for her. "Go right ahead."

She blew him a kiss. "You're a doll. And you, newbie, stay safe out there. Don't get gypped just 'cause you're green!"

All Knox and Taft could do was watch her walk away.

Almost to himself, Taft said, "She sure is something."

Knox thought of the Constance he used to know and wondered if she still had it. Her take-no-prisoners approach to the day, the way she was in bed.

Hell, cathouse girls would ask *her* for tips.

"She sure is."

17

McGuire General Hospital operated like a well-oiled war factory at its best. A rotation of three dozen nurses, Imogene included, were attending to wounded soldiers in the main ward this afternoon. Timony and Constance were in awe, watching them all work. The two of them had agreed to volunteer a few days a week over the next few months, to help ease the burden, and they were amazed at just how many soldiers were recuperating there. Timony looked around and wondered if Nolan was himself recovering in a place like this somewhere overseas. If so, perhaps he was forbidden from sending word to anyone back home. *It's such torture to speculate,* Timony thought, as she let out a faint sigh. What she wouldn't give to know where her son was. But she didn't and so here she was, staying busy, keeping her mind occupied so she didn't wallow over her son's absence.

Constance sensed her friend's mood and gave her arm a comforting squeeze. "Cheer up, darling. Helping out will put you in a better mood, I'm sure of it."

Timony smiled. What fast friends they had become. They were quite the trio — Constance, Imogene, and herself — and Timony was truly thankful to have both of them in her life.

The head nurse came their way, walking fast and snapping her fingers. "Let's not stand around, you two, this is no place to gawk." Timony was whisked one way, Constance another, and the both of them were set to work. They wheeled carts of medical supplies along as the nurses made their rounds. With some instruction, they applied bandages and dressed wounds. They passed out cups of cold water and made small talk with the wounded while doctors checked IV drips and noted charts. All this to the sounds of a radio piping music into the ward. Doris

Day, Bing Crosby, Kitty Kallen. Everyone sang along to The Andrews Sisters' hit single, 'Rum and Coca-Cola.'

Timony, never far from the spotlight, had come prepared for the occasion. She brought along a photographer from the paper and posed for a few snapshots with a willing patient. She flashed her million-watt smile and cocked a hip to one side. Confident and flirty, she never missed an opportunity to make an impression. She was even set to write a feature on volunteering for the paper and figured the photos would help to hook readers. She and Constance had a gas, chatting up the men, raising their spirits, learning from Imogene. The three of them had perhaps a bit more fun than you might expect to find in a hospital ward and none more than Constance. Within an hour, she managed to command the attention of the entire room, perching herself atop a table and holding court as the hospital's resident comic relief.

Constance raised her voice and spoke to the room. "A general says to a private, have you come here to die? No, the private says, I came here *yester*-die!" It got good yuks and laughs, but that was only the beginning. "How do you make a pool table laugh?" No one in the room had an answer. "You tickle its balls!" The room howled. Nurses and doctors went flush with embarrassment. "What do you get when you cross a dick with a potato?" The room gasped. "A dictator!" The room exploded. "What do you call a cheap circumcision?" This time, one of the wounded men had the answer. "A rip off!" he called out and the entire room shook with laughter. No one could deny, it was the best medicine the men could ask for. The wounded in the room ran from needing a few bandages to needing a wheelchair for life and if Timony was honest about it, it was quite depressing. Some of the men were vacant and downcast and it was clear that no amount of joking would change their outlook. She suddenly wished that if Nolan's time had indeed come, that it was swift and painless and that he didn't suffer. What a thought to have about your own child.

Constance sensed her darkened mood. She came over to Timony and kept her voice low. "I think it's time we get you out of here, what do you say?" Timony nodded, embarrassed by her inability to live up to the moment any longer, but more than ready for a change of scenery. She and Constance gave hugs to Imogene, promised the head nurse they would return later that week, and waved goodbye to the wounded soldiers. Hoots and whistles followed them out. To great applause, Constance turned and blew them all a big kiss.

They headed west, out of the city, and settled onto the patio of the Country Club of Virginia. Within minutes, they were sipping gins-on-ice and nibbling triangle-cut cheese sandwiches in the late afternoon sunshine. *Richmond has many hidden comforts*, Timony thought, and feeling a light wind off the river cross your face while the sun sets behind you was most certainly one of them. She felt lucky to be alive, to be at the club, to be with her friend. She chose to let the day fall away and cherish it all.

Constance leaned back into her patio chair and took a hearty sip of her gin. "This is wonderful, Timony, just sitting here like this."

Timony was enjoying herself, too. "I'm glad you're here with me, Constance. I'm just thinking of it, but we should have called Jedidiah to join us."

Constance nodded in agreement. "You know, T, he has a kind of sixth sense about these things. Any minute now, he may just show up!"

Timony delighted at the thought. "You know, the way you talk about him, you and Jedidiah certainly seem to work well together."

Constance nursed her gin. "Is that your way of asking me if Jedidiah and I have ever gotten together?"

Timony was feeling at little coy. "It is."

"Well, I am sorry if this disappoints you, but we have not."

"It doesn't disappoint me, I was just curious."

"Don't get me wrong, T, J is wonderful. Working for him allows me to feel independent. I can drink and dance as I please, I can pay my rent, on time. But working for him also makes me feel, how can I say it? Unconcerned with a man's needs. I'm free and I like it that way."

Timony couldn't help herself. "Still, I can't help but wonder — "

Constance finished her thought. "Has there ever been a special someone who captured my heart?"

Timony nodded — she was on edge.

"Yes, there was. Maybe there still is. Sometimes we just get the one, you know?"

Timony thought of Harrison, the only man she'd ever been with. These weren't the best of times, no, but she did love him so. "What happened to your fella?"

"He went to prison."

"Oh, I see. Is he still there?"

"I don't know. I'm sure that sounds awful. For a time, I wrote letters, I visited, I really kept the torch burning, you know? But he grew more and more despondent. And then I got caught up in something ugly, and when I got out of *that*, I just needed a clean break, from all of it. And then I met Jedidiah and everything changed. And now here I am. I'm still in one piece and I feel pretty good. But I don't know what'll happen if I ever see him again."

Timony didn't want to press further, Constance had shared so much already. She raised her gin and they cheers'd one another. "To true love and what it teaches us about ourselves."

Constance was on the verge of tears.

"Amen to that, friend."

18

Cabbie life ain't bad, Knox thought.

Sure, it wasn't the same as driving for an outfit — no big payday, no on the job rush — but it was steady dough and it sure beat having to look out for the cops at every turn. Still, he did have to be careful. The parole board would have reported him to the police *in absentia* by now and he couldn't afford to be seen by either that preacher man or Walter. But Confederate didn't often run into Jackson Ward, if at all — what with the flags of slavery owners covering their doors, go figure — and Knox had never known Walter to take a cab in his life, he always had his own rides, so on that front, it was so far, so good. Knox had even gone a tad incognito, taking his first shift's pay and buying himself a grey gaberdine work cap which he promptly took to wearing low, to cover his eyes a bit. Per Taft's say so, he had to stay clean shaven, so he couldn't let his bristles show, but he could grow his hair out some and so he would, anything he could do to shield himself from easy recognition.

And so aside from the fear of being seen, things for Knox were looking up. He had dough in his pocket already, care of good weekend tips, he was picking up a few day shifts, like today, getting better fares, and had managed a few square meals, his body starting to feel like itself again after four years of cut-rate slop. Knox used gambling winnings to score a furnished apartment and he was truly grateful because now he had a bed to sleep in and a shower to rinse off in and a way to earn money so he could buy food and drink and the company of a woman.

He got laid, finally, taking some of his tip money and heading straight to Dorris Potter's long-running house of ill repute, a downtown institution off North Adams for more than twenty years that had weathered morals crackdown after morals crackdown, all with the sideways help of more than a few city officials, who were of course themselves regular habitués of Dorris' parlor. Knox could care less, he was just glad it was still open. He walked in and was pegged immediately as just-out-of-prison sex-hungry, Dorris more than happy to pair him with an experienced, mousy brunette who took Knox in her mouth and made him feel like a real man for the first time in years. Knox emptied more than himself that night, he nearly emptied his wallet, too, the brunette willing to go a second time and then a third, for the right price, Knox turning her around and rocking into her harder and harder, listening to the girl moan and scream and thinking of Constance with every sound she made, unable to stop himself even as a storm of guilt washed over him, as if he were cheating on the only woman he ever loved.

And then Knox really couldn't help himself, asking her about Constance when they were through. He felt like a heel about it, sure, but he did it anyway. The poor girl just covered herself with a sheet and shook her head, saying she didn't know her and shoving him out the door, so spent from three turns around the world with an ex-con that she was closing it down for the night. Knox was left to dress in the hallway, panting like he'd just run all the way from Timbuktu. Back downstairs, in the parlor, he mooched a cigarette off a sailor on leave who was waiting his turn, but Doris was none too pleased to see Knox any longer. She shot him a nasty glare for exhausting one of her top earners and told him to scram.

And now in the cab today, all through his shift, fare after fare, all he could think about was Constance. What she looked like now, how she dressed, what she sounded like when she laughed. And then the doubt crept in, like it had ever since he got out. Of course she'd remember him, but would she even want to talk to him? Knox knew that time before was lost. Before he got sent up, before her visits and letters stopped and the thought of her beautifully contoured, no-nonsense face started to fade from —

HONK!

A car horn blared loud then and someone over on the sidewalk yelled as Knox saw the stop sign too late and squealed brakes into the middle of an intersection. His gruff fare got hot fast and yelled at him from the back seat. "Damn, son, watch where you're going!"

Knox went beet-red and shot looks all around — no cops, no Walter, no preacher man. And no accident, he really dodged a bullet. Passersby shot him dirty looks and even dirtier slurs as he put on the gas again. He hoped they wouldn't put in a call to Confederate to complain as he spoke over his shoulder to his fare.

"My apologies, sir, it won't happen again."

"Yeah, well, see that it doesn't, son, or I'll have to write you a citation *and* take your chauffeur's license."

Knox heard the tone in his fare's voice and got wise. Unknowingly, he'd picked up a cop.

"You're a policeman, then, I take it?"

His fare spoke proudly. "Is, was, always will be to some degree or another. Name's Reed, son, Stolmy Reed. But most folks just call me The Cane, on account of this walking sword I carry with me." The Cane held up his rod, so Knox could see it through the rearview. And then it clicked, like a memory from bygone days. Of course, yes, this was the notorious Stolmy Reed, The Cane, with the gruffness in his voice and the limp in his walk. Way back when, he'd been the bigwig over at Second Station before he took up as Chief of Police. Before the war and before Knox got sent up.

"Well, I can't say I've heard the name, Mr. Reed, but I am pleased to know you. I should have known you were someone important, what with our destination being City Hall."

The Cane laughed. "'Important' is a real stretch son, especially given what I do at City Hall every day. Don't be so impressed."

"What can I say? If I read about you in the papers, I say you're a celebrity."

The Cane had to laugh. "Most celebrities, folks run *to*. Me they run from."

Knox laughed, too. It relaxed him. "But it's the devil you know, isn't it? A man like you, I'm guessing you've been at your game for some time. There must be some reward in it."

The Cane had to agree. "Yes, I suppose that's true. And it is most definitely the devil I know, well said. And what about you…" The Cane leaned in to get a look at Knox's chauffeur's license, displayed on the front dash. "… Mr. Smith. Is this the devil *you* know?"

Knox thought of how comforting it was to be behind the wheel of a car, to have control of that kind of power, and how it brought him such peace. Made him feel confident, bold, and reminded him of his father. If driving was The Devil, Knox was its biggest champion. "Yes, Mr. Reed, I suppose it is."

And just like that, they pulled up to City Hall, a wave of relief washing over Knox as he pulled to the curb and relayed the fare price to The Cane — fifty-five cents. The Cane paid him two whole dollars and paused once he got out of the cab, turning back and speaking to Knox through the driver's side window. "I can't help but think, Mr. Smith, that you seem like the knowledgeable type."

"In this line of work, it's not hard to learn a thing or two."

Stolmy handed Knox a card. "Well, if you ever find yourself in a talkative kind of way, friend, give me a call. I'm all ears."

Knox read the card — Stolmy's title and phone number at City Hall. "Will do, Mr. Reed. Will do."

A dozen more fares after The Cane and Knox was through for the night. He clicked on his 'off-duty' light and pulled into a gas station to stretch. Eight hours behind the wheel and he needed someone to pull on each of his limbs like he was a child's doll. He found a hash joint across the street and bought himself a ham sandwich and a beer with tip money.

Stretched out and full now, Knox took up behind the wheel again and steered himself toward a hunch, wondering if Constance still frequented their old haunts. This one in particular had real sentimental value for Knox since it was where they met for the very first time. Tantilla Garden was a ballroom like no other, out west some, on Broad. Knox remembered how he'd never been much for dancing, but before Constance, he'd grown tired of the kind of women he met on the fringes of his old life. The girls always playing an angle, never giving it to him straight, Knox always wondering if he was fodder for a double cross. And so on the very last day of 1939, Knox donned his best suit and took himself to the Garden stag, on the prowl for a woman of a different caliber. Against type, he even tried to blend in some with the New Year's Eve crowd, donning a cheap paper hat and blowing into a noisemaker until his lungs hurt, buzzed and jolly off discount hooch. And then when he saw Constance across the room that night, he felt something change inside of him, as if he were suddenly witness to something that only comes around once in a lifetime, never to happen again. He'd certainly never be the same again after they found themselves drawn to one another across the dance floor, having to shout their names over one of Johnny Pepper's signature numbers, Constance saying her full name so fast that Knox thought she said 'Constantly' and then that became a thing between them, a joke that never got old. Is she coming or going? Constantly! Is she thirsty or making love? Constantly!

Knox had circled the block and was now facing east on Broad with a clear view of Tantilla's entrance. He parked and turned off the engine, now just sitting and waiting. Stewing on old memories and new dreams. And then it was almost as if he'd summoned her there just by thinking of her, the way Constance suddenly appeared, emerging from a car and taking another woman's hand as they skipped along the sidewalk, the two women beaming with glee. Knox's heart skipped three beats. She looked great, she really did, just like he thought she would. Her hair done up, her figure still trim inside a shin length dress, the girls clearly ready for a night on the town. And all Knox could do was just sit there and watch as if he were frozen in stone, his body so overcome with nerves he wondered if he'd ever be able to move again. And then just like that, she was gone, out of sight and inside the Garden. And even though he knew he could just rush in after her, it wasn't time. He wasn't ready. It was enough just to see her, the sight of her enough to sate him for a time before he fired up the cab and drove off.

19

Timony pulled Constance up the steps to Tantilla Garden's ballroom, all smiles and glee, and stopped just shy of the dance floor's frontier, wondering, aside from her Thursday night bridge parties, was there anywhere else on earth she'd rather be? Hollywood, perhaps. Paris, *oui*. In the embrace of my son, most decidedly, but right here, right now, this would more than do. The room swelling with lust, the dance floor doused in sweat. And it had to be a sign, it just *had* to be, the way Johnny Pepper winked at her from the stage before turning the Salt Shakers loose on an uptempo swing. Soon, the entire room was moving and grooving with such infectious force that even the wallflowers couldn't help but swing their hips a little and tap their feet.

Constance was equally ecstatic, her lady-like self all done up in a baby-doll dress and peep-toe pumps, clearly in her element. "I'm so glad you like this place, too, T. I've had some great times here, a lot of memories."

Timony beamed. "Oh, yes, I love it, too. Just ask Imogene."

Constance shimmied in place and scanned the room for a drink with thirsty eyes. "She's coming to join us, I hope?"

"Oh, she'll be here, the selfless doll. I tell you, Constance, I don't know how she does it. One minute she's at McGuire General, patching up soldiers. The next minute she's behind the wheel of a cab, driving strangers all over town. She's a wonder, I tell you."

Constance couldn't hold it in any longer. "Well, for the time being, my new friend, let's stop wondering and start *dancing!*" She grabbed Timony's hands and pulled her onto the dance floor, the two of them caught up in a rush of fun and joy so rich it could light up the entire room if electrified. All around them, bodies contorted and shook as men and women held each other in ways they wouldn't dare in any other public setting. A light, cool breeze blew in through the rollaway ceiling and kept the joint from overheating. It circled the room as if from a genie's bottle, a muse's gift to keep all in good spirits. Which Timony and Constance most certainly were, the two of them locked in a harmonious sync, two lost souls who'd found each other at last, moving through the East Coast Swing and the Jitterbug with ease and then, when Johnny Pepper's drummer snuck a hefty stomp into the beat, something called the St. Louis Shag, which Timony had never heard of but Constance knew like the back of her hand, teaching it to her on the spot. Suddenly they were the stars of the show, the other dancers making room for them to spread out a bit and really work the groove, Timony feeling just like Ginger Rogers, Constance her Fred Astaire. A quick succession of flashbulb pops followed one after the other as the two women twirled in tandem, the both of them quite in sync now, and Timony just knew that one of the shutterbug's snaps would make the paper. Maybe not tomorrow's, but certainly the next day's, and then she'd have even *more* clout at the office, maybe enough to earn her a few more lines for her society column. Just the thought of it gave her a jolt — eat your heart out, Hedda Hopper — and she put every ounce of swagger she had into the last of their dance, the two of them folding into one another as Johnny crescendoed the song to a stomp-out close. Timony was beside herself to find the entire crowd had stopped just to watch them, clapping and cheering now as if they'd just witnessed a great performance by practiced artists. More photos then, smiles and hugs and poses for the camera, Timony and Constance arm in arm with complete strangers, everyone smiling and delighted to join in. Timony even inflated her smile a little, thinking that if it made the papers, she'd buy several copies to save and clip the photo out and place it in a scrapbook to show Nolan once he'd come home, to show how well she'd held up while he'd been away.

"Hi, Mrs. Wells!"

A lively server was heading their way now, a young blonde named Betty. She winked and held up two glasses half-filled with ice and soda water. "Boy, Mrs. Wells, you really bring the excitement with you! This place is always so much more fun when you're around, you must be parched! Here, these are for you and your friend."

Timony winked right back, pulling a flask from her black leather shell bag and filling the two glasses with gin. "Oh, Betty, you sweet thing, you touch me, so! Please, this is my friend Constance Lee, joining me on what I can only hope is another night of mischievous adventure!"

Constance roped Timony in close then, giving her a real friend's hug, as Betty dipped into a playful curtsey and took a healthy swig from Timony's flask. "*Very* pleased to make your acquaintance, Mrs. Lee!" Suddenly, Betty was aghast, exclaiming, "Oh, and Mrs. Wells, I almost forgot! Why, your very own Harrison was here, not one night ago! What a coincidence!"

What a coincidence, indeed. Timony's mood was suddenly on the downswing, deflating like a popped balloon. Harrison was *here*, without her?

"He was, was he? With who?"

Betty searched her mind. "Oh, gosh, let me see. No one I recognized, I don't think. In fact, if I have to be completely honest..." Betty brought her voice down. "The lot he was with that night seemed a little rough around the edges, if you know what I mean. Not the sort we generally see in here."

"Is that so?" Timony was annoyed and altogether perplexed. "Were there women with them, this crowd Harrison was with?"

"Oh, well, sure, all of them were dancing and just having a grand old time." Betty suddenly recoiled. "Oh, my, Mrs. Wells, what have I done... I didn't mean to... "

Timony put on a carefree smile — perhaps her greatest talent — and pulled Betty in for a hug. "Oh, Betty, don't you worry. Harrison is always out and about with one crowd or another. It's part of his life as a public servant. I'm sure he was just blowing off some steam, don't you worry!"

Betty smiled through her embarrassment and apologized before hurrying off to another table,Timony left to consider what she'd just learned. Inside an instant, those joy-filled moments from before — dancing with abandon, bonding with a new friend — fell away as quickly as rotted-through floorboards. She gave Constance a dire look.

"I think Harrison is having an affair."

A familiar voice exclaimed *"He is?!"* and suddenly Imogene was right there, decked out to the nines and ready to play. Timony was glad for her warmth as Imogene brought both she and Constance into a huddle and whispered, with a snarl in her voice, "If it's true, I'll take a scalpel to his fucking nuts and cut them clean off!"

Timony's revelation demanded that she leave Tantilla at once and find a more suitable destination for her mood. Constance knew exactly where to go and before long the three of them were sitting atop the roof of Jedidiah's tobacco factory, avoiding talk of Harrison and enjoying the company of a cool breeze.

"Let's have a drink, shall we?"

Jedidiah's pacifying voice rang out into the night air as he ascended a flight of stairs — balancing a tray of drinks, no less — and stepped onto his rather lavish rooftop with its cushioned seating and its decorative side tables. The three women marveled as he balanced the tray with maître d'-like grace and stopped to see them one by one, handing each of them their martini and repeating their order as he did. "No olives" to Imogene, *"Extra* dirty" to Constance, with a wink, and "Light on the vermouth" to Timony. Jedidiah set the tray down and raised his own martini in a toast.

"To the inevitable end of the war, I say let *it* not come too late and let *us* not come too soon, here here!" The three women laughed and almost spit out their first sips as Jedidiah took a seat next to Timony, altogether pleased with himself and his joke. "Now let's have it ladies, confessions, one by one. What ills besote your hearts and minds tonight? Ms. McKenna, let's start with you. Although I'm sure we all have some idea of what might have *you* in a tither."

Imogene took an appreciative sip of her martini — it *was* quite good — and tried to hide her embarrassment. "Why thank you, Jedidiah, for putting me on the spot."

Jedidiah wouldn't have it any other way. "We're all dying to know."

Constance sipped her drink. "Have you given him an answer yet?"

Imogene held back her reply and for a moment, the air was still and silent but for surrounding sounds — the ceaseless ripple of the James River was not far off, the proud exhaust of nearby tobacco factories purred into the night, and *of course*, she thought, there in the distance, a police siren is ringing out, the peace be damned. How serendipitous.

Imogene rolled her eyes, defeated. "Oh yes, yes, a thousand times yes, I love Bennie Sherwood and want to marry him."

Cheers and claps circled the rooftop, but Imogene waved them off.

"But," she continued, "just listen to *that*," gesturing at the siren, which had grown louder. "Every time I hear that sound, I'm gonna wonder, is that trouble meant for him? I mean, just an inkling of trouble draws him to it, like a moth to a flame. For all I know, that could be him right now and I just don't know if I can handle that every night. I've already been a soldier's wife, friends," taking a hearty sip, "I don't know if I can be a cop's wife, too."

Constance was surprised. "You've been married already?"

Imogene nodded and downed the rest of her martini. "And widowed."

Timony gasped. "My God, Imogene, I had no idea."

Imogene struggled to find more to say until Jedidiah offered, "She is ever the more stronger for it, our incomparable Imogene, who will make us proud no matter what she decides."

Timony and Constance agreed and Imogene was thankful for great friends and the safe space they offered her, since the war had done so much to make everyone feel just that side of unsettled. Jedidiah turned to Constance next. "And you, my dear, I see you most every day but as of late, I know very little about your own matters of the heart. Anything you care to share?"

Constance speared an olive with a cocktail stick and devoured it. "Oh, you know me, J, just point me towards a bar or a bedroom and I'm sure to be quite satisfied. Point me to a room with both and I don't know if I'll ever be the same again!"

Timony blushed at her new friend's frank nature and wished she could be so bold. She always had to be so careful of her position, her stature in the room and what she said. Someone's always watching, her mother said. Someone's always listening.

Constance went on. "But you know what's really got me fired up? We're near the end, friends, we really are. Just think, when we finally belt the Japs, there'll be no more rations, no more drawing our stockings on, no more waiting around for soldiers and sailors like they own the earth." She set her eyes on Timony. "And with any luck, we'll have those we love right back by our side."

Timony shivered and shook and felt as if she might burst like a volcano. Hold it together, child, hold it together.

Jedidiah put a friendly hand on her shoulder. "Whatever it is, T, you can tell us."

"Oh, it's nothing you don't know already. The war has taken my men from me and I don't think I'll ever get them back."

Jedidiah slapped a knee. "That does it. No more wallowing in the dumps. *We* are going to take charge of this night, once and for all. Ladies, follow me."

The four of them trekked the length of King Tobacco's rooftop, maybe fifty, sixty yards, until they arrived at the southernmost side. Jedidiah left them and said to wait as he hurried back about half the distance. He lifted a gate and disappeared into the building, rising minutes later with what looked to be three rolls of fabric. Timony, Imogene, and Constance watched curiously as he went about unrolling them one by one and fastening each of them to its own makeshift A-frame.

"What on earth," Timony muttered, peering at what appeared to be a row of black and white paintings. It was dark and hard to see.

Jedidiah finished with the third frame, knelt down, and flipped a switch. "Voilà!" Spotlights lit up the three panels, each of them displaying a caricatured portrait of an Axis leader. Mussolini on the right, Hirohito on the Left, Hitler square in the middle.

Imogene laughed. "My God, Jedidiah, what is this?"

Jedidiah strode toward them, cradling a small briefcase in his hands. "Just something I offer my most treasured guests." He stood before them and opened the case — three small pistols lay inside. "Take one, please, and set your sights upon the tyrant of your choice."

Imogene nervously took a pistol. "I just don't know, Jedidiah, are you serious?"

"Yes! You three need some serious catharsis. Now, which despot do you wish to fire upon?"

Imogene had to admit, the thought of it did excite her. She studied all three before dialing her gaze on Mussolini's bald, oversized head. Her first beau, Johnny, died in Italy. She stepped to the right. "I'll take Benito."

Jedidiah offered a pistol to Timony. "And you, my dear? Whose lights would you like to extinguish?"

Timony had no idea where Nolan was, but she was certain he was in Europe somewhere. Hitler was dead now, sure, but he was to blame for the entire mess, as far as Timony was concerned. "*That* one took my son from me," she said, squaring her look on Adolf's exaggerated frown and ridiculous hairdo. She lined herself up with the center panel. "I'll take the Kraut."

Jedidiah offered the last pistol to Constance. "That leaves you with the emperor, my friend."

Constance took the pistol and scowled at Hirohito's oversized glasses and buck teeth. She moved over to the left. "With pleasure."

Jedidiah lined up aside them and pulled out his pocket square. "On my count, ladies."

Timony, Imogene, and Constance laughed nervously, the three of them nearly beside themselves.

"Are we really going to do this?" Imogene asked.

Jedidiah called out: "Ready!"

The women cocked their guns.

"Aim."

They fixed on their targets.

Jedidiah waved his pocket square. "Fire!"

Blam, Blam, Blam!

One by one, each of the women emptied a moon clip into their chosen target, six shots a piece, eighteen in total. Within seconds, it was all over.

Constance glowed. "Now *that* was fun! Can we do it again?"

Jedidiah collected the pistols and shut the case. "Not if we want an unpleasant visit from Imogene's suitor. Shall we examine the targets for accuracy?"

Timony clapped. "Yes, let's!"

The four of them rushed to see the targets and admire their gunplay. Hirohito had holes in his teeth. Hitler had no nose. Mussolini looked like Swiss cheese.

Constance shrieked. "My God, Timony, you're an excellent shot!"

Timony feigned a bow. "Why, thank you. My father taught me young."

Imogene started to speak but caught herself. She steadied herself against the panel of Mussolini. Jedidiah moved to her side. "Imogene, my dear, are you alright? You suddenly look unwell."

Imogene took a deep breath. "Perhaps it's the, what do you call it? The cordite? Whatever it is, please excuse me for a moment."

Jedidiah led Imogene downstairs.

Constance and Timony moved back to the cushioned seating and what was left of their martinis.

"I so needed that," Timony said, gesturing at the panels as she downed the rest of her drink. "And *that*."

"Here, here," Constance said, finishing hers.

A shriek came from downstairs — Imogene calling out.

Constance and Timony rushed down the stairs and found Imogene resting against the wall outside Jedidiah's bathroom, a shocked look on her face.

"What is it?" Constance asked.

"I... I think I'm pregnant!"

PART THREE

SHADOWS

20

The dummy tips that came into police HQ over the department's two outstanding murder cases would go down in RPD history as some of the most outrageous ever made. Bennie downed a benzie and skimmed the list, wide-eyed.

A woman in the East End claimed to have seen actual Nazis set fire to the house Scangili was found in. Professed, in fact, to have seen Hitler himself on the scene and would be willing to share more if only we could guarantee her safe passage to a transcendent world called Supernova, vastly superior to our own, with a man named Heinrich, whom she had yet to meet.

An elderly man living in the Chesterfield Apartments off Franklin Avenue claimed to know the *real* killer behind the murders and would tell all, just as soon as the department settled up on the $7.52 he owed a local mechanic.

Another doozie — someone alleged that Mrs. Kleinfeld had been the domineering madam of a citywide sex ring and that Scangili had been her prized gigolo, the two of them murdered by city officials over fears their own late-night proclivities might become front page scandal. And unless someone placed two hundred dollars into an Army duffel and leave it under the westernmost awning of the Marshall Street viaduct, a fifteen page tell all would be delivered to the department within the week.

Bennie had to laugh, unsure of what was more ridiculous — these preposterous claims or the idea the department had that kind of money to throw around. He grabbed a steno and scribbled a note — write an editorial and get it to Archie, remind the public that cops don't negotiate for tips.

More yuks — someone claimed both murders were part of an elaborate Union plot to restart the Civil War and re-oppress the

South. Another winner — it was all part of a grand Negro plan to push out the Jews, overtake state government, and enslave white women. Again with the Nazis — someone claimed that a small army of the Third Reich had overtaken her neighbor's garage and was planning a coup right here in town.

The office phone rang. Bennie picked up quick, hoping for something good. He caught Stolmy's gruff instead.

"Look, Stolmy. I'm — "

"Save it, Bennie. You've had over a month and we're still nowhere close to solving two of the most high profile murders this city has ever seen."

Bennie forced himself not to blow. "No one's talking. Every stoolie we know is tight-lipped, nobody'll tell us shit. The house, the arson? We traced its owner and got a dummy deed. We know it wasn't the Kleinfeld husband because he was at home in bed and if it *was* Walter MacKeye, well, I'd haul him in, only I can't find him. Our two leads, Sutton and this Carroll fellow? Sutton hasn't checked in with his PO yet and Carroll wasn't even on the parole list, which only makes his story more confusing. And it certainly doesn't help morale around here when I'm being vilified in the papers and nearly hung out to dry before I even get a chance to bring the case in. You're not exactly giving me a fair shake, Stolmy."

Stolmy huffed. "I don't remember whining and crying my way through the job."

"For crissakes, I don't even have *the job*! I'm nothing but an *Acting* Lieutenant, remember?"

"You can remember who you're talking to."

Bennie wanted to throw a car across the room. Calm now, deep breaths. One, two, just like they taught him. "What can I say? We're working every angle we can. No luck yet."

"You know I'm supposed to tell you that's not good enough."

"You can always fire me. Imogene would be thrilled."

A long pause.

"Tell me again what we know about Sutton," Stolmy said.

"We *believe* he used to work in MacKeye's crew, before he got sent up. And we think that house belonged to MacKeye, but we can't prove it. Sutton's print off a car near the house? It's too convenient. There's something there, we just haven't found it yet. We may have a lead on Scangili, though, finally. Something from his past."

Stolmy took a deep breath, brought his voice down. "You know, you may need to get a little dirty on this one, Bennie."

Bennie looked at his bruised knuckles, his gut suddenly in knots. "Like my father, eh? Is that a suggestion or an order?"

"If you really want the job, you'll find answers any way you can."

Bennie saw blood trickle down a man's jawline. "You know what separated my father from every other hump on the job, Stolmy? A code. He never hit anyone that didn't deserve it."

Stolmy buried a chuckle. "You really believe that?"

"I do. Why?"

"You have one week. Don't say I didn't warn you."

"Hey, now, what do you mean by that?"

Click.

The phone rang again. Bennie almost threw it out the window. "What?"

"Ben-eh, it's your pal Lenny. Got a minute?"

"That all depends. You got anything for me?"

"Matter of fact, I do. But first, let me thank you, pal, on behalf of some very grateful ladies staying here at the Lodge. They're soon to be *ex*-wives, thanks to you, and looking at simpler divorce proceedings, at that. Whoever you sent to do the heavy lifting didn't disappoint."

Bennie looked at his hands and felt a twitch run up his spine, remembering Lenny's big ask from a few weeks back — to put the hurt on a couple of fist-happy husbands. Bennie had no one to throw it to, not without fear of reproach, so he took it upon himself, donning a homemade mask made of blackout curtain and approaching both men under cover of night. Both men got the same — rights, lefts, ribcage work. Bennie left 'em both whimpering on the ground with a stern warning — leave the women alone or he'd be back for more. Bennie wasn't sure what made him more unsettled — that he'd done it at all or that he'd enjoyed it.

"No problem. What've you got?"

"Had a lady in here the other night who needed to hide out for bit. Another troublesome boyfriend, it sounded like. Well, she gets a little gin in her and starts talking all about him, some guy with a decent spread out west. A barn, even. Says there's quite the party out there on a regular basis. Lotta noise, lotta *talk*. Chants and shouting, she said. Enough to give her chills."

Bennie felt a chill himself. "What kind of chants?"

"She couldn't repeat it, but she swears they were speaking German, pal. She looked out the window a few times when these gatherings were going on. Says she saw fires, marching, some real militant kind of activity, like you see in the newsreels. Hell, it's giving me the creeps just talking about it."

Something else fluttered in Bennie's memory, some thread dangling…

"Klan?"

"She didn't say nothing about hoods and robes."

"She got a name?"

"'Mary' she said it was, but you know how it goes with folks that come my way. I don't always get the straight and narrow."

"She with you now?"

"Nah, she split. Wouldn't talk to you anyhow. Doesn't know I'm talking to you now, but I figure, you did me that favor, well, I knows old Bennie could use all the help he can get right now, so here I am."

Light bulb — Bennie had the tips right in front of him. He leafed through them and found it near the bottom, that bit about the Third Reich and a neighbor's garage. Eyes to the top of the page, an address right there. A spot off Glenside, *way* out west. Bennie's antennae pinged. "A barn, she said?"

"Yeah. Doesn't sound like anything here in Richmond, but there you go."

Boom, another thread hit Bennie dead on. He grabbed the list of addresses Imogene had glommed from Confederate for him and skimmed it, fast. *There*, that address that had stumped him, the one outside the city limits. "Lenny, hold a second." Bennie set the phone down and went over to the map of Richmond on his wall. He tracked his finger along the route of Broad Street on the map. Sure enough, out west, near Glenside.

Bennie almost shouted, he was so excited. Go back a month — the night of V-E Day, The Sunshine Five-and-Dime, that straw of *hay*. He picked up the phone. "Lenny, this lady. You get the sense her boyfriend liked to party with grass?"

"She didn't say as much, but wouldn't surprise me none, the way she talked about herself."

Go back *two* weeks — rock thrower Billy Johnson, that junkie hideaway off Chimborazo, that thread dangling, *there it is*, crystal clear. One of the dopers they arrested said. "Nazis live in my garage."

Bennie wasn't sure if he was relieved or panicked. "You're a lifesaver, Lenny."

Lenny laughed. "Don't think I've ever been called *that* before, but I'll take it."

Dead air.

Bennie needed more before Lenny signed off. "Say, friend. I'm on a tight leash and an even tighter deadline. Any chance you've got any more for me?"

Hesitation on the other line. Lenny's help didn't come cheap. "Like what?"

"Like news on Sutton or Carroll, names I fed you awhile back."

"I've heard nothing on Carroll."

The wild man in the wind, no sight of him since their rooftop chase.

"But Sutton?"

Lenny took a breath. Bennie could tell he was reluctant to say more. "You didn't hear it from me, but you know Ms. Lee, confidant of one Jedidiah King?"

"Sure, Constance. She's a doll."

"She and Sutton used to be an item."

Bennie was surprised, Constance was a top-shelf catch. "Really."

"And Bennie?"

"Yeah?"

"Don't trust Eddie Haden."

Bennie sighed — confirmation. "I won't."

"That's two you owe me."

"Just say the word."

Bennie could hear Lenny smile through the phone. "Adios, Ben-eh. Watch your back, soldier boy."

Click.

Bennie stood up from his desk and almost screamed. High on the news or high on pep, it didn't matter, he had to do something. He hit the squad room and surveyed the manpower. Three patrolmen, plus one detective each for robbery, vice, and homicide. With Annie on the switchboard, that made seven. Bennie stood near the bannister and scanned the room, looking for a trustworthy face. The tecs were low-grade, non V-Squad. Good men, but unimaginative. The patrolmen, though, were more earnest, career-driven, interested in working their way up. More inclined to see Bennie as a leader, perhaps, and not a blight on their record. Bennie pretended to be checking the case board as he looked over at them, looking for a familiar face. *Bingo* — Jimmy Knight was among them, that young patrolmen who assisted at The Sunshine the morning of V-E Day. The one they found outside the store once they arrived.

Bennie whistled, motioned him over. Jimmy rose from his desk and hustled his way, eager to help. "Sir?"

Bennie steered him even farther away from his coworkers. "What's keeping you busy these days?"

Jimmy shrugged. "Tire inspections, accident reports, taking record of all the city parking that's available. The odd field interview, if it's traffic related."

Bennie nodded along. "Exciting work?"

Jimmy knew he was speaking to the boss. With a hesitant crackle in his voice, he said, "Of course. It's an honor to serve the people."

Bennie brought his voice down. "Relax. I know it's a shit detail and so do you. Everyone goes through it."

Jimmy paused before taking on a bold tone. "You didn't."

Bennie smiled, impressed. "No, I didn't. Very good, patrolman

Knight. But if you'd come up under my father like I did, you might well have been wishing for a traffic detail. It sounds preferable to what I went through, let me tell you."

Jimmy just smiled, eager to get along. "If you say so."

"Do you have a wife at home, Jimmy? Or a girlfriend waiting?"

"A girlfriend, sir. We've been steady ten months."

"You have a date tonight?"

Jimmy shook his head. "No, sir. I'm on until ten, and it *is* a Wednesday…"

Bennie laughed. "What's a Wednesday got to do with it?" He looked at the clock, it was almost nine. Imogene was at the hospital tonight, she wouldn't be home until after midnight. Plenty of time to drive out west and run a sneak op under cover of darkness, do some recon.

"How would you like to earn some points here, Jimmy? Help me out with something?"

Jimmy nodded, pure excitement in his eyes. "Yessir!"

"You sure? You can't tell anyone about it. Not them," Bennie nodded at the other patrolmen, "and not your girlfriend. In the vault, understand?"

Jimmy prickled with excitement. "I understand."

Bennie handed him a set of car keys. "Good. These are for one of the unmarked Fords packed out back, license number's on the keychain. Gas it up at the department's pump and meet me in the alleyway behind the Richmond Hotel at ten thirty. Just pull up to the back entrance, I'll be there."

"Yessir."

"Good man."

The pick-up went smoothly. Bennie ducked out of the hotel bar with his duffel a few minutes past ten thirty. He'd taken a cab from the Annex and been there an hour, plenty of time to make himself seen and heard. He chatted up the bartender and one of the waitresses. Made small talk with an insurance salesman, even shared a few laughs with a complete stranger sitting a few stools down. Plenty of good lighting, plenty of face-to-face, more than enough to build an alibi off of. He slid into the unmarked Ford and looked over at Jimmy Knight.

"You ready for this?"

Jimmy nodded. "Just tell me where to, sir."

"Let's get to Monument and head west. We're going out aways, out of the city."

Jimmy pulled out of the alleyway. "Now I know why you asked me to gas up."

"And keep it under the speed limit, Knight. Let's not draw any attention to ourselves."

"Roger that."

Bennie rifled through the duffel as they made time, taking stock of his stake-out prep. A pair of binoculars and his picklock set, both hand-me downs from the old man. A loaded .22, a sawed-off shotgun, a box of shells. A flashlight and a baseball bat.

Bennie used the flashlight to check the address in his steno and the crude map he'd drawn up. Once they were out of the city, it was north of Broad, maybe half a mile out or so. Paved road turned to dirt and gravel and soon they were winding their way on a path to nowhere, tall trees and overgrown brush their only guides. No street lights this far out.

Before long, Bennie saw the makings of a two-story home with a barn out back, a few cars parked nearby.

Jimmy started to brake. "What do you want me to do, sir?"

"Kill the lights and pull over. We'll ditch the car and circle around on foot."

"Roger that."

Jimmy cut the headlights and steered their unmarked just off the road, ducking it behind a patch of oak trees. As he snuck out of the car, Bennie looked at the two-way radio and felt foolish — if they got in a jam, they were done for, too far out to call for help. Jimmy came 'round the back of the car, hunched, his voice low.

"What are we out here for, sir?"

Bennie knelt down and shone the flashlight on the contents of the duffel. "To take stock of what we see and get out without anyone knowing. Look, Jimmy, I wasn't exactly up front about this. I think we've got some fifth columnists out here, Hitler devotees looking to start up their own band this side of the

Atlantic. But it's all speculation at this point and I can't go to City Hall with it until I know more. Look, I didn't want to tell you at the Annex for fear you wouldn't come, but I need backup in case this goes south. You want to duck out now, just say the word. It wasn't fair of me to bring you out on these terms and I won't think less of you if you want out."

A pause, Jimmy thinking. "What I want out of is patrol. Sir."

Smart kid. "Do right by me tonight and I'll put you on track for the detective's exam. I'll even coach you on the questions. Then I'll pair you with one of the older tecs and let you get some arrests under you belt. The rest is up to you."

"The Victory Squad?"

Bennie thought of Eddie Haden — soon to be on the chopping block. "If you want it bad enough."

"Deal."

Bennie handed Jimmy the flashlight. "Good. Got your steno?"

"Always, sir."

Bennie looked over at the cars, four total. "Good. Keep low, get the license plate numbers off those sleds, and meet me on the other side of the clearing. And take this .22, just in case."

Jimmy slipped the .22 against the small of his back and snaked off toward the cars. Bennie popped a few shells into the shotgun, crawled the other way with the duffel at his side, and just like that, he was back in the jungle with a knife and a canteen and a sixth sense for the enemy. It scared him how much he loved the feeling it gave him, kneeing around a dirt clearing to a spot that gave him a good view of the house and the barn. He saw lights on inside the house and heard twang-tinged laughter coming from an open window.

Jimmy crawled up behind him, his voice low. "I got the plates, sir."

"Good work. Now, let's see if we can get a look into that barn."

"Roger that."

Bennie led the way. The two of them crawled on stomachs to the east side of it and came up just underneath a four-paned window. He motioned for Jimmy to stay low as he rose slowly and shone the flashlight into the building. On tiptoes now, a peek —

Boy, did he get a look.

A giant red Nazi flag hung against the far back wall of the barn.

"Bingo."

Anxious Jimmy: "What'd you see?"

"Not enough. We need to get inside."

They crawled around to the front doors and found them padlocked. Bennie went to work on it with the old man's picklock set while Jimmy held the flashlight. Bennie struggled, tricky at first, but eventually he hooked the pin and pulled. The lock gave way, open sesame. "Careful now," he whispered, as they each pulled a door open and slipped inside, closing them slowly behind them. Inside now on soft feet, the both of them, Bennie clicked on the flashlight and shone it around the room. It was spacious and crowded all at once. He and Jimmy took stock of what they saw: a winter's worth of firewood stacked against a wall; a tabled film projector against another, a white sheet tacked to a wall board ten feet in front of it; giant beams leaning against one another, like the kind you'd use to frame a house. Off to the side was a table full of foodstuffs — boxes of cereal, cans of beans — the bounty from The Sunshine Five and Dime theft. Lastly, they found a makeshift printing press in the back. Bennie checked the print king, *whoa:* those hate tracts from the junkie house were made right here. Next to the machine were a few piles of thick cloth, each stacked a few feet high. Jimmy rifled through one and whispered 'Oh shit' as he pulled up a white Klan hood. The flashlight framed it in stark, eerie light against the back wall.

Movement outside — voices, footsteps.

Bennie killed the flashlight. "Oh shit is right."

"What do we do?" Jimmy whispered, the kid looking right scared now.

Bennie looked around the room, searching for hiding places. He saw a crowded corner in the back shielded by discards of oakwood and tented by a flagpole. He motioned for Jimmy to take shelter under the flag while he scurried to hide under the beams, dragging the duffel with him, sliding under them just in time. A couple of men walked in, talking. One of the voices familiar to Bennie, the other not so much.

The familiar voice: "The hell? Did one of of 'em wake up, break the lock, and just head for the woods?"

The other: "It's not like they know where we are or where to go. And anyways, how'd they get the lock open? Ain't any of 'em smarter than a thumbtack. And even that's a stretch."

The familiar voice, again: "I tell you what's a stretch, you calling anyone smarter than a thumbtack, you being what you are."

The other, with something to prove right quick: "What's that now? You got something to say, say it, you rotten shit!"

And just like that, the two men started to go at one another, both of them more talk than muscle. Bennie wrangled his memory — it hit him like a lightning flash. The familiar voice was that guard from the State Penitentiary, Müller he said his name was. A German national. The other voice, Bennie couldn't place. Müller got some kind of edge in the tussle, it sounded like, while the other one slinked away.

Müller: "You done now?"

The other voice: "You just watch it, Tommy. Least you expect it, I'll be on you like stink on a Jew."

Müller laughed. "Is that right? Well, best we get back inside then, don't you think? Finish that card game, see who's *standing tall* then, eh?"

Bennie heard a shove and could just tell, the other man didn't appreciate the 'standing tall' crack.

Müller: "Goddamn it, we're gonna wake 'em, you know that? Now let's get out of here before the boss finds out, or we're both gonna wind up just like 'em."

Bennie listened as the two men left the barn and sealed the lock on the doors, locking he and Jimmy inside. And then he heard it for the first time, the faint ripple of snoring men.

Bennie felt his agency give way — they weren't alone.

Eddie downed an upper and chomped on a toothpick, waiting for the buzz to kick in. He'd caught Sherwood dosing on the sly and figured he had a stash somewhere. He snuck into the Lieu's office when he wasn't looking and glommed a bottle from his desk. *The righteous prick,* he thought. I know your dirty secret and I'm gonna use it against you.

Eddie needed the boost. He'd been tailing Visel three nights running and he was beat. He didn't go for uppers on the regular, he didn't like the come down, but every now and then, it was just what he needed. There it was, that feeling. He could climb a mountain or run to the ocean, it didn't matter. For the next hour, he could do anything he wanted. And right now, he wanted to walk the path he'd studied these last three nights, the one Visel had been driving to after dining at the Occidental and whoring at Dorris Potter's. Eddie had watched him, he knew, Visel hit those same two spots every night and then he came here for some business inside one of these apartments. Eddie figured that whatever was driving Visel — earning him big money on the side, giving him an in at Byrd Airport — it was here. Every night, Eddie had steeled himself more and more. Built up his courage, rehearsed his spiel. The way he figured it, t's time to give them an in with *him,* before it's too late.

It was almost ten thirty now, the night like every other, and as predicted, Visel stepped onto Canal Street, a half a block up. The man a creature of habit, he walked the same path every night. Eddie took a long drag and quickened his pace some, even as he softened his footfall, and had almost caught up with Visel before he finally had the courage to speak.

"Hey, Visel."

Jimmy Visel stopped and hesitated, turning after a moment to face Eddie. A streetlight hit Visel's face and Eddie could see there wasn't a hint of worry on it. Quite the opposite, really. Visel's imposing six foot frame gave *Eddie* a pause and if it wasn't clear before, it was now — this man didn't spook easily, if at all. He did run a prison, didn't he? Eddie only thinking about that now. Visel raised his eyes some and shrugged.

"Yeah?"

"Visel, my name's Eddie. Eddie Haden. I'm a cop on the vice squad. We met a few weeks ago, some of us came to your office."

Visel gave him a long stare. "I remember."

Eddie futzed with his toothpick, he was nervous. "Look, I'm

onto you, pal. You've got something going at Byrd airport and you've got something going on here." Eddie gestured at the nearby apartment building. "I know because I've been on you like a bad habit for three nights straight. And whatever it is, I want in, I want a piece of it. A good one, too. And if you don't want to play ball, well, I'll go to Sherwood, I'll got to Reed, I'll go to the Herald. Take your pick. One word from me and it'll all go up in smoke, capeesh?"

Visel just stared at him. Eddie didn't care, he held his head up high. He was in this, now, all the way, no backing down. Whatever it took for the farm, for a better life, for the life he deserved.

A long beat stretched on and on.

"You want in," Visel said finally.

"Yeah."

"But you don't even know what *it* is."

"Doesn't matter. You're government connected out at the airport. And you've got something cooking here," Eddie pointed at the apartments again, "and between the two of them, you're raking it in. You've got money for women, money for top shelf food and booze. I know the prison doesn't pay for all this, buddy, 'cause I checked your employment file at City Hall, don't play coy with me. And, anyway, I've been at this angle myself for long enough, so don't try and play like you don't have something going. I know every game in town. The players, too. Just ask around. You cut me in on this, you won't be sorry."

Visel took his time before he answered. "And if we don't?"

"*We*? Whose *we*? Alls I see is you."

Visel smirked. "Why don't you tell him who *we* are, Walter. I think he'd like to know."

Someone started clapping then, from behind, and Eddie spun around. He nearly went for his gun when he saw someone emerging from the shadows, walking towards them, and goddamn if it wasn't Walter MacKeye, number one on Richmond's Most Wanted List and one of the very last people Eddie wanted to see tonight.

Walter's clap fizzled out. "Very good, Eddie. You found your way all the way here without my help. Sounds like you're finally getting the hang of this detective thing. It's only taken, you what, fifteen years on the job?"

"Fuck you, Walter. I should have known you were in on whatever this is."

"Should have known, but you didn't. And now, you're gonna make like a bee and buzz the fuck off to wherever you came from and forget all about what you think you know about us. Because this isn't for you, my friend. It's not me calling you at midnight, it's not some last minute tip you just *happened* upon, and it's not definitely some address miraculously left in your mailbox. It's not like old times, Eddie. This isn't for you."

Eddie pulled his gun and pointed it first at Walter, then Visel. Both of them took a step back, on their heels now. "Yeah? Well, what if that isn't good enough? Yeah, I found you, that's right, and I could find you again. You leave me out of this, it's just like I said. I go to Sherwood, I go to the papers. You'll be in cuffs before you know it. Him, too."

Walter just shook his head. "Eddie, I'm telling you…"

Visel put his hands up. "Let's just hold on now, okay? Walter, what do you say we, uh, show your friend here what we're working on. Show him *who* we're working with, what do you say?"

Walter let the idea sink in and Eddie could see it in his face, the way a change came over him. Walter smiled like some kid's parent who'd just figured out the world's best bribe. Eddie didn't trust it, not for a second, but he wasn't backing down.

"Alright, sure," Eddie said. "Show me."

Eddie kept the gun on both of them, not that they looked particularly worried about it, and followed them a short distance to a first floor apartment down at the next corner. Eddie watched as Visel unlocked the back door. He and Walter kept their hands in plain view, neither of them rushing to move or evade Eddie at all. Eddie stayed behind them, his pulse like a gatling gun now, taking it all in. Visel and Walter ushered him inside in total darkness. They moved from one room to another and then *snap*, a light came on. Eddie wasn't sure what he was looking at. He paused, taking it in, and tried to register what he was seeing. People, on the floor, crammed together like sardines in a can. Two, maybe three dozen men, just lying there. Maybe a foot between them, at most. Some of them lay still, some of them writhed in place. Some of them looked up at the ceiling and mouthed words to themselves. All of them looked underfed, emaciated even, their heads shaved, their skin as pale as —

Wham!

Eddie was on his back in a flash. Visel pinned him to the ground while Walter wrestled his gun away. *Goddamn it, Eddie, you let your guard down, you worthless —*

Walter knelt down and reached into Eddie's jacket, pulled out his badge. He t'sked. "Eddie Haden. You know, I really thought you were smarter than this, pal. After all this time, you still don't know to keep us in your line of sight the whole time."

One of the men lying on the floor stood up. The man like a wounded ghost, shaking and stumbling as if he were sick and lost. He moaned and voiced something indecipherable. Eddie caught snippets of 'hungry' and 'please.' Walter punched him in the stomach.

"Lay down, you mutt!"

The man fell to the floor like a dead weight.

Walter hovered over Eddie.

"Here's how it's gonna work, Eddie. I'm gonna keep your gun and your badge for insurance and in return, you're gonna keep your mouth shut about what you saw here. You're not gonna tell The Cane or the papers and you're sure as shit not gonna tell that heel Sherwood. In fact, if Sherwood or anyone on the force catches wind of what's going on here, you are going to run interference, you got it? Whatever you have to do. You keep 'em out of this and away from us. And if you don't, if they come our way, I'll plant these," gesturing to Eddie's gun and badge, "somewhere your fellow cops'll be sure to find them, you understand?"

Eddie could hardly breathe. Visel had him pinned good, the man more than ready to throw Eddie around the room, but after all these years, after all the beatings he'd already taken, Eddie just knew, it wasn't worth it. Play dead, Eddie. Like a dog.

He looked up at them both, nodding. "Yeah, sure. I'll… I'll keep 'em off your backs."

Walter grinned and patted him on the cheek. "That's good, Eddie. That's real good."

They let him up off the floor then and shoved him out of the apartment, shutting the door in his face and leaving him all alone out in the night. There wasn't a soul on the street and Eddie had never felt more naked and afraid as he scurried back to his sled, shooting looks over his shoulder to be sure they weren't following him. He was out in the open now, with no protection. No badge, no gun. He shook, he breathed deep, he questioned every life choice he'd ever made as he hurried back to his wheels, more thankful than he'd ever been that he still had the keys on him, that he didn't have to go back, knock on the door again and embarrass himself further.

He was almost to his sled when he saw a woman carrying a suitcase across the street. She looked to be about his age and the suitcase looked heavy. Too heavy, even, and so perhaps he could help her, make himself useful. Finally act as if he were, in fact, a real cop and not just some lowlife looking to make a quick score. He came up behind her and put a hand on her shoulder.

"Miss? Here, let me help you, I can take that —
Wham!

Again, Eddie was on his back. The woman decked him as if he were some common mugger.

"Get away, you thief! Get away!"

She kicked him again and again. Eddie tried to shield her blows from his ribcage.

"Miss, please, I was only trying to help!"

She jerked her suitcase away and called him an ugly name. Eddie just lay there, hurt, and wondered if would ever be safe for him to get up again. She called back to him as she hurried off.

"You're lucky I don't call the police!"

Marlon brushed the flour from the sides of the pipe, like a baker might clear his surface before baking. Now, this ain't no batch of biscuits, no sir, just your standard twelve inch pipe bomb, friend to delinquent teen boys everywhere, and it isn't for real, not in the least, this one packed with flour and salt, the whole thing all for show. Call it a measurement of sorts, a way to see just how much gunpowder one would need to fill this length of pipe. Marlon tells himself it's just a diversion, something to bide his time with, to play army with in his mind and to remember when. But the thrill it gives him as he holds it in his hand, the excitement of potential, of witnessing the awe-inspiring genesis of an explosion, it's almost too much for him to bear. Forgive me, Lord, but there are some pleasures worth your wrath, and here in my most private of rooms, with a radio on playing the latest white man's music and my candles lit and a sip of ol' Garrison's firewater close at hand, I must admit, I'm most at peace. Away from the worries of our congregation, away from the war worries of the day, of the summer and its inevitable heat, Marlon found himself wondering if beneath all this, the church very much above him and the weight of his sins ever present, would he ever feel truly free of this mortal coil? Because I am shedding, my Lord, I am shedding, like a snake slips from its skin, and what I find underneath is none too pretty.

Marlon plugged wire into the pipe, fitting it snugly into the housing made of chewing gum, just like he might a real fuse, and wondered if he'll ever actually build another real bomb and trigger it for what its worth, light it up and watch it go boom. He allowed himself to appreciate his work, like a proud artist might their own painting or sculpture, and felt confident in his abilities, that if this were the real thing, packed with actual gunpowder, it would absolutely work. And then he began to curse himself inwardly for being so talented and so interested in something that could cause harm to so many. Why, God, did you make me so good at something so destructive, something so harmful? The crater of his left eye itched then and he reluctantly thought back to his fateful time in Ari-zo-nah at Fort Huachuca, where he'd learned to hone these destructive instincts and to manipulate firepower for use in war. Oh, he'd learned to fight, too, but just barely, having all but failed the required physical fitness tests, finishing at or near the bottom of every boot camp challenge, from running to climbing to jumping to, hell, even just crawling under a fence. Coordinated of body, he was not, so much so that he'd begun to wonder if he was even fit to *be* a soldier when his demonstrated interest in chemistry and explosives led a commanding officer to assign him to an artillery posting, a destiny he'd never truly thought possible for people that looked like he did and one that filled him with almost as much pride as his fear of God.

Marlon felt a tear fall from his right eye, the emotions of these memories almost too much for him to bear, the cruelty of it. He recalled how diligently he'd studied the mechanics of guns, mortars, howitzers, how determined he'd been to excel. He worked on his physical fitness, too, at the insistence of their CO, and had begun to craft a soldier's physique, becoming more and more ready to take part in battle and to equip weapons of war with enough ammunition to decimate the enemy. And it's that he got so very close to the front lines that it stung so harshly now, his warrior's pride having been reduced to merely an *almost* of something when a freak explosion took his left eye and sent him not to Italy with his brothers but to the base infirmary for weeks of recovery, robbing him of any chance he'd ever had at becoming a true Buffalo Soldier and fighting the good fight with the 92nd Fighting Infantry. He remembered how he'd screamed and cried and put up a fight, only to be assured he was in fact supporting the war with his sacrifice. He remembered how the white soldiers looked at him and laughed. It took more than a few surgeries to tie up his left eye socket and weeks of bed rest to tone down the shock and horror of what had happened to him. Plenty of time to concoct an elaborate, heroic story of how he lost an eye in the heat of battle. Marlon cooked up a righteous tale about just such a conflict in Naples and how he'd saved an entire platoon of men from a surprise ambush and lost an eye in the process. And then he came back to Richmond and negotiated a loan to buy back his family's old church from Consolidated Bank and Trust. And he wore his eyepatch and told his story to anyone who asked and kept his tragic truth to himself.

He didn't even tell his mother.

Footsteps outside the door, rumblings getting closer.

Marlon grimaced, he wasn't ready to be disturbed quite yet, but no matter, Charles and a man Marlon had never seen before came charging into the room, unannounced. Charles in a way this evening, revved up.

"Hey now, preacher. Not meaning to disturb you, but I gots someone here I think you oughta meet." Charles caught sight of what Marlon had been working on and stopped. "Uh, is that thing... live?"

Marlon held the pipe bomb up with two hands, still admiring it. "I'm thinking we go find those two cops that gave me such a time so many weeks ago. Tie 'em together like they's in a hug, maybe, put this between 'em and light it up. What do you say?"

Charles didn't know what to say. "I guess, if that's what you want..."

Marlon let the moment ride a few beats longer, teasing Charles just a little and enjoying it, before putting the pipe down onto his work table and taking a good pull of his firewater. "The righteous will rejoice when he sees the vengeance. He will bathe his feet in the blood of the wicked. Psalm 58."

Charles wasn't impressed. "There you go now, in your cups again, spouting off bible verse that only you and you alone can make sense of. Ain't nobody gonna argue with you about something they don't themselves understand."

"Then perhaps you should take up your bible more often and study it, educate yourself."

Charles looked around the room, disapproving. "Perhaps *you* oughta get outta this basement, see the sun once in awhile."

Charles had a point. It *was* into June now, and more and more over these last few weeks, when he wasn't preaching or tending to his flock at the hospital or their homes, Marlon had begun to retreat. Away from his church duties, away from Charles, away from Miss Ruby, even, the curious looks she gave him as they passed one another in the fellowship hall an uncomfortable mix of pity and disappointment.

Marlon went on. "Every man needs time to himself. Why, even 'Jesus Himself would slip away to the wilderness and pray.' Luke 5 — "

"*Enough*. Save it for Sunday 'cause I got someone here you just gotta listen to." Charles ushered his friend forward, front and center. "Marlon, this here is Marcus, Marcus Walker. He and I were locked up together, few years back, his sentence a bit longer than mine. He just now got out."

Marlon let Charles steer the moment and took a good look at his friend Marcus, who had the hangdog way about him, just as any man out of prison would have. He had a breadline figure, one that called for several helpings of Miss Garrison's chicken and greens, and he had deep-sunk eyes, too. They must have stared into the abyss of a prison cell for more hours than any man should ever have to endure. Marlon stood up and offered Marcus his hand.

"Pleased to meet you, Marcus. Name's Marlon, but most folk just call me Preacher."

Marcus took Marlon's hand with both of his and gave him a solid shake, the man eager to show himself of worthiness and pride, even as he glanced uneasily at Marlon's latest creation. "Charles has said many great things about you, preacher. Many great things, indeed."

"Has he now. I could say the same about him."

Charles dragged a few hardback chairs over from the corner and the three of them all took a seat, Charles in a way to get on with it. "Now, listen here, cousin, you're not gonna believe what Marcus has got to say. He *knows* this Walter MacKeye, I kid you not. Go on, tell him."

Marcus nodded. "Know him, worked with him, got a grudge against him, too. He's the one that put the cops onto me, got me sent up. Sold me out like I was nothing but cheap dirt, he did."

Marlon's interest perked. "Know where to find him?"

"Even if I did, I couldn't get close enough to do nothing, not with the boys he's gots around him now."

"How do you know?"

"'Cause I seen him, that's how. Just this morning, in fact, 'round an old confectionary we used to frequent, on account of its owner allowed us to imbibe on its premises and play craps out back. Couple of tough boys around him, too, like he's protected. Or paying for it. And then I realized, old Walter *can't* be up to nothing no good 'cause I seen him there with this fellow ain't never should have been let outta prison, no matter how well he might behave."

"Really, now. And just who is that?"

"Fella name of George Carroll, craziest sumbitch ever be locked up in the pen is who he is. Only place he's fit for is the booby hatch. Lock him up and throw away the key."

"Really now, that crazy?"

"Crazy enough to chew off one of his cellmates' ear. I know 'cause I watched him do it. Crazy enough to drink his own pee, least that's what they say. And crazy enough to recite lines from the bible like he wrote it himself. Line after line, entire passages even."

Charles gave Marlon a passing look. "You say he shouldn't be out at all, this Carroll?"

"Hells no. Only way Carroll be let out is if someone let him out on purpose. I know he ain't made no parole, not now, not ever."

Marlon weighed everything he'd just been told. "Let's put Walter aside for a moment. Why do you think this Carroll is out on the street?"

Marcus looked away, wrestling with his answer. "Well, I don't mean to be cursing in front of no preacher, but damn if it ain't gotta be that motherfuckin' super, that Visel. He must of let him out. Meanest goddamn man alive, Visel is. Man threw me in solitary just for picking up a breadcrumb."

Charles shook his head. "Damn."

Marcus went on. "There's more. You know that fella they be writing about in the paper, that Scangili? Well, that's old Carmine and let me tell you, he was just about as mean as the super. Never wasted a chance to whisper 'n______' in your ear or give you a smack when the other guards weren't lookin'. And, well, word around the cells was, he and Carroll..."

Marlon and Charles leaned in, rapt.

"They's were *friends*, if you can believe it. Now that don't line up, no matter where you come from. One man found all burnt up in a house, his crazy to the nines pal out on the street? Tell me that don't add up to a whole barn load of something that just ain't right."

Marlon had to admit, this really was some kind of news. "And your old pal Walter, where do you think he fits in?"

Marcus relaxed in his seat, more at ease now. "Walter's name got bounced around the cells quite a bit and the way I heard it, he and Visel are into something together. What, I don't know, but after what happened to your friend Cornell, well, I'm sure it can't be good."

Marlon sat back in his seat, let it all sink in. Charles looked his way and said, "You heard what he said, preacher. We don't get on top of this, we're gonna get stomped on like a beaten mule."

Marlon said, "Like we ain't already? Cornell ain't been in the ground a month, you think I forgot? And for what? All for some stupid play at Jedidiah's numbers business, which never worked out anyhow." What a foolish idea that had been. All Marlon had wanted to do was bring in more money for the church and just look where it had gotten them.

Charles stood up, he really was in quite a way tonight. "We can't do nothing about that now, God rest poor Cornell. But just think about it. In this town, somebody always finds a way to steer things our way, point the finger *at us*. Now I know we shuttered up that numbers business, but we already lost one brother from all this. If we don't say something and fast, it's just gonna be more of the same, more trouble for our kind and what we'd even do? Try and make a little money, is all. We don't do something and soon, it's gonna be a whole lot worse."

Marlon listened. "And just what do you have in mind, cousin? Say something to who?"

Charles took a deep breath and Marlon just knew it was preface to an idea he wouldn't care for.

"Call that policeman, the one that came to see you. The one they talk about in the papers."

Marlon had to laugh. "Sherwood? Are you out of your mind? I mean, after what I — " Marlon caught himself before saying more, his eyes darting from Charles to Marcus and back again, his cousin holding a look on him now that said *good catch*. Because there were only four other people in this world, that Marlon knew of, who knew that he'd lit up that East End house with a bottle bomb so many weeks ago, the one with that Scangili in it. Charles, Jedidiah, Jedidiah's lovely friend Constance, and Miss Ruby. And there was no reason to make it five. "I mean, after what I'd been through in the street that day, with that boy throwing rocks. You really think I oughta drag the police back into it?"

Marlon knew it was a weak dodge and clocked a miffed look on Marcus' face. Charles caught the gist and helped carry the moment. "All you gotta do is bend his ear a little. Say you heard this and you heard that and you thought it might help, is all. Don't you want to steer the cops away from us any way you can?"

Marlon still wasn't sure. "What if he presses? Wants a sit down?"

Charles harrumphed. "Man, there you go, all worrying again. Look, you convince almost everyone on Sunday to feel better about the lives we're living, even though we're cussed at and spit on and can't get no goddamn jobs worth a damn. You saying you can do all that and not turn that charm onto some policeman? Come on, cousin, have more faith in yourself. Isn't that what you preach every week?"

Marcus nodded. "I hear stories 'bout you, preacher. I know you got it in you."

Marlon sat back in his chair and knew they were right. It didn't sit well with him to call a policeman, it never had, but Charles was right, they needed this. "I'll call him tomorrow."

Charles gave him a hard look. "Yes, well, best see that you do, or we're gonna have us our very own war right here at home."

It was late, near midnight, when Marlon finally got up the nerve to knock on Miss Ruby's door, fueled as he was with more than a few sips of firewater. Liquid courage, they say, and Marlon needed all the help he could get. He knew this was a terrible idea, but he saw her light on and figured she was up. He rapped on her door and stood up straight, his apology all prepared. But he was stunned when Christian Matthews, Cornell's nephew, opened the door, naked from the waist up, a hammer in his hand.

"Hey now, preacher. What brings you here at this hour?"

It was clear in his voice that Christian didn't see this as an inappropriate visit and Marlon could hardly find the words, scrambling for an answer. "Christian, my brother, how nice to see you. I just need to speak with Miss Ruby about music for this Sunday and felt a visit was more appropriate than a phone call. But if I'm interrupting — "

"No, no, not at all, church business is life business. Hold on." He turned and hollered Ruby's name into the house and in a moment she was right there, as stunned to see Marlon as he was to see her wrapped in the rose colored robe he bought her.

"Why, Preacher Marlon. What a surprise."

Christian could see he wasn't needed. "I'll let you two talk. Preacher, good to see you, as always."

"And you, Christian. Be well."

Ruby stepped out onto the porch and gave Marlon a glare. "Well?"

Marlon felt like the biggest idiot alive. "I had no idea you had… moved on so soon."

Ruby folded her arms across her chest. "Moved on from what? I don't remember you asking me to keep this exclusive. And where you been, anyhow?" She brought her voice down. "All those naughty things we used to do and here you ain't hardly spoke to me in almost two weeks. Then you just show up at my door, late at night. What do you think I am, some kind of house cat? Pet me and feed me when you feel like it, ignore me when you don't?"

"Ruby, I… I just been dealing with some things. Lots on my mind these days, I didn't mean to push you away."

"Push me away? You don't control me. I see who I want when I want. And I wanted to be seeing you, but, you're you. So you go on now and deal with your things, Marlon, and when you're ready to see me again, don't come knocking on my door late at night like I'm some kinda hootchie mama. I want a courting for real or this ain't no thing at all, you hear me?"

Marlon could hardly meet her eyes, looking away and back again as he nodded. "I do."

Ruby lowered her voice some more. "And just so you know, Christian is in here helping fix my steps, is all. Only time he can do it, on account of that white family he works for. And that's it, nothing more."

Marlon knew he shouldn't say anything else. "But you got your robe on, I mean…"

"And what about it? He's helping me upstairs and it's *hot* up there, so I wear what I want. And who's to say I don't want to be noticed, huh? Now go on home and get yourself right. And don't you have no more of that godawful shine Garrison makes, it's all over your breath. I mean, really. What'd you think was gonna happen, you come over here like this? I mean, damn."

She waved him off and turned away and just like that, she was back in the house with the door shut. Marlon floated on cloud nine as he walked back home. He still had a chance.

21

Shane strolled up the stairs of the Annex and looked in at Sherwood's unoccupied desk. Odd — the boss was always in early. Shane checked a wall clock to be sure, ten minutes to morning roll call. No way, Sherwood was never this late. He made his way to the main desks of the Annex and called out to no one in particular. "Has anyone seen the boss?"

A few of the morning tecs looked his way and shrugged 'no' as they continued to go on about their paperwork. A patrolman walked by and muttered "Haven't seen him" as Shane looked around the room for a helpful face and found not a one, no one in the room seeming even remotely concerned that their Acting Lieu, always early and expecting the same of everyone else, was nowhere to be seen.

Shane hit the Victory Squad office next and, surprisingly, found Eddie Haden there already, catching zzz's on top of a few desks he'd strung together into a makeshift cot. The morning really was upside down because Eddie was never early. Hell, if he showed at roll call or briefings at all, he was usually late, the man's many years on the force apparently enough to write his own ticket on coming and going. Shane wondered if that was the way it was for any cop, that no matter what path you carved for yourself, it was predetermined that you bottleneck into a jaded mess. He watched Eddie's chest rise and fall, the man in quite the peaceful slumber, it looked like. Shane hoped he deserved it, with his whiskey-soaked odor and his necktie in a mess about his shoulders and his hat over his face. He considered just leaving him there and inviting the other cops to come and watch, make a spectacle of it. Maybe they'd clip his tie in half, draw dirty pictures on this face. Teach him not to snooze in the office.

Shane heard the bell ring out in the squad room, roll call was starting. There was work to be done, so Shane dropped his steno forcefully on a desk. A sharp smack echoed about the room and Shane delighted in Eddie's abrupt awakening, the elder cop muttering something about 'Martha' as he sat up in a daze, looking around and almost missing his hat as it fell from his face, catching it at the last minute. Shane got a good look at the bruise around Eddie's right eye then and saw that Eddie was none too pleased to find himself being stared at.

"'The fuck are you looking at?"

"Not sure I really know. Who gave you the shiner?"

"None of your fucking business. Where's the Lieu?"

Shane shook his head. "Who's Martha?"

Eddie blanched. "The fuck did you just say?"

Someone cleared their throat. Shane and Eddie turned to find Annie from the switchboard standing there in the doorway, watching them with a disapproving look. Shaking her head with a hand on her hip. All these years at the Annex and she still didn't understand why cops had to speak the way they did. "Pardon me, *gentlemen*, but I have a few messages and there's a call waiting, every bit of it urgent."

Shane put on a warm smile. "Tell us all, sweet Annie."

"Well, I've fielded several concerned phone calls this morning from both Ms. McKenna," Annie read from her notes, "and a Judy Strathmore. She goes with one of our rookies, Jimmy Knight. His parents called, too. They all said that neither Bennie nor Jimmy made it home last night."

Shane and Eddie shared a concerned look, Eddie more puzzled than troubled. "Who the hell is Jimmy Knight?"

"A rookie," Shane said. "Helped us out the night we found Mrs. Kleinfeld."

Eddie nodded, remembering now. "What about this urgent call?"

Annie checked her notes again. "Someone on the phone wants to speak with Bennie, but won't give his name. Says he has pressing news about one James Visel, superintendent of the penitentiary, and we need to hear it now."

Eddie tossed his tie, hat, and jacket on the desk and began to roll up his sleeves. Shane impressed, the man suddenly a cop again. Eddie looked at Annie and said, "We'll take the call in here, An. Meanwhile, radio out to every unit on the street and separately to each station, let them know we've got two blues MIA, but don't let on about the Lieu. Tell 'em to keep it quiet, too, no press leaks. If anyone knows anything, have 'em get it to us on the double."

"Yes, sir," Annie said, herself impressed as she hurried back to the switchboard. Eddie pulled the phone over to his desk. Shane dragged a seat over as Eddie clicked on the speaker attached to the phone, the both of them rapt with attention as the call came through.

Eddie spoke first. "This is Detective Haden, with vice. I understand you have some information you'd like to share with the police?

A pause, crackles through the phone. Then, a deep voice. Distorted, as if being spoken though some kind of thick cloth. "I was hoping to speak with Mr. Sherwood."

Shane leaned toward the speaker. "Sir, this is Detective MacDonald, robbery. Our Lieutenant isn't here right now, but we're very interested in what you have to say. You can tell us and we'll get the information to him just as soon as we can. Now, if we've heard right, you have some information about the penitentiary superintendent, Mr. James Visel?"

Another pause, more crackles on the line, their mystery man really taking his time. Finally: "Yes, yes I do. I... I think Mr. Visel and a man named Walter MacKeye are working together."

Eddie almost couldn't believe the timing. He saw those men in the room again, crammed together like sardines. He saw Walter and Visel laugh in his face. "Is that so. And just how do you know this, sir?"

"'Because I've seen MacKeye and another man together. This other man ought to be in prison, that's what I know, not out in the streets."

Shane flipped open his steno, ready for more. "So you saw Walter MacKeye with another man, *not* Mr. Visel. Okay, then.

Where?"

Another pause on the line, their mystery man forming his answer. "A confectionary, out in the East End."

Shane jotted notes as Eddie asked, "Which confectionary, exactly?"

"The one off 30th street. They roll dice games there, in the back."

Eddie's vice antennae pinged: it's true, he knew that spot. He nodded at Shane, confirming it, and went on. "And this other man, the one you saw with Walter MacKeye. Who exactly is he?"

Tension on the line, palpable, the mystery voice even more muffled now. "I believe… I believe the man's name is George Carroll. Man's crazy, ought to still be in the prison."

Shane nearly said 'You're goddamn right' after what he learned about Carroll and their rooftop rendezvous. Shane prayed they could track him down before he caused anymore harm.

Eddie took up again. "When did this happen, sir? When did you see the two of them together?"

Another pause. No answer.

Shane said, "Sir?"

"That's… that's all I have to say. Praise be to God."

Click and the line went dead.

Eddie stood up and kicked a chair onto its side. "The fuck was that?"

Shane jotted notes. "It's something and we should be grateful."

Eddie steamed. "But it wasn't even about Visel, was it?"

Shane wasn't sure either. "Look, as soon as we track down Jimmy and the Lieu, we'll get to this confectionary. We'll print, we'll canvas, we'll get *something*. Come on, even a veteran cop like you can still appreciate an anonymous tip." Shane caught Eddie's look and thought maybe he'd said too much. Eddie's eyes swirled with a dangerous cocktail of desperation and exhaustion, something Shane didn't see earlier. And if Shane didn't know any better, he'd of said that Eddie was after something more than just solving their case. But a commotion out in the main squad room stole their attention and there was nothing more to say on it, at least not right now, the both of them darting from the V Squad office and joining the rest of the day squad to find Bennie and Jimmy Knight limping up the main staircase of the Annex, the two of them like parched souls who'd just come in from a wandering in the desert. Shane ran up to Bennie, helping him up the stairs.

"Holy shit, boss, what happened to you two?"

Bennie leaned against the top bannister for support and looked over at Jimmy Knight, poor Jimmy Knight. For a rookie whose first big assignment had been a real and total shitshow, Jimmy had really shown his true colors, his toughness. *Christ, the kid could even make it as a Marine*, Bennie thought, looking out across the room, hearing the gasps, seeing the widened looks, everyone wondering just what the hell had happened to the two of them.

Bennie addressed his team, best he could. He voice dry and cracked, his energy on reserves. "I'm sure all of you have questions, questions that I will answer in due time. But right now, it is imperative that we mobilize as a team and get to Spring Street, to the state penitentiary. I need the cars gassed. I need everyone charged with a firearm to have one. I promise, you'll understand soon enough. We meet out front in ten minutes. Everyone move, now!"

The room came alive, everyone doing their part, and Bennie wasn't sure he'd ever seen the Annex in such beautiful, harmonious sync. Shane and Eddie were on him like loyal dogs, on his heels as he made for the switchboard. "Shane, Eddie, listen, I'll fill you both in on the way. One of you, grab a sled and meet me out front, we'll ride together." Shane and Eddie paired off as Bennie made the switchboard call room and stuck his head inside.

"Oh, my gosh, sir!" Annie exclaimed. "You're alright!"

Bennie nodded. "Yes, thank you, Annie. Look, would you please call Imogene, tell her just that and that I'll call her tonight, just as soon as this is all over."

Jimmy came up right behind him. "Sir? If it's not too much trouble, my parents, too, and Judy."

Annie nodded, truly relieved. "I'll do it right now, of course."

"Yes, Annie, please, tell them all is well. And call Archie Smith at the Herald. Have him and a news photog meet us at the prison on the double. I'm gonna stuff their entitled stories down their goddamn throats."

Annie, aghast. "Really, sir, such language!"

Bennie grabbed Jimmy Knight and pulled him along, the both of them running on scant fumes. "Come on, kid. Let's see this to the end."

Call it a symphony of noise.

Sirens and red lights and shouts at their parade from the sidewalks, everyone wanting the police to come when called but no one wanting the inconvenience that came from them butting into traffic or stalling a crosswalk. Buildings streamed past along the way, Bennie in the throes of a memory haze. The last seven, eight hours came back to him in a nightmarish blur. He fed Shane and Eddie bits of it, Jimmy confirming with nods, and told of how they listened to the snores of those men, the both of them too frozen to move. They'd stayed like that in the barn for almost an hour, it seemed, until Bennie risked more and more movement. Sliding out from under their cover, crouching, eventually standing all the way up. Jimmy followed suit, creeping out from behind the flag, and then they were right back where they started, still locked inside the barn.

Eddie threaded Broad Street traffic at top speed, a caravan of police vehicles behind them. "How the hell did you get out of there?"

Bennie looked back at Jimmy, sitting behind Eddie, and they both shook their heads. They still couldn't believe it.

Jimmy said, "We crawled out."

Bennie nodded as Shane and Eddie shared an incredulous look, Bennie keeping his eyes straight ahead. They were on Belvidere now, heading south, and all he could see were his hands wrapped around Thomas Müller's throat, the one they called Ghostman. "I found a loose floorboard," Bennie said, "and then another. Eventually, we pulled up three and crawled into the space between the floor and the ground. We pulled the boards back over us and waited."

Shane spoke from the back seat. "For what?"

Bennie didn't exactly know what to say. "For a sign, maybe, for us to make a go of it. We didn't want to wake whoever was snoring and we didn't know what it would take to get out from under there. I mean, how long did we wait, Jimmy?"

"Twenty minutes." Jimmy spoke with conviction, as if he had counted every second.

Eddie hit more traffic and blared the horn. "Police coming through, you jackasses! Move!"

Bennie went on, telling the story as if he still couldn't believe it himself. "I had my duffel with me and my father's old shotgun. I started poking at the boards along the outside perimeter of the barn, looking for more luck, another loose board. It took a minute, but we found one, and started easing it from the frame, best we could. Must have been a half dozen nails holding that thing in, right, Jimmy?"

Jimmy just nodded from the back seat, his face getting whiter by the minute.

Eddie looked over at Bennie, rapt. "Yeah? And then what?"

"And then one of them woke up."

Shane, from the back seat. "One of who?"

One of whoever was sleeping up in that loft, Bennie went on to say. "Whoever it was, we'd awoken them, apparently, with all our noise." All Bennie and Jimmy could do then was not breathe and just listen as whoever it was started to shift about the barn, lifting things, moving things, looking for whatever had caused the noise. And then, with the both of them lying there under the barn, Bennie remembered Jimmy praying to God at that very moment. Bennie hadn't invoked the Lord's name in even so much as a whisper since his mother left his father and him so many years ago, their family-going-to-church-on-Sundays very much a thing of the past. He hadn't even called upon the Lord to save him from the swampy shadows of Guadalcanal, not a once. Bennie looked back at Jimmy, the poor kid almost green now, the both of them remembering what came next, how awful it had been.

Eddie cut onto Spring Street, they were almost to the prison. "What do you want to do, boss? We're almost there."

Bennie was appreciative of how cool Eddie was behind the wheel, his many years on the force sometimes a real plus to his service. He looked up ahead, the prison in full view. He knew Thomas Müller would be there. He knew this because he and Jimmy had tailed him there not an hour ago.

"Just pull up and kill the siren. I'll tell you the rest later."

Twenty minutes later, Bennie stood on the front steps of the penitentiary with a handcuffed Thomas Müller by his side, the one they called Ghostman. Bennie had a tight grip on his arm and was standing tall for the Herald's shutterbug, who was snapping photos of them from a low angle down on the sidewalk. It was a photo op to end all photo ops. No more vilification in the editorials, no more Stolmy breathing down his neck and threatening his job. Bennie looked out over his men and caught mixed reactions. Shock, awe, pride. Eddie looked tenser than usual while Shane looked damn well excited, ready to hear the rest of Bennie's story and get in on Müller's interrogation. Someone yelled "You'll never get away with this!" like they were all part of some predictable Saturday afternoon movie matinee and Bennie turned around to find Visel yelling from the prison's entrance, the man red hot, like a volcano about to blow.

Bennie turned back to address the crowd of fellow cops, newspaper reporters, and Oregon Hill rubberneckers, his voice at full volume. "After weeks of stalled-out leads and dead ends in our homicide investigations, I'm announcing today that the Richmond Police Department is arresting Thomas Müller on charges of sedition, aiding a foreign influence on US soil," Bennie turned to look at Ghostman for this last bit, "and murder." Gasps circled the crowd, the reporters edged in for questions, but Bennie just pulled Müller down the steps and motioned for Shane to get their wheels ready. Müller leaned in to Bennie with a devilish gloat in his eyes. "You don't have shit on me, copper. This'll never stick." Bennie shoved a reporter and got in next to Müller's ear. "Is that right? Maybe I'll just take my chances, *Ghostman*, and see if you fly away to heaven like a little bird." Müller glared at him then with a true look of disbelief, kept looking at him with that same shock in his eyes even as Bennie pushed his head down, saying "Watch it now" with a smile as he shoved Müller into the backseat of the cruiser. Bennie shut the door on him with delight, the questions from reporters coming at him in droves.

"Did Müller kill Carmine Scangili?"

"Did Müller kill Ruth Kleinfeld?"

"Has Müller abused any prisoners?"

Bennie silenced the crowd with a wave of his hand and said, "We'll have answers later tonight, folks. Meet me on the steps on the Annex then and I'll tell all."

Bennie slapped the top of the cruiser and slid inside and they were off, the throng of reporters just standing there like an unsatisfied mob, watching them go.

Knox still couldn't believe how easy he had it as a cabbie. Hell, anything's easier than doing time, but still. Stress-free work. Decent tips. A boss that stayed out of your hair. And perhaps best of all, a front-row seat to the complexities and varieties of human nature he wouldn't find anywhere else. There was just something about getting into a cab that let folks peel off their skin a bit, speak their mind a little more honestly. It was almost as if the back seat became like a confessional every time Knox took on a new fare, as if he were some kind of priest. There were the usual lies and betrayals, of course. Men spoke of cheating on their wives and wives spoke of cheating on their husbands. Lawyers talked of swindling their clients and salesmen bragged about the cons they were pulling off. Vacuum salesmen, bible salesmen, insurance salesmen. It didn't matter, they were all the same. Life's petty arguments came out, as well. Men argued about who would pick up the fare and women argued about where they should go to lunch. Parents berated their children and kids ignored their parents. Things always got a little more sordid on the weekends, the emotions running a little hotter, the stakes a little higher. Soldiers boasted about their sexual conquests while the broken hearted rode solo and cried between pick-up and drop-off, thinking it was the only time no one was watching. And all along, Knox heard all about love and heartbreak, politics and money, what to do with your life and what not to. And when it was all said and done, he still believed what he'd always believed, what his father had taught him — that a working stiff life is for suckers and that you should go big or not at all, in love and money, because with one you can live forever and with the other you can live for now, and who doesn't want to do both?

Knox dropped off a fare and checked his gas gauge, found it running low. He switched on his 'off-duty' light and steered his wheels toward the Confederate Cab lot to refuel. Time to recharge, stretch his legs. Along the way, he saw a parade of police cruisers, their sirens at full volume. *Sure hope they're not after me*, he thought. Half-joking, half-not.

Ten minutes later, he pulled the jalopy into one of Confederate's bays and saw Imogene working a heap in another lane. He motioned for one of the lot rats to gas up the sled, made notes in his fare book, and looked longingly once more at the folded newspaper he'd kept in the passenger seat since yesterday, the one with the photo of Constance and the other woman dancing at Tantilla Garden. According to the caption, the other woman was a socialite, a woman named Timony 'Thursday' Wells, and Knox marveled at the way they looked so in sync in the photograph, at the way the gawkers and onlookers at Tantilla stared at them that night. The picture was from a few nights back and Knox had admired it several times a day since a fare absently left the paper in the back seat. Knox remembered watching them disappear into the Garden that night and guessed the photo had been taken then. Every time he looked at the picture, Knox could hardly contain his own excitement, seeing Constance with such joy on her face. He grabbed the paper and his fare book as he left the cab and made his way toward Imogene, forcing himself to remember what he'd told everyone. When you're here, your name is Smith, Hank Smith.

Slam!

Knox watched as Taft shut his office door in a fit and made like a fox on his way out, in a hurry to be somewhere and get there fast.

"He's been like that all morning," Imogene said, not even looking up from the engine she was working on.

"What's got his goat in such a fuss?"

"Damned if I know. The phone rang, he answered, and now, just like that, he's out the door. For what, I don't know." She looked up at him now, smudges of grease on her face. "What are you doing back, Hank? I swear, your shift just started."

"Had a couple of long fares, needed to refuel. What're you working on?"

Imogene looked up with a grand smile on her face, her hand still turning a wrench. "Oh, just inspecting the gas line, the oil line, the brakes. Whatever it takes to keep 'em running."

Knox was still so impressed. A broad that loved to work on cars? Where was she when he and the old man were running moonshine? "You certainly seem like you get a kick out of it."

Imogene came up for air and started to readjust her bandana, some of her auburn locks had come loose. "Do you have something against a woman working in a garage, Hank?"

"Quite the opposite. I'm thrilled anytime I find a woman interested in something I do. What else do you like?"

Imogene stood tall and tried not to laugh. "I like big breakfasts, I like movies that make me laugh. I like polite people, friendly people. And even though you're cute, Hank, I like a man who knows his place."

Knox put his hands up. "Just making conversation."

Imogene shot him a knowing look. "Sure you were." And then, suddenly, she grabbed at her stomach and bellied over.

Knox tossed the newspaper and fare book on a stool and stepped in to catch her. "Hey now, you feeling alright?"

Imogene rested against the cab and put up a hand, letting him know she was. She took a few breaths, collected herself, and kept her voice low. "Can you keep a secret, Hank?"

Can I ever, Knox thought. I'm getting by on an assumed name, I'm in hiding from one of the most dangerous criminals in town, and I'm stalking an ex-girlfriend in my off-hours. He nodded.

"I'm on the nest," she said.

Knox couldn't tell if she was happy or sad about it. "Congratulations?"

"Oh, don't worry, it's a joyous thing, through and through. I mean, I just found out myself, so I'm still getting used to the idea.

Thing is, my beau doesn't know yet. He's so caught up in his work right now that I haven't been able to tell him."

"He's a policeman, right?"

"Is he ever. I mean, he didn't even come home last night."

"Is he… alright?"

"He is now, apparently. But I don't even get to hear it from him, I have to hear it from the switchboard girl. I'm planning to tell him tonight." Imogene took one more deep breath and stood up. Her eyes grew two sizes when she saw Knox's newspaper. She pointed at the photo of Constance and Timony. "Say! I know them!"

Knox almost froze. "You do?"

Imogene grabbed the paper, beaming. "Yeah! I mean, I was even there that night, but I got there after they did their little show for everyone. Oh, wow, don't they look great?"

Knox nodded. *You all look great*, he thought, keeping it to himself. "How do you all know each other?"

"Well." Imogene pointed at Timony, excited to tell the story. "This is Timony Wells. She writes the Herald's society column. I met her doing volunteer work for the war. Scrap drives, rubber drives, knitting circles, all that kind of thing. She throws these absolutely unforgettable parties and is just a delight to be around. And she knows Jedidiah King, too. You know, the cigarette guy?"

Knox nodded.

Imogene went on, pointing at Constance now. "And *this* is Constance Lee. She *works* for Jedidiah and well, we do everything together. We lunch, we laugh, we cry together. The three of us, we even go out together, too, you know, get into a little trouble. The both of 'em, they make the sour times sweet and the good times even better. In fact, I'm supposed to see her," pointing at Constance again, "at the John Marshall Hotel later tonight."

"Really."

Imogene sensed there was more to his answer. "Is there something about this photo you're not telling me, Hank?"

Knox tried to play it off. "Oh, no, someone just left it in the cab, is all."

Imogene just looked at him. "Hank."

Knox balked as chills ran up his spine. "Okay. The girl you're meeting? She looks like someone I used to know. I saw the picture and it brought back some old memories."

"Then come meet us out! Come on, Constance isn't seeing anyone and let's face it, you are kinda cute, in a rough and tumble sort of way. You've got nothing to lose, come on, what do you say?"

Knox knew he would never have a better chance of seeing Constance. He could finally brace her, come clean. A fresh start. "Sure. What time?"

"7PM sharp, the John Marshall Hotel, don't be late!"

The coupe glass left Timony's hand and sailed through the dining room, missing Harrison's head by mere inches until it connected with the east wall and shattered, the shards like confetti now, all over the floor.

"Who is she?" Timony yelled. "I want to know!"

Harrison cowered and backed away as Timony grabbed another glass from their bar and let it fly, this one very nearly taking out one of his eyes before he ducked and crashed into their China cabinet. Precious family heirlooms fell about the shelves and broke into pieces. More glass fragments hit the floor.

Harrison pleaded. "Timony, please! I can explain!"

"You haven't been to bed with me in weeks. If you're not out with your cronies, you're distant, you avoid me. And even when you're home, it's like you're not even here!" Timony grabbed another glass and smashed it against the bar. Harrison flinched, backing away now as Timony walked toward him, the broken stem in her hand like a lethal weapon.

Timony fought tears, forcing strength into her voice as she stared him down. "I gave you a life, I gave you status. I gave you my heart, my soul, my body. We have a child together, we share a home. And then I come to find out you're parading around with some tramp at Tantilla, in full view of the entire city, doing who knows what! You tell me her name, Harrison, so I can smear her in the columns. And then you pray to God I don't sever an artery because I don't want your tainted, cheating blood all over our floor!"

Harrison held his hands up, pleading like cornered prey as he fell into the wall, sliding to the floor. "Timony, please, I promise you, I'll tell you everything. I just have to do this one thing and then I'll tell you, I promise! Please believe me, it's not what you think! These people, they… oh God, Timony, please believe me!"

Harrison was so vulnerable now, so weak, that Timony didn't know if she could stop herself. It was unexpected, the way she felt, the power over him irresistible, it was like a drug. Her eyes narrowed, her breathing like a wild, rabid animal. "You tell me her name, Harrison, or you leave now and never come back."

Harrison started to cry. "Timony, please. If you only knew what I have to do!"

"I'll change the locks, I'll close your accounts. I'll have someone take the car, just you watch. You'll have nothing. Is that what you want? Is it?"

This, now, this cut him deep — he'd have no status at all. Timony could see it in his eyes, a real sense of hurt.

"Timony, for god sakes, I promise you — "

"Just tell me her fucking name!"

Harrison recoiled and then something registered inside him, as if he could see that she'd gone as far as she was truly going to go, that she was not going to cut him after all. And it's true, she didn't have it in her, no matter how upset she was. She watched as he leaned back into the wall and forced himself up in an awkward kind of shimmy, notching himself up with his shoulders, his eyes never leaving hers, standing before her now with a hard look.

"No."

"You motherfucker," she said.

Harrison brushed himself off, as if he'd been merely play fighting and rolled around in the dirt some, stepping past her now, still careful to avoid her right hand, his eyes on the jagged stem. "And when this is all over, Timony, and I've told you what I had to do, you'll be the one apologizing to me."

"Oh, you arrogant son of a bitch!"

Timony let the broken coupe fly and it isn't even close, Harrison just turning to stare at her as he left the room, a smug look on his face that said he knew she wouldn't do it, not in a million years. And then just like that, he was gone.

Timony let out a scream louder than anything she ever thought herself capable of before falling to her knees, her tears like a broken waterfall, coming in rushes behind the heaves of her chest. She cried and coughed and crumpled to the floor in a ball. And she lay there for a time, there on the floor of her dining room where she'd been eating most of her meals alone and had taken to having imaginary conversations with her son over a bottle of wine, sometimes two. She thought perhaps that Macy would come and comfort her then, but then she remembered that she'd given her the night off. And then she was grateful that Macy hadn't been there to witness their horrible fight, how embarrassing that would have been. And when she had no more tears to cry, she picked herself up off the floor, fixed herself a martini, and went out onto the veranda to watch the sunset.

Knox parked just west of Fifth and Franklin, facing east. He had a good view of the entrance to the John Marshall Hotel, could see folks coming and going. The sun was about to set and there wasn't much light, so he was hidden, somewhat. Out of view.

He watched.

He watched the traffic stream past, he watched the sun fade from the sky, the clouds shadowed with bursts of reddish grey. He watched people cross the street. Men in their business suits, women in their evening dresses. He watched as they disappeared into the hotel and, surprising himself, hoped they had a pleasant evening. His attitude hopeful, for once, optimistic even, like everything might finally be alright.

Shouts from across the street stole his attention — a newsboy hawked the early edition. Knox caught his pitch through an open window.

"Extra, Extra, Read All About It! Prison Guard Suspected Of Murder!"

Pinpricks ran haywire all over his skin. Could that mean they finally nabbed Visel and Ghostman? If so, send 'em to the gas chamber, boys, and cook 'em with all you've got. They deserve nothing less than a gasoline-soaked fry.

A car drove past, parked east of Fifth. Two women got out and Knox's heart stopped. There she was again, Constance Lee, in all of her lovely glory, getting out of the car and running across the street, hand in hand with Imogene. The two of them like giddy schoolgirls on their way to the malt shop, whispering to each other and then walking tall, flaunting their feminine appeal. Men catcalled to them as they drove by.

Deep breaths now. Go all the way, Knox's father had always said, so here he went, steeling himself, priming himself for the big moment. He wasn't ready, not in the least, but this was it, his big chance, years in the making. He'd been rehearsing for it all day and all he could hope for was that she would just listen, hear him out, and with any luck, maybe he could keep Imogene from spilling his tale to her cop boyfriend. *What a world,* he thought. Imogene and the Sherwood kid, just my luck.

Knox started to step from the cab when something caught his eye. Something familiar, that Plymouth, Garfield Green in color, *wait —*

He knew this car because he had seen it driven before.

Goddamn.

There, on the other side of Franklin, someone *else* watching the girls —

Knox's eyes pierced the encroaching nightfall and saw *him* standing just inside a doorway across the way. Walter MacKeye, smoking and staring across the street, watching the girls with a predator's gaze. A moment passed. Maybe two, maybe more, Knox lost count. He felt about his jacket pocket to be sure, but there it was, his snick knife, at the ready. Was *he* ready? Honestly, he didn't know, but he was willing to do anything to keep Constance safe. Knox watched Walter toss the butt of his cigarette and slip into the Plymouth. Knox just knew now, he wasn't going to see Constance after all. No, he was going to tail Walter and follow him wherever he went and then put the snick knife to his throat and force a tell-all. He fired up the cab again, ready for the hunt but tired. This meant more time in the seat, more aches up his back. A long day getting longer as Walter's Plymouth pulled away and started east, Knox doing the same, settling in two car lengths back, shooting a look at the John Marshall as he drove through the intersection, the girls nowhere in sight now. His big chance, gone, blown. And right then, even as Knox knew he was making the wrong choice, he hoped he was doing it for the right reason.

They kept Müller in an Annex holding cell for much of the day, priming him for interrogation. They fed him overcooked food and lukewarm water. Bennie watched from a distance, like he might study an animal at the zoo. Müller didn't budge, not once, he just sat there like a predator in wait.

After dinnertime, they moved him to an interrogation room down in the basement. Bennie chose to put him in number two, his father's favorite, on account of its harsher lighting on the hot seat. He elected to follow the procession, not lead it, and watched as they cuffed Müller and walked him downstairs. Bennie stayed a few paces behind, plotting his approach, and fell in with Jimmy Knight. They shared a most uncomfortable look, the both of them remembering the last several hours.

How could they forget.

Bennie cringed and thought of the moments that unfolded as the both of them laid there under the barn. They prayed and sweated and wondered if they would live through the night when the man above them, the man who had woken up, whoever he was, he knelt down just over them and began to pray. His voice was low enough to the floorboards that Bennie and Jimmy could hear every word, listening as the man begged for someone to come and save him, take him from the awful conditions in which he was being subjected. He called on Ghostman by name to stop treating 'them' the way he did. Beating them, berating them, withholding food and water from them. And all Bennie and Jimmy could do was listen to this man pray, this man who was clearly in a horrible situation, and then continue to listen as others from the loft awoke and descended into the barn's main area, the lot of them woken by this man's act of prayer, themselves both angry and afraid. "What are you doing?" they said to him, "How could you be so foolish?" they said. Their voices hushed and full of fear.

"You'll wake him."

And with that, it was as if they called out to the main house on purpose, signaling to it like a beacon. The sound of others approaching grew nearer and nearer to the barn.

Snap, clang —

The barn doors unlocked again.

Three, maybe four men stepped inside, judging by the footsteps. Müller barked like a rabid dog. "You rotten shits, you're in for it now!"

Bennie and Jimmy listened to Müller and his men work the others over with a beating so brutal it threatened to upstage even the worst of Bennie's clashes in the jungle. Ribs cracked, organs were damaged. The poor men above them, whoever they were, they wailed, they cried, they fell to the floor, begging for mercy. And the one man above them, the first man they'd heard, he must have been turned over onto his back because suddenly he was pleading for his life. And Bennie was sick to his stomach, because he was a cop and he was supposed to be putting a stop to moments like these, this is what he did. Jimmy, too, but all either of them could do was listen as Ghostman leaned above this man and said, "Well, all you can hope for now, you little *scheisser*, is that you fly away to heaven like a little bird." And then *wham*, one wallop followed another, again and again and again, as Müller brought something heavy down onto the man. Inside of a minute, the man above them was no longer whimpering. He wasn't making any sounds at all.

Bennie and Jimmy froze. They felt blood seep through the floorboards and fall onto their shoulders, their hair, their faces. They were wholly immobilized with shock. Above them, Müller ordered the others to return to their beds and stay there, or else, and then he and the men with him left the barn and locked it behind them. They just left the body there, the others inside left to ascend the loft ladder and cry themselves to sleep. Bennie and Jimmy knew this because they listened to the cries of these men, the whispered prayers and the terrified mutterings. And it was perhaps an hour later, Bennie really didn't know, time had ceased to have any real meaning, when he and Jimmy finally felt bold enough to try the side board again, knocking on it gently with the butt of the shotgun and freeing it from the base of the barn. Every breath, every movement, every inching of their bodies out of that crawl space was an act of calculated determination. Hell, it must have taken them twenty minutes to leave that small, unforgivable clearance and crawl all of as many feet, creeping along the ground beside the barn and making their way to the throng of trees from whence they first came. Their first act was to wipe their faces and hair clean of blood, neither of them saying a word as they brushed it away and wiped their hands on the ground. Both of them embarrassed about it, processing it, trying to make sense of such horror. The both of them trying not to cry. Ten minutes must have passed as each man gathered himself before Bennie nodded to Jimmy, their interaction now entirely non-verbal, and motioned that they should crawl back to their sled. Thankfully, they found it undisturbed and pushed it almost all the way back to Broad Street, the both of them running on nothing but adrenaline fumes. The car started just as the sun came up. They decided they should wait, lurk, and watch to see who left the barn and when. They parked in a nestle of brush and waited until a car came down the road from the barn and followed it all the way to the state penitentiary, watching as Müller strolled into work like it was just another day for him.

And now here it was some six, seven hours later and they arrived at interrogation room number two, watching through peekaboo glass as Müller sat in the hot spot, a harsh light shining right into his face. A host of interested parties stood in the wings, waiting for the party to start. Stolmy leaned against the wall and studied the very kind of proceedings he used to command. He said nothing but threw a watchful eye Bennie's way. Archie was there, too. He welcomed Bennie to the show with an optimistic nod. Bennie nodded back but kept his distance. Don't let on that you're friendly with the press, his father always said. It threatens the public's trust in you.

Bennie saw more faces watching him. Some he knew, some he

didn't. Over on the far side of the wall, he spotted Eddie, looking nervy, and could only wonder why. Shane, however, was nowhere in sight, as was the plan. He and two other officers had hightailed it to the barn for recon and confirmation. Ride the lightning, Shane, and let the sirens out. Your brethren needs you and fast.

Jimmy put a reassuring hand on his shoulder. "Get him, boss. Take him down." He fell in with the other patrolmen who had gathered to watch the show and the room quieted down.

All eyes on Bennie.

He stepped into number two, his nerves almost ready to ignite.

Thomas Müller looked uncomfortable. Sweat popping on his forehead, the light bright in his eyes. He was cuffed to the chair, so his movement was limited to shrugs and shifting in his seat. He rolled his neck as Bennie walked in, as if he were flexing for a fight, and gave him a hard stare as Bennie sat across from him. Bennie felt the spirit of his father rush over him. As a teenager, Bennie would stand in the wings and watch as the old man went hard on those that deserved it and donned kid gloves for those who didn't. One look at Thomas Müller and Bennie knew this would go the way of the former.

Seated now, he surveyed the table between them. Müller's effects were laid out before them, everything he had on him when arrested earlier today. Bennie thought they would make for colorful conversation starters and had asked a guard to lay them out pre-interview. A utility belt notched with several buttoned compartments, which Eddie had inspected beforehand and emptied. A .22 Luger, also emptied. A pair of handcuffs, a blackjack, a wallet. And a key ring with maybe two dozen keys latched to it. He leaned back and met Müller's glare with a hard stare of his own.

"Do you prefer Thomas or Tommy?"

Müller just stared at him and said nothing.

"Ok, then, Tommy it is. Tell me, Tommy, why do they call you Ghostman?"

No answer.

"I'm serious. I mean, that's quite a nickname. How'd you get it?"

Müller spat on the floor. "Fuck your mother."

Bennie t'sked. "Joke's on you, Tommy. My mother cut out years ago, haven't seen her in a dog's age. If I saw her today, I might give her an earful myself. But really, why do they call you that?"

Müller glared daggers. "Let me out of these cuffs, you might find out."

"Is that right. Does that mean you beat on the inmates, Tommy? Show 'em who's boss?" Bennie picked up the blackjack. "With this, perhaps?"

More stares, more silence.

Bennie stood up and started to pace the room, twirling the blackjack like he was a beat cop. "What about your old pal, Carmine Scangili? Did he beat on the inmates, too? Did you do it together?"

Müller seethed and yanked on his chains. Still, more silence.

"You said once that you and Scangili were friends. What'd you do together, when you weren't whipping up on inmates?"

More dagger looks, more silence.

"Well, if you weren't beating on the incarcerated, what *were* you doing? Out on the prowl for Jewish-owned businesses, perhaps?"

Müller took a deep breath. The man on the verge of words, but holding back. Bennie reached into his jacket pocket and pulled out the list of addresses Shane had given him, the one he had found in Scangili's apartment. "You know, your pal Carmine, he had this list that he left behind." Bennie held it up for Müller to see. "These are Jewish-owned and Jewish-friendly businesses here in the city. Do you have one of these?"

Müller looked in the direction of the two-way glass and gave it a big, clownish smile. Bennie picked up Müller's wallet and began to sift through it, as if he were looking for something. Unnecessary, really, since an officer had already found an identical list in the wallet and slipped it into an accessible fold so that Bennie could reach it easily, which he did, pulling it out now and confronting Müller with it. "Well, now, it appears that you do. What exactly was your plan, Tommy? Wipe out one business and then the next? Eradicate Richmond of Jews, just like Hitler tried to do in Europe?" Bennie thought of how ridiculously grandiose it sounded. "What made you start with Ruth Kleinfeld?" Bennie's voice rose in volume. "I mean, clearly, you *failed* in the entire endeavor, you only got one notch off your list. What was your downfall? Was it Carmine? Was it someone else?"

Müller yanked on his chains, the man's blood *way* up. "It was that goddamn runt, fuck… You have no *idea* what we're about to do!"

"And what is that, Tommy? Tell me. What are you about to do?"

Tommy seethed. "We are going to set this city on fire and right it for the *cause*, you fuckers! Enough with mixed races, enough with rights, enough with your petty factions of religion! *Enough!*"

Bennie got in close. "Did you kill Carmine Scangili?"

"No!"

"Do you know who did?"

Müller met his eyes. "Yes."

"Did you kill Ruth Kleinfeld?"

"No!"

"Do you know who did?"

"*Ja.*"

A heated pause.

"German, huh? That's cute. So who killed her?"

Müller cooled off and shifted gears. Off a smirk, he said, "I knew your old man."

Tension rippled through the room.

"I'm sorry?"

"Your old man, I knew him. He used to come by the prison, few years back, and look in on those he'd put away. Make sure they were getting what they deserved. And if he didn't like what he saw, well, I'd let him in the cell and he'd get right in there with 'em, make sure they were getting the message."

Bennie felt a vein pop, he'd never heard of his father doing anything like that. "My old man never hit anyone who didn't deserve it. So if what you say goes, well, then I guess he had good reason."

Müller sat back in his chair, confident, breathing heavy. He'd taken hold of the energy in the room and wasn't about to let up.

Right then, someone tapped on the two-way glass. Four taps, to be exact.

Bennie looked over, livid. *Who the hell just did that?*

Müller seemed to relax some. A look of certainty fell about him. Bennie didn't like it.

"I ask you again. Who killed Carmine Scangili and Ruth Kleinfeld?"

"Get me out of this seat, I'll tell you."

"You're in no position to bargain, Tommy."

"Really." Müller sniffed. He kept his eyes tight on Bennie. "What if *I* wanted to know something."

"Yeah, what's that, Tommy?"

"How'd you know?"

"How'd I know what?"

"What I said."

Bennie felt his back tighten. "What about what you said? When?"

Müller smiled. "When you cuffed me."

Bennie had hoped it wouldn't come to this. How foolish he'd been, letting his emotions get the better of him earlier. Please, Shane, please, knock on the fucking door, *now*.

"This isn't about what you heard, Tommy. This is about what you know. If you know who killed Carmine, if you know who killed Ruth Kleinfeld — "

Müller started to laugh. "It was you."

Bennie couldn't believe it. How could he know? "Play all the games you want, Tommy. You're going to tell us — "

Müller loved it. "You were *there*, weren't you? You must have been… "

Bennie could just imagine the wing of the interrogation rooms coming alive with gasps and steps to the glass. "I'm right here, Tommy. I haven't been anywhere else."

Müller yanked on his chains again and Bennie flinched. *Goddamn it, you let him get under your skin.*

Müller simmered. "Are you willing to die for what you believe in, copper?"

Bennie just looked at him and was about to say something,

what he didn't know, when there was a knock on the door. Bennie kept his eyes on Müller's smirk as he rose from his seat and went to the door. Opening it, he found Shane right there, nearly out of breath. Bennie was beside himself, his voice low. "Yeah? Did you find anything?"

Shane had a bummer look about him, like a pitcher who just gave up the winning run. "I'm sorry, boss. There was nothing there. We looked up and down the place, it was all cleaned out. But you're not gonna believe this. We found Holden Taft out there, Bennie, he's dead. Strangled to death. Apparently he owned the place."

Stolmy walked up then and got right behind Shane, a heavy scowl on his face. "What's Müller talking about? What's this all about? Were you somewhere with him?"

And then Shane's eyes grew two sizes and he started to yell. "Boss, boss, get back in there! What's he doing? We gotta get in there!"

For the next few moments, Bennie felt like he was suspended in mid-air as he turned to see Müller chomping his teeth into one of the pockets of his utility belt, really biting into it and then falling back into the chair. Bennie rushed over and got right on top of him, watching Müller's smile grow bigger and bigger as foam began to seep from his mouth, his body beginning to twitch, and Bennie knew then that he'd swallowed a cyanide pill. But by God, where had it come from? They'd inspected the belt, hadn't they? They looked through every pocket before bringing it into the room. *He* would be blamed, the department would be blamed, hell, they would never live this down. Bennie just stared helplessly at Müller, the man with something left to say, the words coming out of his mouth in a deathly spasm.

"We saw the loose board, copper. We knew someone had been there!"

And then Müller was full on writhing, the whites of his eyes rolling back into their sockets, his body arching up off the ground as if he he'd suddenly been shocked with electric wires. Shane was in the room now, Stolmy, too, other cops maybe, Bennie couldn't keep track, what with the clamor and the shouting and the men all standing around them now, watching as the last of the foam eked from Müller's mouth before he kicked out.

Prone now, absolutely dead.

The room swirled, the room spun, the room turned upside down.

Stolmy, right there in his face. "Where did he get that goddamn pill?"

Archie, pushing toward him. "How'd that happen?"

Shane, losing his mind. "Holy shit, boss! What do we do now?"

Bennie grabbed the utility belt.

One, two, three, *four* —

The *fourth* buttoned compartment.

Müller had chewed right through it.

The *fourth* compartment.

Four taps on the glass.

Bennie pushed out of the room. He needed air, he needed a drink, he needed to hug his mother and have her tell him it would all be alright. He found his office instead and shut the door. He stuck a chair under the knob to keep everyone out. He sank against the wall and began to shake. Tears welled up but refused to fall. He'd held his emotions in for all these years, he didn't actually know how to truly cry when he needed to, so he just sat there and pulled his legs up to his chest, wrapped his arms around them, and listened to the chaos out in the main of the Annex, listened to the world coming to an end. And it was like this for several minutes before his phone began to ring, Bennie too afraid to jump up and answer it for fear that it was more bad news. More crime, more death, more heartache. But when it quit and started up again, he figured the switchboard had a real call for him, so he pulled himself up and lumbered over to his desk, picking up the phone as he sank into his desk chair.

And then he didn't know what to say.

What's that word you say when you answer a phone?

Imogene knew that something terrible had happened the minute Bennie said hello. There was a shakiness in his voice she had never heard before and she began to wonder if this was the right time to tell him how she really felt, to share the news of their joy. She'd go crazy if she didn't tell him now, she was about to burst, holding it in this long. But maybe it's just exactly what he needed to hear. That's what she told herself, anyway.

"Benjamin?"

"Imogene? Oh my God, I… I've never been more happy to hear your voice."

"What's happened? You didn't come home last night and I've tried reaching you all day."

"I know, I'm so sorry. Did… did Annie call you?"

"Yes, but that was hours ago. I've been so worried. You don't sound good."

"I'm… I'm not good. It's bad, Imogene, it's really bad."

Imogene heard the sound of someone knocking on Bennie's office door through the phone, heard him bark something unpleasant at whoever it was. "Oh, babe, I… is there anything I can do?"

"Run away with me."

"It's that bad, huh?"

"Yes, and I'm afraid it's going to get worse."

"I… I have something to tell you, Bennie, but I don't know if this… oh, honey."

Bennie came to life some. "What is it? Are you alright?"

Imogene was glad, there he was again. Her beau, her love, his care for her coming through the wire. Just say it already, for god sakes.

"My answer is yes, Bennie. A thousand times over, yes."

She heard Bennie gasp, heard his voice shake.

"Are you sure?"

"Yes, yes. Forever yes. Let's make a life together, Benjamin. And I don't want you to worry about leaving your job, or having that come between us, I… "

"Well, I don't think we're gonna have to worry about that, hon. I don't think I'm going to be a cop much longer."

"Wow, I mean… really?"

"Yes, and I'm not sure I can make it right. I mean, ten minutes ago, I was… oh, Imogene, I just don't want to think about it right now. I can't tell you how happy this makes me. But listen, I have to tell you something, too."

"What is it?"

"Holden, my God. I just don't know how it happened."

"What about Holden?"

"He's dead. I don't know how, but apparently he was a part of it, of *this*, of all of it."

Imogene gasped. "My God."

"I know."

Imogene had to buck herself up. Just tell him, just say it.

"Well, honey. There's more."

"More?"

Imogene took a deep breath and mouthed the words silently before she spoke them.

"Bennie, I'm pregnant."

Bennie made a sound that was somewhere between a laugh and a wild bray. "Holy sh… are you sure?"

They were both crying now. "Yes, I had a test at the hospital. I mean, I've thought it for a few days now, but I just wasn't sure. Oh honey, are you happy about this? Is this what you want?"

Through the phone, Imogene wasn't sure if Bennie was laughing or crying. "Yes, yes, my God. Imogene, if you only knew what I've just been through. Where are you? I'm coming to you."

"I'm at the Wells' house. I'm here with Constance and Timony. Poor Timony, she and Harrison had an awful row. She called us both for a visit."

"Ok, I… I've got to find a way out of here first. I'll see if Shane can cover my tracks for a few hours, I'll be there just as soon as I can. Oh, Imogene, I love you. I love you so much."

"I love you, too, Bennie. Get here fast, hon, please, I can't wait to hold you."

Another knock on the door.

Shane, this time, his voice full of panic.

"Lieu? Hey Lieu, you in there?"

Bennie moved the chair from the door and cracked it open. Shane looked at him wide-eyed. "Boss, you okay? What the hell happened in there?"

Bennie ushered him inside on the quick, shut the door again. Most everyone would still be down at the interrogation rooms, anyway. The medical team would be here by now, maybe the coroner. "What's it like down there?"

"It's chaos, boss. It's madness. The Cane's telling everyone you're out. He's down there making a big fuss about it, too, I mean he's practically having a press conference with all the newshawks around."

"Yeah, he shouted through my door not five minutes ago. Said I was through."

"Geez, is that it? Can he do that?"

"Stolmy's had it in for me ever since Jack died. He's been looking for a way to ruin me and now he's found it. To hell with what he's telling the papers. I'm not through with this. Tell me something, Shane, do you trust me?"

"Yeah, boss, all the way."

Bennie couldn't help it, he smiled. "You'll never believe it. She said yes."

"What? Who?"

"She said yes."

Shane gushed, I-can't-believe-it all over his face. "Are you serious? Holy shit, boss. I mean, now? Like it just happened?"

Bennie nodded.

"Okay, okay. Well, then, shit, you need to get out of here. Where is she?"

"At Harrison Wells' house. She and his wife are good friends."

"I'll stall for you. How long do you need?"

"A couple of hours, tops. I just need to see her."

"You got it. What can I do?"

"You can tell me who tapped on the glass."

"What? Tapped what, who??"

"I don't know. Someone tapped on the glass four times. Then Müller chewed through the fourth compartment in that belt, that's where the pill was."

"Someone planted it, goddamn."

"You got that - " Bennie froze, oh, right, *of course*. "It was

Eddie."

"What???"

"I had him inspect the utility belt and empty it. He was the only who handled it before we took it in the room."

"Jesus, but why?"

"We'll have to figure that out, won't we?"

"Roger that. Look, get out of here, take the back steps. Run if you have to. I'll make a stink if they try to follow."

Bennie cracked his office door open. Amazing — no one waiting. They both slipped out, Shane going one way, Bennie the other. Bennie called back to him. "Stay by the phone, Shane. I'll call you later tonight."

A Jackson Ward alleyway, in between Leigh and Clay. Knox laid in wait near some garbage cans and longed for the day he could shake this life. How many times had he hidden out near a stinking trashcan? He rolled the windows up to kill the stench and set his gaze on Walter's Plymouth, parked a block and a half up. He sighed. Seemed like all he did these days was park in his cab and just *watch*.

He knew something was up, the way noise began to collect out near Broad, out near the City Hall Annex. Maybe they're hauling Ghostman back to the pen, ready to throw away the key. Stick *him* in solitary this time, see how he likes it.

Knox could only hope.

Moments passed, moments dragged.

Somewhere, a dog howled at the moon.

Bennie slipped out of the Annex's back entrance and figured he'd flag a cab once he got far enough away. He'd be too noticeable on a streetcar and with all the hubbub out in front of the Annex, they'd notice if he fired up a cruiser. He had to get far away and fast. He could go north, maybe, into Jackson Ward, see if that one-eyed preacher was in a doing-favors kind of mood and had a sled he could borrow. Bennie started in that direction when he heard someone call his name. He scuffled over near a parked car and ducked behind it. There it was again. Someone was calling out, "Hey, Bennie?"

Bennie didn't recognize the voice right off. It didn't sound like Eddie, Stolmy, or Jimmy. It wouldn't be Shane. Bennie risked a peek through a car window and couldn't believe it.

There was Harrison Wells, right there, his face just visible in the fading embers of daylight.

Bennie stood up, but stayed behind the car. "Harrison? What are you doing here?"

Harrison put his hands up. "Bennie, I know, this is odd, us meeting like this. But I had to see you. I… I need your help with something and I need it right now."

Bennie's cop antennae pinged so hard it could bring down a four story building. What the hell was Harrison Wells doing here, right this minute, after everything that just happened? "How did you know where to find me?"

Harrison walked toward him cautiously. "I know, it's strange. I had been hoping to find you tonight and when I got here, I could see that something was not quite right. So I waited. And after I heard what happened, I figured you might make a run for it. I mean, I've done the same thing myself a time or two, after heated city council meetings, I just duck out the back. I get it, Bennie, I really do."

Bennie took stock of his surroundings — parked cars, no one around, the world getting darker. He took stock of himself — a holstered gun under his jacket, his emotions scattered every which way. His cop instincts told him to run. "I'm just surprised, is all, to find you here. What exactly do you need my help with, Harrison?"

Harrison put on a salesman's smile. "It's silly, really. I'm sure you've heard about the war surplus reallocation I'm overseeing? Well, I believe that some of what I'm dealing with and some of what you're dealing with," Harrison looked over his shoulder at the Annex, "are connected. If we could only talk — "

Bennie looked past Harrison at the Annex. They couldn't stay here, they had to move and soon. He didn't know what to say.

Harrison went on. "Well, I… if you must know, there are documents I'd like you to see, I… I'm really in over my head,

Bennie. And I'm sure we could both use a drink. Perhaps at my office…"

A drink sounded great. So did five. "You know, I'm actually on my way to your house right now."

Harrison lit up, problem solved. "Really?"

"Imogene's there."

"Oh, is that right? You two getting on again?"

Bennie nodded.

Harrison clapped. "How wonderful! Then by all means, let's go together. My car is just over on the next street."

Bennie *knew* it didn't feel right. There was something so off about meeting like this. Didn't Imogene say that Timony and Harrison had a fight? But Bennie had to get out of here and he had to get to *her*. So right now, Harrison Wells was the answer.

"Alright, Harrison. Let's jet. We'll talk on the way. But we gotta move, so come on."

Harrison smiled nervously. "Splendid!" He led them to his car, just a half a block over, off Marshall, and as they approached it, Bennie could see Harrison start to move forward at a faster pace, as if he were suddenly pursued, and it was then that Bennie heard the footsteps behind him and knew it was too late. And then the sap came down on his head, it really smarted, really took the legs out from underneath him, and all he could think of as he faded out was that Imogene was waiting for him, Imogene and their child, and that she wouldn't know.

Knox saw movement in the shadows. He saw two men and could just make our their faces. That's the face of Bennie Sherwood, alright. The other man Knox didn't know. Couldn't see him as well, anyway. But Sherwood's face he remembered. Hell, he'd seen it in the papers these last few weeks, the kid getting dragged along hot coals for those murder jobs. Well, right now, the kid was walking into a trap. This other man he was with probably leading him right to it. Knox couldn't help it, he felt bad for Sherwood, maybe because he was tangled up with Imogene and well, Knox was kinda soft on her. But who was he kidding. Knox wasn't about to stick his neck out for a cop.

Not now, not ever.

They're walking to the Plymouth now and sure enough, Walter sapped Bennie from behind and dumped him into the trunk. The other man, too, the one leading Bennie into the trap. And just like that, the Plymouth peeled off.

And what's a moonshine runner worth his salt to do, then, but follow the prize.

Knox set in behind them, again.

They weaved through downtown. They criss-crossed streets. Knox wondered, *do they know they have a tail?*

It had grown quite dark by then and Knox almost didn't realize where they were headed until it was too late, until he was parking the cab just a few blocks from where he never wanted to be again, in the shadows of the state penitentiary, just a block away from it on Spring Street.

Knox was on foot now, creeping along the side of a building, peeking down the street at the front of the pen. He watched two men lift Bennie and the other man from the trunk of the Plymouth and take them inside the prison. Visel must certainly be orchestrating this, he just knew it. They were disappearing them, like they had so many others. He started to panic, wondering what he should do, who he should tell. Imogene? Lenny?

But it didn't matter, not anymore, because he'd gotten sloppy. And when he turned around and found Walter, right there, knew he was in for it. "What'd I do wrong? Follow too close?"

Walter nodded. "What's a cab doing following *us*, we wondered. Another car length back, we might not have seen you. Very sloppy, Knox. Very sloppy."

Knox sighed as he heard others walk up behind him. This wasn't going to be fun.

Walter took a step toward him. "Where you been, Knoxy? I've been looking for you."

"Have you now." Knox felt hands on him. Two men, one on either side. One of 'em found his snick knife, took it from his pocket. Slid the blade out and held it up to his throat. Not the way he planned it, not at all.

Walter came right up to him, smiling big. Adjusting Knox's lapels, patting them down. "Looks like we're working together again, eh, Knoxy?"

The last thing Knox heard was Walter laughing as they sapped him and all he could hope was that he'd see Constance in his dreams.

22

Bennie etched another slash mark on the wall with a shard of rock he found in the cell. That made ten. It had been at least that many days since he'd last spoken to Imogene. He wondered how she was feeling and hoped that she was comfortable, that she truly welcomed the presence of another life inside her own. What a miracle it is, yes, but what a burden it is, too. She had already lost one child. Was she truly happy about their news, as she had sounded on the phone? Or was she secretly resentful they hadn't been more careful?

Bennie tried to think of more questions, anything to occupy his mind. Save for a glimmer of light far above him, it was damp and dark where he was now, sitting in this tight, small room. He was deep down, he was in the basement of a basement, if there was such a thing. The stench of sweat, urine, and fear hung in the air and made it hard to breathe. Just inside the door, his captors had left him a slab of bread and a cup of water, but Bennie had ignored the offerings, he was too worried to eat or drink anything.

Shuffles, groans, *clang* — a door for the adjacent room opened.

The sounds came hard and fast and meant that Harrison was back, finally, their captors returning him to the next room. Throwing him into it, by the sound of it. Harrison whimpered as his body hit the ground. Quickly, their captors locked his door and started off.

Bennie clamored to the door of his cell. "Hey, you can't do this to us, goddamnit!" Bennie was surprised he even had enough in him to speak this way, he had only the dredges of energy fueling him now. "Who are you? Visel? Walter?" He hesitated, not wanting to believe it. "Stolmy? Stolmy, is that you?" He heard the footsteps move farther away and knew it wasn't Stolmy. They were too patterned, too close to one another. "Goddamnit, whoever you are, you're not gonna get away with this, you hear me? Do you?"

Bennie's words echoed and died, the import behind them lost in the darkness that surrounded both he and Harrison. The vacuum too great, the power of the black too much for even a whisper of hope to survive. Bennie crawled over to the wall nearest Harrison's cell and spoke through it.

"Harrison, what happened?"

Bennie heard sobs through the wall.

"Harrison? Please, tell me something, anything. What happened?" Bennie hated to say it. "What did they do to you?"

Bennie heard a clawing sound, as if Harrison were propping himself up against the wall between them.

"They… oh, Bennie. Bennie, I'm so sorry." Harrison began to weep.

"Harrison, listen to me. Hold yourself together. Come on, now. Don't let 'em get to you this way. Come on!"

Bennie looked over in the darkness and saw Jap faces glowing with devilish glee. They looked as if they were preparing something for him, some ritual. *They're not there*, Bennie told himself. *They're not really there, Bennie, you know this. Come on, come on, come on…*

Harrison fought to speak. "They, they took my hair."

Bennie wasn't sure he understood. "Your hair? They took your *hair?*"

Harrison cried. "Yes."

Bennie didn't know what to say. Keep him talking, anyway you can… "What else, Harrison? What else happened? Come on, what happened next?"

"They… they showed me things…"

"Things? What things?"

"Movies, photographs…"

Bennie thought of the duffel they found at that halfway house, the one that belonged to George Carroll. "Photographs? What photographs? Harrison, I've seen it all, you can tell me." Just keep him talking, keep him going.

"Men, women, children..." Harrison could barely speak. "Hurting each other. I... I don't understand it, Bennie, why? Why would they?"

Bennie looked over at the corner. Those Jap faces were huddled together. Plotting, scheming, organizing against him.

"Harrison, they want to turn you against yourself. They want you to believe what you see in those photographs is right and everything else is wrong. Now, listen, Harrison." *Keep saying his name*, Bennie thought. He knew they would take him next, he didn't have long. "Harrison, why did you do what you did? Why did you find me that night? What did you want from me?"

Harrison wept through the wall. "Oh, God. They said they'd hurt her if I didn't, that they'd cut her up, oh God..."

"Hurt *who* Harrison? Imogene?"

"No, Timony. They had photographs..."

Bennie was confused. "*More* photographs? Of what they showed you?"

"No, no. God, no."

Bennie knew time was running out, they would come for him any minute.

"Harrison, please! Tell me!"

Bennie heard Harrison shift through the wall, as if he were coming to life again, fighting through it. "Bennie, they... they had pictures of me with another woman. These men, they... I'm so embarrassed, Bennie, but they drugged me and took pictures of me with a woman as if I'd been with her. And then they threatened me with them, said that if I didn't cooperate, they'd show them to Timony, to the papers, to my colleagues, whatever it took."

Bennie tried to piece it all together. "What did they want with you? Why? And... and who? Who did this?"

"That man... that man that died the other night, the man that killed himself at police headquarters. That man and men he knew, they want the surplus, Bennie. The war surplus. Weapons, vehicles, supplies, all of it, I don't know why or for who, but that's it... that's what they want!"

A door opened.

Footsteps started their way.

Bennie knew he was in for it.

"Harrison, listen to me. Don't give them anything official, not about the city, not about the war…"

Bennie's cell door opened, there were hands on him now. Someone slugged him good, but he could still hear Harrison shout out to him.

"Bennie, they said they'd hurt Timony if I didn't play along! That's why I did it! I… I'm sorry, Bennie, I'm s — "

Bennie can hear them slug Harrison now, over and over, as hands drug Bennie from his cell, his feet dragging along the ground as they pulled him through the corridor and all Bennie could think then, through his half-open eyes, is that there's light ahead of him.

Rich, glorious light.

PART FOUR

THE LIGHT GETS IN

23

Imogene stumbled into Timony's kitchen, desperate for a drink of something cool. Macy helped her onto a kitchen stool at the counter and handed her a glass of water filled with small blocks of freshly chipped ice. It helped calm her nerves, if only for a minute, and she hoped that it was somehow reaching the child inside her and calming he or she. For nearly two weeks, as she and Timony worried and cried and anguished over just where Bennie and Harrison could be, Imogene's mother had reminded her that she must control herself, control her emotions, that she couldn't let the stress of Bennie's disappearance reach their child. To that end, Imogene had done her very best and would continue to do so, but her body was changing, and along with it, her emotions, her very state of mind. It was as if she were trying to build a house on unstable ground. She held the cool water to her forehead and felt the comfort of Macy's hand along her back as Timony entered the room, all dressed and made up, as if she suddenly had somewhere important to be and were going there.

Imogene couldn't believe it. "You're... going out?"

Macy couldn't believe it either. "My Lord, Miss Timony, where on earth are you off to?"

Timony put her hands up and let the girls soak her in, standing there in a knee length summer dress and a pair of short, buckled heels. Her hair pulled back, her skin done up for the first time in days. "Don't try and put a leash on me, girls, I won't have it. I *must* get out of this house." Timony went about gathering her purse, her keys, her hat. "I have a women's club event at noon and then a coming out party for a neighbor's daughter later tonight. The wheels of society do not stop turning just because men go missing."

Imogene and Macy looked at one another, a weight in their eyes. "Timony, please," Imogene said. "People will be hounding you with questions…"

Timony cut her off. "*People* I can handle. Hell, people are my business. I move 'em up, down, left, right. They're like puppets in my hands. Don't tell *me* about people." Timony knew her inner bitch was on full display, and today, well, she wanted to let it shine. But these were her friends, her confidantes. "I'm sorry, I mean it, please forgive me. It's just that I am… tired of waiting on men. Hell, I'm tired of waiting, period. I need to be out, I need to be seen, I need to put a smile on my face and show others that I'm alright. It's what I do. Now, please, just let me be me."

Macy knew there was no stopping this woman once she had a mind to do something. She looked from Timony to Imogene. "Have you all heard anything more? From the police?"

Imogene hung her head, shaking it. "They called again this morning. They still don't know where they are."

"Who called?" Timony asked.

"Stolmy," Imogene said, her tone unenthusiastic.

Timony sighed, but whatever she wanted to say, she held it in.

"What?" Imogene asked.

"Do I really have to say it? You've said it yourself. Stolmy and Bennie are practically at each other's throats. How do we even know he's looking for them?"

Imogene nearly stood up. "Timony!"

"And how do we know they've been kidnapped in the first place? Is there a ransom note? A demand? What would anyone want with Harrison, anyway? He's a city council member, for god sakes, not the King of England."

Imogene pleaded. "Stolmy says they have reason to believe someone at the prison is behind it. They're doing all they can. Please, T, have faith."

Timony really started to boil. "Faith? You want *me* to have faith? I've had faith for nearly ten months that my son would return to us. I don't even know where he is, for god's sake, or if he's even alive! The government won't tell me, maybe they don't even know! So maybe Stolmy is just feeding us a line of bull to save his own ass. And Harrison, well, you know how awful he's acted toward me these last weeks. For all I know, he ran off with that floozy I heard all about. If you could only hear the way he spoke to me the last time we saw one another." Timony wanted to throw something across the room, a fire had really started to blossom within her. She felt near invincible just then, letting the truths come out of her, finally. No more holding it in, no more denial. But the pain of it was too much for her alone. She needed to siphon it off, to share the burden. She looked at Imogene then and knew this would hurt her, not wanting to say it, but saying it anyway. "And maybe you just need to accept it, Imogene, but maybe Bennie didn't want a baby after all."

Macy gasped and slapped the counter. "Miss Timony!"

Imogene felt the words run through her like a strike of lightning and even as she felt the tears well up and wondered if Timony was in fact saying something true, Imogene could tell her friend was not herself today. And so she just looked at Timony with love in her eyes and let her say what she needed to say. She watched as Timony grabbed her things and stormed off.

"You two tell yourself what you want, but if you ask me, they're not coming back!"

Timony threw herself into the Plymouth and told herself she could get through it, that yes, she could handle the women at the club today and at the debutante party, no problem. Kept telling herself this as she fired up the car and the tears began to fall. She cried harder than she ever had before, harder than she had when her father died and even harder than she had when the first notice of Nolan's disappearance had come to the house. Her body heaved and shook and she knew her makeup was ruined and that she'd have to go back into the house to fix it, but she couldn't stop the tears from falling, couldn't stop her body from hunching over as she clutched the steering wheel for something to hold onto, couldn't shake the voice of her mother running through her head.

Don't be such a fool, child.

You must never let them see you cry.

24

Knox felt Walter's gun stick into his ribs for the third time that day, steering him from the car and into a clearing behind a row of shops. Walter steered him this way and that, as if he owned him, like Knox was his property. In truth, Knox felt more like a prisoner than anything else, Walter having kept a thoroughly watchful eye on him for almost two weeks now, ever since they cornered him just outside the penitentiary. And with no frills, either, Knox having either been locked up for hours at a time or kept within view of Walter and his goons, someone's eyes always on him and a loose gun always just a little too out of reach. Knox had come to feel as if he were being primed for his own execution, the way malice hung in the air about the alleyway they were standing in now, like a storm about to hit. Knox had no idea what Walter was truly planning, but if history was any indication, it would not end well for him if he didn't break free and find a way out of this.

His pulse kicked up, panic started to edge in. He wondered just how far away he was from Constance as he surveyed the back street they were all standing in now. The sun danced through the clouds and there were whispers of orange all around them. A coating of sorts, everything glowed — the toppled over trashcans, the overgrown weeds on the edges of the gravel, it was all brighter, more inviting. It all reminded him of her, how she lit up whatever room she was in, and suddenly it dawned on him, that while he didn't actually know where they were just now, he did know one thing.

That after a life on the run, he never wanted to see another alleyway in his entire life. From here on out, he wanted skyline views, he wanted green grass, he wanted the ocean at his feet whenever he felt like it. No more looking over your shoulder, no more skid row hideouts while you wait out the heat. Get out of this, get *her*, get free.

But unfortunately, at that very moment, the only thing he got was Walter, up close in his face, boring a stare right through him. Rotgut liquor on his breath, too, a real plus. *How much better is this gonna get*, Knox wondered.

"Are you gonna soldier through this, Sutton, or am I gonna have to knock you in line again?"

Knox could still feel the bruising about his ribcage from where Walter had walloped on him earlier in the day. "That's not much of a choice, now, is it."

The barrel of Walter's gun dug in a little deeper. "It's a *choice* to cop the right attitude. So what's it gonna be? You gonna play along or what?"

Knox held everything he wanted to say back. He hadn't the courage yet to ask about Constance and what Walter had done to her. Not with a gun pointed at him, he didn't. "You haven't even told me what I'm supposed to play along with."

"It's a pawn shop. I just need you to watch the door."

Knox nodded. "And then what?"

"And then what *what?*"

"What are you gonna do, lock me up some more? Or are you gonna dump me somewhere like you did before? You *left* me there on purpose, didn't you? With Scangili's body? You never had any intention of coming back for me, did you? What were you gonna do, call the cops on me? Have 'em find me there with him? Don't think I didn't figure it, Walter. Is that what this is, another frame up?"

Walter held his head up and tried to hide his smile. "So you've got some brains on you, after all, eh Sutton?" With his free hand, he toyed with Knox's shirt lapels, opening them and flattening them again. Patting Knox's chest like he was his father, sending him off on some important life journey. "Look, it's not personal, Sutton, you've just got that look about you now, like you're easy to leave behind. If it's any consolation to you, I'll tell the cops to go for your limbs, not your chest."

Knox couldn't believe it. "*Cops?*"

Walter smiled. "I've got friends everywhere, Sutton. Or didn't you pick that up when you were inside?"

Knox felt the world sinking away from him. He looked left, then right. It was too far to run without getting shot in either direction. He was desperate now, he couldn't hide it. "What are you doing this for? You've got cops in your pocket, what do you need me for?"

"The police need a get and I owe them a favor, simple as that. Plus, did you know you're a wanted man? Your name's been on every police blotter for weeks, everyone's looking for you. I give you to them, they're off my back." He patted Knox's cheek like he was somebody's uncle, smiling big now. "Everybody wins. Everybody but you."

Not one but two cars pulled up then, a beat-up Ford and a cop cruiser, one from either direction. Knox watched as two cops got out of the cruiser, one tall, one short. He peered at them but didn't recognize either. The man who stepped from the Ford, however, was Old Butch Donaldson and Knox knew him just fine. Last he saw of Butch, he was sidled up to Lenny's poker table, just after Knox had escaped the fire. Butch was heavy but handsome, always ready with a quip for the ladies, a bit of charm before he wooed them away from a crowd and knocked 'em senseless. And for what — cheap pearls, loose money, cigarette cases? Knox had never understood his crudeness and neither had anyone else amongst their kind. He a crass degenerate, the lowest of lowlifes.

Butch walked over to them. "Walter."

Walter nodded at Butch and slid his gun into his waist. "Keep an eye on him, yeah? Strickland and Halifax just showed, I'm gonna go give 'em the score."

Butch nodded as Walter walked off and then turned a reluctant look on Knox. As if he didn't like what he'd been brought here to do, but he was going to do it anyway. "Why didn't you leave town?"

"What can I say, I'm the sentimental type." Knox figured that if Walter was willing to walk away, it must mean Butch was armed. He tried to glance down as they were talking, see where Butch's gun was.

Butch tried on some small talk. "Have you seen *her* yet?"

"From a distance."

"So no chit chat yet? No face to face?"

Knox thought he saw Butch's gun protrude from his jacket some, as if it were in a holster under his left armpit. "Oh, I'm planning a tea, or can't you tell? Just need to mail the invitation."

Butch looked at him then with a sad, sad look, as if to say, *kid, you should have made your move.* "You hear about Sherwood?"

Knox wasn't sure what to say. "Yeah, of course." He looked over Butch's shoulder at Walter, hobnobbing with those two cops. "Haven't you?"

"Oh, sure. I mean, what a way to go."

Knox played along. "Right."

"I mean, you come up on a car thief, you don't expect to get plugged, you know? But damn if it didn't happen like that. Walter says the cops are keeping it under wraps so as not to embarrass his memory. You know, with what happened to his father and all that."

"Sure." Knox saw how relaxed Butch was now, how easily he could buy into just about anything. "You know, I, uh… I heard something different."

"About Sherwood? And why he's been missing? What'd you hear?"

Butch appeared to have all but forgotten he was supposed to be keeping Knox on his toes, Butch more interested in gossip now than anything else. Knox remembered another story about Butch. He heard once that Butch had strangled a woman for nothing more than refusing to give him a cigarette and so he decided, right then and there, that it was time to go for it, that he'd never have a better chance, and that as long as he could do something about it, no woman would have to suffer another encounter with this man ever again.

"I heard…"

Knox reached in and grabbed Butch's gun clean out of its holster, brought it up and stuck it right into Butch's face. "That you have quite the way with the ladies."

BLAM!

Knox shot Butch in the face, clean and quick. Butch's head jerked back like it had been kicked by a horse. Blood droplets off the blow splattered onto Knox as Butch fell to the ground. His body twitched on the gravel, fighting death. Butch's gun was a .38 and it felt good in Knox's hand. By the weight of it he could tell there were still five shots left as he loosed one toward Walter and his two cop pals. *Bingo* — the shot caught Walter in the shoulder before he could return fire, his face wild with confused anger as he fell back onto the ground. Knox turned and ran, even as he knew those two cops were about to fire on him. Fire they did and *SPLACK* came a bullet through his right arm, his good arm, goddamnit. But it wasn't enough to drop him, his body moving faster than his brain, and before he knew it, he was out on Broad Street, threading traffic from the south side of the street to the north, the *wrong* side of Broad, but the right side of now any way Knox could see it. He dodged a streetcar just in time and caught a blue streak from some woman who nearly ran him over. He made the other side and immediately honed in his stride, hiding his pain and gripping his right arm with his left, trying to keep the blood from dripping onto the sidewalk.

"Hey, watch it!"

Knox looked up, aghast. He'd walked right through a couple, a Negro man who was walking hand in hand with a woman in the other direction. He didn't even look up, he just apologized under his breath and kept moving, hoping that he'd find a sled he could boost and soon.

Marlon and Miss Ruby finished their dinner at the Old Hotel bar, a feast of chicken and potatoes that Marlon had been promising her for a week now, and walked together, both of them sated, both by the meal and their conversation, the two of them just now on a leisurely stroll, going where the night took them.

Marlon tried on an idea. "We could step into Garrison's alley bar, have a nightcap or two. Would you like that? I'm sure they'd be happy to see us and you know we'd see a few friends there."

Miss Ruby smiled up at him, her eyes bright and wide like a full moon. "I have another idea."

Marlon felt himself stir. "Do you now."

Ruby patted his arm, taming him. "Oh, no, sweet Marlon, not that. Not tonight."

"Well, what, then? We done already ate. If we ain't gonna drink and we ain't gonna rock a bed, what are we gonna do?"

"We… are gonna pick out a ring."

"What?"

"It's a surprise. I've worked it all out, we're going right now up to Elwood's counter and we're going to pick us out a ring. I set it all up beforehand, he is expecting us and everything."

Marlon couldn't hardly form words. "Are you serious?"

Ruby crossed herself. "Like a Sunday prayer. It's time, Marlon."

Marlon slowed his pace. "Ruby. I… it's not that I don't want to, you know that." They came to a stop in the middle of the sidewalk. "You know I… I can't afford a ring, I mean, like what you're asking."

Ruby took both of his hands in hers and looked up at him. "Now don't you balk at this, don't you shy away from me on this. And you listen now, when I tell you, that I've been putting away a little at a time… "

Marlon hemmed, hawed, stepped away from her. "Oh, come now, you gotta be kidding with this, *you're* gonna buy it?"

"Marlon. Marlon, you listen to me. Everyone knows, everyone up and down this street," Ruby pointed all over, "and every other street near here, everyone knows you put your money, your *soldier* money, your family money, you put it into the church. And you do it out of love, Marlon, you do it for us. So now it's my time, it's my way, to do something for you, to do something for us. So don't you play like a man on me, not now, don't you resist this just because I'm a lady. I love you, Marlon, and we are gonna do this together."

Marlon was so stunned in the moment that he wondered if he'd been taken back to that time at seventeen when he felt the call of God come through him the first time, there at his father's bedside, when he knew that he was destined to pay service to the Lord throughout his life. He felt weightless, speechless, and some other less he couldn't put into words, all he knew is that he was crying.

He took Ruby in his arms and held her, squeezed her, told her yes a thousand times over. And then he took her hand and began to walk with her towards Elwood's store, more proud than he'd ever been in his entire life, when a man broke their embrace, walked right through them, the man not even looking up as he stormed off in the other direction.

"Hey, watch it!" Marlon called out.

"Sorry," the man muttered under his breath as he kept moving, not even looking up, the man clearly in a hurry and of a fairer skin, thinking he could get just plow through them, no matter what.

Marlon was a forgiving man, yes, but not in this moment, not after the proclamation of love that Ruby had just bestowed on him, no way was he letting her be treated like this. He started after the man and said, "Excuse me. You there, hey now." Marlon got a hand on him and turned him 'round, the man looking straight at him. And in the moments that followed, Marlon would remember later that he wasn't sure if it was God or the Devil that rose up in him so as he started wailing on the man, the very man he'd seen so many weeks ago driving that car on that fateful day that Cornell was attacked.

Ruby pleaded with him to stop. "Marlon, my God, what's gotten into you? Marlon, please! Someone will see!"

Marlon pushed the man out of sight, off the sidewalk, away from the foot traffic. It's just another altercation north of Broad, don't you worry, folks.

But worry, Ruby did, coming alongside Marlon then, looking at him with real fear in her eyes. "Marlon, what's gotten into you? I mean, just look at you. What is this? Do you know this man?"

Marlon had the man up against a wall, holding him there like a pinned animal, Marlon's blows having taken the fight right out of him. The man looked pretty weak, to be honest, as if he hadn't been all that when he came down the street. "It's him, Ruby, *it's him!*"

"Who? Who is this?"

"It's the man I told you about, the man I see in my sleep sometimes. This the one driving that car, the day Cornell got all beaten and shot through."

Ruby wasn't sure how she felt now. "Are you sure? I mean, really sure?"

Marlon had never been more sure in his life. "Yes, it's him. Ain't it, boy, huh? It's you, ain't it?"

The man looked spent and pale, as if were about to faint. He spoke softly under his breath. Marlon leaned in to hear it.

"Constance, please. Please, I'm sorry, Constance…"

Marlon wasn't sure if what he heard was what he heard, but he knew someone named Constance. He knew someone named Jedidiah, too. Marlon fought the urge to help this man and felt about his jacket. He reached in, the man too weak to protest, and sure enough, it was gun.

Ruby gasped. "My God, Marlon, don't touch that! If someone finds that on you, my God!"

Marlon had to wonder, a white man come North of Broad and he ain't use this? Maybe he wasn't planning to. Or maybe he just didn't have the energy. He looked at Ruby.

"Get your momma's car, baby. Please."

"What ? Why?"

"I can't take him to the police, you know they'd never believe me. But there is someone I can take him to, now please. Just help me get him there. This is for Cornell, baby. This can help make it right."

Ruby nodded then, not sure if she was doing the right thing or the wrong thing, but she gave Marlon a good, strong kiss and then started off in the very opposite direction of where she truly wanted to be going, all so she could help the man she loved.

25

Marlon and Ruby pulled the man from her mother's car and walked him over to the front door of King Tobacco, Jedidiah's business on Tobacco Row. Holding him up between the two of them, they rang the doorbell and waited, shooting looks over their shoulders all the while. Yes, they knew Jedidiah, but black folk didn't just walk right up to the front doors of businesses like these, especially not at night. If someone were to see them, why, they'd most definitely run to a call box and ring the police department to come quick. And come quick they would, wouldn't they, especially for a white-owned, money-making business like Jedidiah's. *That's certainly not like it is in our neighborhood*, Marlon thought. He felt himself go tight just thinking about it all, his rage simmering even more. Ruby rang the bell again and the man fell into Marlon some, Marlon trying to hold him up. The man losing more blood now, the color draining from his face. *What a world*, he thought. How many times have I seen this very man in my dreams? How many times have I thought sinfully of the hurt I would bring to him should I ever see him again? But here I am, delivering him not to his judgement but to his reclamation, his recuperation. There truly is no justice in this world, now is there, Lord?

Jedidiah came to the door in a rush and opened it fast, ushering them inside. "My god, Marlon, Ruby, I'm so glad you called me. Come on, now, let's get you inside." Jedidiah peeked outside behind them, just to make sure no one was watching, before he closed the door and cut off the lobby lights. "Here, this way." He guided the three of them, Marlon and Ruby holding the man between them, the man still able to walk but just barely. Jedidiah pointed at a plush, comfortable chair. "Here, set him down here.

You say he's hurt?"

Ruby nodded as she helped the man sit down. "His arm, he's been bleeding. He doesn't look good."

Marlon wanted to ask, *why should this man be permitted to look good at all?* What right did he deserve to *be* good, in any way shape or form, after the part he played in Cornell's demise? "This is him, Jedidiah. The one I told you about, the one I seen driving the car that day. The day Cornell died."

But Jedidiah was already on the phone, talking urgently to someone. He paused, put his hand over the receiver, and looked at Marlon. "Marlon, how you feel about this man is not lost on me, truly. But still, I think we should get him some help. Now I can have a doctor here in just a few minutes. Is that alright with you?"

The entire room paused as Marlon looked from Ruby to Jedidiah, the decision all on him. And while the devil in him wanted so badly to put the hurt on this man some more, have him tell all, have him find some way to make up for what he done, he nodded. He did what was right and he nodded. Jedidiah got right back to the call, saying yes, please come quick now, and now there were footsteps moving toward them, another person coming to join them. Marlon turned and saw that Constance was coming toward them now, the woman somehow even prettier than she was the last time he saw her, all done up like she had just come from a party. Probably everywhere she went, there's a party. And here she was, walking towards them with purpose, cruising into the room with a jug of water and some bandages in her hand.

"Hello Marlon! Hello Ruby! These are all I could find for now, let's see if it helps until the doc gets here."

Constance kept moving through the room, walking right for the man in the chair like a nurse responding to an emergency, and then suddenly she gasped, as if she'd seen the most amazing thing. Marlon heard such gasps at church every so often, when someone felt the touch of the Lord so deeply they could do nothing but cry out. This was like that, the way Constance dropped the jug and the bandages and fell about the man as if he were her dearest, most long lost friend in the entire world. Jedidiah, Marlon, and Ruby watched in awe as it became clear that

Constance knew this man and knew him well, calling him something that sounded like rocks through her tears and the muffled cries she let out as she hugged him and kissed him and caressed his face.

Knox eased his eyes open — contours and shadows came into soft focus. A ceiling, walls, dim light through a doorway. This plush, cushy feeling. *I must be dreaming*, he thought.

He felt about the bed he was in as if he'd never slept in one before and looked around the room. Making sense of it, his eyes adjusting to the darkness. Clean and tidy, it looked like, but too big. Knox didn't like big rooms. Didn't trust 'em, not anymore. Not after four years in a six by eight. Knox had never stayed anywhere this ritzy, not once in his entire life. He always moved around as a kid, the family uprooted whenever the old man felt the walls closing in. And they always rented, never owned. Rundown pads, exclusive.

Click — a light switched on, just like that. Knox had to shield his eyes it was so bright.

"You're awake," Constance said.

She sat on the couch across from the bed and pulled a blanket up around her. She fought off a yawn and pushed her thick, brown hair from her face.

"Getting there. What time is it?"

"It's late."

A long beat, the two of them just looking.

Knox fought off the urge to yell. "Pretty rotten of you just to drop off like that," he said.

"I know."

"Tell me why?"

Constance took a deep breath and pulled her knees up to her chest. "I needed to move on, so did you. A clean break was the only way. No sense in drawing it out. I didn't mean to hurt you."

"And I didn't mean to get locked up again. I was a two time loser, you were right to split."

Constance brushed a tear from her cheek. "When'd you get out?"

"Six weeks ago? Whenever it was the fighting in Europe stopped. I've lost track of the days."

She gestured at his right arm. "What happened?"

Knox saw that he'd been bandaged up and the last day rushed through him in a flash. He saw Old Butch scream, faceless.

"I had some trouble."

"We heard."

"Yeah? I heard some things, too."

Constance's face hardened. "Did you, now."

"Something about Walter?"

Constance sat up straight. She looked cold and rigid, like a piece of metal. "I don't want to talk about that."

"Yeah, okay. Maybe some other time."

Constance weighed the idea. "Maybe."

"You know, he tried to frame me."

"Walter?"

"Yeah. The day I got out of the clink, the very *minute*, he had me behind the wheel for some job, can you believe that? And that preacher, the one that brought me here?"

"*Marlon??*"

"Yeah, the job put me in *his* crosshairs. After it went south, Walter stashed me in some house he owned. Later that same night, who do you think comes to light the pad up with a bottle bomb? That preacher, the very same one. I kid you not."

Constance covered her mouth, she could hardly breathe.

"I'm sure you've seen the headlines," Knox continued. "A prison guard got burnt up in the fire. You can bet I knew him, too."

"You were there, in the house that night?"

"Yeah, isn't that nuts? Got out by the skin of my teeth, been on the run ever since. How's that for freedom?"

Constance nodded, just shy of weeping. "I just can't believe it, that you were there. I'm so glad you're alright."

Knox felt a rush of comfort at her tears — she still cared for him. "Listen, I'm fine." He raised his bandaged arm. "Say, who did this?"

"A, uh, a doctor, a friend of Jedidiah's."

"Jedidiah, okay. King, right?"

She nodded, calmer now. "He's my employer."

Knox just nodded, he had no right to ask.

"And that's all he is," Constance said.

Knox felt a wave of relief rush through him. Maybe there's still a chance. "Gotta ask."

"About?"

"Sadie?"

"Oh, Knox. No, she passed. I kept her as long as I could, but she got sick, I had to, you know. I had to let her go."

Knox fought off his own tears. "I'm sure that was tough. She was such a good dog."

"She really was. She missed you, you know? She wasn't really the same after you were gone. But I can take you to her. I buried her near that spot in Libby Hill we used to go, you remember that hill?"

Knox remembered. "Yeah, okay, sure. I'd like that."

Nods, smiles, a long beat.

She said it first.

"It's really good to see you."

"It's really good to see you, too. And listen, after everything I've just told you, this is gonna sound a little crazy."

"What?"

"We need to call Imogene. I know where they took the Sherwood kid."

Constance made a face.

"Wait, *what??*"

26

Bennie figured he and Harrison were being kept somewhere near the prison's ventilation system, the way their cells swelled with steam. But still, Bennie shivered. It had been almost two weeks since he'd last had a benzie and his body had really started to miss them. He shook, he dry heaved. He had no appetite and slept in fits. His neck muscles threatened to strangle him, they had tightened so along his back.

Laying down made it worse, so he shimmied himself into a seated position against the wall and breathed deep, just like they taught him. It wouldn't be long before they came for him again, to take him and pin his eyes back with threaded wire and make him watch those films again. *How could anyone make such films*, he wondered. Films of torture, films of rape, of murder? Who operates the cameras, runs the labs, who handles the negatives? Nazis, the Klan, *the Japs?*

Bennie shuddered, he knew he'd gone too far. Just the thought of Jap collusion in it all was enough to awaken her and now there's no stopping it, it was just like before. She came to on the other side of the cell, as if spawned from nothing more than thought, and crawled toward him, this ghostly Japanese woman in a threadbare nightgown that revealed too much of herself. Her dark, sunken eyes were somehow blacker than the shadows of their surrounds. *How is that even possible*, Bennie wondered, watching as she came nearer and nearer to him. Her charcoal gray hair fell to just about her shoulders and swayed gently into her tautly drawn face. Bennie looked away, determined to ignore her. He set his eyes forward and breathed more rapidly, more deeply. He tapped a foot on the ground nervously and kept repeating to himself, "She's not real, she's not real, she's not — "

"You took my husband from me," she said. "My brother. My uncle, too."

Harrison called to him through the wall. "Bennie, what's happening? Is someone there? Who are you talking to?"

Bennie heard echoes of her words in translation — 'watashi no otto, no kyōdai, no oji' — my husband, my brother, my uncle. He remembered them from the language dictionary he carried on the island. He couldn't see the faces of these men, no, not after all this time, but he could hear their final cries of life, for they were the very sounds that haunted his dreams almost every night. He jammed his hands up to his ears, trying to plug away their pleas.

Stop it. Stop it, please.

Her hands were on him now and Bennie shirked away, trying to avoid her touch. Suddenly she multiplied, her face morphing into another just like itself over and over again and suddenly there were dozens of her there in the cell with him, every face both the same and distinct, all of them begging for him to recognize their loss and to comfort them in their time of need. Bennie closed his eyes and rocked back and forth.

They're not real, they're not real, they're not —

Harrison called out again. "Bennie, what's going on? Are you alright? Is there someone in the cell with you? Who is it?"

Bennie didn't remember screaming then, didn't remember repeating himself over and over again, saying *don't touch me.* He didn't remember his cell door opening and the men coming to take him again, the men shaking their heads, saying *we really broke this one good* as they hauled him from the cell. He didn't even remember Harrison calling after him, his cries of worry like those of a loving brother.

What Bennie remembered, as they drug him down the dark corridor, the steamy mist and the dim light evoking an alleyway in Shockoe past midnight, was that his fingers hit the ground and drifted along under him. It was as if he were brushing them along Imogene's back, the way he would after they made love. The way she laid there on her stomach, Bennie feeling like the luckiest guy alive, the way he got to admire her and caress her.

27

Call it a meeting, call it a sit-down, call it a strange fucking situation. Knox looked around the room and saw the most diverse group of people he'd even been in the same room with. To his right was the love of his life, Constance Lee. How he'd dreamed of seeing her for the first time after so many years and how unlike those dreams this moment truly was. She was over on the phone now, calling Imogene, telling her and her friend Timony what Knox believed had happened to Bennie. Across from Knox was a man he now knew as Marlon Jefferson, the man who set the house on fire. Next to him was his lovely bride-to-be Ruby, her wide eyes taking all of this in. And to the left of Knox sat Jedidiah King, a man Knox had been prepared to dislike immensely until learning that he and Constance were strictly business partners, nothing more.

Constance hung up the phone and sat down next to him. How intoxicating it was to have her so near him, how deliriously nuts he was going that he couldn't just wrap his arms around her, tell her everything. She took a deep breath and said to everyone, "They're relieved, to a point. They want to know what we should do next." She reached over and put a hand on Knox's back. How comforting it was, her reassuring touch. "Thank you for telling us. I can't tell you how distraught they've been, how worried."

Jedidiah agreed. "How worried we've all been."

But the man across from Knox, Marlon, he clearly did not agree, standing as he did now, looking right at Knox. "I'm glad you all have rekindled and have some gladness to appreciate, but I did not bring you here," pointing at Knox, "to rejoin a circle of friends. I can't take you to the police, but I will if you don't fess up about what you'd done and why."

Knox put a hand up. "Look, I, Marlon, I had no intention of ever bringing you harm. If you knew what I went through that morning…"

"What you went through? Huh? You? What about us? White folk come up in our neighborhood all the time, do whatever they please, and then what, they just walk away clean. Well, that day, son, a man died. A man I cared about." Looking at Ruby. "A man *we* cared about. And I ain't about to let it go unanswered." Marlon looked at the ceiling then, crossed himself. "Praise God, I will not let it go unanswered."

Knox wasn't sure he had the strength to go a round with the preacher, but he might not have a choice. "And just what is it that you want?"

"I want that man Walter MacKeye. I want him to own up for what he'd done." He looked at Jedidiah and then Constance. "Hell, I told you both all this that very night, why've I gotta repeat myself?"

Ruby tugged at his sleeve. "Marlon, baby, you need to remember yourself right now."

Marlon started to say more but held it in, looking 'round the room at every face as he sat back down. Jedidiah stood up then, a glass of bourbon in his hand, and began to pace a bit, walking and talking as if he were a great mediator, a referee for this moment and these very, very tense times. "I think we all have grievances, things we would like to see rectified, and Marlon, my friend, you and Ruby and your community have been wronged, no one disputes it. But right now we need to take this moment and acknowledge something more pressing, that two of our dear friends and two of Richmond's most well-known leaders have been kidnapped and are at this very moment most likely near their deathbeds." Jedidiah looked at Knox. "This is what you believe, yes?"

Knox nodded, having never wanted to remember it himself. "In the prison, there are… cells beyond the cells. Places where you're kept. No light, no air. It's hot, too, you're right under the heating system. They run it in the summers, even, just to make you feel it when you're down there. I don't know for sure, but if I were looking to hide someone and I had access to cells like that, that's where I would take them."

Constance nearly exploded into tears. "And as horrible as it sounds," looking right at Knox, aware now that he had experienced this for himself, "we need to do something, and we need to do it now. Jedidiah, do you know anyone that could intervene?"

Jedidiah shook his head. "I'm afraid my influence just doesn't reach that far, my dear."

Marlon and Ruby hung their heads, the both of them keenly aware they had little to offer.

Knox sat up some — light bulb. "I have an idea."

The other four just looked at him, all of them with the same look on their faces.

"What is it?" Jedidiah asked.

"I'll tell you, but first, I need to get in touch with Stolmy Reed."

Timony hung up the phone in a flash and started to pace the kitchen. She grabbed the bottle of whiskey she'd been abusing and poured another healthy swig into her highball glass. Macy had never seen her so beside herself, the way she walked the room now. Not even after fights with Harrison had she seen her like this. Macy and Imogene just watched her, the both of them nearly beside themselves to know what Constance had told her.

"What did she say?" Imogene asked, her voice dry and hoarse from crying.

Timony could hardly bring herself to say it. "They... someone Constance knows, he has a plan. They need us, we need to be there." Timony downed the rest of her highball and set the glass on the counter. She looked at Imogene. "Do you want to be there, too?"

Imogene stood up from the couch, woozy of mind but fierce of soul. "If it involves getting Bennie out of, God, I don't even want to say, and I can help, then of course, yes, I want to be there."

Timony took Imogene's hands in hers. Macy's, too. "Look, something tells me they're okay, that we can get them. This plan... " Timony almost started to laugh.

Imogene was dying to know. "What? What is it?"

Timony looked at her now, a full-on smile on her face, a look of glee. "We can do this, I know we can." She looked at Macy, who had volunteered her time to help Imogene feel comfortable and to be there for Timony. "Macy, my dear, you are to be here in case we call, do you understand? If it doesn't go as planned?"

Macy nodded as fast as she could, she had never been more ready. "I'm here, Miss Timony, you know I am."

Timony took Imogene now and guided her out of the sitting room and through the hallway. "Come on, now, we need to go. You can drive, you're good at that. I'll tell you all about it on the way. But first…" Timony had steered her through the labyrinth of her spacious home and stopped now before a large gun cabinet. They were in a drawing room, a room Imogene had never been in before, and her eyes grew wide and then wider as she watched Timony open the cabinet and grab two handguns, slipping one into her purse and then another into the waistband of her pants. She took a third from the wall of the cabinet and handed it to Imogene.

Timony smiled. "Come on, now. It's not like you don't know how to use it."

And then Timony and Imogene were off, out of the house and into her car. Imogene barreled into town and listened to Timony tell her all about how they were going to break the men they loved out of prison.

PART FIVE

PRISON BREAK

28

Stolmy Reed listened.

He listened to a man he'd met only once before, a man who had done him no more a courtesy than drive him a short distance in a cab. Yes, he listened to this man tell him the most fantastic story. At the start, Stolmy was convinced that it would lead to an easy arrest, that he'd lucked out, finally, and could bring this man Knox Sutton before a judge in the morning and have him locked up for not only wasting Stolmy's time but for any number of offenses he was already wanted for, the man's name having been bounced around the department's wanted list so many times in the last few weeks it was practically etched into the typeset of the daily police blotter. Still, Stolmy listened, and as Knox went on, he was surprised at how his story grew more and more believable. There was talk of the man Scangili again, and then the man Müller, the one they called Ghostman, the one who had killed himself at the Annex almost two weeks ago. This man Knox, he knew things, a great many things, and as he went on, Stolmy had a few questions about just how he knew these things, but the longer Sutton talked, the longer Stolmy became convinced that he was telling the absolute truth. And what a truth it was, that Bennie Sherwood and Harrison Wells were being kept in the darkest reaches of the state penitentiary. Sutton was not only convinced of this, but the man had a plan, a plan to not only get inside the building but to get right back out again, with Bennie and Harrison in tow.

Knox picked up a piece of gravel and skipped it along the steady ripple of the James River. They were east of the city, down near the water, just this side of a boat dock moonshiners used to use. A truly remote spot where an ex-con and a cop were unlikely to be found talking together. Somewhere even Stolmy, a lifelong

Richmonder who thought he knew every alley and hidden enclave in and out of the city limits, had never been before.

Knox pressed. "So, what do you think?"

"I don't know what I think. You want to do this now, tonight?"

"Why not?"

"There's a hundred why nots, son. What if Visel doesn't let you in? What if he doesn't believe me?"

"He'll believe you."

"And just why are you so sure?"

"Because Visel has a yen for controlling people and keeping them under his watch. You'll tell him all about how I couldn't go straight, how I couldn't make it going my own way. That it was only a matter of time before I slipped into the old life. He wants it to be true so bad, he'll eat it up on the spot."

Stolmy shook his head. "We have a jail for guys like that. He'd never go for it."

Knox breathed deep. "Then tell him you've got me for murder and don't want me in the jail for fear that friends of the guy I shot who are already *in* jail would go after me once the lights go out." Which, if it happened that way, would be true.

Stolmy hesitated. "You didn't say anything about a murder, son."

"You find a man last night, his face half-blown off?"

"We did."

"Yeah, that was me. That's Old Butch Donaldson, if you didn't know already. You probably have him down for at least a dozen breaking and entering jobs, only you could never quite catch him in the act, could you? If we make it out of this, I'll look over old case files with you, tell you which ones were his."

Stolmy just couldn't believe it all. "You know, I'd have to… "

Knox turned around and looked at him. "You'd have to what? Turn me in? Who's to say I don't ditch you right here? Who's to say I don't go to the papers with all this? I'm coming to you because Jedidiah said… "

"Jedidiah's in on this?"

"Jedidiah agreed with me, he said you were the only person who could get us into the prison like this. Last minute, late hour.

Look, I know that place all too well and as much as I don't want to ever step back inside, I haven't been one iota of free since I got out. Could be, the only way for me to truly get free is to go back in one more time. The woman I love? Friends of hers are in there. And hell, I'm bringing this all to you, aren't I? I help you with this, that oughta square me, get me a clean slate. And think about it, you get to play hero, too. Way things are in town, I'm sure you could use the praise. I certainly don't see a lot of that going on, at least not where the cops are concerned."

Stolmy let it all sink in. The kid was right. *What a get*, he thought, what a rush it would be to bring all this in. My God, there'd never be another case like this in his life. For a minute there, he really had wondered if Bennie had just skipped town, especially after that debacle with Müller. But if the kid was in danger, in *real* danger, hell, Harrison, too, he couldn't look the other way on that. Even after all that business with Jack, Bennie was like family. A surrogate son.

"Alright, I'll go along with this. But there's one more thing."

Knox didn't like it. "What?"

"We're gonna need another body, another cop." Stolmy banged his cane against the steps of the boat dock. "I'm a cripple, remember?"

Knox felt sorry for him. "Who've you got in mind?"

Shane walked a length of Belvidere Street before ducking into the shadows of a side street that led to the penitentiary. The Cane told him to take as clandestine a path as he could and to look for him just across from the prison's entrance, he'd be sitting in a cab. Shane ran through it all again as he walked, everything he was supposed to have on him. His badge, his cuffs, and, as requested, two department issued handguns, fully loaded. Something about the way The Cane had asked for those over the phone, the way he'd lowered his voice and said this was an off-hours operation but still V-Squad related, it had really put a knot in Shane's gut. But he didn't balk, no way, not to the boss of bosses. Through and through, Shane was a company man. Had been in the Navy and was now with the department. Which was coming apart, by the way. Bennie had been MIA for almost two weeks now. Eddie, too, for that matter, but that was a different story. Eddie had been the one who tampered with Müller's belt that day. And just yesterday, they found Eddie's badge at a crime scene where a man's face had been blown off. Shane shook his head, remembering it all as he walked up to the cab that Stolmy had described. There looked to be two men inside, one in the driver's seat, another in the back. Shane steeled himself as he rapped a knuckle on the back window.

A man Shane had never seen before got out of the front seat and opened the door for Stolmy, who edged out of the back with his rod and his bum leg bumping on the door as he lumbered out and stood before him.

"MacDonald. You're a good man, son."

"Sir."

The Cane gestured toward the other man. "MacDonald, this is Knox Sutton. Knox, this is Shane MacDonald, one of our up and comers on the Victory Squad."

MacDonald almost shook Knox's hand before he thought it through. "You mean this is… Sutton, sir? The one on our list, the one we've been looking for?"

"Yes, well, wouldn't you know. Turns out he's been looking for us, too. Got your cuffs on you?"

MacDonald pulled them off his belt, held them up. "Yes, sir."

"Good, cuff him."

MacDonald relaxed some then, maybe this was all going to be easier than he thought. "We're making an arrest, sir?"

The Cane started toward the prison, tapping his rod on the sidewalk like he was just off for a stroll. "No. We're about to break two men out of prison. Come on!"

Knox, cuffed now, MacDonald behind him, looked up the street as the three of them walked up to the penitentiary. Knox could just make out the car that Constance had said they'd be in, a ritzy Buick, the one with her and the preacher. Knox still couldn't believe Marlon offered to help them, how willing he was to create their diversion. Knox smiled then, thinking of it — he still hadn't told the preacher that he'd been in the house that night. The fire and Scangili and all that. Maybe once this was all over, he'd have a chance to truly come clean, tell Marlon how sorry he was about the day he got out.

Knox looked up at the imposing cascade of the prison's entrance as the cop muscled him from behind. MacDonald putting on a show just like he'd been asked to, the both of them following The Cane up the steps.

This had better work, Knox thought.

This had better fucking work.

Stolmy rapped on the front doors of the prison, really hitting 'em for a moment. He didn't get much of a chance to do that and well, right now, he was quite enjoying it, hitting them again and again, making a real noise about it, too, and then watching though the small glass window on the outside door as a guard came out of an office down the hall and started hustling toward them. The man rubbing sleep from his eyes, it looked like. Waking him from a nap, are we? *Well, all the better*, Stolmy thought.

The guard looked through the glass window, looking at all three men outside, wondering if he should even open the door in the first place, but once his gaze settled on The Cane, he knew it was serious and then set about fussing with his keys. There was an inside door, too, and the guard had to open one before he could open the other, the man really having to go through with it all, and finally he opened the outside door and stood there with a hand on his pistol, vexed.

"Director Reed, what can we do for you at this late hour?"

Stolmy flashed his best politician's smile. "Well, son, you know how they say crime doesn't pay? It doesn't sleep, either. Got us here the worst of the worst, a real tried and true career minded thief," Stolmy shot a good snarl at Knox, "and well, what does he go and do? He murders someone. Someone he used to know, at that. And we can't lock him up in the jail over on Marshall Street because the man he murdered has got one too many friends over there already. And I need this one," gesturing at Knox again, "I need him to make trial." Stolmy pulled a piece of paper from his jacket, a phony document he hoped the guard wouldn't ask to see.

"Got me here a 'writ of incarceration' if you need to see it. Just need a good old six by eight for him, for maybe a week, tops. Jimmy'll understand."

The guard didn't like it. "I understand all that, sir, I truly do. It's just, we don't take admittance without the warden present. It's our standard policy, as I'm sure you know."

Stolmy nodded. "Oh, he's aware, son, he's aware. I spoke with him not an hour ago. His signature is right here on the writ." The guard inspected the document while Stolmy gave him a harder look. "I've asked nice just this once, son. I won't do it again."

The guard looked at the three men, caught Stolmy's glare and figured it wasn't worth the trouble he'd get for not complying with a city bigwig. "Alright, okay. But sir, you'll all have to wait inside here, inside the lobby while I get the admittance roster."

Stolmy smiled. "That's just fine, son."

The guard looked at Knox and then Shane. "Your man, there? He's an officer?"

Stolmy nodded.

"He have a firearm on him?"

Shane nodded.

It was enough. "Alright, then," the guard said, easing open the outside door. "Bring him in here and just hold back a minute while I get it all together." The guard started to lock everyone in between the two doors, trying to keep some sense of protocol.

The Cane protested. "Son, it's late. Can we just get on with the proceedings? No need to lock us in here, we'll be out in a jiffy. Come on, now! There isn't time to waste!"

The guard didn't like it, but The Cane could see he didn't like arguing with someone more powerful than himself even more. "Alright, sir, just a few moments." He looked at Shane. "Protocol is to keep your firearm ready at all times until the prisoner has been secured inside the penitentiary's main fencing, do you understand?"

Shane nodded again, thankful that all he had to do was just nod.

The guard turned and started back to the office, his holster and his keys jangling as he started off. Knox watched him go and wondered just how long —

KABOOM!

Outside on the street, a car blew into flames. The guard turned around and started back toward the front doors. "Oh my God," he said, saying it again and then saying it once more as he came all the way to the outermost door and looked out. "Oh, Jesus, what was that?"

Shane raised his gun on the guard, hoping to God he was doing the right thing. "Put your hands up, now!"

The guard turned around. "Oh, oh God, what... oh no!" He started to go for his pistol when Shane stepped toward him.

"Keep your hands up! I mean it!" Shane had never been more scared in his life, he just hoped it didn't come through in his voice.

The guard just balked. "I mean, what... what is this?"

The Cane walked up to him. "I apologize, son, truly I do." The Cane took the guard's pistol and then his ring of keys. He tossed the keys to Shane and then held the guard's own gun on him. "Don't move, son. It ain't worth it." He called to Shane over his shoulder. "You're up, MacDonald."

Shane unlocked the cuffs on Sutton. "You better be in the right here, pal."

Knox rubbed the sting out of his wrists. "Or what? You think I wanted to come back in here? Plus, you've got the gun That was the deal, remember?"

It was true, Shane couldn't deny it. "Alright, then. What next?"

"Next, we go inside. Come on."

Knox and Shane nodded at The Cane as they started to run, incredibly, *into* the prison.

Keys, doors, gates.

Opening, sliding, running.

Soft feet, no footfall.

Getting from one corridor to the next didn't really bother Shane. It was the silence that really started to put the edge in him. It was late, so sure, most of the inmates were asleep, but every lock they turned, every gate they opened, it all echoed so hollowly, as if there were nothing really here at all. And Knox knew where all the guards were and how to tiptoe around them, how to move from one passageway to the next. When to duck, when to move, when to slip this way and that. The farther into the prison they got, the more cavalier they could be, and soon Shane realized they were moving beyond the cells. Beyond the inmates, the guards. Wherever they were going, it was not somewhere they were meant to be. And even if Sutton had forgotten the way, the smell would guide them. The scent was foul and rank, Shane almost gagged. And just when he thought their journey couldn't get even more darker or more remote from the entrance, Sutton stopped and whispered, "We're here."

Sutton took the keys then and studied them with his fingers, one after another, and it became clear to Shane that Sutton knew these keys, knew which one came before and which one came after. It was almost as if he were a meticulous craftsman who had suddenly rediscovered his greatest work. Before long, he found the one he had been looking for and used it to open a door that almost didn't appear to be there at all, as dark as it was. It was like Sutton just knew it was there.

Sutton motioned to Shane to say nothing as they descended even more stairs, their hands on the wall for guidance. Sutton felt along the walls as they crept, as if feeling for something secret, something only he could find. He stopped, he'd found it. Shane heard Sutton open a door and call out with a whisper. "Bennie? Harrison? You guys in here?"

Shane didn't know what to think when he heard an 'uhh' and then another, the sounds of someone sick and weak. Clearly, they had found them.

They had found them at last.

Knox knelt down and patted the floor, feeling for them, and sure enough — a foot, a leg, a man. Whoever it was eked out a few feeble grunts. Knox whispered to MacDonald, "Got one," as he leaned in and started to feel about the man, not sure which one he had. "Harrison? Bennie?" The man groaned as Knox propped him up against the wall.

"MacDonald, can you hear anything else? There's supposed to

be two of them. Check the other rooms, there's more."

Shane opened doors and shuffled from one to the next and then whispered back that he couldn't hear anyone else and that no one else was there. Knox didn't like it. He didn't like not delivering on the plan, but they couldn't risk being inside the prison any longer. Knox helped the man up, whichever one he was, and wrapped a strong arm around him. Together, the three of them shuffled away from these rooms, slowly. "Follow me," Knox said, as he led them back up the darkened stairs. And then to the right, to the back of the penitentiary, just like it had been the day he got out.

MacDonald protested. "What is this? Where are we going? What about Stolmy?"

"Don't worry, kid. The Cane knows the plan."

29

Knox kept a look out as they snaked through the rear of the penitentiary, holding the man up best he could. With any luck, the fire out front would have drawn a hefty crowd. Plenty of cover to sneak out the back door, just like he had so many weeks before.

"Come on, kid, this way." Knox led them toward the back corridor and thought back to that day, the morning he got out, and how he should have chosen to go out the front and taken his chances. But there was no time to think of that now as he lifted the dead weight of the man under his arms and arrived at their exit. Knox still couldn't tell which one of them they had with him, the man just grunting and holding on as Knox handed Shane the key ring and told him to just try one after the other. Luckily, it only took the kid five tries to get the door open and then holy shit, they were outside, edging out of the prison darkness into a moonlit night, Knox finally able to look down and see that it was Bennie Sherwood he had under his arms and not the other one, the one Constance told him had been so terrible to his wife. And the MacDonald kid, well, he was more than relieved at being free of the prison. Hell, he looked like he was just now seeing the world for the very first time, he really must have been some kind of spooked. Knox felt for him, sure, but wanted to tell him it was nothing like being locked up for good. You only had four minutes, kid. Try four years and let me know how you feel about it then.

They were almost out to the street now. Knox held Sherwood up best he could, wondering just what exactly were the odds of it. Sherwood's old man sends you up the river and then here you are, putting yourself voluntarily *back* into the penitentiary to pull his kid out. *It's like a movie,* he thought, *you should write a script and send it to Hollywood.* Knox laughed then and allowed himself to keep laughing. The laughs kept coming as he pulled Sherwood to his feet and then they just waited there on the sidewalk. If they'd timed it right, it wouldn't be long.

Shane couldn't believe it. "What's so funny?"

Knox just smiled. "You know, kid, you wouldn't believe me if I told you."

Sherwood came to some, his eyes half open. "Where are we? Who... where is Imogene?"

Knox straightened him up, wanting him to look tall for his lady, to stand proud. "She's coming, pal. She's coming."

No sooner had he said it and there was Jedidiah's ritzy sled, creeping up the street, inching toward them with its lights off. Knox waved to it to let them know they were in the right place. The sled stopped and two women got out, Imogene from the driver's seat and the woman Knox knew as Timony Wells from the passenger side. They both rushed over, beside themselves with grief and worry and glee, Imogene grabbing Bennie and holding him tight. Timony tried to be as excited.

"Where's my husband? Where's Harrison?"

Knox looked at Shane and could tell they both felt awful, horrible that there was only one. Knox tried to find the words. "He... there was only him, we only found one."

Timony fell to the ground and cried out. Her agony was enough to waken the whole of the prison. Knox lurched forward and brought her back up, shushed her. "Careful, please. You must — "

"Where is he? Why isn't he here?"

All Knox could say was that he didn't know as Timony fell into him, sobbing beyond control, Knox just holding her and telling her it would be alright. Sherwood came to life some then and held onto Imogene for support as he tried to speak.

"Ai..."

He was trying to form a word and Knox could hardly believe it, how much of a time he was having trying to speak. What all had happened to him in there?

"Air..."

He said more and more of a single word, one piece at a time.

"... por..."

Imogene tried to make sense of it. "What, baby? What are you trying to say?"

"*AIRPORT*," Sherwood blurted out finally. "They took him... to the airport. They thought I couldn't hear, but I heard it all, that's where they're going. We have to go. Now."

Knox was amazed, just listen to the man now, speaking in full sentences. Maybe he was as tough as they said. Timony gathered herself and wiped tears from her eyes. "My God, yes, let's go."

Imogene could hardly make sense of it. "I mean, you just... Bennie, are you sure?"

Bennie started to stand on his own some, pulling his arms from Imogene and taking a few steps on his own. He lurched toward the car and rested against it for support. "We have to... Harrison, he..." Bennie looked at Timony. "Whatever you think he did, he didn't do it. He was drugged then and he's drugged now. There are more of them, too, come on, we've got to go." Bennie opened the passenger side door of the Buick and threw himself in. He looked over at Shane. "Call it in, Shane, call it in fast. We need everyone there."

Shane stood at attention, proud. "Yes, sir!"

Timony freed herself from Knox, giving him a look of thanks as she looked at Imogene and then the two women just held each other's arms for a moment. Imogene nodded, as if she understood her friend without having to say anything at all, Imogene rushing now for the driver's side.

Shane started to move again, too, giving Knox's back a pat as he moved past. Patting it with some urgency, a notion to move. "Well?"

Knox just stood there. "Well, what?"

"Are you coming?"

Knox looked back over his shoulder at the prison, amazed he'd made it out a second time. The last thing he needed was more trouble. "I'm done for, kid. I worked it out with your boss, Reed. I'm square."

Shane slowed. "You sure? You've come this far, you don't want to see this through?"

Knox had never felt more sure of anything in his life.

"Whatever it is, it's out of my hands, kid. I've done what I came here to do."

Shane nodded. He knew there was no persuading him. "Suit yourself."

Knox watched as MacDonald broke into a run and was pretty impressed with the kid as he darted off, hoping he played some winning part in whatever came next. And even though he knew he was risking being seen, Knox really took his time walking now and felt centered in a way he never had before. For the first time in his life, he felt gravity's pull and it made him feel honest, as if he'd done something good and deserved to be here, alive. He picked up his pace and hoped they were still waiting for him.

Stolmy, Marlon, and Constance watched as a fire truck and several police vehicles swarmed the front of the state penitentiary. They were huddled up inside Jedidiah's Buick Century and they watched as a controlled chaos built around the car that Marlon had set on fire. The flames weren't difficult to contain. Marlon had set the bomb with just the right amount of explosive, so that it didn't get out of hand. Stolmy watched as the prison guard they'd made a sucker of directed the firemen around the blaze. Stolmy promised the guard a promotion and a raise to keep his mouth shut, they didn't need this getting out. Would anyone believe him, anyway? Stolmy looked over at Marlon, the man looking proud.

"You say you… learned to do this in the war?"

Marlon nodded. "The Army taught me how. Even paid me to study it, to learn it."

Stolmy nodded, incredulous. "And you're a preacher now, is that right?"

Marlon crossed himself. "Called by God at seventeen, praise Jesus. Been his servant ever since."

Stolmy watched as the car bomb's flames rose higher and higher. "Well, in any case, I'm not supposing that this here will find its way into Sunday's sermon."

Marlon couldn't help but smile. "You'd be surprised at all I can put into a sermon, Mr. Reed. Very surprised."

The Buick shook as a car door opened and then here was Knox, sliding into the back seat. Stolmy and Marlon turned to look at him, the both of them wide-eyed. "Did it work?" Stolmy asked.

Knox answered them with a nod but kept his gaze on Constance, sitting there so far away from him on the other side of the seat. It was like she leapt across an ocean the way she pushed herself toward him and wrapped her arms around him. *What a feeling it was*, Knox thought, to feel her embrace, how wondrous it was to have it spread throughout his body, his soul.

"Did you find 'em both?" Marlon asked.

Knox shook his head. "Only Sherwood."

Constance gasped. "Oh, no, Timony!"

Knox went on. "But Sherwood, he said they took Harrison to the airport."

Stolmy was surprised. "*Byrd* airport?"

Knox shrugged. "He just said airport and that's where they're going. He said that's where they took Timony's husband."

Stolmy looked back at him with urgency. "That's where they're going? You're sure?"

Knox nodded. "It's what they said. They just left."

Stolmy breathed deep, as if called to duty once more. "Then, this, my friends, is where I leave you." He addressed each of them in turn with a stern look. "I trust we're in agreement here? About what we've all seen and experienced tonight?"

Knox, Constance, and Marlon all nodded, the three of them fully aware that this unique arrangement was unlikely to ever happen again. Stolmy lurched himself from the car then, shutting the door and hobbling his way towards the fire and the men surrounding it. Knox, Constance, and Marlon watched as Stolmy took command of the scene, directing the firemen and talking to the policemen with authority. Over the next few minutes, the firemen succeeded in smothering the fire. Knox cracked a door window and they listened to Stolmy mandate that the police drive him, right then and there, to Byrd airport. And before long, they were off, all of them — Stolmy, the cops, the firemen and their truck. It went from full-blown mayhem to a ghost town in minutes.

A silence took up in the car then and no one spoke for a

moment. *What can you even say about what we've just done?*, Marlon wondered. He looked back at Constance and Knox and sensed the warmth in their embrace. Never far from the call of duty, Marlon slid over to the driver's seat, very aware that he was about to play chauffeur to a man who not yesterday he had wanted to find and strangle and reign all manner of vigilante justice upon. But having spoken to this man Knox and heard his story, Marlon had softened on his quest for retribution and lucked out on a task for which his unique talents had finally proven useful. As he fired the car up, he could hear Constance nestle herself further into her man's embrace and he hoped then, he prayed, even, that such an embrace was waiting for him at the end of tonight's long, demanding journey. As Marlon steered the car from the curb, he laughed to himself. No matter what they'd just been through, if some policeman saw him driving this car, this ritzy car of Jedidiah's, why he'd be arrested on the spot. He'd just have to drive real slow, then, and hope no one saw him. As they pulled away, the three of them looked with some astonishment at the lingering embers of the car fire as they drove by it, it's last remaining sparks rising and disappearing into the night.

30

Eddie sized up his current digs at Lenny's Lodge. Stained carpet, fold-out Murphy bed, no window. It wasn't the nicest room at the Lodge, but Eddie was grateful, truly. Sitting there on the bed, all by his lonesome, he was overcome with loss. Martha, his job, his self-respect. Tears welled, but Eddie held them off. No time to wallow. He was on the run now and for good, maybe, so he had the room for just one night, two tops. Lenny had comped him out of pity.

Eddie came to the edge of the bed and sifted through his knapsack. He had two guns — a .22 the old man had kept under his pillow, every night until the day he died, and a .38 he'd bought off a fence just yesterday. He had near eight hundred dollars cash, his life savings. Hopefully it was enough to get him somewhere far away and keep him there. He had his mother's bible, too, not that he read it, but it was the only thing she'd left him when she died and so he kept it with him, always. He also had the clothes on his back, the hat on his head, and what was left of himself after being framed by Walter and Visel for Old Butch Donaldson's murder. They'd left his badge at the crime scene and the word was out. Eddie was now #1 on Richmond's Most Wanted List. He was the hunted now, no longer the hunter, and he didn't like it. No tears for Butch, though. The man was a terror with the ladies, good riddance.

A rap on the door — Lenny's face peeked in.

"You good in here? It ain't ritzy, but then again, neither are you."

Eddie yukked. "I won't be here long. Two nights, tops."

Lenny's look said *you're lucky to have that.* "You've got heat on you. That I don't need."

"What can I say? It wasn't me, honest."

Lenny studied him. "Yeah? You didn't clip Old Butch, like they're saying?"

Eddie put his hands up. "I don't know who did Old Butch, honest. Not that I'm sad to see him go, mind you."

Lenny smiled. "Nobody's sad to see him go." He had more to say, but wasn't sure if he should.

"What is it?"

Lenny shrugged. "You're still a cop, yeah?"

Eddie thought of his badge and department-issued gun, neither within reach. "I don't know how to be anything else."

Lenny leaned into the doorframe. "Well, if you've still got a yen for someone I *think* the cops are looking for, I've got a prize for you, Mr. Haden. A delightful prize, indeed."

Eddie didn't follow. "A prize? What prize?

Lenny opened the door wide, inviting Eddie to join him outside. "Come with me, I'll show you."

Two minutes later, they were both looking down on another man housed at Lenny's Lodge, this one scrawny and babbling a bit under his breath. He rocked back and forth on the bed in what looked like an uneasy slumber, as if he were lost in a dark kind of daydream.

"Who is he?" Eddie asked.

"*This* is George Carroll," Lenny said.

Eddie remembered Carroll's name from the blotters. "Yeah? This is *the* George Carroll?"

"In the flesh. And I was hoping that, you know, since you're a cop and all, you might do something about him."

Eddie wasn't sure he could do anything at all. "How long's he been here?"

"A week, maybe? I can't remember exactly."

"Did he come on his own? Or did someone leave him here?"

"You know I don't kiss and tell."

"Oh, come off it, Len, I'm up against the wall here. This could save me from a life of looking over my shoulder."

Lenny weighed it. "He says Jimmy Visel put a hit out on him

and that he needed somewhere to lay low."

"Yeah? How'd he know to come here?"

"He said —" Lenny started to say more, but was suddenly distracted. Distant sounds, like those from a radio, came from another room. Lenny put a hand up, as if to say *I'll be right back*, and hustled off down the hall.

Eddie looked at George and pitied him. The poor looked broken and Eddie thought of those men packed into a room like sardines. Men who had been vacated of life. Men who could be controlled, manipulated.

Lenny slipped back into the doorway. "As I was saying, Carmine Scangili told him to come here."

Eddie couldn't believe it. "You serious? What were they, chums?"

Lenny shrugged. "Beats me. It's just what he said."

Eddie mused on an idea. "What do you know about brainwashing, Len?"

Lenny almost laughed. "That it's not something I care to know anything about. You know, I tried calling Bennie to come and get him, but, well, you know. Him being MIA and all that."

Eddie did know. Hell, everyone knew Sherwood had gone AWOL after what happened with Müller at the Annex. Eddie cringed at the part he played in the interrogation. Four taps on the peek-a-boo glass and bye bye Müller. He heard Visel growl, "Do it or else." After everything he'd ever pulled to get a solved, that was the worst, the lowest he'd ever sunk as a policeman. And now here he was, a chance at redemption, a chance for him to do right, make good by his oath. He could take Carroll in, his name had been on every blotter for weeks. Been on the lips of every CI, too, everyone was trying to get a bead on him. Eddie mulled on it, trying to find the answer, when Lenny cut in.

"There's more."

Eddie wasn't sure he could take any more. "Yeah?"

"Chatter just came over the police band. Everyone and their mother is headed out to Byrd airport."

Eddie felt his body almost go numb. He'd chased that lead and missed it altogether. *The big score*, he thought, the one that would hit pay dirt for him. Send him off to a farmer's mansion and the life of a full-time porch sitter, if he did it right. He had two choices now, one big, one even bigger. He looked at Lenny. "What would it cost me for you to keep him," gesturing at George, "safe and out of harm's way?"

"Fifty bucks oughta do it."

"That's steep, Lenny."

"And this is wartime, last I checked."

"I may not have that on me..."

"Oh, please. I saw your knapsack. I know what you've got."

"Aren't you the snoop."

"What can I say. You snore."

Eddie had to agree. Martha always said so. "Okay, a century. You keep him fed, you keep him out of view, and you keep him away from other cops, yeah?"

Lenny nodded. "And if you don't return?"

"Take what's left in the duffel, set him up somewhere safe."

"You got it."

"Good. Now, what's a gassed up car run these days? Cause I need to get to the airport and fast."

Another fifty bucks, apparently, Eddie lamenting just how dry Lenny was bleeding him as he made time out to Byrd airport, the wind rushing past, the windows down as he drove. He was draining his life savings and for what, a chance at a cop's glory, to bring the big case in? Or did he want to clear his name, make a fresh start? All he knew is that he wanted to put a stop to it, whatever had befallen those empty, soulless faces, and George, too. If he could stop them from enduring any more pain, any more of whatever they were feeding them, Walter and Visel and whoever else, then yes, he would try and put a stop to it. He may not be a cop anymore, at least not a real one, but he wasn't so far gone that he didn't care. And so he leadfooted it and drove as fast as he could. His dignity barely intact, the world flying by.

Timony looked every which way from the car as they barreled east. Her instincts up, on high alert. She looked over at Imogene, driving with such confidence, pregnant as she was. She looked back at Bennie then, afraid to, really, the man clearly having endured something terrible. His head had been shaved, he had no color in his face. He didn't look emaciated, really, but Timony could tell, he hadn't eaten a real, full meal in days, the way his awareness looked all off, his rendering of things. What a horror, then, to be in a situation like —

KERCHING!

Something hit the rear of the car and bounced off. Imogene jerked the car just a little. "What the hell was that?"

Something else whizzed by the car, it sounded like a juiced-up dragonfly. Timony and Imogene looked at one another, aghast.

"Someone's shooting at us!" Timony exclaimed.

Imogene dug into the gas then, really putting her all into it. Timony just sat there in the passenger seat, feeling helpless and not wanting to, wishing she could do something, and not just anything, but something that would make her son proud of her, make her think she had made an effort all these years, that she hadn't just primped herself up and put on a face and drank herself silly with worry over where he might be. And so she looked down at the guns they brought with them, her father's guns, and she grabbed one of them and made sure it was loaded, just the way he had shown her to, and she rolled down the window and lifted herself out of her seat just enough to point the gun behind them.

"Timony, my God, what are you doing?" Imogene called out.

Timony fired off a round behind them, and then another, and then, wow, just look now, the car behind them careened and turned and ducked off the road. She must have hit a tire, she must have made an impact. She held the gun up, still watching behind them, truly sated at having derailed their aggressors. "I got 'em!" she called out, just letting the air rush through her, sitting proud and mighty like a warrior on the hunt. She wouldn't let anyone come between her and her men ever again and that most certainly meant Harrison, her husband who hadn't done the things she thought he had done. She would be with him again and soon. She ducked back into the car, her hair all around her now.

How I must look, she thought.

"My God, Imogene, did you see that??"

Bennie had about as much energy in him as a fly must have after he's been swatted but isn't all the way dead. He's not even sure where he is, but he knows that Imogene is driving and wishes she weren't. Hell, he hardly said a personal word to her since being carried out of the prison by someone he didn't even know and now here he is in the back seat of a car, the speed and the wind and chaos of it all threatening to make him nauseous. And then, even more incredulously, Timony, of all people, had leaned out the window and shot a gun at a car behind them. Stopped it, sent it off the road and off their tail. He saw her beaming in the front seat. She looked proud, secure. Bennie didn't even have the strength to sit up, so he breathed deep, just like they taught him, and tried not to close his eyes. Because if he did, he'd see the pictures and the movies again, the ones they made him look at over and over, and then he'll see the jungle, too, all of it meshed together, all of it like some nightmare art, bodies and death and women being strangled, all of it in one total picture, a haunting scene he was forced to look at again and again and again.

The car screeched, Imogene was clearly braking, the car coming to a stop. She got out of the driver's side and came around to him, pulling him out of the back seat. She leaned in to him, her face beautiful and concerned. "We're here," she said, "and something is happening, but I," she started to break into tears, "I don't want you to be a part of this, you've been through so much already, please baby… "

Bennie heard her, but he had to look, so he propped himself up against the car and watched as maybe four, five hundred yards off, at Byrd airport, a throng of men moved boxes and canvas-strapped bags onto the back of a wide-winged cargo plane. Bennie watched these men move like obedient soldiers. And even though Bennie couldn't see him, something inside of him burned with the idea. "Harrison is one of them, he's out there."

Timony sunk to the ground and kept her voice low, mouthing 'my god' over and over. Bennie had to lean against the car for support, he was so weak, but he tried to make out which one of the men was Harrison. Out on the tarmac, a militant voice carried through the air and a man stepped from behind a truck, barking orders and pointing at the plane. Bennie peered to be sure and there he was, Jimmy Visel, waving a gun at one of the men and speaking to him angrily. Bennie was sure this was the war surplus Harrison had described, it was Visel and his men who had blackmailed Harrison into securing it for The White Shadow and the Nazi sympathizers they were courting for a new stateside army. Bennie watched as Visel quit yelling and then *Blam!*, he pointed his gun at the man and shot him dead, point blank. Timony shrieked and folded into the ground, her muffled cries filled with terror. Imogene sank against the car, aghast, and Bennie felt hopeless and incompetent and wished he'd never chosen a policeman's life at all, watching the dead man's body fall to the ground, hoping and praying that it wasn't Harrison's. The other men just kept loading the plane, the lot of them clearly unbothered by the turn of events.

Sounds rang out in the distance. Sirens, it sounded like, growing louder and louder. Bennie and Imogene and Timony looked at one another, incredulous, as an army of rescue made the scene — a fire truck, police cruisers, even some unmarkeds. *Who's minding the city*, Bennie wondered, as he looked at almost the entire police department, as far as he could make out. Even Stolmy Reed had come, emerging from the fire truck and hobbling admirably along on his cane, looking at Bennie and nodding, as if he'd known all along that Bennie would make it out alright. Bennie couldn't believe it, it was all too much. He felt himself go light headed and fell into the car. Imogene caught him before he hit the ground. What a terrible feeling it is, to be a person in charge but unable to lead. Just have to let it go, let the men show their worth.

Or their perfidy, Bennie thought, watching as Eddie Haden came charging to the scene and strolled over to join them.

Eddie made the airport and wondered if something ethereal had driven him there, given him reason to be there, even, as he pulled up to a throng of his own kind.

Stolmy hobbled toward him, on the edge of livid. "What are you doing here, Haden? Don't you know you're wanted for murder?"

"Then arrest me, already. All I can tell you is that I didn't shoot Old Butch. I heard the call, I came to help."

Stolmy accepted it, for now. He gestured at the tarmac. "Visel just shot someone, so we're holding back. I don't know who he's got out there working for him, but I think they're moving the surplus, that's what this was all about."'

Eddie felt a sting in his gut — he never had figured what they were after. "What surplus? What's out there?"

Stolmy looked over at the airfield. "Masks, guns, ammunition, provisions of every kind. My god, they could equip a small army with everything they have out there."

Eddie peered at the runway — he saw men on one side, the plane on the other. Some of the surplus was on the plane already, some of it had yet to be loaded. Eddie looked at Stolmy. "If I can get in there first, can you get in behind me? Get to the men?"

Stolmy studied the airfield, curious. "Maybe, I don't know. What do you mean?"

Eddie darted for his sled. "Just get in behind me, you hear me? I'll create a diversion." And before Stolmy could protest, Eddie was off. He slid into his wheels, fired it up, and there he was, driving past the crowd of cruisers and fire trucks and his fellow policemen. He broke through the fencing and made a beeline for the stash. Run a guess — whatever's in there, something's gotta ignite.

Up ahead, Visel and his men stood gobsmacked. Visel fired at Eddie's sled. Bad aim — the bullets dinged off the hood. The men scrambled toward the plane, but it was too late, Eddie had picked up good speed and was aiming right for the pile of guns and ammo and fuel. Good on Stolmy, here they came after him. Over to the right, Eddie could see military police jeeps headed their way, their sirens ringing out. They stormed past a row of P-47s onto the tarmac.

You're too late, Uncle Sam. Eddie steered his wheels right for the bay of the plane. No time to think, just do it. He jerked open the driver's seat and threw himself onto the runway, rolling and rolling onto the ground. Holy shit did it hurt, holy shit was he old, but it didn't stop him from rolling onto his back and watching as the sled hit the surplus and rolled onto its side.

Smoke, gas leaking now —

KABOOM!

The car, the surplus — all of it exploded.

Bennie watched as Eddie's car hit the pile of supplies and burst into flames, the fires reaching to the sky. He saw Stolmy lead the trucks and the cruisers onto the airfield. The fire department got to work fast as the military police zoomed to the scene. They spilled from their jeeps in formation and cornered Visel and his men. And just like that, it was over, the surplus all charred up now, all of it a waste. It was no good to anyone now.

31

Timony pulled into her driveway and wondered how she ever made it home. Never in her wildest dreams did she imagine she would play a part in such an affair. Did she really fire a gun out of a moving car? At other human beings? She collapsed into the steering wheel, thinking about how wild and absurd and terrifying the night had been. Harrison was safe now, safe at McGuire General, and safe in her heart, but the look in his eyes… Timony winced, thinking of how frail he seemed, how starved and empty. Gone two weeks and he looked as if he had been lost at sea for months. Timony had made such a fuss at seeing him in that throng of lifeless men, she couldn't help herself. She wondered now if she had made a fool of herself in any way, embarrassed herself. And if she had, well, what did it matter now? *I did what I had to do to save my husband.* Me, a woman who coordinates parties and writes columns about what people wear and the beaches they go to on vacation. *I did this,* she thought. And while she was beyond relieved that her husband was safe now and the truth, as he told it, the way it came out through Harrison's rambling, that he had been drugged and framed and that he hadn't been with that floozy at all, that it was all a setup, she wished she could share the moment with Nolan more than anyone in this world. And so rather than sink into the dumps about it, rather than drown herself in a bottle, she would write a letter to her son and tell him everything that had happened that night. The thought of it delighted her and she stepped from the car suddenly more aware of almost everything within reach, as if the entire ordeal had awoken some magical gift within her to appreciate every touch, every smell, every sight. The way her feet touched the ground, the look of the daffodils in her yard, the way her house seemed to tilt as she looked up, the smell of her car's engine as it cooled. It was as if everything were more alive today than it was yesterday and she relished it, thankful that she could experience it, live it, write about it.

She stepped into her home and felt so grateful then, buoyant and lucky. And as she peeled off her heels and slipped the jacket off her back, letting everything just fall to the floor, she heard a sound she never expected to hear at this hour.

Laughter.

Someone was laughing in her home, here in he middle of the night. Timony traced its source, the sound of it luring her down the main hallway and back towards their entertaining rooms, back towards the kitchen. It was as if *she* were now the sailor, lost at sea, hearing sounds of life for the first time in weeks. She followed the sounds all the way to the kitchen, hearing Macy's high pitched laugh, of course, and her cousins, too, Robinson and Christian. Timony loved to hear them laugh. And she was so excited at seeing them all, hoping they would share the joke with her, include her in their joy, that she almost didn't see him at first, the way Nolan was just standing there, all six feet of him, his mouth chomping into a chicken leg, talking and laughing as he ate. He still had that same goofy, innocent look he had worn for years, the one that looked as if he had stolen it from a Norman Rockwell painting, and just then Timony could hardly move, so stunned she was that she stopped breathing, just looking at the four of them, wondering if somehow it had all been a dream, the ordeal at the airport and now this, but then Nolan saw her and nearly jumped out of his skin.

"Mom!"

They would tell her later that she had a look of pure amazement on her face as she fell, as if she'd just seen the world's greatest magic trick, but the only thing Timony could remember thinking as she began to faint was that *my son is home, my son is home, my son is home.*

CLASSIFIED INTELLIGENCE
RIVER CITY HERALD / AUGUST 10, 1945
BY TIMONY 'THURSDAY' WELLS

Ring those wedding bells, folks! The one and only Miss Imogene Angela McKenna is set to wed Benjamin Thomas Sherwood of the Richmond Police Department in a public ceremony on the steps of City Hall. Can you believe they're finally tying the knot? Bennie, as he's commonly called, has been away for most of the summer on a special assignment for none other than Uncle Sam! Details of his top-secret venture are locked away tight, but I have it on high, dear readers, his union with Miss McKenna is a go! Look for them to make it official just as soon as we call it quits on the war. Best wishes to them both!

*   *   *   *

The ever delightful Miss Constance Lee has been recently spotted in the company of a former beau, one Mr. Knox Sutton. Look for them most any night on the town, especially on the Tantilla Garden dance floor, where they light up the room like fireworks! A more compatible couple you're unlikely to find.

*   *   *   *

Speaking of Tantilla Garden, can you say Hollywood? Rumor has it that none other than Tantilla's hot-hot-house band, Johnny Pepper and The Salt Shakers, are being courted for an appearance in a new MGM musical! Be on the lookout friends, because Johnny and his fellas are soon to be 'The Top of Tinseltown!' Coming soon to a theater near you!

*   *   *   *

Spotted: Jedidiah King at The John Marshall Hotel with not

one but two lucky ladies on his arm! Our city's most flamboyant philanthropist never seems to do without, now does he?

*   *   *   *

Can you say Bachelor-In-Demand? Nolan Byron Wells has been home from the war since late June, ladies, and he has been diligently following in his father's footsteps, oh yes he has! You all know, from previous columns, that my loving husband Harrison was chosen for an overseas appointment and has been away for some time. In his absence, Nolan is currently serving on not one, not two, but three city committees! When not called to duty, you can find him almost any night of the week holding court at either The County Club or The Commonwealth Club. Take a look, ladies, I think you'll like what you see!

PART SIX

VICTORY IN JAPAN DAY

WEDNESDAY, AUG 15, 1945
RICHMOND, VIRGINIA

32

Bennie peeked through the see-through glass window of the sanatorium room where George Carroll was being held and watched as he sat at a table and drew a picture with the focus and intensity of a young child. An attendant looked on, they didn't want Carroll to try and hurt himself with one of the pencils. How peaceful Carroll looked, how at ease. The doctors had allowed him, under watchful supervision, to draw and write for an hour a day and Bennie was amazed at the body of work that lined the walls of his padded room. There were poems, diatribes, scribblings of prose and verse, proclamations and declarations. And there were drawings, apocalyptic visions and renderings of biblical stories that played out on large swaths of canvas sheets, each one with its own eye-opening and alarming attention to detail. In one, lightning bolts emanated from the sun as fires rose up from the Earth, men and women fighting above them, warring with one another on a battleground made of flames. In another, a God-like man held a Jewish soldier by his throat and pierced his heart with a jagged Star of David. The soldier's blood poured over the dozens of soldiers that lay dead on the ground below. Bennie wondered: if Carroll saw these things in his dreams, would he see them, too?

He hadn't yet and didn't want to know if he would. Bennie stepped back from the glass and checked a wall clock. It was almost ten 'o clock in the morning and he had to make this quick — in just three hours, he'd be wedding Imogene on the steps of City Hall. Carroll's doc rang him this morning, said they had a few breakthroughs and to come if he could, that Carroll might be on the verge of remembering something useful. Bennie caught a look at himself in the reflection of the window while he waited and took stock of himself. He was still a bit haggard, he knew that. He'd only recently started to eat full meals again. He was exercising again, too, getting his push-ups and sit-ups in twice a day. Maybe it wouldn't be too long until he looked more like himself again, looked the way he did before they took him and locked him away.

The doctor attending to Carroll came out to the waiting room and shook Bennie's hand.

"I'm Doctor Neville, thank you for coming."

Bennie nodded and gestured at Carroll. "How's he getting along?"

"Somedays he's talkative, somedays he's not. When he is, well, what he has to say isn't always pleasant, but little by little, we're getting a sense of who he was before he had a breakdown. Or at least, that's what we think happened."

"What about the pictures, the writings? Does it help to let him do that?"

"We think so. It allows us to see what's happening in his mind. We can't help him if we don't know what he's thinking. And while we're not forcing anything on him, we're slowly introducing material that could help steer his mind in a more positive direction. Art and literature that's educational, uplifting, less provocative."

"What do you think happened to him?"

"By our estimation, just the opposite. We think someone tried to brainwash him. Of course, we don't know the details, but what we've gathered is that someone fed him a steady diet of just what you see now on the walls. Hate, discrimination, us-versus-them. A steady diet of religious persecution, too. And whoever did this to him, they did it so often and so persuasively that," Doctor Neville snapped his fingers, "he turned, just like that."

Bennie thought of the films and images Visel made him look at after he'd been taken, how they'd pinned his eyes open and made him watch movies of women being strangled and pictures of men being sodomized against their will. Made him watch these things over and over, for hours at a time, before throwing him back into the prison cell to sit in the darkness. He tried to shake off the memories and failed. "What about the other men, the ones we rounded up out at the airfield?"

Doctor Neville appeared more hopeful. "They're likely to recover, I believe, although it may be longer for some than others. We don't think they were exposed to quite as much damage for as long as Carroll was."

Fifteen men, Bennie remembered. Fifteen drones, men who had been stripped of their cognition and re-programmed as soldiers for whatever new world army Visel had been trying to create. Fingerprint checks had identified many of them as ex-convicts, men Visel must have gotten to know, men he must have believed he could manipulate.

Neville could see that Bennie was lost in thought. "Detective Sherwood? Would you like to try and talk to Carroll?"

Bennie brought himself back into the moment. "Yes, of course."

Neville ushered them into George's room. The attendant looking after him walked over and told him his time was up, he had to surrender the pencil. George did so willingly and then looked up at Dr. Neville, as innocent as can be. "I made a new one, doc. Want to see?"

"Of course, George."

George held up his latest work of art. It was a fully-realized depiction of a dragon disemboweling a horse. Blood was splashing everywhere, entrails were being ripped out. The horse's legs had been amputated and the dragon was feasting on one of its hooves. The whole nine yards.

Dr. Neville just smiled. He'd seen it all before. "Very nice, George. George, I've brought someone to see you. This is Detective Sherwood, he's with the police department. Is it okay if he asks you a few questions?"

George looked at Bennie and seemed to recall him. They had seen each other just once before, nearly three months ago. Carroll had led them on a rooftop chase after ditching that halfway house. Carroll looked at Neville. "Could the policeman and I step outside, have a cigarette together?"

Neville turned to Bennie. "That ok with you?"

"Works for me."

A few minutes later, Bennie and George were seated on hardback chairs just outside the sanatorium, sitting in the shade of the building's eastern wing. Bennie pulled a pack of smokes from his jacket pocket, one of Jedidiah's top brands. Bennie had a few packs of them at home now, one of Jedidiah's many gifts to him since he'd been on the mend. Bennie took two, handed one to George, and lit them both with a match.

George took a drag and exhaled with deep satisfaction. "That's a good smoke. You can afford these premium sticks on a cop's salary?"

"Matter of fact, they were a gift."

"Is that so? A top cop like you, I sure hope that isn't code for taking a bribe."

"Well, now, listen to you. For what it's worth, that's not something you need to worry about."

George nodded and kept his gaze on the woods out past the sanatorium. "I remember you. That day on the roofs? I thought to myself, now there's a copper gonna do alright for himself. You and that other fella gave good chase, I'll give you that."

"You sure seem to remember a lot."

"I've been locked up in one place or another since I was sixteen, Mr. Detective. Gives a man a lot of time to think. And to remember things."

"By the looks of the drawings in there, what you think about doesn't sound very pleasant."

"Oh, I don't know about that. One man's nightmare is another man's dream, eh?"

Bennie thought of his own nightmares — hand-to-hand combat in Technicolor. "Well, you certainly seem pretty lucid for someone in a sanatorium. Dr. Neville said you were on the verge of a breakthrough. If I didn't know any better, I'd say you broke through a long time ago."

George sneered to himself and looked down at his feet. "Is it that obvious?"

Bennie couldn't believe it. He leaned over, kept his voice low. "You gotta be fucking kidding me, this is all an act?"

George held out his hand, palm down, and shook it like he

wasn't sure. "Some days I know exactly what's going on. Other days, well, not so much. You can take my word for it or not."

Bennie shot a look over his shoulder — through a window, he saw Dr. Neville reading a chart. He couldn't be more than ten yards away. "And what's stopping me from ratting you out right now?"

"'Cause then you won't find out what happened, Mr. Detective. And that's what this is all about, yeah? You want to know who shot the nice Jewish lady. *And* who put a slug in old Carmine. Isn't that right?"

Bennie took a long drag. Goddamnit — what is the truth, anyway? He checked his watch — *shit*. "So dish, George. Tell me what happened, or I rat you to the doc."

"You want it all?"

Bennie made the gimme sign. "Everything you got."

"Ok, Detective, here it is. When I was sixteen, I used to run with my cousin, down in southern Virginia. We stole a little, robbed a little. Nothing big time. But then my cousin, well, he raped these two girls and set fire to a church, just for fun. I didn't have any part in that, God's honest truth, but he ran off and left me to take the fall. The local cops knew we ran together and they figured I must have had something to do with it. So, I got locked up as a teen for something I didn't do. I was pretty mad at first, I'll admit it, but life inside wasn't so bad. Three square meals, a bed. Hell, it was better than my life on the outside, 'cause I grew up poor. Like real poor. Dirt floors and nothing to eat for days at a time, that kind of poor. So I didn't mind it on the inside. And then I got to reading and taking these classes, all so I could get my high school diploma. I did seven years and got pretty used to it, before they cut me loose."

Bennie wasn't sure he heard him right. "Cut you loose?"

"Yeah, my cousin eventually got nabbed out in Kentucky and he wound up confessing to all these crimes he'd committed so that maybe he'd get a lighter sentence. He didn't, he's locked up for good now, but after he told the judge about raping those two girls and burning the church, well, they cut me loose. So I was on the outside again. Had my diploma, sure, so I could have made a real go of it, gotten a job and all that, but, I gotta tell you, Mr. Detective, I didn't like it much."

"So you got yourself locked up again *on purpose?*"

George smiled, proud. "I broke into these people's homes while they were sleeping. I had fun with it at first, but then I just wanted to get back inside, so I did this real sloppy burglary job and they nailed me for all this jewelry I stole. I even told 'em where they could find it all so it could be returned. You see, I never wanted to hurt anyone. I just liked the order of being inside, you know? Every day's the same, no surprises."

Bennie wasn't sure what to make of it. "Doesn't sound like much of a life."

"If you grew up the way I grew up, you'd see it differently. Anyways I got locked up again and this time it's the Virginia state penitentiary. I got my squares back, my bed, I'm right as rain. But then, well, on account of me always being alone, you know, I start to get these ideas. That what people are saying to me isn't what they mean. Same with the books I was reading, I started to get the sense that there were these what you call subliminal messages being pushed on me. And well, I guess you could say I started to crack a bit. And that just happened to be the same time I met Carmine."

Bennie checked his watch — wedding bells loomed. "Who killed him, George?"

George flicked his cigarette butt into the grass. "We're getting there. See, Carmine took a shine to me because I reminded him of this kid brother he used to have. The brother, he was kinda dim, if you know what I mean, and he got killed by some other kids when he was just a boy. Carmine, well, he never got over it and when he met me, I'd started to crack a little with all those ideas, so it was like I was kinda dim, too. So we got on and I got pretty used to seeing him around the penitentiary, you know? He was like a friend."

"This doesn't sound like the Carmine we've heard about."

"Oh, Carmine was plenty mean, alright, and he let the other inmates have it all the time. That was also on account of Carmine being, how can I say it… He didn't like girls, you know? And he was all frustrated about it, like he felt wrong all the time. But it was Müller and Visel, really, they were rough on Carmine and so he was rough on everyone else. And Carmine, well, he didn't have any family around, so those two were his family. And it was what you might call a real dysfunctional arrangement, at that. Anyways, Müller and Visel, they see the curtain fall on the Nazis, but they've still got these fascist tendencies, these beliefs, you know? They think they're going to keep the cause going and Visel, well, he rigs all this paperwork behind the scenes to get these inmates freed from the prison, he's trying to build an army, can you believe that? I know this because Carmine told me. And they wanted Carmine to be a part of it, too, you know? And he wasn't sure, but he didn't want to disappoint em, either, because they're family, like I said. So they give him this initiation, he's got to go kill that Jewish woman. They want to see if he has it in him, see if he's got what it takes. I could see him leaning towards going through with it, because he wants to prove to them he can, but I don't want him to kill that woman. I plead with him, over and over. But it doesn't matter, because Müller still took him to the five-and-dime that night. Carmine couldn't do it, so Müller shot her."

"Carmine told you this?"

George nodded. "He was spooked something fierce, I tell you. He was convinced Tommy was gonna hurt him and he didn't want anyone else to die, so he went behind Visel's back and snuck me out of the prison. And he gave me all those photographs you found in my duffel. Told me to get 'em to the authorities, to rat out Visel and Müller and all their criminal plans."

"Why didn't you?"

"Because Visel shot Carmine and left him in that house that burned up. I wasn't exactly a free man at that point and I didn't think anyone would believe me, anyhow. Plus, I wasn't used to being on the outside and that made me crack even more, just the pressure of it, of having to make decisions every day, it was too much. I had a decent spot at a halfway house that was good, that felt like being inside, but then, well, you found me there and then I was on the run."

"Did you see Visel shoot Carmine?"

George nodded, tearful. "Yeah. After he snuck me from the prison, I met Carmine at his apartment later that same night. We made a plan to come see you, of all people, the very next day, but Müller and Visel broke in, in the middle of the night, and shot him in his bed. I got out through the fire escape, they never saw me."

Bennie stared at George, dumbstruck. "That is a hell of a story, George."

"Yeah, it really is. Say, you want to take one of my drawings? I bet it would really liven up your office."

33

Imogene smoothed her wedding dress, having pressed it and sewed its loose ends and ran her fingers over every inch of it several times now. *It's perfect*, she finally concluded, and hung it up on the door of her closet, being careful that it didn't touch the floor. She'd had to open it up a bit, give it some room, because she was starting to show now, just a little, and she didn't want the photos to reflect it. *Better they show I've just put a few on*, she thought, than think I'm pregnant out of wedlock. She sat on the edge of the bed and looked at herself in the mirror, sitting there in nothing but her slip and wondering if she were ready. Not just to be married again, but to be married to a policeman.

It had been just over seven weeks since Bennie had been rescued from the confines of the state penitentiary, six weeks since he'd been returned to Imogene in a state she could only call fragile. They had shaved his head, they had shown him things, images, movies, things he said he would never be able to unsee. For weeks, he had slept on his own in another room. He said it was just temporary, that he didn't want to disturb her and the baby and make anything more difficult for her while she went through the changes overtaking her body. But she heard him, every night, thrashing and struggling to sleep, crying out in the night and pacing in his room, hitting himself, even, talking to himself and having conversations with people that weren't there. She had listened to him do this for weeks, pretending to sleep but unable to truly relax while he muttered and paced and went for days without any rest. He had no appetite, either, eating nothing but a single piece of bread over an entire day, a fried egg, maybe. Imogene had to practically force water into him those first few weeks, he didn't want to put anything into his body. All she could do was wonder what they *had* put into him while he was locked away.

She had tried to care for him, but it was near impossible. After three weeks, she was ready to call it, move in with Constance and look in on him from afar, but that night he came to her as she pretended to sleep. She remembered how scared she had been when he slipped into the bed, finally, wondering if she had let it go on too long, that he was too far gone, he needed real, professional help and he was going to hurt her, but all he did was slip into the bed and lie flat on his back. As if he was trying to assimilate back into his old life a step at a time, that it had finally dawned on him that he could try and do that. Every day and night since then, it had gotten better and better, he had started to eat more, drink more water, he even started doing push-ups in the morning again, like he used to. She was impressed at first but then afraid at the way his bones showed through his skin. How weak he must feel, how depleted. But press on, he did, Imogene was truly amazed as every day became better than the one before. It was like she was rehabilitating one of her patients at McGuire, the way he ate a little more, smiled a little more, touched her a little more. Caresses at first and then touches on her back as he moved past her through a room, every touch a little more affectionate than the last. And then three nights ago, he'd slipped into bed and pulled her close to him for the first time in forever, she didn't even know how long it had been. It started slow at first, the two of them both finding their way around each other's bodies for what felt like the first time, and then they were on each other like a pair of lovers in heat, Imogene surprised the room didn't catch on fire the way they went after one another. It was raw, it was carnal, and it was full of love.

Imogene allowed herself a smile, thinking of it. In the last several days, he had come alive, even more. His hair had started to come in, too, and he was ready to take a crack at going to the office. "Just want to stop in," he'd said the first time, and then the second time went on longer and then the third time went on even longer than that. He was checking case files, he told her, he was getting what's new from Shane and Eddie and all the other cops.

And then he surprised her yesterday, telling her that he had asked Stolmy for no less than a demotion. That he wanted to remain a detective and stay a detective for as long as he could stand it, that he did not want to assume control of the department. Not now, not ever.

"It's what I know. And it won't keep me away as long, from either of you."

Imogene hated the thought of him giving up more for her. "But, didn't you want to move up, don't you want more?"

Bennie shook his head. "I can't change who I am. But I can make that part of me easier to be with. I don't want more responsibility for the city, not when I've got you.. " Bennie looked at her expanding belly, "… and Sam waiting on me."

She was taken aback. "Oh, it's Sam, is it? You've decided? How do you know it's a boy?"

Bennie wrapped an arm around her. "Call it wishful thinking."

"Yeah, well, we need to have another name ready, in case it's a girl."

"That's easy. Sam."

"I'm sorry?"

"It's Sam either way. We'll name him Samuel if he's a boy, Samantha if she's a girl. Either way, the kid's name is Sam."

Imogene smiled, surprised that she actually liked the idea, and glad that Bennie had found his sense of humor again. He was more like himself, finally.

A pause.

"Are you sure you're okay with it?" she had asked him. "I thought you wanted to be chief someday."

"No, not anymore. But, it's a detective's salary I'll be on. Can you live with that?"

Imogene kissed him, hard and full. And then she gave him a look.

"What's that for?" he asked.

"I'm not giving up driving a cab or working at the hospital just because we're having a baby."

Imogene remembered how he had looked at her then, how he must be mulling it over but keeping it to himself, that man-works-while-woman-stays-home spiel that every new family must contend with. But then he just smiled and said that he didn't care, that as long as she was happy, he was happy. She had remembered that smile for days.

The memory helped bring her mood up and she looked up then, into the mirror. She had just been sitting there, watching that entire conversation play out in her mind, right there in their room, and thinking of his smile, she just knew that it was the right thing. She looked over at the clock, it was almost noon. She leapt up and grabbed her dress. It was time, finally, to get ready.

34

Timony stood before her vanity dresser in nothing more than a lace-trimmed slip and took stock of herself, unimpressed. She had always been slender — good genes and bones, passed down from mother — but her figure now was gaunt and infirm. She'd hardly eaten of late and had had no real appetite for weeks. She could remember being this slim only twice before — once for her debutante coming-out party at seventeen and then again for her wedding at twenty-one. She starved herself both times with crackers and champagne. The difference, of course, was that she had chosen the limits on both occasions. This, her current state, was less voluntary.

Truth was, the events of the summer had been all too much, plain and simple. Nolan was home, yes, and to that she was eternally grateful, but the events of that horrible night at the prison and then the airfield had all but eclipsed his homecoming. Since then, she'd woken several times from vivid nightmares in a sweat. Visions of Nazis and gunfire filled her head. She cancelled her Thursday night bridge parties weeks ago, until further notice, and had leaned on Constance as a ghostwriter for her weekly column. She had groceries and beverages delivered. She ignored phone calls and blew off appointments. She slept in most days and drank more than she ate. And she didn't leave the house unless it was to visit Harrison.

Poor Harrison. The 'ordeal,' as she had come to call it privately, had taken too hefty a toll on his well-being. He was now shuttered away under an assumed name in a private wing at the Medical College of Virginia, just downtown. Timony had arranged, under the strictest of confidences, for Harrison to be seen by one doctor and one doctor only. She wasn't about to trust Harrison's care to anyone who might leak his current whereabouts and condition to the press, so she employed the services of a private detective to vet both the doctor and his rotation of nurses. Timony was relieved to find they were all honest, hard-working professionals, and she paid them well. She wanted as much control over Harrison's care as she could get, even if his current state was dire.

On that last thought, she shuddered. How ironic it was that her son, who had known countless fears and unfathomable tragedies across Europe, was now safe at home with her, while her husband, who had been caught up in a twisted, nefarious scheme just miles from their home, was not. She could hardly begin to think of what Harrison had endured, kidnapped and locked away at the penitentiary, but she was very much aware of how 'the ordeal' had left him. He was often vacant and unresponsive during their visits together at the hospital. He said very little, if he spoke at all, and was easily distracted by his own stray thoughts The doctor encouraged Timony to recall their happiest memories together and share them with Harrison, in the hopes they might bring him back to life. But not only was she dismayed to find that revisiting the past did not achieve said result, she was herself gutted to find there weren't a lot of happy memories to call to mind. Turns out, two adults living lives of purpose in the public eye didn't leave a lot of room for the moments that truly counted. Making dinner together at home. Cuddling on the couch and listening to the radio. Going to the movies and then for a cocktail afterwards, just to talk. Sitting with Harrison in his hospital room as he stared out the window, Timony grieved for those moments the most, for not being able to appreciate what had been right in front of her this whole time.

She was exhausted just thinking about it. *How long have I been standing here?* she wondered. She threw a look at her bedside clock and nearly shrieked. *My God, we have less than an hour!*

She pulled on her patterned housecoat and rushed to the hallway, calling for her son. "Nolan! Nolan, dear, are you — "

And there he was suddenly, standing just outside his bedroom in the navy blue suit he had worn for his junior year dance. Timony gasped. "How handsome you are, my goodness. And I can't believe it still fits!"

"Wild, right?" Nolan swung his jacket over a shoulder and began to walk towards her in a playful strut, like a model on the runway at a fashion show. Timony giggled, she loved it. Nolan laughed, too, amused with himself. He did a little twirl at the end of the hallway and took her hand and kissed it. "What do you say, mother, fancy a night on the town? The Japs are gonna fold any minute now, I'm sure of it. We ought to get a jump on the celebrations."

Timony's stomach fluttered. "Goodness, I... I just don't know. I'm not sure I'm ready for all that. Are you sure you want to?"

"Why of course! People are beginning to talk, they think you're a shut-in. Come on, let's get out there and show the world your face again." He winked at her. "Everyone misses you."

Timony felt a current run through her. It *did* sound like fun. "It would be nice, wouldn't it?"

"Come on, what do you say?"

Timony took both of his hands, held them tight, and rested against his chest. He was a head taller than she was, he had Harrison's height. He kept his thick blonde hair rough and slightly unkempt. He was lean from the war but still strong, she could see it in his arms. He had a fair complexion, an inviting smile, and dusty brown eyes that were a bit older now that he was home. They had more depth. They had seen real darkness. She looked up into them and wondered if he saw the same qualities in hers.

"We need it, don't we?"

"Do we ever," Nolan said.

"Okay, then, yes, yes, yes!" Timony raced into her bedroom and made for her walk-in closet. "I think light blue should do it, it'll match your suit. Here, let me see." She began to rifle through her many dresses, searching for the right one. She felt giddy all of a sudden, like she just heard some wonderful news on a bright, spring day. *There* — one of her favorites, a chambray button down with a slit neck. Just the right mix of friendly and flirty and perfect for a warm, summer day. She eased her closet door shut and called out to Nolan as she dressed.

"Where do you want to go tonight, sweetheart?"

"Where *don't* I want to go, is more like it. Let's do the Commonwealth Club, let's do Tantilla. Westwood, Tillie's, the Jefferson — "

Timony laughed. "You weren't kidding!"

"It'll be a night we'll never forget, mother. We'll make some new memories, you'll see."

Timony emerged from her closet, all ready in her dress and a pair of brown-buckled heels. "We certainly need some new ones, I'll give you that." She put a hand on her hip and struck a pose. "What do you think?"

Nolan whistled. "You'll never stop turning heads, mother."

Timony sat down at her vanity and started with her make up. "You're too good to me, son. Have I told you what a joy it is to have you home again?"

"Only once an hour."

"So you've noticed? Best get used to it, then. There are no limits to a mother's love."

"Apparently not. Say, should I drive us tonight?"

"A sweet thought, but no. I've hired a driver. And he'll certainly get his money's worth, with all these places you want to go."

"Do you think Bennie and Imogene will join us? Afterwards, I mean."

"I'll insist on it! I'll call Jedidiah, too."

"I like him. Think he'll, uh, bring Constance with him?"

Timony looked at Nolan through the mirror with a knowing smile. "Smitten with Ms. Lee, are you?"

"There's no denying it, she's a looker."

"She is, indeed. She's also *very* spoken for, I'm sorry to tell you."

Nolan grinned. "Figures. Not to worry, though. I'll find a suitable match, yet. Perhaps even tonight!"

Timony applied the last of her foundation and lipstick and stood to face him. "Oh no, not tonight, you won't. Tonight, you're *my* date, you hear me?"

Nolan laughed. "The only thing I hear is my stomach rumbling. Say, why did you cut Macy loose?"

Timony helped Nolan into his jacket. "Because it's high time I learn to do things for myself, that's why. It's time for a change, don't you think?" Harrison's 'ordeal' had stirred within Timony a real need for self-reliance. But Macy, Christian, Robinson, they were all still friends. She wanted the best for them and she was helping to see to that, any way she could.

"I suppose I just miss her," Nolan said.

"As do I." Timony smoothed Nolan's lapels. "But we'll be seeing plenty of her, don't you worry. Imogene and I are helping to coordinate a nursing school at her church, sort of an apprentice program, so they can get better jobs and better serve their families."

"You're one of a kind, mom. A true rebel. But what will the ladies at the country club think?"

"I don't give a *damn* what they think. Hell, they need me more than I need them, anyhow. And believe me, they're all too chickenshit to talk about *me* behind my back. Nobody wants to end up a sour item in my column."

Nolan made a face. "Did I say rebel? You have all the makings of a ruthless killer, mother."

Timony winked. "A girl's gotta make her way in this world the only way she knows how. Now, the car's gonna be here any minute. There's sandwich fixings in the icebox, so we can eat a snack on the way. You ready?"

Nolan help up his right arm at an angle. "Ready."

Timony hooked her left arm through and they were off, arm in arm, to see Bennie and Imogene married on the front steps of City Hall and then for a night on the town. Timony gushed, she was so happy, she had just what she wanted — her son, all to herself.

35

Marlon looked out over the crowd assembled there on the steps of City Hall and marveled at the faces, the smiles. The onlookers, too, everyone just walking by and cheering. It was, after all, a day to celebrate, in more ways than one. The Japanese had surrendered, finally, and the world was rejoicing. Richmond was awash in celebration, everywhere you looked, and as intoxicating as it was, Marlon began to wonder if he had made a wise choice, after all, having agreed to officiate this wedding here in the midst of such a large gathering of people. He could only hope that in the midst of such fervor, such jubilation, that this crowd, filled with white folks, mind you, he hoped they didn't suddenly see him as a threat and then storm after him, carry him off and string him up in a noose, all because they were just riled up and had nothing better to do. And he thought again of where was he standing, on the steps of a building that never seemed to care much for his kind, never made decisions that did his folk any bit of good. But here he stood, proud, and being the dutiful servant of God that he was, well, if this is where he was supposed to be, then so be it.

Marlon clutched his bible and watched as Bennie and Imogene made their way to the steps and started their way up toward him. How beautiful she looked, with her reddish-brown mane and her fitted dress and her lipstick just like her hair, my God. He harbored a man's thought then and hoped that Bennie was a worthy companion for this heavenly creature, but watching him now as he came up the steps and knowing what he knew, that Bennie had endured some severe hardship and that he had been in recovery, well, watching him now you wouldn't know that, the way he walked tall, the way he held the hand of his bride-to-be, the way he admired her and looked at her with love in his eyes.

You look good, Bennie Sherwood, thought Marlon, as Bennie and Imogene came up to the step just beneath his and looked to him to seal their union.

"Oh, Lord!" Marlon said loudly, letting it ring out over the crowd. "We are here today to bear witness to the joining of this man and this woman in holy matrimony. Does anyone have reason to say otherwise or reason to speak ill of this union?"

Marlon heard cheers and laughter, he heard joy. He heard no dissent. He looked out over the crowd. He saw many faces he did not know, but among them he saw familiar faces, too. The man Stolmy was there, the one they called The Cane. Jedidiah was there, too, and Constance. And her beau, the one Marlon had come to know as Knox.

"No? Then let us proceed! But before we commence this union, let me offer to the crowd a few words about the bonds of matrimony." Marlon adjusted his eyepatch, just to be sure it was in place, and looked at Bennie and Imogene with his good eye, his right eye, before he looked out over the crowd and tried not to think too gaily about what was truly on his mind. "In theory, matrimony is unbreakable. It is a bond like no other, bonded together by love. True love, and what is stronger than that, I ask you? What is stronger than true love?"

The crowd had no answer for him. Marlon heard cheers, he heard people milling about, all up and down the street, but none offered an answer to his question. And so finally he answered it himself.

"Nothing," he said loudly, so that everyone could hear, "Nothing is stronger than true love. But forces beyond our control, well, they seek to break it. They seek to tear it apart, to render it obsolete."

Right at that very moment, in a neighborhood just west of the city limits, Miles Strickland got into his car, started it, and then felt the world rush up against him as the engine went up in flames. He staggered from his vehicle, trying to stamp out the blaze on his clothes. He fell to the ground, shrieking, and felt the burning on his skin.

Back on the steps of City Hall, Marlon smiled. "Nothing is

stronger than the bonds we build together, the bonds we form between us. But the world," he looked up then at the sky, really selling it, "it will try and break you down. It will try and crush you."

In the very next moment, at his home on the south side of the city, Astor Halifax got into his car, started it, and then felt it shake underneath him until it came alight and then there he was, rolling out onto the street, his clothes all in flames. He writhed back and forth, screaming at the sky.

Marlon smiled again and looked at Ruby, who he saw now in the crowd. Like him, she didn't like it, either, being around a big horde of white folk, but she had wanted to be there for him. Their time was coming. They had gotten a ring, finally, and had a date set for September. Marlon felt his love for her rise up inside him and spoke again to the crowd. "For it is together that we rise from complications, from disagreements. It is together that we build ourselves up. Do you hear me?"

Bennie and Imogene looked at each other then, neither of them just exactly sure what they were hearing, but happy nonetheless to hear the crowd rally to Marlon's cry, to be a part of this moment, their moment.

Marlon looked at Imogene. "Do you, Imogene Angela McKenna, do you take this man to be your lawfully wedded husband?

Imogene beamed as she slipped a ring on Bennie's finger. "I do."

Marlon looked at Bennie. "Do you, Benjamin Thomas Sherwood, do you take this woman to be your lawfully wedded wife?"

Bennie started to cry as he slipped a ring onto Imogene's finger. "I do."

"Do you promise to cherish one other? To love one another, in sickness and in health?"

Bennie and Imogene nodded at one another. "We do "

"Do you promise to forsake all others, to ignore temptation and to stay true to one another?"

"We do."

"Then by the power vested in me…"

Marlon locked eyes with Knox just then, wondering if he'd been able to do it.

"I now pronounce you…"

Bennie and Imogene had never been more ready.

"Man and wife."

Bennie and Imogene kissed then and it seemed as if the whole of the city erupted into joy, everyone clapping and cheering, and they weren't sure if it was for them or for the end of the war, but it didn't matter, they were together now, for good or ill, for now and forever, and they'd had hundreds of witnesses see it come through.

Marlon found Ruby and started to make his way through the crowd, eager to be out of it, but more eager to know, if what he hoped was happening was in fact a reality. And as he took Ruby's hand and kissed her and started to move north, to their side of the street, he came upon Knox, the one who had haunted his dreams for so long, and saw Knox's nod, his very direct nod, and Marlon knew that it had happened, after all, that it was true.

What Marlon knew now was at that very moment, Walter MacKeye was leaving an apartment he thought only a handful of his cronies knew about but that, in fact, a cop named Eddie Haden knew all about, too. And now Eddie and a few other other cops were standing around Walter's car, marveling at the explosive paraphernalia found in the back seat and trunk. The remnants of gunpowder, the pipe casings, the strands of wire. And the addresses of Miles Strickland and Astor Halifax, scribbled onto a piece of paper and just found there, in the front seat. Knox had said it would happen like that, that this cop had a grudge with Walter and would be happy to play along, and so Marlon let it sink in, this feeling of getting even. It didn't feel right at first, Marlon ashamed that he couldn't do it himself, that he'd had to call in help, from white people at that, to get it done. But then he thought of Cornell and of Charles and of Marcus, men who had been jeered at, spit on, called names. He thought of their fathers and brothers, too. Men who had been locked up for longer sentences than their crimes deserved. Men who had been denied jobs on account of their skin color. Men who, like himself, had been made to feel lesser of themselves by the mere presence of statues lining Monument Avenue.

Marlon smiled and looked at Ruby and knew that today's joy would not last. That even though they were part of something, that they had been included in this celebration today, it would not be for long before they were spit on again, denied again, made to feel lesser again. And right now, he could not let it matter, he had to go on, he had to put on his preacher smile and show his world that all was well, that there was much to be rejoiced upon. He kissed Ruby again, excited that she would become his wife, and looked at the crowd they were now approaching, everyone outside now, the lot of them on Second Street, all of them knowing what he knew, that this happiness would not last, not any of it.

"Let us celebrate!" he shouted out. "And let us praise the Lord, the war is over!"

36

Knox stepped into the apartment he'd come to know over the last six weeks and wondered if he'd ever truly get used to it. Four years in a prison cell and the idea of more space just felt wrong, as if he couldn't let himself trust it. It had been a drab setup upon arrival, but now it was all jazzed up with Constance's touch — bright curtains over the windows, a sitting room arranged just so. Everything a shade of peach and red. She saved up quite a bundle working for King and now she was spoiling Knox with it. Nights on the town with dinner to the nines and brand new threads to boot. Being with her was the tops, she was like a bottle of champagne, always fun and bubbly and ready to celebrate. But the rest of his life, Knox wasn't so sure about yet. He quit driving a cab and got into the home-building business. It was a ground floor gig in construction that didn't pay much, not yet, but if he played his cards right, he might be able to score he and Constance a pad all their own. It was a good job, but he was struggling with the idea of working for a living. His old life was lost to him and he had no purchase there, not after everything he'd done to offend it. He shot Old Butch in the face and left him for dead, not that anyone missed him. He saved a cop, which was tantamount to betrayal, really, at least from where he came from, no going back from that. And he framed an old cohort, Walter, just today. So maybe he *was* still in the old life, even if he really wasn't. He'd never really leave it, at least not in his mind, not as long as he had a taste for the big scores.

Knox looked out the window at the crowds outside, at everyone celebrating — the Japs had finally cut out of the war. A crowd of people blanketed the streets, everyone cheering, laughing, dancing with one another. Knox opened the window and let the noise in, he didn't mind it. They'd gone to see Sherwood and his gal pal tie the knot at city hall and now he was waiting on Constance. She'd told him to go ahead of her and wait, she had a surprise. What, he couldn't imagine, but did it matter? She was in his life again and that was everything. They'd moved fast, after the prison ordeal, and made up for lost time. Evenings together, weekends, extended time in the bedroom. And the both of them felt productive, they were both working. She had a good thing going with King, a good job. The man was like a magnet for money, the way he carried himself and ran his business. She even hinted that *Knox* could have a job with King, but so far, he'd had too much pride to take her up on it. He wanted to make his own way. Prove to himself, and her, that he could go straight on his own and stick with it.

A knock at the door — there she is, back with his surprise. Knox opened the door and was surprised, alright — Bennie Sherwood was standing right there.

"I sure hope this isn't an official visit," Knox said.

"It is and it isn't. Could I come in for a moment? This won't take long."

Afraid to say no, Knox motioned for Bennie to step inside. "I did wonder if I was truly in the clear."

Bennie gave him a thumbs-up look. "You are. In fact, that's part of the reason I'm here. I've squared things with your parole officer, you're officially out of trouble."

Knox was stunned. "I don't know what to say. I mean, I... Butch, I mean. I... I killed a man."

"In self defense. And your heroism in the face of grave danger went a long way to clearing your record. That, and a few choice words from Jedidiah."

"I had no idea he had so much pull."

"He does. And he clearly thinks highly of you. A word to the wise — take advantage of that when you can, you'll thank me later."

"Noted. You know, you could have called me with this." Knox almost laughed. "Didn't you just get married?"

Bennie smiled. "Yes, and I know this might be strange, me

showing up here like this. But we're not leaving until tomorrow and I wanted to get a few things off my chest. First, I wanted to thank you. For coming in to get me that night."

"You've expressed your gratitude."

"Not properly. And not face to face. Truly, I can't thank you enough. I might not be here if it wasn't for you, Knox. I mean it. You have my thanks and then some."

Knox thought of the prison and felt a shudder. "Ok, then. I'll say 'you're welcome' and we can leave it at that. I'm sure you can understand, I never want to think about that place ever again."

"I do. So, what's next for you?"

"Is that your way of asking me if I'm going back to my old ways?"

Bennie couldn't hide it. "In a way."

Knox took a deep breath and looked around the room — there was love in this room, there was comfort. He was richer now than he'd ever been after a score. And after that day with Butch, well, he'd made a promise to himself. "The answer is no. I wouldn't risk this, risk losing her, for anything. Tell your buddies at city hall, they don't have to worry about me any more — I've gone straight, for good."

"That's good to hear."

Someone came running up the steps, or rather, some *thing*, whatever it was shuffling and running up into the apartment and then all of a sudden, there was a dog, right there, climbing all over Knox and sniffing him. Compact and hardy, it was a boy and it looked like a beagle with its brown splotches and white paws. Knox patted it good, they'd had beagles and hounds all growing up. They were always good at alerting the family when the cops came snooping around the stills.

He looked up and saw Constance coming into the apartment, all done up still from the wedding, a bag of groceries in her hand. "I got him from the pound, I think he answers to Jefferson but we can call him whatever you'd like." She was stunned to find Bennie in their apartment. "Well, hello there, Mr. Groom. What on Earth are you doing here?"

Bennie smiled and gave her a kiss on the cheek. "I wanted to say a word to your boyfriend before we hit the road tomorrow. Take care, you two. I'm sure we'll be seeing you before long."

Constance beamed. "I certainly hope so! You two have fun, now!"

"We will," Bennie said as he made his exit.

Knox knelt down and let the dog lick his fingers and his face. It made him so happy. "We could have picked him out together, you didn't have to go on your own."

Constance swatted the idea away as she went about putting the groceries on the counter. "Well, you know, I just remembered how much we liked having a dog." She pulled out a few pots and pans from the cabinets and went about making a fuss near the stove.

"Are you making dinner?" he asked.

"I am, indeed. There's too much commotion out there for us to go out tonight, I'm doing steak and potatoes right here at home." She gestured toward their well-stocked bar cart. "*You* are in charge of the martinis."

Knox saluted her. "Aye aye, captain. Say, I'm gonna take old Jefferson out on the porch and just take it all in for a moment."

She grinned and winked at him. "Don't be too long."

"We won't," Knox said. He and Jefferson moved out onto the fire escape. The sounds of celebration were all around them. The entire city had come alive to celebrate the war's end and Knox couldn't care less. He had Constance back in his life and now he had this dog, he had it all. He tried to laugh but it came out wrong and he started to cry instead. He just sat there, listening to the sounds of joy all around him, and let the dog lick the tears from his face.

Acknowledgements

I'm forever indebted to three great friends — Eric Miller, Evan Moore, and Dave Patteson — for reading an early draft of *Shine A Light*. Their notes were invaluable in helping to improve and strengthen the manuscript. My deepest thanks, fellas.

To my wife Amy — your love, patience, and support mean so much. Thanks, babe.

And thanks to you, dear reader, for reading *Shine A Light*.

About The Author

Ward Howarth is the author of the novels *River City Blues* and *Shine A Light*. He was voted 'Best Local Author With A New Book' for *River City Blues* in Richmond Magazine's 30th Annual Best & Worst Issue, August 2017. A television professional by day, he's also a passionate cinephile and coffee devotee. He lives in Richmond, Virginia.

www.wardhowarth.com

www.ingramcontent.com/pod-product-compliance
Lightning Source LLC
Chambersburg PA
CBHW030937120726
47906CB00002B/616